TAKE A GREEDY, POWER-MAD DIC-TATOR AND A MYSTERIOUS, CHAR-ISMATIC REBEL LEADER AND ADD—

Alec Fletcher—in this black republic, his black skin goes together with shrewdness and courage to make him invaluable to American intelligence

James Gerard—torn between his duty to his partner, Fletcher, and his desire for Nora Lund

Suzanne Forrest—a woman of unashamed passion and unselfish love, she wanted only Alec Fletcher—any way she could have him

Eleanor Lund—strong-willed, beautiful, demanding Nora wanted Jim Gerard on her terms.

A HAIR-RAISING STORY OF CORRUPTION AND COURAGE, POWER AND PRIDE!

Jack Hoffenberg

A Thunder At Dawn

 AVON
PUBLISHERS OF BARD, CAMELOT, DISCUS, EQUINOX AND FLARE BOOKS

This book is for
my brothers, WILLIAM, HARRY, *and* ALBERT
and my sisters, ROSE, SHIRLEY, *and* EDYTHE
with deepest affection

AVON BOOKS
A division of
The Hearst Corporation
959 Eighth Avenue
New York, New York 10019

Copyright © 1965 by Jack Hoffenberg.
Published by arrangement with E. P. Dutton & Co., Inc.
Library of Congress Catalog Card Number: 65-11609.

First Avon Printing, July, 1966
Tenth Printing, December, 1972

AVON TRADEMARK REG. U.S. PAT. OFF. AND
FOREIGN COUNTRIES, REGISTERED TRADEMARK—
MARCA REGISTRADA, HECHO EN CHICAGO, U.S.A.

Printed in the U.S.A.

CHAPTER 1

1. Port Amitié, Liberté

Sunday mornings at the American Embassy in Port Amitié were usually quiet. And dull. And this Sunday, Clark Shannon thought, was no exception to the rule. He sat in his own small office in the chancellery, coat off, in a short-sleeved white convertible shirt, the knot of his brown tie pulled down about three inches from its unbuttoned collar, feet cocked up on the pullout leaf of his green steel desk. Over the soft whining of the ceiling fan he heard the electric coffee pot on the cabinet behind him begin bubbling noisily. Shannon yawned, put down the DIB file he had taken from Suzanne's desk, swiveled himself around, and grunted as he stood up to pour a cup for himself, wishing he had an ounce or two of "revitalizer" with which to lace the strong black coffee.

The telephone rang, the first call of the morning. He lifted the receiver and said, "Duty officer. Shannon speaking." He listened for a moment, then said: "Sorry, Mrs. Lund. No, haven't heard a word. No idea where he could be. Sure. Sure, I'll ring you right off if I hear anything."

He hung up, reached for the cup, and sipped at it. Damn it, he thought, a whole week gone by and not a word from Alec. Now they were beginning to get edgy. A few others had mentioned his absence, but when Mrs. Lund began asking questions the damned thing took on a semiofficial air.

Shannon put the cup down, reached across the desk, and tapped a cigarette free from the rest of the opened pack, lighted it with his Zippo, vintage World War II, ran a finger mechanically over the worn engraving that spelled out his name, rank, and serial number, 0-920724, now faded and hardly legible. For a brief moment his memory of those war years returned. Years of greatness. Major Clark Shannon, Base Provost Marshal. Receiving

5

brisk salutes, taking reports, giving orders, conducting investigations, the final commendation from General Galbraith . . . The memory faded with the rich odor of the coffee in his nostrils. He threw his legs up again, sipped at the rim of the thick messhall-type cup, and began scanning the Daily Information Bulletin file for the preceding week.

The door opened, and the inch-long crew-cropped head of First Sergeant Jake Walker thrust itself through the opening with a broad grin that was both inquisitive and accusatory. "Hi, Clark. You still with the living?"

"Hi, Jake. Cup of java?"

"Sure. Thanks." Walker came into the room and went directly to the coffee percolator. "You got the watch today?"

Shannon snorted mildly. "Now, what the hell else do you think I'd be doing here on a Sunday morning when I could be corking off—"

"Okay, okay. Don't snap my head off. You must have hung a beaut' on last night."

"You know anything better to do on a Saturday night in a dump like this?" He rubbed a hand over his blood-shot eyes, suppressed another yawn. "Boy! If I opened my eyes wide right now, I'd bleed to death."

"Yeah. I saw you tossing off a few with Old Man Reed at Le Tambour."

"I didn't see you. Why didn't you sound off?"

"You couldn't have seen me if I had. You must've been three sheets to the wind by then. Besides, that old crumb gives me the creeps. Anything I can't stand is an ancient mariner telling me how it used to be back in the days in the *old* Marine Corps, the iron-men-and-wooden-ships routine. Living in the past is strictly for rummies like Reed. How can you stand him?"

"He's not so bad, Jake. I kind of feel sorry for the old guy."

"Christ! You're sorry for *him?* With that sugar spread of his, set for life?"

"He's had it rough. Besides, he don't live on the plantation and he might be set for life, but who wants to live like a rumpot?"

"I guess there's worse things. But if I had his setup, I sure could make out."

Shannon voiced his contempt with a "Phui! Here?"

"What's wrong with here?" Walker helped himself to

6

one of Shannon's cigarettes. "You know, Clark, you got it figured all wrong. You get yourself one of those long-haired sleeping dictionaries, shack up with her, and you've got it made in spades. Takes care of every problem a man can have."

Shannon threw Walker a look of disdainful rebuke. "You goddam Marines can't see beyond the ends of your peckers."

"Hell, nobody's got you chained down here, Clark. Why don't you put in for a transfer back to the States? Just think, you could be enjoying all that clean fresh snow and sleet, getting up mornings and putting chains on your tires to get to work, paying full price for cigarettes, liquor, gasoline——"

"Okay, okay," Shannon growled bleakly, "knock it off, will you? I'm on orders same as you. I go where they send me, spin my wheels, and gripe my head off, no different from you." He put the file and coffee cup down, yawned and stretched. "Two years and seven months more, friend, and I kiss them all goodbye. I've got a little house on the Severn River near Annapolis waiting for me, with a tenant paying me rent and keeping my two acres in shape. Comes my sixty-fifth birthday, I retire, boom! Fish all spring, summer, and fall, and sleep all winter. I might even wind up writing my memoirs, Jake. How about that?"

"That's okay with me. Just spell my name right and say nice things about me, will you?" Reflectively: "Four years and three months and I go out on thirty. Only, I'm not looking forward to it. The Corps has been damned good to me, but I'll only be forty-eight, and that's too young to check in my chips. You know, Clark, I got a theory about retirement. I think——"

Shannon was only half listening. He had passed his sixty-second birthday, a man of average ability, average looks, average height and, sadly, over-average weight by about twenty-five pounds, mostly in a noticeable paunch. Nearly two years on the bright, sun-drenched island of Liberté, and he still had managed somehow to retain his pink-and-white Stateside paleness, a full head of wavy, reddish-blond gray-streaked hair, with lower and upper dentures replacing an average number of missing teeth that made his mouth sag with a humorless quality. His features were coarse and granitelike, his stubby fingers those of a workingman, despite the fact that he did no physical labor.

7

Clark Shannon was the embassy security officer. A former policeman, MP officer during the war, he had transferred to State Department Security in 1946. He considered himself secure in a safe, comfortable billet, and prayed he would never foul up so badly that he would miss out on retirement at sixty-five; with retirement pay and social security, what else could a man want or expect out of life? Walker's theories on retirement interested him not at all. He had his own plans for living out his days in a world that had passed him by with a brief nod. Life today was for the young and quick. The roosters. Take it easy, check out quietly, and to hell with it.

Walker's voice came to an abrupt end in the middle of his dissertation. Shannon looked up toward the door and saw Thorne Truscott, the embassy counselor and chief executive officer, entering the room. Walker leaped to correct military attention, and Shannon stood up.

Truscott was a youngish man in his early forties, quietly brisk in manner and tone, intelligently alert, tall, well tanned, and elegantly turned out in a crisply pressed dark gray suit of fine, iridescent material. In freshly starched linen, expertly knotted tie, and gleaming black loafer shoes, he made Shannon seem aged and untidy by comparison. Truscott smiled in his usual friendly way to Walker, the senior noncom in charge of the embassy Marine Guard, then to Shannon. Walker replied to Truscott's "Good morning, Jake," and went out.

"Do something for you, Mr. Truscott?" Shannon asked.

"Clark, has there been any word from Alec Fletcher?"

"Why, n-no, sir. No. Not since he left a week ago. Mrs. Lund called about ten minutes ago to ask the same question."

"Did he give you any idea where he was going?"

"He didn't say exactly, sir. Just took off to make some routine calls in the south. That's all he told me."

Shannon saw the unspoken "Damn!" that formed on Truscott's lips. "Did he give you any inkling, any reason for making the trip?"

"No, sir. Only that he hadn't been down there for a look around in over two months." With an almost too careless shrug: "He's been out this long before. Should be back in a day or two." A moment of silence hung between the two men, then Shannon asked casually, "Anything I can do, sir?"

"No. No," Truscott replied slowly. Then, "You've no guess where he might be contacted, I suppose."

"I wouldn't know. He didn't leave an itinerary." Hesitantly, "Is something up?"

"Possibly. Washington's signaled the ambassador to come up for a talk. No special reason indicated. He's exploring the possibility that some of these recent hit-and-run raids in the interior, so close to election time . . ." Truscott's voice trailed off.

Shannon said, "I've been catching up on the DIB's." He pointed to the circulating file. "The Old Ma—ambassador said in Wednesday's staff meeting that they were just local back-country flare-ups, nothing to get worked up about, that they generally happen with an election coming up—"

"I know," Truscott said with a hint of impatience both in his voice and in his manner. "Just between us, I think the ambassador privately disagrees with that theory." He smiled again as if in apology for his impatience. "And, like most of us here, I agree with his disagreement. I know Alec does." Truscott turned to leave; then, as an afterthought, he said, "I thought Alec might have kept you posted . . ." Again his voice trailed off, and Shannon knew it was the counselor's way of prompting an answer without asking a direct question. Truscott walked to the percolator and poured a cup for himself.

Shannon said: "You know how these Intelligence people work, Mr. Truscott. They tell you only what they think is safe for you to know. If Alec is onto something, he wouldn't tell an"—his next words were spoken in a harsh, self-deprecating tone—"an ex-cop like me anything."

Truscott flashed a curious look toward Shannon. The Security Officer, he knew, was no great shakes, an aging man who moved from one post to the next every two years, playing a minor role, lost in a world that had speeded up and left him behind. Shannon was meticulous in his work, went by the rule book, and showed little initiative beyond that. He could run security checks on the local Libertéans employed by the embassy, make the rounds to be sure the office safes were properly locked after hours, alternate night watches with Walker. When it came to outside work . . . "Just the same," Truscott was saying, "I'd feel a lot easier if I knew where he was and what he's been up to. The ambassador hates surprises, and a sudden call to fly up for a talk with the Undersecretary, without a given reason—"

"Yeah. You can step into a lowered boom that way."

"All right, Clark." Truscott put his cup down. "We'll just keep this between us, eh? If you hear anything, ring me up at once, will you?"

"Yes, sir. When is the ambassador taking off? I'll be off watch at 1600 if he wants me to drive him to the airport."

"No need. I'll see him off. Thanks for the coffee." Truscott went to the door, hesitated for a moment, opened it, and went out.

Now it was Shannon who remained standing, his mouth forming the same expressive "Damn!" He drained the rest of the coffee in his cup, put it down with a mild bang, and sat down. He opened the top drawer of his desk and drew out a map with a tracing overlay that was marked in red crayon. Seven names were underlined in red on the thin tracing, showing the cities and towns of Petite Aiguille, Gran Aiguille, Royan, Carcasonne, Dondon, Cap Grande, and Gironde Sud. A heavier red line connected the names in an almost complete circle, except for the one town: LEONE.

Shannon sat for a moment, wondering if he should have shown it to Truscott. If he had, he would have been forced to admit he had found it under the blotter on Alec's desk the other day when he had been nosing around just for the hell of it.

2. Leone, Liberté

The small seaport city of Leone, on the extreme southwestern coast of Liberté, slept in the heat of a three o'clock sun. At its single, sun-warped dock, a rusty tramp freighter dozed beside a three-masted lumber schooner, both waiting for an end to the afternoon siesta and the return of the stevedores to resume loading. Two small coastal vessels and several fishing craft were tied up close by, their crews asleep in the shade of overhead awnings.

A dilapidated, crowded, open-sided bus, its roof rack piled high with bundles, packages, four squealing pigs, and two crates of protesting chickens, rattled to a stop, with much creaking and wheezing, in front of an iron-roofed shed that was its terminal, throwing up huge clouds of fine, choking dust. The passengers clambered down, calling to the indifferent driver to hurry with the release of their belongings. It was the only area of activity in sun-baked, sleepy Leone.

The last passenger to descend was a tall black man whose attitude toward the bustle around him was one of incurious apathy. He carried a light-colored jacket tucked under one arm, and the brim of his straw hat was pulled down to shade—or conceal—the upper half of his face. The tight short-sleeved cotton jacket he wore exposed the quiet power in his muscular arms and shoulders, just as the black cotton trousers could not conceal the strength in his legs. He walked with a loose, easy grace away from the bus, since he had no baggage to claim.

He crossed the dusty, unpaved surface of the small, nearly empty public square to a café, and sat in the shade of an awninged veranda and rested until a sleepy waiter came eventually to take his order for a glass of beer. Though it was lukewarm, it helped slake his thirst, and he ordered another, drank it quickly, then dropped two francs on the table and strolled toward the upper part of the town, past the police station and a clutch of stores that were closed down for the siesta period. There were, he noticed casually, a few small offices of shipping, import-ing, and exporting companies, the civil administration of-fices, combination courthouse and jail, the usual ocher-walled enclosure that was the military garrison, and a lumber storage yard. The small drab church caught his eye, then the private dwellings that surrounded it. He headed in that direction.

Along the way several beggars slept on the street, their backs to the shaded walls, wearing disreputable cotton garments and old, cracked sandals, straw hats inevitably pulled low over their faces. One old man held up a filthy, broken hand and whimpered for a coin, but the man passed by with unseeing eyes.

From the shaded veranda of the only other café on the main street, a shabby affair with only three outside tables, one of the two men who sat there looked up suddenly and motioned to his companion. The second man stared, and said in a whisper: "He is not from Leone. I have never seen him before."

The first man said: "Follow him carefully, Meurice. He could be the one we seek."

Meurice got up, pulled the rope belt around his dirty trousers a little tighter, and walked northward slowly, his head down. The bigger man had reached the church and

11

circled around toward the rear of it. Meurice followed, then disappeared inside the empty church. He walked down the single center aisle, crossed himself as he passed the altar, and went behind it, found a window, and peered out.

The big man was standing some twenty-five yards behind the church, scanning the clutch of weather-scarred shacks that seemed to be huddling together to keep from collapsing. He appeared to be making a count, or selection; finally he chose the seventh house to his left. After standing before it for a few moments, he apparently found what he had been looking for—a thin strip of red ribbon that hung from the latch of the front door. He nodded with unsmiling satisfaction, then pushed the door open and stepped into a dark room. Before his eyes could adjust to the dim interior, he heard a movement. A soft voice said, "M'sieu?"

"I seek a man," the newcomer said.

"There are many men in Leone, M'sieu. By what name is he known, the one you seek?" the voice asked.

"He is known as—Poignard."

"Ah." The man came forward out of the darkness, sheathing a knife inside his shirt. There was expectancy in the fleeting smile and tone of voice as he said, "I am Poignard. Welcome to Leone, Chalumeau."

"Then you have had word from M'sieu Duclosse. Your people are ready?"

"We wait only for you."

"How long will it take to raise them?"

"There are twelve and myself. By nightfall I can have them assembled."

"Good. I am hungry. Is there food?"

"A little. There is no money."

The man called Chalumeau reached into his trouser pocket and withdrew a sheaf of franc notes. He peeled off several and handed them to Poignard. "For the moment, this will do. Buy food for all. And four bottles of rum. Let me eat what you have now and I will sleep. Will I be safe here?"

"You will be safe, Chalumeau. Come. You will eat, then rest in my bed."

From inside the church, Meurice watched as the man called Poignard, whom he knew as Jules Fabreau, boss stevedore on the Leone docks, left the house and walked

12

toward the main street. He waited cautiously in the doorway of the church, then followed him as far as the café where he rejoined his companion who sat at the table waiting. "Eh, Meurice?"

"He is in the house of Jules Fabreau. It is likely that he is the one you seek, M'sieu Alec."

"Then keep an eye on the house. I will be close by. If there is to be a gathering, find out where, and how close we can get to it without being observed."

"*Oui*, M'sieu Alec," Meurice replied. "When Fabreau returns, I will be on his heels."

Night had fallen like a heavy mourning veil. Thirteen men sat on the ground in the thick woods beyond Leone and listened as Chalumeau outlined his plan of action in meticulous detail. Poignard, his host, sat facing his twelve followers, nodding his head in agreement. When Chalumeau's low, strong voice came to a halt, Poignard stood up and said: "You have heard. Are you willing?"

A murmur of general assent came from twelve throats as though they were one. Poignard said: "Then we will go now. One at a time. You know your stations. Go slowly and do nothing to attract attention to yourselves." He called out six names. "When you see me approach the police station, hold yourselves in readiness. Then, watch carefully, move swiftly. You others. When you see Chalumeau reach the entrance to the garrison, that will be your signal to follow him. Do your jobs well, and in less than an hour we will return here, well rewarded for our work."

The men rose and began to drift toward the center of Leone. Chalumeau and Poignard waited for perhaps ten minutes before the big man said: "Go now. I will follow."

Alone, Chalumeau removed his light-colored jacket and turned it inside out so that only the black lining was visible. From an inside pocket, he took a black cloth and held it in one hand. He pulled his hatbrim down lower on his forehead and began to walk toward the center of the town. At a safe distance behind him, the man Meurice trailed along, unseen in the shadows. From between two warehouses, Alec Fletcher watched.

It was nearing nine o'clock, and a wan quarter moon looked down feebly on Leone. Stores and offices were again closed. The only people abroad, aside from the one uniformed policeman and usual beggars, were seated at the outside tables of the two cafés. Music and drumbeats came from within, a high shrill laugh of a woman, a man calling across a café room to another. A sleepy sentry stood at the entrance to the garrison, two small dogs pawing at each other in play at his feet. His rifle rested against one gatepost where the sentry leaned at approximately the same angle, arms crossed over his chest, smiling at the puppies.

Inside the police station, a hundred yards away, a sergeant dozed behind a small desk, his feet crossed at the ankles and resting on the top leaf he had pulled out, hands clasped behind his head.

At exactly nine o'clock, the man Chalumeau began his approach on the garrison. Poignard, a few yards from the entrance to the police station, turned to one side, bent over and struck a match, then touched it to a cloth wick that had been inserted into a bottle of gasoline. When the wick flamed up, he turned back to face the police station, and hurled the bottle through the open window. As the bottle exploded, sheets of flame spread out quickly, licking hungrily at the old dried wooden floors and walls. Before the sergeant could collect his wits, a second bottle came flying into the room and exploded within six inches of where he had fallen to the floor, igniting his clothes.

Behind the building, three men entered the small storehouse and began handing out the rifles and ammunition belts to their companions, who carried them swiftly to the small pickup truck in the alley. Within seconds, the six men were joined by Poignard, who drove the truck toward the garrison through a back lane.

Patrons of the two cafés rushed into the street and began running toward the police station. Alec Fletcher, on signal from Meurice, moved quickly in the opposite direction toward the garrison. The startled policeman on the street was the first man to arrive at the station, but could not enter through the curtain of flame. He stood helplessly at the fire-shrouded entrance, then began to scream senselessly.

There was little need for the sentry at the garrison gates to sound an alarm. At the roar of the first explosion and the sight of flames soaring high into the air, the lieutenant in command came on the run, shouting orders to his men to follow him to the scene of the conflagration to keep order and to aid the small volunteer fire department operate its one piece of antiquated equipment.

No sooner had the twelve soldiers dashed out behind

14

the lieutenant than Chalumeau, his head and face fully covered by the black cloth, led the balance of Poignard's men into the garrison. The lone sentry at the gate was overpowered, and his carbine was used to hold the remaining nine soldiers at bay. Quickly, they were herded into an unused storeroom and locked in. At that precise moment the small pickup truck arrived and was backed up to the central warehouse and loaded with what arms, ammunition, and canned foods were in sight. On leaving, the men exploded gasoline bombs in the empty barracks, the headquarters building, and garage.

Within twenty minutes, the band of guerrillas was back at their earlier meeting place. Under Chalumeau's direction, the load was placed in a trench that had been dug earlier, covered with a canvas tarpaulin, and filled in with dirt and covered with brush. The pickup truck was already on its way back to the edge of Leone, and was abandoned near the point from which it had been stolen. The remainder of the men sat on the ground passing rum bottles back and forth, tasting with it the fruits of their swift victory. Chalumeau sat with them, quietly exulting. When a few minutes had passed, he spoke to them quietly, reassuringly.

"You have seen what can be accomplished by unarmed men against the police and military if you will organize and learn to operate under competent leadership." Flushed with victory, the men voiced enthusiastic endorsement and approval.

Chalumeau continued: "It is not yet over, my friends. You will return to your work in the morning and act as everyone else will act in Leone: surprised, shocked, even fearful, but never nervous. Do not volunteer anything, and speak with caution when you are spoken to. You have your alibis prepared. Use them wisely. You will be questioned by the local police, the military commander, and by security police who will arrive from Port Amitié. They may threaten, even beat a few people, you among them. Remember well that if you are persistent in your innocent denials, no harm will come to you. If you succumb to beatings, threats, or promises, you are fools and your families will suffer. You will be thrown into prison, your wives and daughters violated. Swear on your lives that you will remain silent."

The men swore fervently and in unison.

"Good. You have arms for each of you now, more for

those whom you will enlist in our cause. Poignard will instruct you in their use. Heed him well and learn everything you can. Your lives will one day depend on that knowledge and your response in the fight for freedom that lies ahead of us.

"I came to you today and I leave you within the hour. What you have seen and done tonight has been done elsewhere by your unknown, unseen brothers, men like yourselves. In other villages and cities on Liberté, men are arming. They wait for *L'Aube*, The Dawn, the day of our liberation. When that day nears, I will send word to Poignard. You will come, with many others from many villages and cities, into Port Amitié. You will come by bus, by boat, by wagon, by horse, or *bourrique*, or you will walk; but you will come with your rifles well hidden under a load of straw, in a box or bundle, concealed in rags.

"Then, on the day of *L'Aube*, we will together take back our country and return it to the people who have been robbed by the thieves and tyrants who rule us now. We will conquer those who have defiled and debased us and destroy those who would destroy us. *Do you believe me?*"

Low hoarse shouts and upraised fists demonstrated their belief. *"Will you follow me?"*

"We will follow you!" Poignard shouted.

"We will follow you!" twelve other voices chanted in unison.

When the jubilant band of maquis dispersed, Meurice came out from behind a tree and gave a short soft bird whistle. He waited, heard it repeated, and moved in its direction, where he met Alec Fletcher and led him back to the clearing, then to where the arms and ammunition and canned foodstuffs had been buried. As Fletcher stood staring at the spot, Meurice said, "You wish to take a part of this with you, M'sieu Alec?"

Fletcher replied: "No, Meurice. Leave it and do not return here. I do not want them to know they were observed. You have done well. When I have need for you again, I will send word to you through M'sieu Lebrun. For the time being, we have done all that needs to be done. When I have changed clothes, you will go home and forget what you have seen."

16

Later that night, Jules Fabreau led Chalumeau through a valley, up a hill, down through a treacherous ravine, and across a spiny ridged mountain. Far below them, Fabreau pointed out the road that led inland to La Rochelle. "When you reach the valley, Chalumeau, you will be well beyond the Leone military checkpoint. In mid-morning, the bus from Royan to Romizeau will pass. The driver will be instructed to stop for you. If you do not get off before you reach La Rochelle, you have nothing to fear. I will send word ahead by drums to tell them you are on your way. *Au 'voir, cher ami*. It has been a joyous, profitable night. We will await your word."

Chalumeau nodded. "Train them well and keep them hidden, Poignard. *L'Aube* draws near. When that Dawn comes——"

With a wave of his huge hand, Chalumeau began making his way down the hill.

At the almost dry creek, Alec Fletcher washed away the grime from his face, upper body, and hands. He threw the towel to Meurice, stripped off his workingman's denims, then took his own socks, shoes, and trousers from Meurice, and put them on quickly. They went up the steep incline to where the black Ford stood, and Fletcher put on shirt, tie, and jacket. He got the .38 revolver from under the driver's seat and tucked it into the special holster that was attached beneath the dashboard, then unlocked the glove compartment and took out his wallet. He extracted a thick wad of franc notes and handed most of them to Meurice, then got into the car and drove off. Within seconds, Meurice had disappeared into the woods.

Fletcher drove through Leone slowly and saw the smoking ruin of the buildings inside the garrison, the near hysterical activity of the soldiers attempting to make some order out of the chaos. He passed the police station that had virtually disappeared, where the crowd watched as four or five brass-helmeted men ran a chain line of buckets from the water trough next to the well, attempting to put out the last of the fire. He inched his way through to the street that paralleled the waterfront, went past the bus depot, then headed north on the road toward Port Amitié. He came onto the checkpoint and braked to a stop when two armed soldiers waved him down. A sergeant, carrying a clipboard, came up beside the car.

"Your *carte d'identité*, M'sieu," he demanded.

Fletcher lowered the sun visor to display the small official seal of the United States Embassy, and pointed to it. "Your *carte d'identité*," the sergeant insisted briskly. Fletcher reached into his jacket pocket, got out his wallet, and flipped it over to his embassy ID card. The sergeant examined it closely, made a scrawling, laborious notation on the ruled sheet, then similarly recorded the license-plate number. With a flashlight, he and the other soldier examined the inside of the car. "The keys to the trunk, M'sieu," the sergeant said.

Fletcher handed the keys over. The two men examined the trunk and returned the keys. "You may continue, M'sieu," the sergeant said politely.

As the Ford disappeared into the night, the sergeant picked up his clipboard again and studied the name and license number he had written down. Then he walked to the sentry hut and picked up the telephone. To the operator, he said: "Port Amitié, *le Quartier Générale d'Sûreté. Lieutenant Falot. Oui. Claude Falot. Vite, no?*"

A little over two hours of fast driving brought Alec Fletcher to the Port Amitié military checkpoint. When he braked the black Ford to a halt, an armed sentry stood in front of the red-and-white striped barrier next to the inspection hut. Fletcher got his ID wallet out, pulled the keys out of the ignition lock, and handed them to the man. The sentry studied the ID card, made a note of name and license number on a ruled sheet. Another sentry came out of the hut, took the keys, and inspected the trunk. Satisfied, he returned the keys.

"From where are you coming, M'sieu?" the first sentry asked.

"Ah—from Gironde Sud."

"And your business there, M'sieu?"

"I am the assistant commerical attaché at the American Embassy. I have been in Gironde Sud on business, visiting the representative of the Apex Oil Company."

"And you now are returning to your domicile in Port Amitié?"

Fletcher nodded through the familiar routine. "Yes."

"*Bien, M'sieu.* You may pass." The second sentry raised the barrier and waved him on.

So far, so good, Alec Fletcher said to himself. He picked up speed now, and half a mile ahead, branched off toward his left, out of the heavier stream of traffic. As he

18

turned into Rue des Mille Fleurs, his eyes automatically went up to his rear-view mirror. Another car had turned off the main road behind him and was some sixty yards away. Natural instinct or caution took over. He turned left at the next corner, making no effort to increase his speed. The car followed. He made another left turn. The car made the turn behind him, but kept its distance. Two turns in the same direction were almost too much of a coincidence for Fletcher. He made another turn that would bring him back into Rue des Mille Fleurs, and saw the headlights of the car as it came around the corner.

Fletcher turned to his right quickly and raced back toward the main highway at an accelerated speed. There, he made a left turn just before a long line of vehicles reached him, and headed toward town. All the way in, for more than three miles, he kept his eyes glued to the rear-view mirror, but could not pick up his follower.

He came into Rue Pavillon and, before turning off it, checked the traffic behind carefully. No sign of the black Plymouth. He drove past the Café Excelsior. The outside tables had already been taken up and were stacked on the veranda. At this late hour, he knew the remaining patrons would either be in the bar or the inside dining room. He turned right at the next corner, then right again into the alley behind the Excelsior. Next door to its rear entrance he parked in the space reserved for employees of Chez Martal, which dealt in cut flowers and gift items for tourists. He got out of the Ford, locked it, and went to the back doorway. He lifted the sign that read MARTAL. Beneath it was a lock into which he fitted a key, and went up the flight of stairs. At the second level, he unlocked another door and entered a room, shot the bolt, and turned the lights on.

The room was furnished as a bedroom: double bed, two dressers, lounge chair, table, two straight chairs, and a wardrobe closet. There was another door that led to a bathroom. Fletcher went to a second light switch and flicked it up and down twice, then lay down on the bed.

Ten minutes later, he heard a sound coming from the direction of the wardrobe. He raised himself on one elbow and watched as the door to the wardrobe opened and a man stepped out.

"Alec! M'sieu Alec!" the bulky man said anxiously. "Where have you been? Over a week has passed without word. I have been worried."

Fletcher smiled and said: "Until tonight, there was nothing worth while to report. Everything is fine, Emil. Your man, Meurice, was excellent."

But Emil Lebrun was not so easily reassured. "Something is wrong," he stated flatly.

"I am tired. Also, someone trailed me in from the checkpoint, but I was able to elude him in the traffic. It is possible he may be cruising about looking for me. At this hour, he could pick my car up easily if he should see it."

"What can I do, Alec?" Emil Lebrun asked.

"I want to leave my keys with you and take Etienne's car. He can make the exchange later. I'll leave his car outside the embassy gates and he can leave mine there, the keys under the rear floor mat as usual."

Emil nodded, his face still sober. "The bar is nearly empty. I will take over for him."

"Thank you, Emil."

"What news from the south?"

"Good, Emil. I have seen him. Not only seen him, but I have been close enough to hear him, see him in action. A formidable man. Strong and quick. Tomorrow you will hear that the police station and military garrison at Leone were attacked and raided, the eighth such raid within three months. But the important thing is, I have seen Chalumeau. I know now that there is a definite pattern behind the raids that has all the signs of a revolution behind it. I've got to get back to the embassy and send off a message."

"Give me the keys to the Ford and I will bring you those for the Citroën. It is behind the building?"

"Yes. And thank you, Emil."

3.

At one in the morning, Alec Fletcher sat beside Roland Baker, the embassy communications officer, while Baker tapped out the last of the coded message to Minos 1 from Paros 9, Fletcher's code signature, and concluded with the customary MESSAGE ENDS. He turned off his shortwave set, removed the earphones, and said: "Man, you're really hopped up on this one, aren't you? Something hot?"

Fletcher folded the sheet with the coded message and placed it into an envelope. He scrawled his name across the flap, sealed it with transparent tape, and handed it to Baker. "Keep that in your safe for me until morning, will

20

you, Rolly? I've got to get something to eat and I don't want to carry it around on me."

"Sure, Alec. Anything up?"

Fletcher grinned. "Maybe, but it's not for me to tell. I've got to keep it fresh and pure for the ambassador in the morning." He changed the subject quickly. "Sorry I had to pull you away from the club for this. Come on down to Leonardo's with me and I'll buy you a steak and a drink to make up for it."

"No dice, buddy. I had to leave my date among a flock of hungry wolves to get this off. Incidentally, Suzanne was there tonight."

"How does she look?"

"Beautiful as ever. Come along?"

"And watch somebody else romance my girl?"

"Your girl? With all that competition, is that your brand on Suzy that keeps 'em panting?"

"Next time you see her, take a good hard look. It might just be."

"Well, lucky you. May I be the first to—"

Fletcher laughed. "Too soon, buddy, too soon."

"Nothing official?"

"Not yet. In my job, I've not only got to win the girl, I've got to get parental permission, then approval from my chief of service."

"That gives you both an extra in-law most people never enjoy. But you'd better hurry and ask before somebody crowds you out."

"I'm not worried yet. And I don't mind her dancing with you guys as long as she comes back to me. Go ahead and have your fun. I'm beat. All I want right now is something to put inside this empty cavern I call a stomach, then home and to bed."

"Okay. I'll tell Suzy you're back. She's been anxious."

Fletcher waited until Baker locked the Com Shack and the two men walked together to the parking area where Baker got into his sporty Facel-Vega that Alec regarded with envy. He got in beside Baker. They drove out through the Marine-guarded gate, and Fletcher saw his dusty black Ford parked half a block away. Etienne's car was gone. "End of the line, Rolly," he said. "See you in the morning."

"Night, Alec. Take it easy."

Leonardo's would be open until two o'clock. Alec got the keys from under the rear floor mat, checked the holster under the dashboard to make sure his .38 was intact. He drove along Rue des Américains, then turned into Montaigne, heading toward his goal, Rue Pavillon. In the middle of the next block, a black Plymouth shot out of a side street, roared up from behind, and pulled sharply ahead in front of the Ford. Alec threw his brakes on and came to a squealing stop within inches of crashing into the side of the Plymouth. Angrily, he leaned out of the window to shout an imprecation at the occupants of the offending car, then realized it was the same one that had tailed him from the checkpoint. He leaned back, right hand in his lap dangling over the edge of the seat in case he needed to make a fast move toward his service revolver. One man had remained behind the wheel of the Plymouth. The other threw open the door and came back to the Ford, leaned over, and peered inside. "It is M'sieu Fletcher, no?" he asked.

Fletcher at once recognized the grinning face. "Lieutenant Falot," he said. "You drive very badly. A policeman would arrest you for your carelessness."

Falot's grin broadened. "I thought I did very well, M'sieu Fletcher."

"Then suppose you tell me what the hell this is all about? I damn near rammed you. Why did you cut me off?"

"It would not be the first time we have been close tonight, would it, M'sieu?"

"Ah, so now we play the *énigme*. Riddles."

"Get out of your car, M'sieu."

"On what authority, Lieutenant?"

"Come, M'sieu Fletcher. It is not a game we play. Do not waste my time. Get into the back of my car."

Fletcher leaned back against the seat and said: "You are a stupid man, Falot. You can't get away with this. I'll have an official protest filed—"

"Do not argue, M'sieu." Falot's hand was reaching inside his jacket. "I will give you exactly five seconds to move. If you do not—" His hand was outside the jacket now, a flat automatic in it.

Alec glanced up and down the street. It was useless to resist or argue. There wasn't a moving thing in sight, human or vehicular. He reached for his keys. "Leave them," Falot ordered.

Alec got out of the car and slammed the door shut. As he started toward the Plymouth, Falot said, "One moment." While Alec stood still, Falot ran one hand over his legs, then patted it over the upper part of his body. "Very well. Move." As he got in beside Alec on the back seat, he said to the driver, "Plage Etoile."

Alec said, "I don't have my swimming things with me."

Again a sardonic grin from Falot. "Everything you will need, I can furnish, *M'sieu Espion*."

"Espion? I, a spy? You're crazy, Falot. Does Major Lamonte know anything about this?" He saw the reflex reaction in Falot's quick sidelong glance. "I thought not. You can be damned sure he'll find out soon enough. He and General Batraville as well."

"Do not threaten me, you black traitor. How can a man of your color work for the *blanc pou?*"

"Falot, you didn't get your head screwed on properly this morning. I am an American. If you want to discuss color—"

Falot's voice was contemptuous. "A black man who sells his soul to the whites. You are a traitor to your race."

Fletcher said: "Falot, you sad, ignorant animal, we're not even in the same race. Now listen. If you're arresting me, let's go to Police Headquarters where you can file charges against me. Why are we going to the beach?"

"You returned to Port Amitié tonight after an absence of a week. From where, M'sieu Fletcher?" Falot asked abruptly.

"From Gironde Sud." Even as he said it, Alec knew with a sinking feeling that this was the careless lie that had given Falot the courage to take him into custody.

"Ah, so. Gironde Sud. So you told the sergeant at the Port Amitié checkpoint. At what time did you leave Gironde Sud?"

"About ten-fifteen. Perhaps ten-thirty."

"Then, M'sieu, how do you explain that at that same time, you could be leaving Leone? And only half an hour after the police station and military garrison were raided and destroyed?"

"And will you explain what that has to do with me, Falot? You must be out of your mind to accuse—"

"I have reason to believe you were in some manner involved in what happened tonight in Leone. If not, why was it necessary for you to lie?"

"Whether I lied or not has nothing to do with what

happened in Leone. What I was doing there and where I have been are none of your business."

"That, M'sieu, is exactly the point. I have decided to make it my business and I intend to find out exactly what you know and why you were there."

The car was approaching the military checkpoint that guarded the city's southern exit-entry. The driver pulled up at the barrier. A corporal flashed a light inside the car. Falot spoke to him briefly, and the corporal drew back, saluted, raised the barrier, and waved them on. They were curving in the direction of Maréchal and Anse à Goulet along the shore road. Plage Etoile was only six kilometers south, a sparsely developed beach town that fronted the sea. The car picked up speed, shot past a few isolated shacks, a small fishing village, then a long stretch of palm-bordered beach, a tangle of woods. The road rose into a hilly area and dipped into another valley, then straightened out as they came into the village of Etoile. The car glided through the sleeping town and turned toward the beach.

Fletcher knew that Falot's act was one of desperation. The security police had long been conducting a hopeless chase, offering rewards and bribes for any information concerning the whereabouts of Chalumeau, the man who had made a laughing-stock of General Batraville's security police and military forces. If the ambitious Falot could bring some definite knowledge, which he now believed Fletcher to possess, to Batraville, his personal rewards would exceed even his own dreams.

Fletcher also realized that his situation would become hopeless once they reached their destination. Wherever it was he was being taken, Falot would have the time, by physical torture or starvation, two methods not unknown to the security police, to force any knowledge of Chalumeau from him. And once he had accomplished that much, how would it be possible for Falot to permit him to remain alive?

That the only importance of his trip to Leone was to refute the ambassador's belief that Chalumeau's raids were more than "little local flare-ups" would mean little to Falot, desperately hungry to learn the man's true identity, his whereabouts, his contacts; which, in this case, would be Jules Fabreau, known as Poignard.

They came out into an open stretch now. In the distance was a community of residences, perhaps thirty or forty, more pretentious than those in the older village they were leaving behind. The car pulled up beside a two-storied house that, like the others, was dark. Falot threw the left rear door open and got out, motioning Fletcher to follow him. The driver sat erect, looking toward the beachfront. Fletcher started to slide across the seat, Falot's back still toward him.

As he reached the door, he raised his right hand and brought the side of it down in a sharp, slashing arc against the base of the chauffeur's neck. The man slumped over the wheel with a grunt. Falot wheeled around at the sound as Fletcher leaped toward him. Falot stepped back quickly, and slipped in the loose sand. As he fell, Fletcher was on him, reaching for the automatic Falot held in his right hand, but before he could get a firm grip on it the pistol skittered across the sand. Both men dived for it, Fletcher on top of Falot. Someone came running from the house across the sand just as Fletcher's fingers touched the roughened pistol grip. Falot turned over then, facing upward, and threw the palm of his right hand under Fletcher's chin, snapping his head back. Fletcher made one more desperate lunge toward the automatic. Through sand-blurred eyes, he saw the foot of the newcomer as it stamped down hard on his knuckles. The automatic disappeared in the sand. He tried to tear out of Falot's grip, driving his knee into the lieutenant's groin, felt himself released. He rolled away from Falot just as something crashed against his skull. He fought to get to his knees in the cloud of mushrooming sand, shaking his head to clear it of the fog. From behind, another blow smashed into his skull, and as the night splintered into a million bright, stabbing flashes, he felt another and final blow.

The world suddenly returned to silent darkness as he fell forward in the sand.

CHAPTER 2

1. Havana

Outside, the lights in the buildings that surrounded the Plaza de Libertad had come on to add a touch of sparkling tinsel to the velvet dusk. At her desk in the Office of the Ministry of Defense, Consuela Sándoz reached the end of the Report of Ship Arrivals and Departures. In the center of the bottom of the page, she typed the words SECRETO! and APREMIANTE! and pulled the four sheets of carbon-interspersed paper from her machine, tugged the extended corners of the carbons at the lower right-hand corner. She laid the carbons in the upper right-hand drawer of her desk and closed it, then glanced over the typed matter for errors, checking against her shorthand notebook.

The man sitting in the chair that was tipped against the far wall moved his thick body forward, and as the front legs hit the carpeted floor, stood up and looked at his wrist watch. He wore an ill-fitting suit of cheap white duck, light tan shoes, a striped shirt, and a flowered tie. He was swarthy and short, with shiny black hair that swirled at the back of his neck and over his forehead in tight curls. He was about the same age as the attractive girl on whose trim back he had been concentrating during the hour or more she had been typing the urgent four-page report for the deputy minister.

The girl assembled the four sets of typed matter in proper order and clipped them into separate units. The man said, "It is finished, Consuela?"

"Finished," the girl replied shortly.

He came to the edge of her desk and took the four sets from her, glanced at the top sheet appraisingly. "You do a clean job, *chinita*."

"Thank you. I am paid to do a clean job. And please do not call me by that name."

26

"I am sorry, Consuela." He hesitated with boyish embarrassment at the rebuke. "Will you wait while I take these to Señor Urbana? Then perhaps we can—"

"We cannot, Juan. I have another engagement."

In a surly tone, petulant with disappointment, "Always it is 'another engagement' when I ask you—"

"Always," Consuela replied briefly and without encouragement. "Go along, now. The deputy minister is waiting for the report." To emphasize her words, she pointed to the line at the head of the top sheet: SECRETO! APREMIANTE!

Juan flushed darkly, turned away, and started for the door to the inner office. As he reached it, the girl said, "Wait, Juan." He turned with a look of sudden, hopeful reprieve, but it turned to quick defeat when she said, "You forget the security regulations too easily. The notes."

He walked back to the desk where she stood holding the notebook. He took it from her, tore out the several pages of shorthand notes, and added them to the typed reports. "Please do not forget next time," Consuela said. "You can make trouble for both of us." She smiled roguishly and added in a conspiratorial whisper, "There are spies lurking everywhere, didn't you know?"

Juan hooted with mild contempt. "Consuela—" he began with a new plea in his voice.

"No, Juan. Now, run along."

When the door closed on his broad back, Consuela moved quickly. Foregoing the usual lipstick, powder, and comb ritual, she opened the top drawer again and lifted out the sheets of carbons she had been using. Every third sheet had been used only once, and she counted off three of the smooth sheets and replaced the rest in the drawer. She folded the clean sheets gently in half, then into quarters. Now she lifted her skirt and slip high and inserted the wad into the top of her stocking, using two bobby pins to clamp them securely in place. She pulled the slip and skirt down, then picked up her flat purse, pulled on the tam over her dark hair, and walked to the door that led into the main corridor. Before she could open it, Juan burst into the room again, his face red and contorted. "Consuela! Wait!" he called out.

For a second she felt a tremor of panic. "What is it, Juan?"

"The carbon sheets. Where are they?"

"In my desk, of course. Where else should they be? Why?"

"You know the security regulations so well, you should know. They are to be burned with the notes. All SECRETO! documents—"

She laughed with relief. "It is of no use, Juan. They are old carbons and have been used over and over again."

"It is the order of the security chief."

Consuela shrugged her shoulders. "Very well." She went back to her desk, Juan on her heels, his face still flushed by the verbal lashing he had just received from the security officer in the deputy minister's office. She opened the drawer and took out a thick sheaf of heavily used carbons. "Take what you like, Juan. It makes no difference. These have been typed over so many times it is impossible to know which to give you."

"How many sheets did you use?"

"There were four copies, so I used the three sheets that are on top!"

Juan took the three top sheets from the pile, turned them over, and tried to read through the layers of typed matter. He shrugged, grinned, and said, "Of what use it is, I do not know, but if they must be burned, I will burn them."

Consuela picked up her purse again and started toward the door. *"Bueños noches,* Juan. I must hurry now. I am late."

He stared after her longingly. "Consuela—" but she had already stepped out into the corridor. She turned into the next long hallway and walked down one flight of steps toward the arched exit where two armed security guards stood checking identification cards. As she approached, she automatically opened her purse, took out the green card, and held it up for inspection with a bright smile. The guard scanned it briefly, lingered with more interest over the original subject. She brought her opened purse up a few inches to remind him of his inspection duties, and the man glanced into it, his eyes searching for possible documents. Satisfied, he nodded with an oily smile and she snapped the purse shut, then walked out into the open, down the remaining steps to the ground level, where she joined the pedestrian traffic.

Three blocks north, Consuela Sándoz entered the Librería Ramírez. The bookstore had only four customers in it. She looked over the stack of newspapers on the front counter, then went to the back of the store to one of the empty aisles. She glanced to either side quickly, then bent over and extracted the wad of carbons from her stocking, picked up a paperback book, and inserted them between its pages. She selected two thin paperback volumes and sandwiched the first book between them.

At the cash register on the front counter, she handed the three volumes to the small, elderly man and picked up a copy of *El Mundo*. Without more than a casual glance, he took the three books, extracted the center volume, and placed it on a ledge beneath the counter. He wrapped the other two, returned them to her, and rang the amount up on the register. She paid him and went out. At the next corner, she joined a queue that had collected to board the bus that was just arriving.

From a darkened doorway across the street, a seedy-looking man in rough work clothes watched for a few minutes after the bus had departed. His attention now turned back to the Librería. He saw Simón Ramírez go to the display window and pick up a book that had been lying flat on top of a stack of similar books. Ramírez opened the book and stood it upright on the pile and went back to his cash register. Across the street, the man moved out of the shadows of the doorway, crossed over at the corner, turned right, and sauntered slowly toward the store. He paused to examine the books in the window, looked to left and right, then entered the store. He went directly to the counter and asked for a copy of *Hoy*, which Ramírez took from the stack. As he folded it over twice, he picked up the paperback book from the ledge under the counter and deftly inserted it into the folds. The seedy man dropped a coin on the counter, tucked the newspaper under his arm and went out into the street. At the corner, he turned into Avenida Mercedes. Four blocks away, at the corner of Calle de Torres, he saw the dark gray 1956 Chevrolet sedan parked at the corner, the driver sitting nonchalantly behind the wheel, smoking a cigarette, the older man reclining on the rear seat. He opened the back door, got in, and said to the driver, "The *finca,* Pedro. Quickly."

As the car moved out smoothly, the man beside him on the rear seat said, "It went well, Jaimie?"

"It went well, Luis. No one followed her."

A mile before they reached the City Gate, Pedro Sándoz pulled the car into a small side road and ran it up a narrow lane, no more than a cowpath. In the rear of the car, Luis Sándoz stripped off his outer clothes while Jaimie lifted the rear seat and got out a uniform. As Luis traded one article for another, Jaimie stuffed Luis's civilian garb under the seat. When he had buckled the belt around his waist and put the automatic in its holster, he got out and exchanged places with Pedro. In good humor, he said, "It is not fitting for a man of my age and distinguished looks to be a mere lieutenant."

Matching Luis's tone, Pedro said, "When we took him, I was thinking of myself, Luis."

"Ah, well, perhaps the next time you will find a major or a colonel who is my size." He got behind the wheel, backed the car out of the lane, and headed it back toward the main highway. At the military checkpoint a sentry dropped the white bar in a horizontal position as he saw the approaching headlights. When the car came to a stop, he walked around to the driver's seat, saw Luis, and saluted. *"Paso, Teniente,"* he said smartly, then backed away and raised the barrier. The Chevrolet glided through smoothly. At Marianao, they cut off onto a branch road, empty of traffic, and Luis depressed the accelerator. The car leaped forward with a remarkable burst of speed. Pedro said with youthful pride, "She goes well, eh, Luis?"

"And why not, my little brother? Did we not spend many pesos to give you a mechanical brain?"

A little more than five miles passed without conversation. Luis began to slow the car down as they approached a farm gate. In front of it, Luis cut off his lights, and Pedro leaped out to hold the gate open. The car passed through; Pedro closed the gate and got into the car again. They ran on for another hundred and fifty yards before they came to a low, sprawling farmhouse, pulled to the right of it, and headed for a barn. When they reached it, unseen hands opened one of the two doors to permit the car's entry, then closed them.

Luis Sándoz's flashlight made a brilliant path of light and picked out Miguel Gómez, who exchanged *embrazos* with the three men, then produced his own flashlight and lighted their way up the ladder into the loft. Pedro was already lifting a canvas-covered frame that had been buried under a pile of hay. Beneath the frame was the shortwave radio. Jaimie switched the set on and found the desired waveband.

"Minos 1. Minos 1. This is Argos 3. Come in, please.

30

Come in, Minos 1." He waited, then heard the relay station cut in.

"Argos 3, this is Chieftain. This is Chieftain. I have an urgent message from Minos 1 for Argos 3. Do you read me, Argos 3? Over."

"Argos 3 to Chieftain. I read you loud and clear. Proceed with message. Over."

"Argos 3 from Minos 1 via Chieftain. Message follows: EXIT ALTERNATE PLAN TWO URGENT AND IMMEDIATE MESSAGE ENDS. Do you read me, Argos 3? Over."

"I read you, Chieftain. Secure. Over and out."

2.

Long before dawn, they came into Bahai Honda, dressed in the garb of fishermen. Luis and Pedro Sándoz had dropped Jaimie Dominguez and Miguel at the house of Estaban, and now Estaban and Miguel were guiding Jaimie to the beach where the commercial fishing boats waited for first light. Jaimie carried two bait cans, Estaban the ice, and Miguel the fishing gear. Just as a dozen other crews were doing, they first made their boat ready, then drank the coffee Estaban had made over a small fire, got into their boat, and poled out beyond the buoy before Jaimie raised the sail. They were the third boat out, and kept a close watch on the small, fast gunboat that lay tied up to the pier. One man, carrying a rifle, guarded the government craft while its crew slept below.

During the day, they cast their nets, drew them in, called to other fishing boats, and exchanged disgust over the bad fishing luck they were having. They circled farther and farther from the others, trying to find a good spot. At two o'clock they rigged an awning and curled up for a siesta, but allowed the boat to drift southward with the wind. By late afternoon they had lowered the sail and removed the mast to make themselves smaller and lower in the now choppy water. They peered over the side at the gunboat that was making its third trip among the fishing boats, taking the angry insults from the fishermen who ordered them to keep the hell away and stop driving the fish off. Thus far, the threesome had not been noticed. And then the sun began to go down. The sky's violent colors became a spectacular performance, and within a few moments darkness fell.

In their boat, Miguel and Estaban reached under the

broad seat aft and hauled out an elongated shape covered by a tarpaulin. They untied it and exposed a heavy-duty outboard motor, which they lifted over the stern and fastened into place. From the fish box, Jaimie got out the tins of gasoline and handed them over to Miguel, who filled the tank. Estaban primed it, adjusted the cord, and as all three men prayed, pulled the cord in a long, sweeping motion. The motor turned over, coughed, sputtered several times, and quit. Estaban coiled the cord around the flywheel and pulled again. It spat, caught, and died again. Jaimie silently wished for Pedro's mechanical ability until, on the third try, it caught and held. Miguel smiled happily. He brought out a package of food and distributed it in equal shares, gave the course to Estaban, and they were on their way, three pairs of eyes keeping an alert watch for patrol boats, north and east.

"When you return, Jaimie, you will bring cigarettes with you, eh?" Estaban asked.

"And for me, a pair of the glasses that see into the night, Jaimie, yes?" Miguel added.

"When I return, it will be with more than that, I promise you. For you, Estaban, you, Miguel, for Elena, Luis, Pedro, Consuela, Ramírez, all of you who have meant so much to me these months."

"*Colego mío*," Miguel said simply, "you are our brother. We honor you."

"Honor me? Why?" Jaimie asked.

Miguel shrugged, showing some reluctance to elaborate on the sentimental note. "A man risks his life for a cause that is not his own, and asks why he should be honored?"

"Your cause is my cause as well, Miguel, the cause of the whole free world."

Estaban nodded. "I know little of the world, Jaimie. Also, I know that it is not every man who willingly risks his life for one of another country, of another language and culture."

"It has been done before by many, *amigo*. In South America, Europe, Africa, and Asia men have laid down their lives in the cause of freedom. They do it today."

"But," Miguel observed, "you are not one of us, Jaimie. I do not understand this entirely."

Jaimie smiled wearily, an aching tiredness showing in his face. "*Amigos*, it is said that a man passes through a lifetime on this earth but once. If he does even one good deed for another, his passage has not been fruitless. To

32

help free your people here, one helps free people everywhere. So, for a while, I have become one of you. Let us say a member in good standing in the human race."

Estaban and Miguel seemed to be thinking this over for a few moments, then Miguel said, "Eh, so. Like many of your people, you are a true sentimentalist, Jaimie. I am a simple man without education. I do not profess to understand the full depth of your philosophy, yet you have taught us much. For myself, for my people, I am grateful to you. When the *liberación* comes, many of us will remember."

"God's will," Estaban said.

"God's will," Miguel echoed.

During the night they saw the insidious shapes of several patrol boats. A plane roared by overhead. Another. Anxious eyes turned upward until they had passed, even though they knew they would not be seen from such heights and distances. On through the night they plowed northward, correcting their course by stars and compass, moving slowly, steadily through striated seas in the open craft. God, Miguel said to himself, was being good to them. When they delivered Jaimie, he hoped God would be equally merciful to Estaban and himself on the return trip.

Shortly after dawn, while the sky was still overcast, they heard the motor droning overhead, probing through the clouds. All three men were awake now, alert and anxious. The sound of the motor faded, then came back. The plane was flying in a wide circle over them, but they could see nothing. An hour passed. The cold wind began buffeting them about as the boat shipped water. And then they were coming into a stretch of sea that was sunlit through a break in the clouds. They heard the motor overhead again and knew it could mean either safety or death. No one spoke. The outboard thrummed on, driving the bow through gray-green seas. Waves slapped against the side of the boat and shook them, making it difficult for them to keep their seats. They came into the sunny patch. Miguel raised his head, one hand up to shield his eyes from the sun.

"There!" He was pointing toward the huge, awkward shape, waiting for Jaimie to follow the direction of his extended arm. Estaban's eyes were on Jaimie, too.

"It is ours," Jaimie said finally. "A seaplane."

Miguel stripped his shirt off and tied it to an oar, raised it, and began waving back and forth. The seaplane passed over them, dipped its broad wings in recognition, and began to make a ponderous circle back. It lost altitude over them, then lowered its long body on the surface of the choppy sea, taxied toward them slowly, and came to a stop about two hundred yards away, rising and falling with the motion of the water beneath. The small boat headed its nose toward her happily, bouncing as it cut across the wake the seaplane had left behind.

Within minutes, the port door was flung open and a short ladder lowered. Jaimie got up on the gunwale and stepped nimbly across the short open space and felt his wrist in the grip of a strong hand. He turned and shouted, *"Vaya con Dios, amigos,"* and saw the regret in the faces of Miguel and Estaban as the latter shouted, *"Vaya con buena suerte, mío hermano."*

In the cabin, a Navy lieutenant commander in gray greeted him with a formal salute, then a grin and handshake. "For the record," he said, "you are Jaimie Dominguez?"

"Yes, Commander."

"Your name in the clear?"

"James Gerard."

"Code name?"

"Argos 3."

"Any further proof?"

Gerard raised his left wrist and held the watch for the lieutenant commander to see. It was a *Jaeger-Le Coultre* wrist alarm with two stems. Directly beneath the trademark was the tiny word ARGOS. Gerard raised the upper stem and turned it so that the small triangle indicator moved counterclockwise around the dial. When it reached the figure "3," he stopped it, then pushed the stem in.

"That does it," the lieutenant commander said. "Welcome aboard. I'm John Wheeler."

"Thanks, Commander. Smoking lamp lit?"

"Sure. Have one." He pulled a pack from his pocket and offered it to Gerard, gave him a light, and saw the look of pleasure as he took his first puff and exhaled the smoke. Wheeler pushed the rest of the pack toward him and said, "Keep 'em. We've plenty aboard."

When they came ashore at Key West, a knot of officers and enlisted men stared at Gerard with curiosity. Surrounded by the seaplane's crew of four as they moved along the dock, Gerard saw the Navy sedan pull up and recognized Prescott Richards when he got out and began to walk toward them. Even from this distance, Richards was unmistakable: an erect, commanding figure with broad shoulders that tapered down to an athletically trim waist, leaning forward as he walked in the manner of a man who knew exactly where he was going and what he would do when he got there. As he reached the group, he threw a casual glance in the direction of the five men, looked away toward the seaplane. He took another full step before his head snapped back quickly with a half-smile and came to an abrupt halt.

"Jim?" There was still a note of doubt in his voice. "Hey, Jim! Is that—"

Gerard had turned toward him. *"Perdone, señor. No habla Inglés,"* he replied blandly.

Richards's look was one of complete bafflement. Then, "Jim! God Almighty, Jim, is that really you?" He made a quick motion forward and raised an arm to envelop Gerard, but Gerard backed away as he warned him off.

"Hold it, Pres, or you'll have to be deloused and fumigated along with me."

"Man," Richards exclaimed with unrestrained glee, "it will be a pleasure! Damned good to see you again, Jim. How do you feel?"

"Mortally tired and thoroughly starved."

"We'll take care of the food part right away. While they're refueling our plane."

"And I need a bath and a shave and a change of clothes in the very worst way."

Richards threw him a clinical glance and said: "You were never more right in your life. Well, let's see what the boys in the back room can come up with. I brought along a suitcase with some of your things, but we'll have to depend on the Navy for the balance of the restoration."

Jaimie Dominguez, code name Argos 3, had disappeared down the drain of the shower room in the bachelor officers' quarters, along with mustache and wads of clipped hair. In his place, dressed in his own clothes that felt wonderfully strange and soft, Jim Gerard preceded Prescott Richards aboard the Army jet transport. Richards said: "You look a hell of a lot more human now, Jim. Welcome home."

"Thanks, I needed that. What's all the fuss, Pres? Why was I pulled out so suddenly?"

"Something new has developed, Jim. Dix wants you in on it."

"Big?"

"Big enough to pull you out of Cuba. Did you bring anything out with you?"

"A few dozen strips of negs that we'll have to process and blow up before I can do much talking about them."

"We'll have the lab on it as soon as we get in. The Old Man is anxious as hell to see you."

"You make it sound loaded."

"It could be. We've got an URGENT on this one. Green light all the way. Choice of manpower, the whole bloody works."

"Do I go back to Cuba?"

"Quit fishing. You'll find out when we get to Washington."

"Can you tell me where, at least?"

"No harm in telling you that much, I suppose. Liberté."

"Liberté? That two-bit banana republic?"

"That two-bit banana republic is about to give us a ten-dollar case of acute indigestion any minute now."

"Liberté," Gerard mused. "I thought you'd sent a man there a short time before I got the Cuba assignment."

"We did. Alec Fletcher. Did you know him?"

"I think so. A tall, rangy boy— Sure, the bright kid from Tuskegee Institute. What's happened?"

"To be honest with you, Jim, we don't know. He was out on loan to State for the Liberté assignment. We didn't have a full-fledged fieldman, so we picked on the Investigative Division and came up with Alec, who'd been trying to transfer to Field."

"And?"

"A few nights ago he filed a message that he was onto something and thought he would have a complete answer to send by the next day. By morning, Alec was reported missing. After he filed the message with Baker, the embassy communications officer, he said he was going out for something to eat. And that was it. No Alec Fletcher."

"Any police reports?"

"Nothing more than what I've told you. It's as though he were swallowed up by something from outer space."

Gerard waited for more, but Richards was apparently

finished for the time being. He leaned back in his seat, let the drowsiness take over and promptly fell asleep.

3.

In Dixie Harrington's office, Richards was going over the photographic blowups the lab had made from the miniature negatives Gerard had made with his cigarette-lighter camera. Each blowup had been numbered by Gerard, who was speaking into a neck microphone that had been plugged into a tape recorder. Harrington came in, a slim man with large bright eyes that took in the scene in one quick surveying glance. He was about sixty, perhaps a year or two more, his hair combed neatly to one side; as always, he was immaculately dressed. His suit was solid gray; his tie and socks matched. He could, in most cases, have defied accurate description by a casual observer, which was the way he wanted it. Few people in the building knew, when they passed him in the hall or sat near him at a table in the Joint Intelligence Agency dining room, that this was Dixie Harrington, deputy director of the Special Operations Branch. It pleased him to know that among so many who saw him daily, few knew his position.

"Jim," Harrington greeted Gerard, "I can't tell you how delighted I am to see you again. You look extraordinarily well. Lose a little weight?"

Gerard took the long, artistic hand and gripped it firmly, felt the strength in it. "Good to see you, sir." He patted his flat stomach with his left hand. "I must have starved off a good ten pounds."

Harrington rubbed his own small paunch and said self-consciously: "It's becoming. How do you feel?"

"Fit. But I could use some sleep."

"You'll get it." He looked toward Richards. "Do we have everything, Pres?"

"Yes, sir."

"Well, then, gentlemen, shall we get on with it?"

Gerard spread the rest of the blowups out on the long table in proper sequence, then looped the neck mike over his head again, and began to mark and identify each print as the recorder picked up his voice. One small stack of the blowups had been previously identified and sat to one side. When he finished recording, he watched Harrington's crag-lined face for some reaction, trying to read something

37

into the intent, scholarly expression he had come to know so well over the years.

Harrington ranged back and forth over the photographs, scanning, studying, impressing them on his phenomenal memory. Gerard thought of the graying, gentle-voiced man with a particular kinship. He had seen the deputy director involved with perplexing matters that would have driven another man into a frenzy, admiring his amazing ability to hold others in check with a calm, unruffled exterior. Harrington seemed always at ease: at work, over a meal, in pleasant off-duty hours (if there were such a thing in the man's life), seldom revealing or projecting his true feelings.

Harrington held in his hands a series of photographs of Havana harbor, showing various Russian and satellite ships jammed closely together at the docks, cranes and slings unloading deck and hold cargo; the tanker *Dubrovnik*, carrying propane; the freighter *Ivan Polsunov*, with Czech field guns and ammunition; the radar-equipped trawler *Stalingrad*, about to leave port with a deck cargo of mine-laying equipment. There were shots of missile and radar and heavy-artillery installations in the more remote areas of the island; trucks, tanks, personnel carriers, and Czech buses to replace the American types now abandoned for lack of replacement parts; additional anti-aircraft emplacements installed in the port areas, near industrial plants, sugar mills, refineries and oil storage tanks; new types of commercial and military jets; some recently unloaded and not yet serviced for use, their cases bearing original markings in Russian.

Next came a series of close-ups; of Cubans in the streets of Havana, girls and boys in uniform, wearing side arms as they patrolled or guarded military and government buildings, an air of youthful bravado and pride about them as they swaggered about, looking like schoolchildren playing at an adult game of some sort. Where trouble seemed more likely to erupt, at nationalized stores and food markets where shortages were common, self-conscious older men and women stood guard, trying to look as tough as the youngsters.

Dock, refinery, airport, and industrial workers carried side arms (to protect themselves from saboteurs) as they labored. Armed police and militla were everywhere, while the dreaded *policía seguridadas,* Gerard explained, were forever stopping each other to check identifications and their right to wear a bulge under their left armpits or over their right hips.

In that second group of photographs, Gerard had centered his miniature camera on individuals; strange, un-Cuban-looking men whom he identified as Russian "technicians," "advisers," and "training instructors." There were several Chinese dignitaries being welcomed by Fidel Castro, his brother Raúl, President Dorticós, Che Guevara, and others of the important hierarchy; shots of visitors from several Central and South American countries being given the VIP treatment at outdoor receptions; sitting at sidewalk cafés, entering and emerging from tourist-free hotels or Castro's headquarters, carrying the inevitable bulging brief cases, at public rallies and parades or inspecting military groups and installations.

"Fine, Jim," Harrington commented. "Simply great. No recon planes could have picked this out of the air." Harrington put the last of the photographs down and turned his attention to the smaller stack Gerard had put to one side. "What about these?" he asked.

Gerard picked up the picture that lay on top of the pile. "This man," he said pointing to one of the men in a group of four.

Harrington and Richards studied the photograph together. "What about him?" Harrington asked.

"I don't know too much about him, but I think I'd like to. He's important. His name is John Mosher, American, mystery man of some sort, but closely connected with Domingo Urbana, Castro's Moscow-trained expert on arms. I couldn't get a solid line on him there, so I sent a query back by radio, but no one here could identify him from the description alone."

Richards said: "I recall the query and the name. We didn't have a thing on him, nor could any of our refugee contacts come up with what we wanted."

"Here"—Gerard took up another photograph from the special stack—"he's on the stand at the anniversary parade of the Revolution, Urbana on one side of him, Guevara on the other. Here he is again with Raúl. From their expressions, these boys weren't discussing a baseball game. Here's another with Fidel himself, Fidel's arm around him, smiling as though Mosher were a long-lost brother. Here is one with a couple of—" Gerard broke off suddenly and exclaimed, "Liberté!"

Harrington dropped the photograph he was holding and

jerked his body around quickly. "Liberté? What about Liberté, Jim?"

Richards said, "I mentioned it to Jim on our way up from Key West."

"What about it?" Harrington repeated.

"It comes back to me now—"

With a note of rising impatience, Richards pressed the question. "What comes back to you, Jim?"

Gerard held up the photograph again. "This. Here. This name John Mosher, this time with these two. One in uniform, the other in civilian clothes."

"Who are they?"

"The one in uniform is General Benoit Batraville, a wheel in Liberté's Defense and Security Organization. The other one is Charles St. Germaine, the foreign minister, and a member of the Libertéan Council of State. Consuela Sándoz identified them for me. They were there by invitation of Urbana, with all the stops pulled out. Full red-carpet treatment."

Harrington was studying the faces in the photograph, gripping it tightly with his hands. "Batraville and St. Germaine in Havana," he mused. "That's an interesting little item that got past Alec."

"He might have been elsewhere when this took place," Gerard said in soft apology for Alec Fletcher, "but it's an intriguing prospect since Liberté seems to be getting itself involved. Now that we have the photograph of Mosher, we might be able to turn up something on him."

Harrington didn't seem to be listening. He turned to Richards and said: "Get Chesler and Abel in here, will you, Pres? I'd like them to check these out."

Richards went out and returned a few minutes later with the two men. Harrington said: "Take a good look at these, will you, fellows? And tell us if you recognize anyone in them."

John Abel and Dave Chesler bent over the small stack of blowups and began to inspect them carefully. After a quick first-time-around scrutiny, Dave Chesler began to re-examine them more meticulously. He hesitated over the third blowup, then picked up a large magnifying glass and peered closer at one of the men in the picture. "Anything, Dave?" Richards prompted.

"Well," Chesler replied in a low voice, "if it isn't, it could be his twin."

"Which one?" Harrington pressed.

40

"This one." Chesler pointed to the face of the man Gerard had identified as the mysterious John Mosher. "I'd swear this guy is Craig Madden."

Harrington circled around and stood over Chesler's shoulder. "Craig Madden. Are you sure, Dave?"

"I'd swear to it in any court. If we had our hands on him, that's what I'd be doing. I was one of the team that trailed him the night he dived into the Potomac and got away."

"Who," Gerard asked, "is Craig Madden? The name has a familiar ring to it, but I can't place him."

Harrington, from behind the magnifying glass he had taken from Chesler, said quietly, "The playboy ex-captain who was picked up in an affair that involved some documents relating to our Polaris program."

"When—"

"About six months after Batista was routed by Castro. If I'm not mistaken, you were in the Far East then, weren't you?"

Gerard nodded, recalling the name Madden vaguely from the JIA reading file.

Harrington continued: "We'd never seen him in person, and there weren't many photographs of him available other than the Army ID shots that were published in the press after he defected. There's a resemblance of a sort here. He's put on a few pounds and his hair is somewhat thinner, but the look around the eyes and mouth is the same. We'll check it out more thoroughly with Defense and FBI."

"How did they get to him?"

Richards picked it up from there. "Madden was up to his neck in financial and marital difficulties after he came back from West Berlin. He liked to live it up, gambled quite a bit, was involved with a mistress and a divorce, all adding to the heavy drain on his finances. Back in '60, a Russian Embassy attaché, I don't remember his name—"

"Marenkov," Harrington interjected.

"Yes. Marenkov. Anyway, Marenkov got his orders to return to Moscow. That night he slipped out and asked for asylum. Among other disclosures, he named Craig Madden as the man who had been supplying their GRU man with various types of classified information. The Defense Department and State kept that part of Marenkov's disclosures a secret and set up a trap with some faked missile deployment schedules and saw to it that copies became available to Madden. Dave Chesler was with G-2 at the time.

"One night soon after, Madden was shadowed to a house in Virginia along the shore of the Potomac where he'd gone to meet his contact. When our people broke in on them, Madden crashed through a rear window during the first confusion and made it to the river. He got away in the dark. Right so far, Dave?"

Chesler nodded. "He dived into that cold black river with all his clothes on. Before we could get a search going, he was gone."

"Some time later on," Richards continued, "he was reported having been seen in Mexico City. We sent some people down to help look for him, but they were never able to track him down. We suspected then that he'd been flown to Russia. This photograph is our first knowledge of his whereabouts since that time."

Chesler said, "Wouldn't Defense be happy to get their cotton-picking mitts on that bird."

Harrington said: "For the time being, Defense will have to wait. We need to know just what he's doing in Cuba at the moment and how much, or what, he's got to do with the Libertéan situation. This photograph makes him the hottest prize on our agenda right now. You don't have anything else on him, Jim?"

Gerard concentrated for a few moments, then said: "According to Consuela Sándoz, he came to Havana about five or six months before she got her job at the Defense Ministry. That would put him there about two years ago, give or take a few months, the same time Urbana returned from Moscow. Her assumption is that he'd come direct from Moscow. Probably from their GRU training grounds. One thing is definite; he's in with the top boys and plays for big stakes. He comes and goes as he pleases, has the use of an official car and an armed chauffeur. He headquarters with Domingo Urbana as his deputy, and since Urbana is in charge of the entire Cuban arms program, it presupposes that he also directs their disbursement to Cuban-trained subversives in other Latin countries."

Richards said musingly, "Liberté." Then again, "Liberté."

"Tender nerve, Pres?" Gerard asked.

"It couldn't possibly be more tender right now."

42

"Clue me in, will you? I've been out of contact with things for the past five months. And I'd like to hear more about Alec Fletcher, if you have anything."

"We may have something more by tomorrow morning, but I wouldn't count on too much," Richards said.

Harrington looked up, checked the time, and said: "Pres, why don't you take Jim along with you and bring him up to date. And remember, we're due at the Undersecretary's office at ten in the morning."

By morning, they had received reports from both FBI and Defense. FBI was satisfied the man in the photograph was former Captain Craig Madden. The Defense people would not commit themselves; they hedged over making a positive identification, noting that the only photographs available for comparative purposes were Madden's World War II official ID prints that were smaller than passport size and had been taken under less than satisfactory conditions at a time when tens of thousands of men were being processed simultaneously. Harrington, however, readily accepted the FBI decision, based on Dave Chesler's identification.

On their way over to the State Department building, Harrington said: "Jim, we're going to do a lot of listening this morning. Undersecretary Emerson had Ambassador Chance fly up from Port Amitié last night for this talk, and we're going to sit in on part of it. However, since the ambassador isn't very cordial to the idea of Intelligence operations, we're to keep out of the discussion until we're invited to put in our two cents' worth by the Undersecretary. Understood?"

"Understood, sir."

Richards merely nodded.

4.

Undersecretary for Latin American Affairs David E. K. Emerson smiled with genuine warmth at Ambassador Extraordinary and Plenipotentiary William Ross Chance, Chief of Mission to Liberté, and blended a greeting and two questions into a single sentence. "Hello, Buck," he said extending a welcoming hand, "how's Katherine, have a nice flight?"

Chance telescoped his reply in the same manner. "Hello, Deke, she's fine, I did, and why the sudden smoke signals?"

"Sit down and unwind, Buck. Grand to see you again. How's your latest hurricane?"

Chance sat in the indicated chair beside Emerson's and pulled out a nicotine-stained white pipe and tobacco pouch from his jacket pocket. Emerson moved his own tobacco humidor within reach. "Try this for a change. Highly recommended by my gardener. I think it's his own special blend of grass cuttings and compost he manufactures on our place."

The ambassador dipped a thumb and two fingers into the walnut box, picked up a few brown shreds gingerly, sniffed critically, and dropped them back into the humidor. "Too fragrant for me, Deke." He settled back with his own pouch and began the process of filling and tamping, sucking at the stem, finally applying a wooden match to the discolored pipe. Through the window, he eyed a bleak winter sky and the naked tree branches to which clung the remains of a two-day-old snowfall. And shuddered slightly. Washington was steely-gray on this chill day; wind-whipped clouds feathered out over grimly stark granite buildings. Lawns were lifeless with stiffly frozen spikes of grass that were unappealing to the eye; men and women walked briskly into the wind; new buildings jutted upward from among the old, looking uncomfortable and out of place, like a woman waiting on a street corner for some-one who was very late.

His pipe properly fired, Chance said, "If you want to know about Hurricane Linda, she missed us by a coun-try mile. If it's our climate you're interested in—"

Emerson's smile had faded slowly. "Buck," he said, "I think you're in for some trouble."

"And you also think I've been deluding myself that everything was just dandy-peachy."

"However you feel, I think the picture is somewhat less rosy than you believe it is. The Secretary himself brought up a few questions at our last staff meeting and marked them for my special attention and action. I decided to have you up for this chat."

Chance said: "You could have come down and skipped a few days of your usual miserable weather. And got to see Katherine personally and enjoy a sample of our Carib-bean sunshine and hospitality."

"I might do that later. If Peggy had her way, we'd be

44

there right now instead of entertaining you here. You did bring Katherine with you?"

"No, not for so short a stay."

"Then let's get on with it, shall we? Seriously, Buck, the way things are going in your neck of the woods, I couldn't fly down without raising some press speculation about our sudden interest in Liberté. You know how they react when they believe we are holding out on them. Out come the clubs, and the clobbering begins."

Chance's smooth forehead wrinkled into furrows: "Then you tell me. Just what is all this sudden interest of yours? And the Secretary's?"

"First, this disturbing business of Alec Fletcher's disappearance, which seems to tie in with your earlier reports of scattered hit-and-run raids in the interior."

Chance's reply was an indistinct growl. Emerson continued. "Have you learned anything more?"

"No more than I've already reported. He's either missing or dead. I had Shannon investigate the matter thoroughly. He came up with exactly nothing. The police don't know anything, either."

Emerson picked up two sheets of closely typed matter and handed them to Chance to read. "This is the decoded report Alec filed the night he disappeared. Read it."

Chance took his time to read the report, then handed it back to Emerson, who said: "Now we know a little more about what Fletcher was chasing down. Evidently he linked it up with more than mere hit-and-run raids."

Chance said defensively, "Deke, you know how these things take on an air of greater importance this close to the Libertéan election—"

"This is more than local brush fire, Buck. Alec's disappearance, or death, points it up all the more."

"Damn it, I know that. To have a boy like that die uselessly—"

"Hold it," Emerson said. "We don't know for sure that he's dead, do we?"

"Oh, come off it, Deke. You don't really believe he's alive, do you?"

"I don't know that he's dead, either."

"Goddam it, Deke, what else can you expect? You ship in an Intelligence man who goes chasing around the island without my knowing what he's up to, where he's going, or whom he's in contact with. Now, when he gets himself—involved—and disappears, I'm called on the carpet to explain. All right. I was opposed to it from the very outset, remember? You just can't hide an undercover agent anywhere in the world today. He's prelabeled. Suspicion alone is enough to get him killed—"

"Take it easy, Buck, you're coming on too fast for me. You're not on anybody's carpet, and we're not asking you to assume responsibility for anything. Except to know exactly what is going on down there. Fact, not surface appearances, not rumor. Fact."

Chance snorted impatiently. "You know the situation as it exists. Aside from those raids, that island is secure. President Fontaine hasn't been any more of a joy to me than he has to you, but I've managed to keep him contained. Now, with their election coming on soon, he'll be out of office and—"

Emerson finished the sentence for him. "—it's all the more important to keep a close watch on those brush fires. That name, Chalumeau, should be interesting to you. Also, something that has come to our attention from Havana that involves General Batraville and Foreign Minister St. Germaine."

"What?"

Emerson smiled. "That's exactly why we're meeting shortly with the people I've asked in. They have something very interesting to show you." He looked at his watch, and added, "Should be here in a few minutes."

He had no sooner uttered the words than a light flashed at the base of his intercom set. He depressed the lever and heard his secretary's voice say, "The three gentlemen are here, sir."

The three men from JIA had shown the photographs, and Jim Gerard had spoken quietly, with undeniable clarity, and conclusively. Chance was at once interested and impressed with Harrington's introduction to the problem that undoubtedly tied Cuba and Liberté together, followed by Gerard's line of reasoning and Richards's summation. His earlier rebellious attitude faded when he saw the photograph of General Batraville and Foreign Minister St. Germaine together with Domingo Urbana and the American defector, Craig Madden, alias John Mosher. He sat examining the set of photocopies of the carbon sheets Gerard had gotten from Simón Ramírez that listed various ships scheduled for loading and departure, or awaiting instructions.

Gerard was saying, "—the name *Jewel*, sir, is the most recent code name, and appeared shortly after Batraville and St. Germaine left Havana. We believe it is intended to identify Liberté. And since it comes from Urbana's department, we can assume that a loading of arms and ammunition is indicated for the near future."

"*Jewel*," Chance repeated. "It could just as well be one of half a dozen other countries Castro is interested in, couldn't it?"

"It could," Harrington said softly, "but I would rather rely on Gerard's educated guess, taking into consideration the visit of Batraville and St. Germaine at that precise moment."

And then, as quietly as they had arrived, the three men from JIA were gone, leaving their report, photographs, and recommendations for Emerson and the ambassador to mull over.

Chance burrowed deeper into his chair, knowing what was about to come. More agents. Young, overeager men running around the island posing as attachés, upsetting normal routine, creating embarrassing situations that he would have to explain under the harsh, antagonistic stare of the foreign minister or president. It had happened before, the very same damned thing, with CIA agents in the Middle East when he had been notified that he was no longer welcome and must return to Washington. The thought of that experience curdled something inside him.

"Well, Buck," Emerson broke in on his thoughts, "what do you think now?"

"I've had a pretty fair-sized dose of the unpleasant side of the picture—" Chance began, but Emerson was pressing his point.

"Why don't we take the realistic view," he said, applying the pressure gently. "Our image in the Far East is pretty dim at the moment. In Europe, we're still in a battle over East Berlin, and De Gaulle isn't making our position any more pleasant or easier. Africa is a tinderbox ready to flare up at the drop of a match. We haven't nearly enough hoses to put out the brush fires they've got started there right now. In our own back yard, our allies as well as the Red bloc are trading with Cuba and making our trade embargo look rather weak and silly. Our own face hasn't been made any cleaner since the wheat deal with Russia. At the moment, the administration is particularly concerned that no overt or covert act takes place to worsen our position, especially in our own immediate sphere of influence. Defense is just as skittish about it as the White House is, the Men on the Hill, as we are. And you, my very dear and old friend, are sitting in the catbird seat."

"The what?"

"The catbird seat. First row, center. Liberté seems to be next on the list. And you'd better believe that."

"Why?"

"Because if you don't, and it comes off, heads will surely roll, including mine. You've got nearly twenty-five years and a hell of a fine record going for your career, and I, for one, think too highly of you to want to see it washed down the drain. I'll be honest with you. We've had you pegged for bigger things, but if we have a bad guess on our shoulders now—"

The catbird seat, Chance thought. More like the seat in the gas chamber, waiting for the pellet to drop. And then he remembered Ambassador Nathan Childress, whom he had replaced in Port Amitié. One diplomatic error and they'll be accepting my resignation, just as they did Childress's, "with regrets," and put me out to pasture. Good God, where does it end?

He heard Emerson saying, "How does it feel to be a primary target?"

"I've been there before, Deke, and I still don't like it. All right, suppose I agree that everything is packaged into a mess of trouble, that the whole thing is Cuban- or Russian-inspired. Or admit to the possibility of a purely internal revolt. Where do we stand at the moment?"

"Right at the barrier. I want you to take on someone to replace Alec Fletcher and start digging in hard and deep."

Chance emitted a small groan. Emerson said quickly, "Don't fight me on this, please. You've lost a man—"

Chance said heatedly: "*I* didn't lose him, Deke. Goddam it, he was *your* man, sent in by you. Maybe—"

"Maybe," Emerson cut him off curtly. "And maybe nothing. I can't help it. That's the way it's stacked up and that's the way it's got to be."

The two men sat staring at each other for a few moments in silence; then Chance said: "All right, Deke. You're calling the shots. How many do you want to send in?"

"Only one. The younger of the three people you just met. Gerard."

Chance nodded, not too unhappy that there would be one man and that the one man would be Jim Gerard. "Since I have little choice, it does make me feel a little more comfortable. He seems older and better equipped and qualified than Fletcher."

"He is. He's JIA's top man. We're going to give him a crash briefing, and he'll probably show up in about a week. How about a cover for him?"

"Well, we had Fletcher in as assistant commercial attaché. I suppose we can put him in as assistant press attaché to Ray Ferriss, but all these covers seem a bit silly. Why not just play it straight and let him work with our Security Officer, Clark Shannon?"

"Perhaps. If he won't have to stumble over Shannon."

"I'll see to that."

"Then suppose we keep it open and let Gerard take his choice."

"All right. Just keep me posted." Chance stood up. "Are we finished? If we are, I'd like to get over to Andrews Field and start back. I've got a lot of loose ends to look into now that I know what the climate is."

"Good. I'll have you driven over right away."

5.

Prescott Richards had a luncheon appointment with the head of the Human Factors Section, which left Jim Gerard to dawdle over his meal alone in the JIA dining room. It was filled almost to its vast capacity, and he had the feeling of being a complete stranger among the many new faces he saw at the surrounding tables. One or two were vaguely familiar, but he made no effort to join them. Nor, in accordance with customary practice, did anyone approach him.

Until the waitress came to take his order, he played an old familiar game of separating agents from lab technicians, scientists, executives, and administrative personnel in the room. Practice had made it an easy game. The agents were usually men of average height, weight, looks, and features. They dressed modestly and would more readily fit the description of senior clerks, accountants, barbers, dentists, lawyers, or fall into any of a hundred indefinite and nondistinguishable categories—any

49

rather than that of highly skilled and trained men in a very specialized field. They were less prone to engage in deep, serious discussions, unlike most of the others who worked and ate together in small cliques that carried on their work even at mealtimes.

The waitress came and he gave his order. The game was broken off as he returned to more objective thoughts. It was obvious that he would be asked to take another foreign assignment, and at once. The deputy director had not indicated a decision in so many words, but he had little doubt that he would be included in the Liberté operation that had begun to cloud the horizon. Nor would Harrington make his choice lightly.

To be chosen for a special assignment by the deputy director was in itself a tribute to a man's ability. Special Operations Branch, the élite of JIA (and known, quite naturally, as Harrington's S.O.B.'s), was a small, closely knit corps of specialists. The S.O.B. man frequently worked alone, established his own contacts in the field, ran his own risks and, as it had happened in the past, died by his own miscalculations. In a service where there were few rewards beyond the satisfaction of accomplishment, with no drums or bugles or medals to herald success, the fatality factor had been relatively light, a credit to Harrington's uncanny second sense in picking the right man for the right job.

In his own case, he had come fresh from Penn State to Army G-2, having given up further thought of a career in law when his father was killed in a tragic motor accident. To give himself time to think, Gerard decided to take his Army training, get it over with, and then decide on his future. Because of his law schooling and an exceptional facility for languages, the Army had commissioned him and assigned him to Intelligence work. At the end of a year of intensive training, he had spent his next two years in the operational field abroad. He was elated when, by order of General Dixie Harrington, he was transferred to the Pentagon for a tour of domestic duty.

Gerard was at the point of resigning his commission when Harrington retired from active duty and moved over to the Joint Intelligence Agency as deputy director of the Special Operations Branch. He had Gerard in for a long talk, which resulted in Gerard's move over to JIA.

In S.O.B., he had been put through further technical

training by a handful of specialists, progressing through the parachute school at Fort Benning into advanced skills in self-defense, domestic and foreign weaponry, updating his knowledge of explosives and demolition, communications equipment; he also kept up with his language studies.

Among other qualifications, he was required to be well read, currently informed, and his mind converted into what his chief called "a storehouse of miscellaneous information, both useful and useless." He learned the fascinating art of improvisation. Experts in all manner of trickery taught him to keep alert for the unusual and different, to be suspicious of the commonplace. Step by step, he became actor, reporter of fact, wire-tapper, forger, saboteur, escape artist, expert in photography and microphotography. He was required to mingle with and operate at top, intermediate, and lower social, diplomatic, and military levels with equal tact and ease; to handle large sums of cash for buying, hiring, or bribing; to make use of the special tools devised by JIA's lab experts. Also, to kill unflinchingly when it became necessary. And always, he remembered the deputy director's valediction on the day of his first field assignment abroad:

There is always the enemy—overconfidence and carelessness. Not necessarily on your part, but on the part of someone in whom you have put your faith, trust, and life. And never underestimate the living enemy. He is there, always, waiting patiently for you to make one small slip. Tell yourself each morning that HE IS THERE! *And he is as well trained, intelligent, and resourceful as you, regardless of race, color, or culture. He will never give you a second chance, so be sure you don't give him the first one. If you do, you could very well be giving your life with it.*

One-thirty. Time for another cup of coffee and a cigarette. Again he examined his memory for the scanty scraps he remembered of Alec Fletcher. From the file he had seen in Richards's office, the recorded facts were familiar: Fletcher was twenty-six, Alabama-born, a graduate of Tuskegee Institute, *summa cum laude*, selected for unusual ability and leadership in the Army. Excellent performance in local security and investigative work, sent to Liberté because of his knowledge of French and his color, which would permit him to mingle with local natives without undue notice. Liberté, then, was Fletcher's first foreign assignment, chosen because of a shortage of men with qualified field service, and because he had volunteered after the danger potential had been pointed out to him.

Gerard thought again of the day Harrington had given him the Cuban assignment, with Pres Richards as his co-ordinator; and Harrington's last words before he took off for the rendezvous with the submarine off Norfolk that would bring him within swimming distance of the isolated Cuban shore where he would meet Luis Sándoz for the first time. They had shared lunch in the executive dining section of this very room, and Harrington had said, rather than asked, "All set, Jim."

"All set, sir."

"This will take several months. You know what we need and need badly; the observations of refugees, however willing and helpful, are prejudiced and therefore not reliable. The U-2's and RB-66's can't get close enough for the minute and detailed confirmation we need. It will be up to you. Anything you can send out to us will be important. When you get the word to pull out, get out by one of the three plans we've outlined. We won't pull you unless it is vital. When the word comes, get out as fast as you can with as much as you can."

"I understand, sir."

A few moments passed before Harrington said, much to Gerard's surprise, "You know that Pres Richards is retiring soon."

"I hadn't heard that, sir."

Harrington's brief nod was an affirmation. "I seldom make an assignment in advance, Jim, but when you are finished with this one, I want you to step into Richards's shoes. If I weren't so greatly in need of you on this Cuban thing, I'd have you in as my assistant now, but I've had to ask Pres to stay on until you're back."

It was as close to a voiced commendation as Harrington had ever come beyond a "Well done, Jim," and Gerard felt a surge of pride sweep through him. All he could think of to say was, "Thank you, sir."

And now the Cuban assignment was completed: at least for the moment.

6.

The six days that followed were too completely filled to give Gerard time to think of anything but the assignment at hand. He had finished with the briefings at State, devoured every research detail JIA's investigators could come up with, gone over the demo refresher course, and was being checked out by small-arms expert Brian Howell on the pistol range in the basement of the headquarters building.

"Ready, Mr. Gerard?"

"Any time you are, Brian."

Howell pressed the button on the panel in front of him. The sweep second hand on the large dial began to move as the silhouette target of a man turned from its narrow side view to full front and began turning back to its side. The revolver in Gerard's hand leaped to life. He got off five of the six shots as the lights went out in the target area.

"Still pretty good for an ailing old man, eh, Brian?" Gerard said.

"I've seen worse. A few more sessions and you'll be able to get that sixth shot off with half a second to spare."

Gerard nodded noncommittally, knowing there wouldn't be "a few more sessions," the reason why he had asked the chief instructor to speed up the clock action and allow him two seconds less time in which to get his six shots off. From behind him, Pres Richards, dressed as Gerard was in sweat suit and tennis sneakers, said: "Not bad. Glad we're on the same side, Jim. I don't think I could hit a bag from the inside of it any more."

Howell's tongue cluck-clucked against teeth and lips. "Mr. Richards is trying to con you into a bet. Don't take him on. Never known a better shot than him in his day."

" 'In his day,' " Richards repeated with a smile. "Well, that classifies me pretty well, even if it doesn't cheer me up much. How about the steam room, Jim?"

"Sure. I'm finished here."

"Go ahead. I'll catch up with you."

Gerard unscrewed the blunt attachment from his .38 and weighed it in the palm of his hand. "Neat gadget. Best the lab's come up with yet, Brian."

"Getting a lot of good reports from the field on it, Mr.

53

Gerard. Not only noiseless, but flashless. And small enough to be practical. It's got a lot going for it. Are you going to take that one?"

"I think so. I'll let you know how it works in the field."

"I'll have to charge it out to you by number. Stop in on your way back and I'll have the memo receipt for you to sign."

Gerard walked down the hall to the locker room, got out of his sweat suit, socks, and tennis sneakers, wrapped one towel around his waist and draped another over his shoulders. He slipped on a pair of wooden-soled clogs, clomped past the tiled shower compartments and into the steam rooms. John Nero, the old attendant, was holding a glass door open for him. "No. 6, Mr. Gerard," he said. "Mr. Richards telephoned. He'll be along in a minute or two."

"Thanks, Emperor," Gerard said. Nero went inside with him and adjusted the steam outlet valve, which began to hiss immediately. "Get your muscles in shape, Emperor. I'll want a stiff rub after."

"I'll be here, sir."

Four minutes later, Richards entered, a towel around his middle. He lay down on the shelf below Gerard with a sigh, and after a bit of shrugging his body into a comfortable position, said, "You're getting out tomorrow morning, Jim. All set?"

"If you mean the briefings and boning up on Chance's and Fletcher's reports, I'm as set as I'll ever be. I still don't know what I'm looking for besides Alec."

"You'll get clued in by Chance. More likely by his counselor, Thorne Truscott. You're going out on Pan Am's 106 at 7:10 in the morning. Play it cool and keep in touch. It's just possible something may come in from the Havana end on *Jewel* that could be useful. Try to get hold of any papers Alec may have left behind. Chance said they'd cleaned his safe out, which means that if they had access to it, he wouldn't have left anything valuable where anyone else could find it."

Gerard nodded his response, even though he knew Richards couldn't see him on the upper ledge.

"One thing more, Jim. I—I held this out on you."

"What?"

"It's a personal matter. You'd better know about it."

Gerard didn't say anything, but waited. "It's Eleanor

Devlin," Richards said. Gerard almost jerked himself upright, caught himself in time. "You were once engaged to her, weren't you?"

"Not officially."

"Yes. Anyway, I thought it best to mention this to you. I don't want you walking into a surprise. Eleanor is Ambassador Chance's administrative officer in Port Amitié."

Gerard sat up and swung his legs over the step. "What? Nora?"

"Yes. But you'll find she's Eleanor Lund now. She left her job at State about six months after you went to Vietnam. Married Braden Lund who'd just come up from Buenos Aires for leave and reassignment. They went on to Rio, where he was first secretary in the political section. Lund died almost two years ago. Leukemia. State offered Eleanor a commission in Foreign Service when Chance, an old friend of Lund's, asked for her. She's been in Port Amitié ever since. About eighteen months."

Gerard leaned back against the wooden shelf, sucking the hot air through his mouth, feeling his pulse race. "Why didn't you tell me about it before I went to Cuba?" he asked in a tight voice.

He could almost sense the shrug in Richards's reply. "She wasn't *in* Cuba, so she couldn't affect your work there. But she *is* in Port Amitié. I don't want to expose you to the sudden shock of walking in on her without a warning."

Never underestimate Harrington or Richards, Gerard thought ruefully. So they'd known about Nora Devlin and himself all along. How much? he wondered now. If she weren't in Port Amitié, they'd probably have said nothing about her. Almost four years had passed since he'd seen her last, the morning of the same day he'd caught the plane for Vietnam. Nora. How much difference would there be after four years? She would be what?—twenty-seven to his thirty-two. How would it be between them now? What—

"I hope you understand," Richards said after the long silence.

"Thanks, Pres," Gerard said dryly.

Richards got up and adjusted the towel around his waist. "That's all I can take of this." Then: "Jim, you know I couldn't tell you before. It wasn't mine to tell."

"Sure, I know," Gerard said, trying to make it come out light and easy, but failing to hide the small anger and sudden resentment that had welled up inside him. "It's a tough service."

Richards had slipped into his clogs and gone to the door. He had one hand on the handle, ready to pull it open, then turned back. "I'm sorry, Jim." A pause, then: "One thing more. When this one is through, I'm getting out. Retiring. And this is out of school, so keep it to yourself. Okay?"

Gerard nodded laconically. By the code under which they operated, he would not mention the fact that Harrington had spoken to him of Richards's retirement before he went to Cuba.

"Dix and I have been discussing my replacement as his assistant."

"So?"

Richards smiled and said: "You're it if you want it, Jim. Come back healthy." Before Gerard could reply, Richards had pulled the door open and was heading toward the showers.

CHAPTER 3

1. Liberté

The island of Liberté is about the size of Maryland, with somewhat less population, but more densely populated per square mile in its habitable areas because so much of the land is given over to mountain and jungle. From high in the air, it is a rich, many-hued jewel set in an erratically shaped blue-green mounting, glistening with brilliant highlights of white beaches that are frequently interrupted by stretches of lush, wild foliage, occasional picturesque coastal towns, and sudden sheer cliffs that thrust majestically upward out of the Caribbean Sea. Shimmering heat waves add the illusion of movement to its mountain ranges, shaped somewhat like the huge spines of cumbersome prehistoric behemoths who, having overfed upon the valley's succulent growth, have begun to grope slowly and awkwardly toward the sea to quench their thirst.

Certainly the first breath-taking view from such a height is startlingly magnificent, and at once recalls enchanting descriptive passages from the works of C. S. Forester, of Cook, Nordhoff and Hall, or Michener; and brings to mind such stimulating and exotic names as Papeete, Bali, Bora Bora, thousands of miles distant from these West Indian islands; to conjure visions of graceful, dusky houri, unbelievable tropic sunsets, ancient sacrificial rites, tribal wars, pig hunts, song, laughter, feasting and indescribable pleasures that reach all senses.

But beauty observed from thousands of feet in the air can never reveal, or hardly suggest, the steaming heat and violence of interior jungles and swamps that lie below in contradiction to its peaceful appearance, camouflaged by deceptive tangles of thorny thickets and strangler vines that entice and trap and kill when one's sense of awareness and respect for Nature's grimmer side becomes momentarily sluggish.

From such a height, it is impossible to see into the poisonous marshes that are alive with yellow-legs, plover, curlew, and heron, the hundreds of other colorfully plumaged birds whose strange native names the average traveler would scarcely have heard before; birds that racket, shriek, and halloo in deafening cacophonic symphony; nor see, as the roar of the jet wakens them from their slumbers, the scarlet flamingos that rise in fright out of the canebrakes, the ibises, egrets, jaconas, and coots that come suddenly and furiously alive; nor the rest of the world of abundant life that, once wakened, begins to surge toward known feeding grounds or a watering hole, possibly to encounter the fearsome crocodiles that lay in shallow ooze, peering through malevolent eyes, waiting hungrily, ready to snatch, crush, and devour an unwary prey between steel jaws.

As the plane lowers its landing gear and noses downward in descent approach to Port Amitié, the capital city of Liberté, one's attention is diverted to the colorful mosaic of white, pastel pink, blue, green, and ocher dots and squares and oblongs that quickly materialize into hillside homes; and only then is one returned to reality as he contemplates that the rewards of a successful sugar, coffee, cocoa, or sisal plantation must indeed be considerable if such grandeur and opulence are examples of a way of life here.

From the center of Port Amitié, the core of which is the gleaming white Presidential Palace, other government buildings encircle its beautifully kept and well-guarded grounds; behind it, the *caserne*, or military barracks, houses the Palace Guard; on either side, and facing it across the broad Champs de Révolution, various ministries and Army administrative buildings are more somberly clad in ocher. These in turn are surrounded by commercial buildings and establishments; Port Amitié's banks, hotels, office buildings, stores, restaurants, cafés, and every other manner of enterprise.

To the west lies the crescent-shaped harbor with its two long docks that finger out into the sea, where ships of many sizes and tonnage and registry huddle close, linked by heavy umbilical cords as they load and unload cargo. To the east, where the city begins to rise along the slope that reaches to the top of Mont Couronne, the homes and estates of the *haut volée* begin, each with spacious grounds and formal gardens, mounting higher and more pretentious until they come to a halt at the base of the crest where the summer home of the president, known as Bellefonte (often as *le petit palais*), commands the most magnificent view of the city and open sea. Thousands of royal palms arch upward amid groves of trees and exotic varieties of colorful shrubs, waving their shaggy, explosive heads over acres of flowering bushes in the soft breeze.

To make the picture more delectable and appealing, the jet passenger is spared a close view of the teeming *quartier misérable* that covers an area of some five blocks in depth immediately adjacent to the waterfront, and runs for several miles north and south of the busy port. Seldom do visitors penetrate this vile, disease-ridden slum of hungry, appallingly poverty-stricken natives; in fact, it is a rarity indeed when the Port Amitiéan who lives outside this ghetto of misery is seen close to it; for, despite years of foreign aid and surplus food allotments to bolster and improve its incredibly low standard of living, the slum remains—not only remains, but thrives and worsens with a constantly exploding population.

2.

Pan Am 106 put down smoothly on the center strip and taxied the length of the field to a concrete building beside the tower structure. Gerard was last off the plane, enjoying the stretch of his long legs as he crossed the black-topped walk to the reception area. As he entered the hot, open shed, he caught a glimpse of a familiar suntan uniform on a Marine First Sergeant who stepped up briskly and saluted smartly. "Mr. Gerard?"

"Yes."

"First Sergeant Walker, Embassy Security Guard. Mr. Shannon is waiting at the car. If you'll give me your checks and passport, I'll clear your baggage in a minute. The stuff you shipped in the other day is in locked storage at the embassy as you requested."

"Thanks, Sergeant." He handed over checks and diplomatic passport, turned, and came face to face with a rumpled man who smiled as he extended his hand. "I'm Shannon, Gerard. Glad to see you. Welcome to Port Amitié. We'll have you out of here in no time. How was Washington when you left?"

They skirted the Customs shed and went into the air-conditioned main building. Gerard was grateful for having been spared the temporary purgatory of the corrugated iron-roofed inspection shed.

"Freezing," Gerard replied to Shannon's question. The older man permitted himself a small, tight smile of satisfaction. "Ah, the poor peasant bastards," he said. "How I do bleed for them." Then, "You don't look as pale as the rest of them, more like you'd been hitting the beaches at Miami."

Gerard winked conspiratorially and said, "Sun lamp." He turned to watch Sergeant Walker and two Libertéan workmen manhandling his small trunk and two suitcases into an olive-green pickup truck that stood beside the black sedan with diplomatic plates. Shannon was saying: "Mr. Truscott would have been here to meet you himself but something came up. The Old Man had to go over to the palace, and Truscott's minding the store, so I was elected to do the honors."

"Thanks. It's Clark, isn't it? Mine is Jim."

"Glad to know you, Jim." He looked around them to make sure he would not be overheard, then said, "Truscott clued me in on you—"

"Fine. We'll talk about it later," Gerard warned him off. "What is the quarters situation like?"

"Damn little available. Decent billeting is tough down here, and we've got a full staff." He glanced around again and said in a lower tone, "Of course, there's Alec Fletcher's house—"

Gerard said quickly, "I'll take that."

"—if it's okay with Billeting," Shannon concluded. "We'll stop by the chancellery first and pick up the keys. Okay?"

"Okay." Sergeant Walker was standing beside them, and handed the passport back to Gerard. "Ready to roll, sir."

"Let's go, then," Shannon said. "Chancellery first. You go ahead, Jake, and I'll follow."

Shannon got in behind the wheel of the black sedan and waited until Walker's pickup truck with the two Libertéans pulled out in front of them. They came into the city from the north, paused at the ornate arch where all traffic stopped to exchange words with the military guard. The pickup truck, recognized by its color, was waved to one side and permitted to pass. The sedan had to wait its turn in line. When they finally reached the sentry hut, they were passed through quickly when the sentry caught a glimpse of the diplomatic tags and the American flags flying from both fenders. "Checkpoint," Shannon explained. "Everybody's so damned jittery around here, they've got these things up all over the place. Bloody nuisance, but Fontaine's got a wild hair up his ass about rumors of invasion or revolution or one thing or another." He slowed down and turned halfway toward Gerard, then threw a quick look out the rear window. "I thought so," he chuckled. "We've got our escort."

"Escort?"

"Honor guard. Take a look. The black Plymouth."

Gerard turned and saw the car about fifty yards behind them. "A tail?"

"Sure. Security police. Meets all trains, planes, ships and buses. Standard Operating Procedure No. 1. Particularly when a new man comes in from Washington. You'll probably have company on your tail until they make up their minds whether you're legitimate or CIA." Shannon laughed abruptly. "You'll get used to it. Gets so you miss 'em if they aren't around."

"How would they have known I was coming in?"

Shannon shrugged. "Not necessarily you. Could've been anybody. One thing, we've got local people working at the store. Two: when I went through the checkpoint to meet you, the sentry probably called the word into Lieutenant Falot, General Batraville's bird dog on the arrival detail. Don't worry about it."

Shannon's nonchalance, affected or otherwise, was beginning to annoy Gerard. Now, whether to impress his passenger or indulge himself, Shannon began taking elaborate evasive measures to lose their rear escort. He dodged in and out of traffic somewhat recklessly, turned up narrow side streets, and emerged into the heavier-trafficked avenues, circled one block twice, and finally lost the black Plymouth. Gerard watched the clumsy game with mild amusement, and nodded when Shannon grunted to let him know they were in the clear, but later, when they entered the embassy grounds and took the salute from the pair of Marine sentries at the open gates, Gerard noticed, as Shannon had not, that the black Plymouth was standing at the curb about thirty yards beyond the entrance.

3.

The American Embassy was a huge, splendidly colonnaded mansion whose twelve tapered columns rose from ground level through two broad verandas to the fretted roofline three stories high. It had been built in 1890 by Jonelle Pitou, an enormously wealthy shipping magnate whose judgment, money, and influence had correctly backed four presidents in quick succession, including Armand Lapere, in exchange for certain valuable commercial privileges that had raised the presidential fortune along with M'sieu Pitou's.

Five years after Lapere had entered office, Pitou received a quiet signal one night from his patron in the palace. Quickly, the two men moved their families aboard the shipping magnate's palatial yacht and led a parade of several well-filled vessels to a safe Mediterranean port. Thereupon, they proceeded to live as only multimillionaires of that period could afford.

Unfortunately for ex-President Lapere, he became bored; and with boredom came a failure in his reasoning. He came to believe that time heals not only wounds but also memories of grand theft and heinous crimes with which he had been charged by the junta about to overthrow him. Three years after his abdication, he decided to return to Liberté and finance a revolt against his successor. This slight miscalculation cost him his life. Within four hours after his presence in Port Amitié became known, Armand Lapere was murdered in his hotel suite.

Shipping magnate Pitou's abandoned mansion became the official residence of the current president, but in time, aware of the danger in having to travel twelve blocks from Rue Montrez to the palace, the president decided to give up this adventurous daring, and converted a large wing of the palace and went to live there in comparative safety. In 1910 the Pitou Mansion was leased to the United States Government for a period of ninety-nine years for use as its embassy. To commemorate the occasion, Rue Montrez was renamed Rue des Américains.

The stately mansion had defied the compulsive efforts of successive ambassadresses to redecorate and remodel its interior into "a touch of home away from home" ever since the first American flag flew over it. After more than fifty years of such effort, Katherine Chance spent a full year restoring it to its original colonial beauty, elegance, and charm. Rugs were taken up to reveal handsome Moorish tiled floors in the broad entrance hallway and rooms on the lower level; layers of paint were burned and scraped from its walls until original mahogany surfaces were eventually restored, then waxed and polished. Its rooms were large, high-ceilinged and thick-walled for coolness. Those on the ground level opened onto broad, mosaic-tiled verandas, and one wing had been converted into a suite of offices for the ambassador's private use.

The broad entrance whose wide, exquisitely carved and balustraded stairway swept regally up to the formal ballroom, dining room, library, and the ambassador's private quarters, was a splendid example of the artistry of an earlier day blended with architecture. Every room blazed with flowers, changed daily so that when one stepped from the outside in, both color and atmosphere were nearly the same. The dozen rooms on the third floor had been made into suites for guest use, or, should an emergency arise to make it impossible for anyone to leave, bedrooms for the embassy's American employees.

Behind the embassy stood the chancellery, added in 1925, where the various attachés and officers of lesser rank performed their duties. Separated from these two buildings by a formal garden, tennis courts, and a swimming pool were four small guest houses. At the far end of the grounds were quarters for the small contingent of Marines assigned to embassy security, the motor pool, garage and other utility buildings.

At the chancellery there was a momentary problem with Ben Green, who seemed to be the most harassed individual among the staff whom Shannon had introduced to Gerard. Green's small office appeared to be the catchall for personal problems and woes. To him fell the duty of providing quarters, engaging household servants, arranging air, sea, and ground transportation, hiring native personnel employed by the embassy, supply information regarding doctors, dentists, schools for children, where to buy what, how much to pay for it, and, in general, to take care of the more or less personal needs and requirements of the embassy's officers, attachés, and staff.

"I have a memorandum here"—Green shuffled through a pile of green, blue, white, pink, and yellow papers— "yes, here it is," he exclaimed with subdued glee, "yes. Mr.

James Gerard. Let me see. Disposition—open." He looked up brightly. "Until we can make a permanent arrangement, there's the Hotel Métropole, the—"

Shannon said, "How about Alec Fletcher's house, Ben?"

Green shook his head disconsolately. "I have no authority—"

"Then call Mrs. Lund and get the goddam authority, can't you? We can't crap around here all day."

"But Mrs. Lund—" Green began indignantly.

"Are you going to call her or shall I?" Shannon demanded.

Green regarded Shannon with cold distaste and looked to Gerard with round, helpless eyes. Gerard smiled and said, "I hate to upset your routine, Mr. Green, but if I may see Mrs. Lund, perhaps—"

"I'm sorry, Mr. Gerard. Mrs. Lund is in a conference with Mr. Truscott."

"Then get on that goddam horn and talk to her, for Cris'sakes," Shannon insisted. "Hell, she's easy to talk to."

Green shrugged, cradled the receiver between ear and shoulder, and dialed the extension, then turned his back on Gerard and Shannon as he spoke into the instrument. There were a few questions they could not hear, then a series of soft expostulations, a "But, Mrs. Lund, you—" and another, "But—" then, "Yes, Mrs. Lund, of course." He hung up and turned back to Gerard, dejected with fatigue and defeat. "Mr. Fletcher's quarters are available, Mr. Gerard. No. 11 Rue Perrigeau." He wrote the address on a slip of yellow paper and pushed it, with two keys, across the desk. "There's a phone installed, and I'll have service connected this afternoon. You'll find a button at the base of the instrument. In a vertical position, you dial 'O' to get the embassy operator. Someone will be on duty around the clock. In a horizontal position—"

Shannon snickered. "I'm sure Mr. Gerard knows all about telephone operators in a horizontal position—"

"—you are connected with the outside operator," Green continued, ignoring Shannon's vulgarity. "If there is a language problem, it's best to go through the switchboard. The two household servants we employed for Mr. Fletcher are still in residence, if that is satisfactory, and—"

"Thank you, Mr. Green, I'm certain it will be," Gerard said.

"And about transportation, Mr. Gerard—" Green was

shaking his head, a man about to deliver a piece of discouraging news.

"He doesn't have a car, Ben. You'll have to scrounge one up for him," Shannon said.

"I'm afraid—"

"Sure you are, Benny. Let's go, Jim."

Outside, Shannon laughed and said: "Poor Benny. All you have to do to get a hammerlock on his nervous system is to ask him for a car. Or something else hard to get." Walker had already gotten the wooden box and two cartons that had been shipped earlier and was waiting in the lobby for them, talking to the marine on duty at the information desk.

"No. 11 Rue Perrigeau, Jake. Alec Fletcher's old quarters," Shannon said. Gerard steeled himself when he heard the word "old," recalled that Ben Green, in mentioning Alec's name, had lowered his voice. Shannon added: "You take Mr. Gerard up with you, Jake. I've got to get back to the office." To Gerard: "See you when you're squared away, Jim. Take your time. No rush."

The small house that had been assigned to Alec Fletcher was on a sloping hillside almost a mile east of the embassy. It was fully furnished and showed signs of Fletcher's recent occupancy. The grounds were enclosed by a six-foot wall of weathered brick, with a wide, wrought-iron gate of intricate workmanship. A path of crushed stone curved in a wide circle for some thirty or forty yards through a lush garden to the entrance steps of the house. On each step of the four, and along the fully screened veranda, rows of blue, pink, and red pots of flowers were massed in colorful profusion. Deep purple bougainvillaea trailed downward from the roof and hung like an erratic frame above the upper edges of the screening. Inside, the house was cool, comfortable in size, and furnished in simple, pleasant taste.

On the first floor were a broad living room, dining room, study, and kitchen. In the entrance hallway, a narrow stairway ran along the left wall to the second floor to two bedrooms, master bathroom, a separate shower, and a small room lined with Alec's books, and which he no doubt used as his workroom. About twenty yards behind the house were two small hutlike buildings for servant and utility use, as well as an open carport.

Jacques, a tall, brawny black man, naked to the waist,

wore a pair of white pants that ended just below the thick calves of his legs, an oversized pair of crudely made sandals, and a wide-brimmed straw hat. He held a wicked-looking, well-honed machete in his hand, and had evidently been working in the garden. He took off his hat and grinned a broad welcome to Gerard, delighted that the *blanc* could speak the language so fluently. Yvonne, his wife, was a short, round, smiling woman who wore a single garment that was tied around her ample waist with a cord, and stood waiting for orders. Jacques lifted one of the heavy wooden boxes from the truck and placed it on her head, while he took Gerard's dispatch case and carried it inside the house.

The rest of the baggage was unloaded by the workmen and brought to the spare bedroom, where it lay unopened. "That's fine, Jake," Gerard said. "I'll unpack these later."

"You got a car coming down, Mr. Gerard?" the sergeant asked.

"No. What form of transportation did Mr. Fletcher use?"

"A Ford sedan. It's at the motor pool. Cars are short, so if you've got any ideas about using it, you'll have to fight Ben Green for it." He winked slyly. "Of course, if you get to rate any pull with Mrs. Lund, you've got it made."

"Thanks, Jake. From the way people use her name around here, anyone would think she was the ambassador."

"Well, not exactly. She's administrative officer and—well, she's kind of okay. She gets things done."

As he suddenly remembered her, Gerard nodded his head. "I get it. The embassy den mother. Okay, Jake, how about a drink?"

"Not during duty hours. Got to set an example for the boys. They get enough ideas of their own without any encouragement from me."

Gerard took out a key ring and unlocked the trunk and found a fifth of Scotch. "How about taking this along for later."

"Sure, thanks. By the way, you could've saved yourself some money buying this stuff here instead of bringing it down from the States. We've got an exchange at the factory. No duty, no local taxes."

"I'll have to remember that. Let me lock this trunk and I'll ride back to the—uh—factory with you."

4.

In the executive wing of the embassy, Thorne Truscott slouched in a large leather chair as he worked over some papers at his desk. When Gerard entered the room behind the counselor's secretary, Miss Sarah Bennett, an attractive, briskly efficient woman in her mid-forties, Truscott rose to greet his visitor. The room, like the outer entrance hallway, was paved with richly colored tiles and was paneled in native mahogany. There were two large and two small Oriental rugs scattered over the broad expanse of floor, several pieces of statuary on heavy bases, and a number of handsome, hand-carved cabinets against the walls. A half dozen primitives by Libertéan artists hung on two walls, dark and brooding in theme and mood.

Truscott came out from behind his desk, moving in an easy, loose-jointed manner, smiled pleasantly as he shook hands, and indicated a less formal conversational area on the far side of the room away from his desk, to a long, upholstered sofa and three matching chairs. Miss Bennett disappeared and returned a few moments later with a coffee tray that she placed on a low table before them. She went out again and pulled the shuttered doors closed behind her.

"Welcome aboard," Truscott said as he poured the coffee. "That makes it official now. Did Shannon get you settled?"

"Yes, thank you. He checked me in and I've already stowed my gear in Alec Fletcher's quarters."

"Fletcher's?" Truscott's alert eyes opened a fraction wider as his eyebrows moved upward in question momentarily. "Well, glad you're settled. The ambassador is at the palace at the moment, but I expect him back shortly. He and I have discussed this assignment of yours. So far, only Shannon and Mrs. Lund, our administrative officer, have been told." He paused, sipped at his coffee, then added with a resigned half-smile, "Naturally, we'll try to keep this among ourselves, but it is inevitable that others will come to know, or suspect. And of course, there will be the usual rumors among the water-cooler set, particularly since you'll be occupying Alec's quarters."

"I don't see that it really matters," Gerard said.

"All right, then let me bring you up to date, which is practically nowhere. There's still no word of Alec. Washington told the ambassador about the report he filed the night he returned here from Leone and what happened there. I'm sure you've seen that. The thing we don't know is what he was going to follow up on after he sent the report in. That, I suppose, is the second thing you'll be looking into."

"The second thing?"

"Yes. I assume that locating Alec—or his body—will be your first thought."

"Yes," Gerard replied slowly. "What has been done with Fletcher's personal effects, sir? Were there any papers among them that might be helpful?"

"Not to us. Any documents in his office safe and quarters were packed up and are locked in my safe now. Most of it is harmless and unclassified. I'll turn them over to you before you leave."

"Thank you. I'm very interested in that material. How about Shannon?"

"I don't think you'll find much help there, Gerard. Clark is—well, the night-watchman type, but little beyond that. He's just marking time until his retirement. Not up to your sort of activity."

"I understand," Gerard said with a certain sense of relief. Shannon, at least, was safe and wouldn't get in his way. Far better than having an eager beaver to trip over.

Truscott began dealing with political matters and background. As he listened, Gerard sensed that he was dealing with a man who was forthright, dedicated, intellectually mature, and honest. In Washington, the State people had spoken very highly of him as a Foreign Service Officer whose sixteen years of service were untarnished; a man without political obligations to anyone for his appointment and quick to rise to counselor, and who would one day represent the Department as Chief of Mission in an important post. He was forty, affable, courtly, married, and in a rugged sort of way, barely missed being handsome. Neat, was the word Gerard thought to describe him in the overall. Neat in his clipped phrasing, appearance, and perceptivity.

For the greater part, Gerard had already been briefed on the situation, but it was the brisk, clear manner in which the counselor led him from the past into the present that held his interest in the sadly familiar and violent history of an island emerging into modern power politics, a growing pattern in the Caribbean sphere.

In 1957, a military junta of four Army General Staff officers, Generals Josef Lebec, Louis Laroque, Paul Martine, and Colonel Theron Dessez, entered the palace in Port Amitié to attend their regular monthly meeting with President Jean Dubonnière. Also present was Louis Fontaine, then Chairman of the twenty-one-man Council of State. As usual, President Dubonnière listened to General Lebec's dreary recital of mounting unrest, anger, and increasing demonstrations against police and military authority throughout the island in protest against government indifference to rising unemployment, deplorable working conditions, and a growing apathy toward the basic needs of the people. And, as usual, President Dubonnière smiled with that same irritating, tired smile and made the same bland statement: that his hands were tied by the National Assembly, which was reluctant to act on the recommendations he had submitted through his Council of State to the legislative body for approval. However, he promised he would again submit—

"The time grows short, Your Excellency," General Lebec said ominously. "Too short. The people—"

"I have my ministers to keep me fully informed on the climate and temper of the people, M'sieu le Générale," Dubonnière replied with stiff formality. "I need neither reminding nor warnings from you."

"We are far past the time for warnings, Your Excellency," Lebec said with equal rigidity in his voice. Dubonnière looked up quickly. Something in Lebec's tone caused him to look from the Chief of Staff to the faces of the others assembled at the table. Written upon them was the same implacable, hostile coldness. Nor was there more warmth in the face of the man he trusted most, Louis Fontaine. As he turned in his chair toward the least ranking member, he saw the P-38 in Colonel Dessez's hand, its barrel aimed directly at his chest. Globules of sweat began to bead up in a glistening row at his hairline, and his mouth began to quiver. He raised a shaky hand before him and said in a cracked voice, "Gen—gent—lemen—"

"It is too late, M'sieu le Président," Lebec's voice tolled hollowly. Dubonnière looked hopefully toward Fontaine, the man he had personally appointed, over many objections, to the Chairmanship of the Council. He may well have spared himself this further humiliation. Fontaine, he saw at once, was part and parcel of the junta. Louis

Fontaine said: "It is over, Jean. Do not make it necessary for us to spill your blood."

Dubonnière's short, thick body sagged backward like an emptying sack of grain. His breathing became labored, his face purpling darkly. "Louis—you—you—" he gasped, then collapsed. His eyes fluttered and closed. The clenched fist slipped from the table and hung loosely at his side. Fontaine rose and went to Dubonnié's side, took a limp wrist between his fingers, then leaned over and placed an ear to the stricken man's heart. The others remained frozen in their chairs, waiting. Dubonnière's head suddenly fell forward and to one side, fluid dripping from between his lips.

"Gentlemen," Fontaine said quietly. "Fate has joined the cause of Right."

The reins of government passed into the hands of the four-man junta. Its first official announcement after the state funeral of Dubonnière suspended the weak National Assembly and dissolved the twenty-one-man Council of State. Next, it voided all existing trade pacts and government concessions that had enriched the holding companies of the Dubonnière family and a small, tight coterie of his personal friends. The takeover was hailed in the United States as a stunning victory against Dubonnière's left-leaning policies and was at once denounced by Russia, Red China, and their satellite nations as illegal and typical of American imperialist influence and support, hinting broadly that the Central Intelligence Agency had been the prime mover in the affair. The Communist press of the world stormed and raged at such arrogance and interference in the affairs of a small, independent republic by the great Western power.

In the eye of the storm, United States Ambassador Nathan Childress smiled modestly, waved aside charges and suggestions that he had been the principal architect and supporter of the move. Childress blandly pointed to Dubonnière's death, and observed pontifically that God needed no support, guidance, or inspiration from CIA, GRU, or intervention from other earthly sources.

The State Department in Washington was in a small quandary. Happy to be rid of the man who had flirted openly with Russia, it was forced to maintain its policy of suspending all economic aid to a country ruled by junta. The decision came as a serious blow to the economy of Liberté.

Early in 1958, there began a series of conferences between Ambassador Childress and Generals Lebec, Laroque, Martine, and Colonel Dessez, which resulted in the re-establishment of a new Council of State. With Childress's blessings, Henri Delacroix, a wealthy planter with marked influence among the people, and prominent in government and political circles, was chosen as its new chairman, with Charles St. Germaine as his chief deputy and with the portfolio of foreign minister. Within a few hours, the new Council met and elected Louis Fontaine to the presidency. The four-man junta stepped down and returned to their military duties, and the National Assembly was hastily recalled into session.

Without question, Nathan Childress was the man of the hour. His image was featured on the covers of *Time, Look, Newsweek, Life, Paris Match,* and front-paged on every newspaper of importance throughout the world, praised by the heavily favorable Western press, and scored bitterly by *Izvestia* and *Pravda*. He was alternately applauded and damned in the United Nations, and even as the Cuban representative raised his voice loudly in condemnation of such meddling in Latin American affairs, and cried out in anguished protest against Gestapo and gangster tactics, Louis Fontaine was busy decorating Childress with Liberté's highest civilian honor, the Medal of Merit. On the following morning, Childress flew to Washington to urge full restoration of economic aid, plus a certain amount of military assistance "consistent with Liberté's need to protect herself from outside evils and influences being generated by a notoriously ambitious dictator neighbor."

His requests and recommendations were approved within the week.

During the next few months, it became apparent, even to Nathan Childress, that President Fontaine's oft-stated promises and much-talked-about programs for the public good and welfare were hollow echoes of the sweeping reforms he had declared would follow his election. Only one had been kept: the military establishment had been strengthened by heavily increased budgets and by shipments of small arms, some obsolete antiaircraft guns, two outmoded World War II bombers, an ancient destroyer, and a considerable number of trucks, personnel carriers, pieces of road-building equipment, and spare parts. The two bombers fell quickly into disuse by lack of need and capable hands to keep them in repair. The destroyer was at once outfitted lavishly for Fontaine's personal use, and a crew of Libertéans was sent to the United States to be trained to man it.

Economically, Liberté saw little improvement. The same deplorable conditions of Dubonnière's regime were perpetuated under Fontaine's rule. The cronies and associates of the former had merely been exchanged for those of the latter. Nathan Childress was forced into embarrassing explanations, found himself linked with the deficiencies and failures of the new government. When he attempted to reply, it was necessarily from the defensive. Those who once hailed him began now to ridicule him, abetted by merciless lashings from the Communist press.

Urged by Childress, General Lebec began to pressure Fontaine to act to relieve the desperate conditions among the suffering peasants, live up to his promises of tax reforms, to build schools and hospitals, explore new industrial possibilities, invite outside investments, make proper use of the modern agricultural and road-building equipment that had been supplied by the United States foreign-aid program, permit American instructors to train Libertéans away from primitive agricultural methods and practices, and a score of other measures designed to lift the country out of its quickening decline. Fontaine pleaded for time, and promised to form a National Economic Council to put such a program into motion within six months.

When three months had passed without action, Lebec sent a quiet reminder to Fontaine. The president's memory of a similar warning to Dubonnière was firmly fixed in his mind. He invited the general to a private luncheon at the palace to discuss the matter.

An hour later, Lebec was dead. Dr. Cadeus Fombrun, Fontaine's personal physician, certified Lebec's death by heart attack. Colonel and Madame Batraville were the only other guests present.

Within a month, General Louis Laroque was shot and killed by an unidentified enlisted man while inspecting troops being trained on the rifle range. Colonel Batraville, who had accompanied Laroque as an observer, conducted an immediate investigation, and declared the tragic mishap an unavoidable and regrettable accident.

General Paul Martine was sworn in as Chief of Staff.

Two months and three days later, his body, together with that of his chauffeur and two members of his immediate staff, was discovered at the base of Mont Guérite. Fontaine appointed Colonel Batraville to head an investigating team. It reported that there was every reason to believe that a truck or bus had forced the general's staff car over the cliff on a particularly treacherous stretch of road during a night trip from the Trémont garrison to his Port Amitié headquarters.

Colonel Theron Dessez, whose daughter was married to Benoit Batraville, was promoted to the rank of general and appointed Chief of Staff. In that same Order of the Day, Colonel Batraville rose to a general's rank and was placed in charge of National Defense and Security. At once there were angry rumblings in high places in the Army. Dessez, at fifty-two, had leaped over a considerable number of men far senior to him in rank and length of service; but even greater was the undercurrent of feeling among the old professionals over the promotion of Dessez's thirty-six-year-old son-in-law to equal rank.

With the scathing criticisms and denunciations came the renewed whisperings of indiscretions involving Fontaine with Batraville's wife, Lénore, spreading from Army circles to private clubs and public cafés and restaurants. When the gossip and rumors reached the palace, Fontaine angrily ordered sweeping changes in the Army establishment. Seven senior officers and a host of junior staff members were court-martialed and convicted of disloyalty. Others were imprisoned, demoted, dismissed, or transferred to isolated garrisons of little or no importance. Some thirty or more fled into hiding or escaped the island to seek refuge in voluntary exile.

Taxes on land and on imports and exports increased. American, British, French, Italian, and German businessmen complained to their respective trade representatives that the new and strict government measures were tantamount to nationalization or expropriation. Ambassador Childress, now shut off from personal contact with Fontaine, received sincere sympathy from Council Chairman Henri Delacroix, but little satisfaction. From Deputy Chairman and Foreign Minister St. Germaine, Childress got little more than polite indifference. When strong representations from London, Paris, Rome, and Bonn were made to the State Department in Washington, Nathan Childress flew north for consultations. A few days later, he announced to the press that personal financial pressures made it mandatory for his return to private law practice in Detroit.

Shortly thereafter, the cancer that was Cuba metastasized into a broader and more insidious threat to international peace as Castro's agents began fomenting unrest among his Caribbean, Central and South American neighbors. Ambassador William Ross Chance, recently rebuked and declared *persona non grata* by a Middle Eastern government, was hastily sent to Liberté to replace Childress, whose resignation was accepted by the Secretary with customary "regrets."

Within a month, Chance had cut the embassy staff by one-third, brought in several men and women with whom he had worked closely in the past, and set about to mend his fences. He established a close, cordial, and no-nonsense rapport with his like numbers in the embassies of other Western governments, made official calls on President Fontaine and Foreign Minister St. Germaine, and at once let it be known by both that the store had changed hands and a new management was functioning.

Chance's reputation had preceded him. He was logical, honest, and firm. *Va bien.* The international diplomatic corps stood aside and waited for the inevitable locking of horns between the American and Fontaine. Chance's month-end summation report to Deke Emerson ended with: "—and to sum Fontaine up, this is a clear-cut delineation of a man thoroughly corrupt, well steeped in autocratic concepts, one who has flouted every legality in his roughshod ride to power and who, having arrived at his desired destination, has consistently sacrificed the interests of Liberté on the altar of his own abundant appetites. I anticipate an attitude of considerable resistance toward any effort to achieve a cooperative climate. Detailed recommendations follow. Report ends."

Truscott stretched his long legs out, crossed his ankles, and locked fingers behind his head. "Interested in more, Jim, or am I boring you?"

"Not in the least. It's far more illuminating than the three-foot stack of reports I had to wade through. What happened next?"

"The situation didn't improve much, a sort of stalemate, until the ambassador, about six months ago, took the bull

74

by the horns and insisted that all economic aid be cut off. Just about that time—"

From exiles in Florida, Panama, Puerto Rico, and Mexico, statements began appearing in the press, predicting that the Fontaine government would soon fall by combined external and internal resistance. Shortly thereafter, a series of simultaneous bombings and raids took place in a number of widely separated cities on Liberté. In l'Arcachon, the president's resort home was virtually destroyed by fire while a small band of men raided the military garrison and removed a substantial quantity of rifles and ammunition. At Gironde Sud, four Molotov cocktails were tossed into the military-police headquarters, while some twenty men entered the government warehouse on the dock and helped themselves to arms, ammunition, food, and clothing. To add insult to injury, they used a small Coast Guard vessel to escape, abandoned it at a lonely spot near Cap Grande, with a large hole chopped in its bottom. At Montbousonne, the captain-commander in charge of the garrison and four enlisted men were killed when a well-armed band of marauders attacked with rifles and incendiary grenades and virually emptied a warehouse of its entire contents of food, medical, and military supplies.

Fontaine made a rare personal appearance before the National Assembly to ask for powers to act without restriction "in this time of dire peril and crisis." The rubber-stamp Assembly at once approved his request. Immediately, Fontaine declared martial law throughout the island and ordered a sunset-to-sunrise curfew. Before sundown of the first day, enraged merchants, hotelkeepers, café and restaurant owners were venting their indignation and wrath to all listeners, since most of their business came after dusk. Tourist trade, already falling off at an alarming rate by recent bombings, plummeted to zero.

Students from the university and schoolchildren took advantage of the turmoil to clog the streets of Port Amitié, shouting, screaming, and creating disturbances wherever they could find an excuse or materials for mischief. They threw rocks through windows, strangled traffic, overturned cars, tore up park benches, and shouted defiance at the already harassed police. General Batraville took command and ordered his security police to break up the mobs with tear-gas bombs. Two hundred and sixty children were arrested and held in tightly packed compounds at the Pénitentiaire Nationale, their names made public in a list posted on the bulletin board in front of Police Headquarters. When parents arrived to seek their release, they were themselves arrested and fined, then warned they would be held responsible for the future conduct of their children. On the following day, police trucks picked up dozens of university and school teachers who were accused of inciting their students to riot.

François Courdet's *Le Temps,* long a harsh critic of President Dubonnière, later of Fontaine, began a series of editorials suggesting that the bombings by alleged terrorists might well have been politically inspired to permit the president these long-sought powers of unlimited and unrestricted dictatorship; that Fontaine's declaration of a national crisis was unmitigated nonsense; that martial law was merely a device to give security police unprecedented license to enter homes, schools, and business establishments to search and arrest critics of a failing, blundering administration.

Within twenty-four hours, several small bombs were exploded in the grounds and on the veranda of the Courdet home. At once, Henri Delacroix ordered a military guard set to protect the property and family of his old and devoted friend Courdet, who was also his close neighbor on the Boulevard de Couronne.

In retaliation, crude gasoline bombs were thrown into the palace grounds, at military vehicles and checkpoints. Eight of Port Amitié's forty-one miles of railroad track were torn up and either carried off or buried. Batraville turned his security police loose, and within a few hours the city's jails were once again filled with students, accused of sabotage and treason. That very night, as if to prove that the students had nothing to do with the bombings and raids, new attacks were made on military outposts and the docks.

One large group attempted to sack the heavily guarded Arsenale Nationale, but the assault was repulsed by machine-gun fire, resulting in sixty-two deaths and an unknown score wounded. Urged by Henri Delacroix, Fontaine began to see reason and declared an end to the martial-law decree, and removed the curfew.

Within a week, smoldering public resentment flared again. Fontaine, now shaken and unnerved, dissolved the National Assembly until the climate of hostility, "encouraged and supported by exiles and known government detractors," improved. Liberté, meanwhile, would be governed by the Council of State, thus refuting the oft-printed claim of François Courdet's *Le Temps* that the government was headed for total and absolute dictatorship. Public demonstrations continued.

Infuriated, Fontaine ordered confiscation of the properties of twenty-two prominent exiles. He jailed some thirty "known government detractors" who had opposed him politically in the past. "Others," he threatened, "will do well to re-examine their thoughts and convictions before they attempt to spread their volatile poison throughout the land."

Courdet's reply was a stinging rebuke in an editorial that suggested Fontaine had acted in the manner of a man with a mental disorder. Fontaine responded by ordering confiscation of *Le Temps* and the arrest of François Courdet and his son, Marcel.

When the word reached Henri Delacroix, he at once tendered his resignation as Chairman of the Council of State. Eight members followed his action in protest. The international press began to focus its critical spotlight on the president, casting him in the role of the ruthless, unconscionable dictator who was, as one national weekly news magazine put it, "a somewhat doughy, pompous caricature of his bearded neighbor in Cuba who is attempting to sculpt himself into the image of a Caribbean strong man, falling far short of the mark."

Fontaine seethed, and ordered the magazine's reporter and photographer out of the country. He sent for Ambassador Chance, and blustered, fumed, protested, and frothed, but received little consolation. Other embassy officials stood coolly apart from the fray, watching the contest between Chance and Fontaine with concern and some amusement.

In the end, it was Fontaine who gave in. He backtracked in a face-saving statement, sent for Henri Delacroix and asked him to resume as Council Chairman and bring his eight followers back into the fold. Delacroix, now in a firmer bargaining position, balked; a compromise was effected. The names of François and Marcel Courdet and those of political opposition still remaining on Libertéan soil in hiding must be expunged from the arrest-and-seizure list, their properties and assets restored, safety guaranteed. Further, the Courdets must be permitted to publish *Le Temps*. Fontaine gave in finally, but the names of those already safely in exile outside the country would remain on the list, under threat of arrest and dire punishment if they returned.

During the next three months, Fontaine trod with caution. To allay fears and growing suspicions that he was attempting to maneuver himself into another six-year term for which, by law, he was ineligible, he permitted Charles Du Faure to make several high-level statements to the press concerning government policy. Within a short time, it became surprisingly apparent that Du Faure, Fontaine's Minister of Education, was being groomed for succession to the presidency.

Du Faure, an obscure, distant relative of Fontaine's late wife, Berta, was little known to the official or public world. The shy gnome of a man had few duties and almost no voice in a ministry long neglected by a lack of funds, organization, or powers to act. Now, suddenly thrust into prominence, it was generally conceded that while Du Faure would never reach noble heights, he might possibly be led by the wisdom and influence of Henri Delacroix if elected.

Meanwhile, as the local furor died down, the attention of the international press was focused on other and more important crises brewing elsewhere in the Caribbean. With the approach of Libertéan elections, Port Amitié grew quiet; the only disturbances came from isolated areas in the back country.

5.

Foreign Minister Charles St. Germaine sat in the large chair as though it were a ceremonial throne, staring across a wide, mirror-polished desk at United States Ambassador William Ross Chance. St. Germaine was a short stub of a man, known principally for his variable and unpredictable moods that ranged from coldly phlegmatic to short-fused explosiveness. That he held no real power in his own hands was well known to those closest to the diplomatic arena. He was Fontaine's message-bearer, and little more; completely faithful to his sponsor, who had rewarded his total loyalty and subservience with high office.

He was a dark, almost wizened man who, even in his better moods, wore a perpetual scowl. In his early sixties, his nose, lips, and ears seemed exaggerated in size, principally because his hair of gray caracul was trimmed so close to a skull that was small and knobby. His face had a spongy, porous quality. It would seem that no amount of careful tailoring would ever improve his chunky figure.

Any impression of warmth or friendliness in St. Germaine's benign, forced smile was denied by a keen, appraising gleam of distrust in the pair of beady eyes that peered out from under thickly hooded lids. He reached out and raised a cam on the intercommunication set, making no move to hide his action; and Chance was at once aware that their conversation would be recorded, or that President Fontaine, in his own office nearby, would be listening in on their conversation.

"Your return to Port Amitié is a welcome one, Mr. Ambassador," Germaine said glibly. "I trust your visit to Washington was pleasant."

Chance, in perfect French, replied, "Considering everything, it was indeed, M'sieur le Ministre. The change of climate was invigorating."

"Ah, yes. When I represented my government at your late president's funeral last November, I found it extremely so. I hope now that the shortness of your stay there is an indication that everything went well and that the news you bring is favorable."

Chance's eyes never wavered. "I regret, M'sieur St. Germaine, that I am unable to report any action on your request that our foreign-aid program to Liberté be resumed. I am certain you have been so advised by Ambassador Levesque."

"Yes." The word was a brief hiss. "However, it was believed that your visit would perhaps speed action with your State Department and Foreign Affairs Committee—"

Chance said flatly, "I made no such recommendations, M'sieu."

"Ah, so. I had assumed, when I spoke to your President Johnson at his reception that followed President Kennedy's funeral and told him of President Fontaine's willingness to co-operate, that some mention would have been made—"

"In our last talk, President Fontaine recommended that I take some such action, but I did not concur with his suggestion." As St. Germaine's face clouded with restrained anger, Chance continued smoothly, "I could see no useful purpose in urging my government to take favorable steps to restoring aid unless we can first be assured of your willingness to comply with our need for a full and accurate accounting of all aid funds, supplies, materials—"

St. Germaine's tightened lips drooped wearily at the corners, exhibiting open disdain. "A nation of bookkeepers, Mr. Ambassador, can hardly hope to lead a world in the democratic principles it preaches."

"It is not my government's desire to lead the world, M'sieu St. Germaine. To assist free nations in need, yes—"

St. Germaine's laugh was short, harsh, and derogatory. In a half-wheedling, half-taunting voice, he said: "So that they will refuse aid from the Russians or Chinese? Or from the Cubans, M'sieu Chance? The benevolent parent extends a hand to a needy child, but withdraws it unless the child renounces its individuality and obeys with slavelike devotion and without question. Is such indignity and humiliation necessary to encourage lasting friendship? And tell me, sir, if your government imposes similar strict and exact accounting requirements for the billions it has poured into—let us say Korea, Indonesia, Laos, and Vietnam?"

Chance's color deepened. "M'sieu St. Germaine, as I have said to His Excellency on another occasion, my government does not expect to buy love, gratitude, popularity, obedience, or loyalty with the assistance it offers, but it cannot continue to dispense unlimited millions of dollars to a country that refuses to allow our representatives to see that such aid reaches those for whom it is intended. I am sure you are better aware than I that tens of thousands of your countrymen go hungry and are in need of medical aid, housing, schooling, and training, among other basic necessities, while a handful enrich themselves privately at the expense of your people and my government. We cannot permit—"

St. Germaine's fingers had burst into a furious fit of drumming as Chance spoke; now they curled into a tight fist that he brought down hard on the top of his desk. "*You* cannot permit! Then let me advise you, Mr. Ambassador, that *we* cannot permit your government to send its commissioners and advisers and regulators and CIA spies to stand over our shoulders to dictate where and how each penny or pound will be put to use."

Chance said wearily: "M'sieu St. Germaine, I feel we are getting nowhere in this discussion. Indeed, we seem to be losing ground."

His chin lifted imperiously, St. Germaine retorted stiffly: "You are correct, sir. These talks grow increasingly dull and repetitious with your reluctance to resume the economic aid your government promised and which, through your recommendation, it has withdrawn. His Excellency grows weary with impatience over your stubborn refusals, denials, and evasions, sir."

"His Excellency has left my government with no alternative, M'sieu."

"Nor does your government leave us with an alternative."

Chance looked up quickly with a feeling of quiet apprehension. St. Germaine noticed the change in his visitor. The foreign minister leaned back in his chair, more at ease; the anger evaporated as his voice grew softer, oilier. "Fortunately, M'sieu Chance," he continued with a crafty smile, "our position is not nearly so desperate as one might suppose."

"Sir?"

"You have been frank, M'sieu, and I will be frank with you. Our patience has been drawn out to the point of exhaustion. While you play exasperatingly on words, our neighbor in Cuba enjoys the fruits of a profitable alliance that you North Americans have, perhaps incautiously and unwittingly, placed into his hands. I am a great admirer of the swiftness and efficiency by which Cuba has become the second strongest power in the Western Hemisphere, with the most able leadership among our sister Latin countries."

Chance said: "Militarily and momentarily, I must agree with you, M'sieur. But in what way has Señor Castro's alliance reduced the poverty and misery of his people? By placing them under obligation to a foreign government? By drastically rationing food? By restricting their freedoms? And if you are correct, why have so many tens of thousands of Cubans fled their homeland at great personal cost and risk of life?"

St. Germaine smiled coldly. "As one in whose hands that alliance was formerly held, you should know very well that miracles do not occur overnight. We have all learned valuable lessons from the Cuban. First, the need for military strength. The economic benefits follow soon after. If you will remember the history of your own great revolution, you will recognize the wisdom and validity of my words."

"And am I to take those words as a—threat, M'sieu?"

"As you wish, M'sieu Chance. While we sit here and exchange fruitless words, the Cuban exchanges sugar for arms and machinery and technical assistance. Your own government trades wheat for gold with Russia, wheat that will eventually find its way back to Cuba. Her position improves each day with trade agreements with Britain, France, Belgium, Yugoslavia, and Red China. Soon, she will be trading with the entire Western and Eastern worlds. Would I be wise to recommend to President Fontaine that we do less?"

For a moment, Chance held back in silence, then calmly, "Be that as it may, I am sure His Excellency and you, M'sieu, realize that my government cannot, and will not, permit a second foreign foothold in this hemisphere such as you seem to be suggesting under the veil of trade."

St. Germaine's thin smile broadened. "Foreign? Foreign, M'sieu Chance? Is the Russian more foreign to us than the American? At least you will agree that the Russians have given the Cubans strength and not weakness. You speak of threats, yet your own words 'cannot and will not permit' constitute a threat, one I find extremely distasteful and unacceptable." St. Germaine paused to see how the American was taking his words, but Chance remained calmly bland. "How amusing it is," the foreign minister continued, "for you to sit and speak so bravely while even at this moment Russians and Cubans embrace each other in friendship, and scorn your futile efforts to drive them apart."

Chance said: "M'sieu, permit me to remind you that despite what you have said, little economic progress has been made or felt in Cuba. Its imports arrive in pitifully small amounts, nor does Russia or Red China provide the gold for her to trade broadly elsewhere. Her credit stands at near zero, and when she is unable to pay for her purchases her stature with the Western powers who now trade with her will fall to the level of her credit. She exports a sideline of subversion among her sister countries and runs screaming of oppression by the United States, hoping to win sympathy and friends, but the free world knows her for what she is. One day, M'sieu, the inevitable must happen. Cubans will settle their problems themselves, from within or without and—"

"M'sieur Chance," St. Germaine interrupted, "you tread on dangerous grounds. Nor can I accept such an outrageous statement from the representative of an imperialistic nation with dreams of a colonial empire in the Caribbean."

Before Chance could reply, the door was thrown open. Chance rose to his feet as President Louis Fontaine entered the room. St. Germaine got up and moved to one side as the president walked to the desk and sat in the chair. Without apologizing for the interruption, Fontaine said, "Your conversation has interested me very much, Mr. Ambassador. Please be seated and let us continue."

St. Germaine busied himself with a long, flat box that he held open for Fontaine, who took a cigarette from it, accept a light from his foreign minister. Fontaine wore a uniform of white silk material with a single splash of red ribbon that ran from his right shoulder to his left side, held in place by a brilliant medal pinned just below his left breast. He was tall and dark, but not nearly so dark as St. Germaine. He carried himself with a true military erectness, although he had never served his country in the uniform of the Army. His figure and features showed the strength of a proud man, and his eyes reflected scorn and a mildly aroused hostility for the American. He seemed to take it for granted that eavesdropping by an intercommunication set was a natural part of the diplomatic game.

Beyond that, Fontaine's face showed an immense capability for cruelty. His eyes were penetratingly sharp and set deeply into a narrow face that appeared long because his hair was straight and combed back from a high forehead. Both cheeks were lightly pocked from a childhood disease; the nose was long and straight, his mouth wide and harsh over a hard, unyielding chin. The overall impression was one of firm, formidable authority.

"Your Excellency," Chance said, still standing, "I believe M'sieu St. Germaine and I had concluded our talk."

Fontaine autocratically ignored the remark. "Seat yourself, sir. I am interested in your statement concerning your country's views of any friendship we may seek to establish with another nation, M'sieu."

"I believe I made our position clear on that point, Mr. President."

Fontaine's smile was cool and brittle. "Then perhaps you will amplify the point for us. If, as we have repeatedly requested, your government continues to ignore its obligation and trust to restore aid funds to Liberté, why should it have a voice in any friendship we choose to make with any other nation in the world, whether in this hemisphere or another?" When Chance did not reply at once: "M'sieu, we tire of being treated as a dreary and unwanted stepchild or a backward colony. England has learned her lesson. France, Belgium, and the Dutch have likewise lost their colonies in many parts of the world, and will lose those that remain. These are changing times, Mr. Ambassador, to which your government must adjust. One day, just as Africans and Asians are doing, as Panama seeks to do, Puerto Rico will rise against you and destroy your dreams of empire. Nor is it unreasonable to suggest that one day a world federation of black men will form that may well crush and grind you as we crush and grind cane—"

"Bury us, Your Excellency?" Chance asked coolly.

"Yes, perhaps even that, if you persist. Let us understand one another, sir. Your government has proved, as the Russians and Chinese have, that force and power are themselves the greatest deterrents to war. Or invasion from an enemy. Cuba is proof of that, if proof is necessary. Russia and the United States meet and talk in fear while their guns and submarines, nuclear bombs and missiles lie idle. Why disarmament, which can lead only to unpreparedness and war? Strength is all, M'sieu Chance, strength. Cuba has become strong, and your country dares not attack her. Then why should we permit Liberté to remain weak?"

"A free nation, Your Excellency, does not remain weak. She becomes strong through alliance with other free nations. If she becomes weakened, it is from within that such weakness stems—"

"Pray spare me your sophomoric lecture, Mr. Ambassador, on freedom. We have heard too much of the freedoms guaranteed by your amazing Constitution, just as we have known of French *liberté, fraternité, and égalité;* but these, as we have also learned, are mere words behind which a strong nation practices intolerances and cruelties while shouting the cause of freedom to the rest of the world. Therefore, whom does one trust? Am I wiser to trust your government, sir, or the governments of Russia, China, and Cuba? It is a simple matter of selection, of semantics, is it not, M'sieu?"

Chance was finding it difficult to wade between sophistry and illogic, and decided it was sheer nonsense to try to defend against Fontaine's quibbling. "Your Excellency," he said, "have I your permission to withdraw?"

"In a moment. But let me first warn you, sir, that if we decide to look elsewhere for friendship and assistance, we shall expect no interference from your government." His voice became hard, and his smile evaporated completely as his eyes narrowed. "If the United States Government foolishly decides to move against us, I promise you it will find only the ashes of a country. But glorious ashes. I will burn Port Amitié and our coastal cities to the ground and raze every inch of earth as we leave it behind. Not a single building will remain standing, nor a field that has not been burned black. Then the world will be witness to what happens when a major power forces its unjust will upon a smaller, weaker, helpless nation. Latin and South Americans, as well as the rest of the world, will see how it profits them to align themselves with a great, proud, and arrogant power.

"Your government is extremely sensitive to the reactions of the rest of the world, is it not, M'sieu? Then what will be the feeling of Asian, African, European, North and South American black men, do you think? How much quicker will you drive them into one another's arms in a federation of black against white, eh? You may then learn that there are untold millions who believe in a world where God is black."

Chance said heavily, "Mr. President, I have taken too much of your time already." Without waiting for a reply, he rose and walked out of the room.

6.

Fontaine's frown deepened as he watched Chance disappear through the door. He had taken well into account the ambassador's well-placed remark regarding the hands of the Russians that were clasped about the throat of the Cuban, and knew that this, should he accept Ambassador Vossolofsky's stepped-up offers of aid and technical assistance, was what he would face himself. How much simpler, better, he thought, if he could force the American to restore the aid that had been withdrawn, than be forced to deal with the Russian. The thought was like the pinch of a tight shoe. He walked back to his office, leaving a disturbed St. Germaine to stare at his back and contemplate the seriousness of the damage that had been done here by widening the ideological distance between Port Amitié and Washington.

Seated at his desk in his own office a few moments later, a red light flashed. Fontaine depressed a cam on the ivory-toned box and said, "Yes?"

"It is Dr. Fombrun, Your Excellency," the voice of his secretary replied. "He insists he has an appointment, but the Callers' List—"

"Send him in at once, and see that we are not disturbed," Fontaine commanded harshly. He stood up and came around to the front of his desk to await his visitor with renewed eagerness.

Cadeus Fombrun entered the room quietly, a thin, solemn man dressed entirely in funereal black, even to his shirt, which was topped by a narrow white clerical band. In one hand he carried a leather medical bag, his black hat in the other. His skull was clean-shaven, his small ears flattened against his head. A short, bridgeless nose broadened at the nostrils, and his protruding lips were drawn in a tight line. His angular frame moved slowly across the room to where Fontaine stood.

"You had a safe trip, Father?" Fontaine asked.

Fombrun put the black bag on the president's desk, then placed the tips of his long, gnarled fingers together, raised them tentlike in Fontaine's direction, and made several passes in an up-and-down motion. "I bring you the blessings of Damballa, Ashtar, and Lazarillo, Divine One."

"And good news?"

Cadeus Fombrun's nod was noncommittal. He turned back to the bag, opened it and removed a black cloth that was embroidered with silver and gold designs; a huge, coiled serpent in the center, surrounded by numerous mystical signs and symbols. In one corner, a human skull in red silk; in another, a rooster in red, white, and green; in the third, a hornless goat; in the fourth, a lizard about to strike at an insect. From the bag, Fombrun now took four vials, and from each he poured a small amount of powder into the palm of his hand, then distributed it in pinches to each of the four corners of the cloth. He brought out a short, thick candle that he lighted and placed in the exact center. Now, from each corner, he took pinches of the powder and allowed them to sift down into the candle flame. The flame leaped up to lick at the powder grains, changing color momentarily to green, then blue, deep violet, and finally, brilliant red. Cadeus, meanwhile, had begun to speak.

"The one you seek, Divine One, is not a spirit, but mortal man. In Leone, where my followers told me he had visited, I went to the ruins he had created and called upon our Gods. They spoke to me. Nine times I called upon Them and nine times They denied him. Therefore, he is a matter for men and not Gods; nor for a *houngan*."

"Did anyone *see* him, Father Cadeus?" Fontaine asked anxiously.

"No, Master. He is seen only by those who serve his evil purposes. He moves secretly and swiftly, this Chalumeau, and it is undeniable that he is a source of true danger to you as long as he lives. Therefore, my son, I have created for you a *ouanga* to protect you from him. Wear it upon your body, and no harm will come to you. It has been blessed by our sacred Gods, Damballa, Ashtar, and Lazarillo, to bring you long life without harm, with good health and the wisdom and courage to fight and defeat your enemies."

Fombrun withdrew a smoothly polished stone that was suspended from a thin silver chain. The stone was as flat as a coin, multihued. In its center a green brilliant sparkled. Fontaine leaned forward. The priest hung the chain around his neck and placed the stone in the president's hand as he muttered a prayer over it. Then he reached up and loosened Fontaine's collar and dropped the stone inside his shirt.

"To capture this Chalumeau, Father—" Fontaine began.

Fombrun repeated: "He is not a matter for the Gods, my son, but for men. I would rest now and think."

7.

Strange, Chance thought to himself as he walked toward Truscott's office. Damned strange. How did it happen that Charles Du Faure's name had not once been mentioned? So close to election day, and we talked as though Du Faure didn't exist. It was as if Fontaine had only just come into the presidency, instead of standing in the doorway on his way out.

He paused reflectively at the door, then threw it open and went in. "Sorry if I held you up, Thorne," he began, then saw Truscott's eyes turn toward the far end of the room where Gerard sat. Gerard rose and came forward.

"Mr. Ambassador, may I present Mr. James Gerard?" Truscott said. "Mr. Gerard, Ambassador Chance."

Gerard took the ambassador's extended hand and said, "Good to see you again, sir."

Chance smiled briefly. "Nice to have you with us, Gerard. Make yourself comfortable. I'll have a longer talk with you later." He turned back to Truscott. "Thorne, I'd like to see you privately. And you'd better have Major Bissell stand by for a quick flight to Washington with a special report I want to draft."

"I'll be with you in a moment, sir." Truscott called, "Sarah." The ambassador smiled again at Gerard and began walking toward the door that led to his own suite.

Sarah Bennett came in from her adjoining office and handed the counselor a ruled yellow pad and several freshly sharpened pencils. "Thank you, Sarah. Will you entertain Mr. Gerard for a while? If there's anything he'd like to know—"

"Of course."

"And ask Mrs. Lund to come in, please. At once."

Sarah Bennett stepped to Truscott's desk, depressed a button at the base of the telephone, spoke into the instrument softly, then replaced the receiver. Truscott, following the same path Chance had taken, said: "I'll be with the ambassador. Call Reception and ask them to have Major Bissell stand by for a quick trip north. And you might see about a card to CI for Mr. Gerard, eh?" With another brief nod and a fleeting smile, he was gone.

Miss Bennett called Main Reception, passed the messages along, then asked, "More coffee, Mr. Gerard?"

"No, thank you, Miss Bennett. Another cup and I'll begin floating. What, if I may ask, is CI?"

"CI is the Club International where, as the radio comedian used to put it, the élite meet to eat. Also to dance, swim, exchange social and intellectual amenities. It is also known as the Watering Hole where, at the end of the day, our thirsty brother and sister workers gather to restore the salt they've dissipated in the course of their duties. As a Foreign Officer, you're entitled to membership, but until you apply formally I'll have Ben Green issue a temporary card for you." Her pleasantly modulated voice broke off as she turned in the direction of her own office with a smile. The woman who entered the room through the double doors walked directly to the desk without having seen Gerard sitting on the sofa on the far side of the room.

"Hello, Sarah," she greeted. "Where's the fire this time?"

Sarah indicated the door to the ambassador's suite with a quick toss of her head. "They're waiting inside. You'll need these." She held out a wire-bound notebook and pencil. "By the way, Mrs. Lund, have you met Mr. Gerard? He's just in from—"

Gerard had risen and was crossing the room toward her. Even though he had been forewarned by Richards, the suddenness of the meeting brought a certain shock with his first sight of Eleanor Devlin Lund. She wore a mist-blue sheathlike dress, sleeveless, with a wide and deep V-neck that ended at her waist. Beneath it was a white blouse with a high, open collar. Her exquisitely formed legs were encased in sheer nylon, and she wore narrow, square-toed blue crocodile shoes. On her left wrist was a heavy gold bracelet with a watch recessed in a nest of diamonds, at her throat a double strand of pearls. Tiny gold-and-pearl earrings peeked from beneath her thick, burnished-gold hair. On the ring finger of her left hand she wore a large baguette-cut diamond in a platinum setting, but she wore no wedding ring. Her face, happily, was as he remembered it, oval, faint hollows below the cheekbones, slightly tilted nose and full, generous lips, finely drawn eyebrows that arched upward as her eyes opened a bit wider when she turned with a half-smile of recognition. Her hand came up almost mechanically as Gerard raised his.

"Hello, Nora," he said quietly.

"Hello, Jim. It's—good to see you again. We've been expecting you. You look—very well."

Sarah Bennett cut off his reply with a brisk, "I think Mr. Truscott is in a hurry, Ellie."

Eleanor Lund replied, "Yes, of course." To Gerard, "I'm sure we'll see each other soon, Jim." As she turned to leave, he felt a sense of inadequacy in his brief, "Yes. Yes."

Not until the door closed on her back and he had turned back to Sarah's quizzical look did he realize that the exchange of so few words had not gone wholly unnoticed. "Coincidences," Sarah Bennett observed, "aren't nearly so remarkable at home as they are so many miles from home, are they?"

Gerard stared blankly for a moment, nodded without comment, then walked slowly out of the room.

In his quarters, Gerard showered leisurely, patted himself dry, then stretched out on the bed to relax. At once, his thoughts went back to Nora. And Sarah Bennett's words: *Coincidences aren't nearly so remarkable at home as they are so many miles from home.*

In his profession, coincidences could be the most unsettling, unnerving, and devastating of all perils. The unexpected was always hardest to defend against. He felt a sense of gratitude toward Richards now for having warned him against the surprise of the encounter.

Even with the foreknowledge that she was here, he had felt the deep shock of the first sight of Nora, coming out of a past he had thought long dead. The meeting had given him the same feeling he always experienced when confronted with sudden danger: dry mouth and throat, constriction across his chest, the over-all feeling of impending doom, an impact about to occur— He closed his eyes and tried to compare the Nora Devlin of six years ago with the Eleanor Lund he had seen today.

8.

Gerard seldom thought of the past with happy memories. Not that his boyhood in Connecticut had been markedly unpleasant. It was that sooner or later he must come to certain portions of his life he would rather not think about. His mother had died when he was in his second year at Penn State. Leland Gerard remarried within a year, to a woman only a few years older than Jim, and a good seventeen years younger than his father.

"You don't like her, do you, Jim?" his father had asked the morning after he arrived for the wedding; and Jim, with unkind honesty, or because he was comparing Lucille with his mother and found her too youthful, too flashy, and too quick with smile and kiss, replied, "No, Dad," adding weakly, "I'm sorry."

A year later, Leland Gerard telephoned and asked Jim to drive up to New York to meet him at the Plaza. His father seemed gaunt, drawn, and years older; unsmiling and unhappy. He scarcely mentioned Lucille, but Jim knew instinctively that she was the reason for the remarkable change he saw in his father. It took quite a while before Leland came to the point. There would be a divorce. And

90

a court battle. His charges of infidelities. Countercharges of mental cruelty. Sordid scandal in a normally quiet, respectable community.

"Can I help in any way, Dad?"

For a moment an old closeness was back between them. "I think not, Jim." He went to his overnight case and brought out a package and handed it to his son. "Here are some securities that belonged to your mother. About $42,000 at current quotations. I don't know how I'll come out of this mess, but I want you to have them, no matter what. Lucille doesn't know they exist."

The divorce never came off. A few weeks later, there had been an accident following a conference between Leland, Lucille, and Leland's friend and fellow attorney, Phil Stewart, at the latter's home. Driving back sometime before midnight, the car went out of control on Miller's Hill and smashed through a guard rail. Finish. Funeral. Dry-eyed mourning for the sad man his father had become. The law practice taken over by Phil Stewart, the house sold. Gerard never returned to Connecticut. Back at Penn State, there was the graduation with no one to share his award as an honor student; then the decision to go into the Army. Intelligence. Harrington; the offer to go along with him to JIA.

Bill Noyes, whom he had known at Penn State, was with the Washington *Tribune,* and showed his disappointment with Jim's decision. "It's a lousy show, Jim," Noyes had said then. "You've got to live like a hermit and have fewer friends than one. No life of your own, and even if you get married, no wife but your job. Nobody you can talk with for fear you'll spill something accidentally. Let me find a spot for you on the *Trib.* You can take a few courses at Georgetown and—"

He could have put it all behind him then and returned to normal civilian life. No money problems. No marital or family involvements. But even after all of Noyes's arguments—and his own—against it, he had taken the job with Harrington. Had it really been a need to flirt with danger? Guilt? A death wish?

Through the next two years, he had thought often of Bill's words and wondered why he hadn't listened. In the Far East, he had walked, run, and crawled with Death in a strange land among strange people. He had learned to fear, experienced intense cold, pain, hunger, and desperate loneliness. He had tasted danger and killed in violence.

91

Survival had become an all-consuming game; the awakening to a certain fascination and attraction for making use of his developed skills and techniques instead of putting them aside forever and, if possible, out of his mind.

His advanced training in JIA had been tougher and more exacting than anything he had ever known before, so demanding of his physical and mental powers that there was little or no time to devote to pure leisure or personal pleasures. So that when Bill Noyes introduced him to Eleanor Devlin, and he had at once been captivated by her open friendliness and pert, Irish good looks and humor, he had come up against an emotion he thought had been cut out of him. Love had become a luxury that must be given up; like weekly poker, bull sessions, parties and sports; all for the purpose of Work, the intensely jealous mistress who had moved in and taken over his life.

Nora Devlin.

Five feet and four inches and 115 pounds of attractiveness and personality. Sensual, joyful, warm; half-girl, half-woman; enticing, understanding, in love with life. Her laughter, like her presence, could fill a room as easily as it filled the void created by the death of his mother and the suspicion that his father's death had not been an accident. She dissolved his first standoffishness like snow melting in the palm of a warm hand, and he began to remember again how to smile and laugh in happiness. The problem, he recognized now, was not his job, not Nora, but himself; how could a man of his dedication to a profession of danger and secrecy afford to lower the defenses and protective guards that had been building up within him for so long?

Nora had a responsible job as secretary to the Assistant Secretary of State for Inter-American Affairs. She could no more discuss her work with him than he could talk about his own to her. Of himself, she knew only what he had told her, that he was employed by the Department of Defense in work that took him out of town frequently; and Nora was sufficiently Washington-indoctrinated to know better than to pry deeper.

He was away often on "business." His trips might last a few days, a week, or longer, and caused no major problems because they had entered a period of undeclared love and quiet understanding. The first jarring collision came on a New Year's Eve when, groomed and gowned with special effort for a special occasion, a party at the Shoreham, Nora spent the night alone in her apartment. Jim Gerard had failed to show up. He returned to Washington a fortnight later without having written, phoned, or cabled. His simple explanation was that an unexpected emergency had come up, one he could not discuss. It took a full two weeks before the thin crust of ice in Nora's voice melted.

His job moved him from the Pentagon to somewhere within the city, then into the Maryland countryside, later to Virginia, then back to Washington. He called her often when he could, but the only number through which she could reach him was his apartment telephone.

In the summer of that year, when they had known each other for some eight months, they began to talk around the fringes of marriage. Then Gerard became an even greater puzzle to Nora, enthusiastic and receptive one moment, reticent and withdrawn the next. She had reasoned by now that he was with one of the Intelligence services, but little more.

It was late that autumn, when the countryside flamed explosively with rare and magnificent color, that they managed an entire weekend to themselves. Early on a Saturday morning, they headed for Front Royal and Virginia's spectacular of spectaculars—the Skyline Drive. It came to an end at Charlottesville in a blaze of football excitement with a hard-fought homecoming victory for the University of Virginia. Inflamed old grads and students, with their alcohol-ignited wives and sweethearts, filled fraternity houses, hotels, motels, and restaurants, snake-danced through crowded streets, locked car bumpers, bashed fenders, and halloo-ed from one end of town to the other.

Nora and Jim were caught up with the virulent fever. They finally managed a meal at a table in a hotel, jammed together with eight other diners, enthusiastic alumni. They drank from bottles of bourbon, rye, and Scotch, danced —if it could be called that—in a crush of human bodies, and by midnight, managed finally to escape into the fresh air.

At a gasoline station, they decided it would be foolhardy to attempt the trip back to Washington at that late hour. They drove along slowly for over ten miles before they found a motel with a vacancy. One room. Double bed. The sleepy, gap-toothed woman behind the office counter waited, knowing or suspecting, and uncaring, one hand behind her on the open slot that held the key. Jim glanced down at a silent Nora. She had heard the woman say it. "Only one left. Double bed." Nora looked up at him, and smiled. Jim turned back to the woman and said, "We'll take it."

How many times, hundreds of times, had his mind turned back to that night, the Sunday morning when he awoke and heard the shower running in the tiny bathroom. He got out of bed and went into the bathroom, stood at the sink, and rinsed his mouth with cold water, then began washing his hands and face to drive out the sleep that remained in him. No razor. No toothbrushes. Only what they had worn. He heard the shower turn off, and the fogged-up glass door opened. "Don't look," Nora cautioned.

But he had caught sight of her lovely body as she reached for the small motel-type bath towel, her hair bound in a small hand towel to escape the shower.

"Of course not," he said, eyes fastened on her figure in the partially steamed mirror.

"You're cheating, Jim," she accused.

"Of course I am," he replied. He rinsed his hands and took the towel out of her hands. "Turn around and I'll dry your back."

But instead, she had moved into his arms, damp and more desirable than ever. "I love you, Jim," she said with open honesty. As he held her closely, she added, "Will this make a difference between us?"

"Yes," he whispered. "Yes. It certainly will. I've always wanted you and now I'll never be able to stop wanting you."

She lingered in his arms for a few luxurious moments, then pulled away. "I'm starving. And you need a shave. Let's get something to eat and start back."

But they hadn't at once. There was the bed, warm, intimate, and inviting. An hour later, they had breakfast and started for Washington.

Sometime in midafternoon, he began to tell Nora as much as was permissible about his work with JIA as a field agent, and Nora didn't require much to understand the hazards; that he was putting his life on the line every time he took an assignment in some distant, troubled area.

"Do you want to keep on with it, Jim?" she asked. "Do you like that sort of thing?"

"Like it? No. I don't like it in the way one normally

94

associates like or dislike for a job. Let's say I look at it the way I did my Army service, something that needs to be done by people who are best qualified or able to do it."

She fell silent and looked at him sadly, so unlike her. He said: "There's so much at stake, Nora. If men like me turn our backs on the job, we'll soon be pushed out of Asia, then Africa, then Europe, and South America. One day we'll find ourselves backed up against the walls of our Fortress America, isolated from the millions crying for the simple freedoms we know will be dead. The foreign trade we depend on will go to the Communists, and by the time the rest of the world realizes they've been completely suckered, it will be too late to recoup our losses. That's why West Berlin is so important an issue between Russia and ourselves."

Nora said: "In the time we've known each other, I've suddenly discovered how really little I know about you. It's so—funny—peculiar funny, I mean. I can't even explain it—"

"Does it make any difference in how you feel about me?"

She thought for a moment before she said: "No. Not in how I feel about you. The uncertainty of it is what bothers me; the insecurity in the feeling that you'll go off somewhere one day and I'll never know where, or when, or if I'll ever see you again."

His eyes were on the road ahead, but he knew from her voice that she was distraught; and that, too, was so unlike Nora. He drew her closer to him across the seat, and for miles they sat huddled together without a word between them.

They spent that Sunday night in Gerard's apartment. Nora set the table and made the salad and a dessert while Jim broiled the steaks; and later, as if to avoid the subject of themselves, Jim turned on the television set and they watched a program neither wanted particularly to see. During one of the commercials, Nora got up suddenly and turned the set off. "Do you want to take me home now?" she asked.

He said quickly: "I never want to take you to any home but mine. Our own. I love you, Nora. I—"

She was in his arms instantly, crying. "I know, Jim. And I love you. All the more, the most I could ever love anyone. But suddenly, I'm frightened. It terrifies me, now that I know. Your job—"

"Don't, Nora. Don't cry. Please." He held her tightly, feeling the sobs, then said, "I'll turn my resignation in. Tomorrow morning."

"And what will you do then?" she asked.

"I don't know at this moment. Everything is coming up too fast. But I'm not so old or so crippled that I can't find a job. I suppose Bill Noyes might find a spot for me on the *Tribune*. Hell, there are a dozen other jobs I can—"

"Like selling insurance or vacuum cleaners door-to-door? Jim, if you quit your job on my account, you'll hate me for it one day."

"Nora—"

"Let's not make any hasty decisions. We'll think about it."

In the morning they were up early and had breakfast before Jim dropped Nora at her apartment. She kissed him before she got out of the car, and said: "Don't do anything rash, Jim. We'll work it out."

It was noon when he telephoned her from an outside booth to tell her he was going "out of town," their code for a foreign assignment. "For how long, Jim?" she asked.

"I don't know, Nora. It was waiting for me when I came in this morning."

"You'll write?"

"When and if I'm able, but you know—"

Her last words were: "Take care, Jim. I love you very much."

The assignment, living underground in Far East jungles and among rice paddies, seeking, being sought, marked for death, passing needed information back, hungering, thirsting, once almost dead from an infection caused by a knife wound, lasted almost two full years. On his return, all contact with Nora Devlin had been broken off. Her old apartment on M Street was occupied by a strange couple who had never heard of Eleanor Devlin. At her State Department extension, he was told that Miss Devlin was no longer employed there. State Personnel advised him that Miss Devlin had resigned her post earlier in that year. Bill Noyes was gone, assigned to the *Tribune*'s Rome Bureau. New faces had replaced old friends at JIA. Why should he have expected Nora to wait?

Fini l'épisode.

Then had come Vietnam. Cuba. Liberté.

96

Now, the dream of a hundred tortured nights had come alive again with electrifying suddenness. In the sparse moments of their brief reunion, he had seen the change in her. The pretty-girlish attractiveness had been transformed into the ripened beauty of mature womanhood, her deeply bronzed hair now combed in an upsweep to make her appear taller. Closer, her skin was as flawlessly clear and creamy as he had remembered it, her spectacular green eyes thickly lashed, the regular spacing of her nose, mouth, and chin an artist's delight. The tilt of her head, slimness of waist, the same provocative walk, with each step outlining her perfectly rounded legs from hipline to ankle, all were there. But the greatest change was in her eyes. Behind their Irish emerald color, the life and sparkle seemed to be missing, as though only that part of her had aged.

Was she, he wondered, aware of what their brief contact had reawakened in him? And if she were, how much would it—could it—matter?

At six o'clock he felt fully rested. And hungry. He thought of phoning the motor pool for a car to take him in search of a restaurant, reached out and picked up the receiver; but when he heard the chancellery operator's voice, he said, "Mrs. Lund, please."

He waited, heard the intermittent buzzing, a click, then, "Mrs. Lund here."

"Nora?"

He heard the soft intake of her breath. "Jim?"

"Hi. Still busy?"

He felt the hesitation over the wire, then, "Well—yes. Are you settled?"

"All squared up and starving. Any recommendations?"

"Oh, Jim. I'd like to, but I'm afraid I'm busy tonight."

Disappointedly. "I see. How about a raincheck?"

"Of course. Tomorrow night?"

"That's a deal. Will I see you at the chancellery?"

"Of course. Drop by any time."

"I'll do that." The pause lengthened. "Nora—" he began.

"Yes?"

"Nora, I—I'll look in on you sometime tomorrow."

"Do that, Jim. Incidentally, I've had Alec's Ford assigned to you. Ben Green will give you the keys if you'll stop by."

He hung up after thanking her, feeling his pulse racing, remembering the musical quality of her voice, wondering if she still laughed in that same wonderful way. He got off the bed and began to dress.

Don't let it break wrong for me this time, he prayed softly to himself.

He decided against going out for dinner, and ate the meal Yvonne had prepared: red snapper that had been wrapped in a large leaf, then coated with clay, and baked over a charcoal brazier; a combination of rice and red beans, heart of palm salad, and strong coffee.

In the upstairs study, he got out the dispatch case Sarah Bennett had turned over to him on Truscott's order, and spread Alec Fletcher's papers out on the desk. Neither the material in the clear nor that in one of the simple, basic JIA codes contained anything he had not already seen in Washington. He opened the sealed envelope with Alec's name scrawled across the flap and found a copy of the last report Alec had had Baker transmit to Minos 1 before his disappearance.

Where, he wondered, were Fletcher's other papers? There should be some record of the contacts he had established, a notebook of "switch codes" used from time to time for security reasons. If this were the sum total of what he had kept in his office safe, the chancellery could be ruled out. Nor would Fletcher have left important material with an outside contact. Therefore, the only logical place would be here, where he lived.

He locked the papers back in the dispatch case and went back to the bedroom and put it away in his trunk, then went downstairs and began an expert search of every room. An hour later, he went through the same procedure on the second floor, with no better results. He lay down on the bed and closed his eyes. Relax and think, he told himself. Put yourself in the place of the lost horse; go there and find him.

Gerard decided to give up for the night. He got off the bed, stripped, and went into the bathroom to shower. In the morning, more refreshed, he would give it another whirl.

As he toweled himself dry, the problem was still firmly fixed in his mind. He came out of the bathroom, and his fingers caught the outside edge of the door as he closed it. Less than a pace away from it when it slammed shut, a dull sound caught his ear. A strange rattle. He stopped and turned to stare at the door, then opened it, slammed it shut again, this time a bit harder. Again he heard the rattle. He grasped the edge of the door with his hand and shook it. There it was. The rattle.

Gerard went to the clothes closet, opened that door, and went through the same motions, slamming it closed, shaking it; but the curious rattle was not there. He tried the door that led into the hallway, and that was solid, too. With a sense of growing elation he came back to the bathroom door, examined the long, vertical edge. Solid. He drew up a chair, stood on it, and felt along the top edge, but there was no evidence that it had been altered or tampered with.

He began rapping his knuckles along the top of the door, then the sides and center. There was no indication that it was anything but solid. He bent down and rapped the lower panels and listened carefully as he continued to move back and forth across it and—*pay dirt!* A hollow ring. He shook the door and rocked it back and forth on its oiled hinges. The rattle was more pronounced now.

Gerard now examined the three hinges that held the door to its frame. There were a number of scratches near the pins. He unlocked his trunk and got out a kit of small, specially hardened tools. With the screwdriver, he forced the top, middle, and bottom pins out of their slots and put them to one side. He lowered the door carefully to the floor, then examined the bottom edge. There it was! Two countersunken clasps, about twenty-four inches apart, held some sort of a container inside the hollow portion of the door.

Breathing heavily with excitement, Gerard snapped the clasps open, used them to lever the container out. It was made of wood, hinged like a dispatch case, about one and one-half inches thick, twenty-four inches long and about eighteen inches deep. He picked up the container lovingly and placed it on the bed. When he lifted the lid, he found himself looking down on several files, a sheaf of notes that were clipped together, and the familiar black notebook that contained Fletcher's JIA codes.

Fletcher, Fletcher, bless you! Gerard prayed. He gathered up the material and began poring over it. There it was. Fletcher's work of months. A file marked: RADIO CONTACT—CODES. Another, CHALUMEAU. Others: DELACROIX-

FULLER, FONTAINE, BATRAVILLE. A thick file, TOM REED. He thumbed through the latter file curiously, saw the collection of letters, photostats of birth records, military service, a long and detailed report from EMB PORT-AU-PRINCE. He put the file aside and began examining the RADIO CONTACT—CODES file, transferring some of the symbols and information to his own notebook.

9.

In the morning, Gerard busied himself getting settled in the office assigned to him, separated from Clark Shannon's by a smaller room that was occupied by a secretary, Suzanne Forrest, whom they would share. Suzanne, Gerard guessed, was about twenty-five. Her soft Southern accent fell pleasantly on his ears, and with his first appreciative glance he knew she would be a marvelous sight to behold in a bathing suit. Or in bed.

Her coloring was a warm, rich tan. Her face was oval and framed by jet-black hair that was cut boyishly short against the heat and fell in soft comma-like wisps over her forehead. Her features were petite and regular; large brown eyes, straight, slender nose and full lips. There was an athletic quality about her lithe figure that expressed the virility of resilient youth with every movement.

It was when she crossed her long legs and held her notebook and pencil in the approved manner, her head tilted slightly toward him, that Gerard became consciously aware of the obviously unhaltered upper portion of her exquisite body, and concentrated on her face to keep his mind from dangerous distraction. Shannon had said, "Suzy knows as much about everything in this joint as anybody, and that includes me." He shook his head then, and said: "Look out when she wears a tight dress. You can practically read her mind." He had then departed to, as he called it, "make the rounds."

"Put the book away, Suzanne," Gerard said. "Let's just talk for a few moments."

"Yes, Mr. Gerard." There was the hint of a question mark that dangled at the end of her words. For a while they talked in general terms, and Gerard was impressed by her deep interest in local affairs; then he realized that it was not extraordinary that she would take such an interest. She had majored in political science. Her knowledge of the language was excellent. As a "lady of color," she had been made welcome in upper- and middle-class Libertéan circles, mingled with native business people, circulated among the Libertéan employees of the embassy staff, and was accepted with cordiality in their homes on an equal basis.

As the conversation progressed, Gerard began to feel a note of reticence when they reached the subject of her work, her feelings toward her job, as though she resented being questioned from a so-recent arrival. He tried another tack. "Suzanne, I need help," he said simply.

"If I can be helpful, Mr. Gerard," she began, then stopped.

"What do you think happened to Alec Fletcher, Suzanne?" He saw her fingers tighten into small fists, the skin drawn across her knuckles.

"I don't know, Mr. Gerard."

"You knew him well, didn't you?"

"We were—yes, I knew him very well."

"Do you think he is—dead?"

She flinched, relaxed slowly, and said calmly, "No."

"Do you know that for fact, or have you some reason to suspect other than what I've been told by Shannon or Mr. Truscott?"

"No."

"Then what makes you so sure? Just how do you feel about his—disappearance?"

There was a long pause. Gerard waited. Suzanne expelled a deep breath. "I can't explain it logically, but I don't believe Alec is dead. He may be hurt somewhere, waiting until he can make it back safely." As Gerard's lips pursed up, she seemed to take this as an expression of doubt. "I don't blame you—or anyone else—for thinking what they want about it, but I knew Alec. Don't write him off the way the others have, Mr. Gerard. They don't even mention his name around me, as if he never existed, but I have a—feeling." Again a pause. "Are you going to look for him?"

Gerard said: "Alec was one of our people, Suzanne, and I'm going to do everything I can to find out what happened to him. Can you suggest anything that might help me?"

"Only that—well, I thought Alec took too many risks. I think Mr. Shannon thought so, too. It was as though he had to prove something."

"What did Alec have to prove to anybody?" Gerard asked.

She said it with open honesty. "The same thing any Negro has to prove to everybody, including himself. The way I've had to prove that I can take dictation faster, type neater, and do anything my job calls for better than a white girl. I've done that and I'm accepted here. Alec hadn't reached that point yet. This was his first field assignment, and because he was anxious to make good on it he took more risks than anyone else would have taken. Or asked him to take. Not that anyone demanded it, but he had to—had to—"

"I understand, Suzanne."

"Do you? Then maybe you can understand why he might have had to expose himself to danger a little more than he would if he were white."

"Or perhaps because he knew he had a certain added advantage going for him that a white man couldn't possibly have had."

"Like what?"

"Like his color. Knowing the language, he could move around this island like a native any time he chose—"

"He did. He did it often, just to test whether he could get away with it. He made a lot of friends and contacts, but he made enemies, too. Lieutenant Falot—"

"Who?"

"Falot. A security-police lieutenant. For some reason, Falot suspected that Alec is a CIA man, a spy working against the Fontaine government. Whenever Alec and I were out together, at the Bacchanale, CI, the Excelsior, or somewhere else, Falot managed to find an opportunity to be close by. Sometimes he'd just nod and smile; sometimes he'd even come over and say a few words, as if he wanted Alec to know he knew Alec wasn't just an assistant commercial attaché. It's a stupid cover, anyway. Nobody believed it among the embassy staff or the local police. Alec always kidded about it and said that Falot was following us because he was jealous, that it was me he was interested in. I—"

Gerard said it quietly. "Were you in love with Alec, Suzanne?"

Her eyes were moist as she flashed a look of annoyance. "Were? You're doing it, too, Mr. Gerard. Don't put Alec in the past like the others. Yes, I love Alec. We were engaged—unofficially. Alec and I—" But she didn't finish the sentence, nor was there a need to.

"I'll do my best, Suzanne, believe me. I hope you're right, but I can't allow what you feel to make me believe something that remains to be proved."

"I'll pray for you." Suzanne stood up and turned away from him. "If I can help you, Mr. Gerard, I'll do anything."

"Thank you, Suzanne. In Havana, a friend of mine often used an appropriate expression. I'll say it to you now: 'God's will'."

10.

He found Jake Walker in the chancellery lobby, and asked if Jake would like to join him on an exploration tour to familiarize himself with the city and surrounding area. Walker was agreeable and brought the black Ford around to the main entrance. Gerard picked up a map from the information desk, and they were on their way.

As Walker drove and pointed out the various key points of Port Amitié, Gerard checked them off on his map. They drove through the hilly sections where Jake pointed out the entrance to Bellefonte, the president's summer home, at the top of Mont Couronne, the homes of Henri Delacroix and François Courdet on the Boulevard de Mont Couronne, among the larger estates that sat behind walls and fences or jutted out spectacularly from mountainsides in seeming defiance to the laws of gravity. Later, they drove south through the small town of De Cossett to Maréchal and Petite Aiguille, then swung over to Gran Aiguille and returned northward along the coastline, past a large sugar mill, a rum and alcohol distillery before reaching the plantation country that stretched for miles between sea and mountains.

Walker's assessment coincided with what Gerard had read and heard of Liberté: a land of ancient mystery, of tribal customs more closely related to Africa than to Western cultures, of beliefs in the supernatural that were so frightening to the uninitiated; even to the army of anthropologists who had come and gone over the years, shaking their heads in bewilderment and disbelief. Locally, those rare few who had actually witnessed a voodoo rite were reluctant to speak of them lest they be charged with gullibility, naïveté, or plain drunkenness.

Yet, records existed of men and women who had been pronounced medically dead, and who were seen alive weeks later; others had disappeared from villages only to return by night to roam about as "zombies," or walking dead; human sacrifices were still not unknown; evil *ouangas,* or fetishes, were designed and sold by *houngans, mambus,* and *gangans,* priests and priestesses, that were powerful enough to kill, cripple, render helpless or senseless, create love powers, make the rich poor, the poor rich, bring on fertility or impotence in man, woman, animal, or the earth itself, subject a selected victim to slavery and bondage to another. The renowned mysteries of the East were no stronger or effective or more feared than those of voodooism on Liberté. Or Haiti.

So powerful were these beliefs that stringent laws, carrying the death penalty, were passed, notably Article 249 of the Penal Code, to prohibit its practice among these descendants of the Yourbas, Ashanti, Dahomeans, or Whydas, Fanti, Congolese, Ibos, and Mandingoes who had been brought to the West Indies by the first Spaniards to work the land, and whose numbers were later increased by the French.

Walker sat behind the wheel of the Ford with a certain aloofness toward the native traffic, a small wad of tobacco lumped in his left jaw. He was in his late forties, with twenty-six years of active service that had begun just prior to World War II. Soft embassy duty had taken little of the hardness from him, had merely gentled his manner and voice. Clean-shaven, but with a light blue-black residue in evidence, clothes sharply pressed, shoes shined to a brilliant glow, his round bullet head sat on a pair of massive shoulders, from which dangled a pair of thick, well-muscled arms and large hands. His khaki tie was pulled firmly against a short, thick neck and dropped down over the curve of a broad chest. His voice rolled on and on with a catalogue-like quality.

"That's the Hampton place on our left," Jake said with a nod of his head in the direction of the coast, then added from personal knowledge—or gossip—"a limey. Wife died a long while back, daughter went back to England to get married. A real witch. He's alone out there. Plays the field. Got it made in spades. Get a load of his 'housekeeper' some day and you'll know what I mean. That's Belle Roseau coming up next. Tom Reed, ex-Marine from the days of iron men and wooden ships. Been here twenty-five or more years. Bamboo American." When Gerard looked at him questioningly, "Married a gook gal. He's a lush. Drops around to con some of the boys about how they did it in the old days with bows and arrows. You'll see him floating around the gin mills all over town. Shows up at the Club once in a while. Makes him remember he's white and American. Wife lives out there on the place. Got a thing going with her headman, a spick. Used to be a looker, from what I hear, but nobody ever sees her. Up ahead another mile, we'll be coming to the big one. Terre Delacroix. American boy name of Mark Fuller fell in soft. Married to Old Henri's oldest daughter, Eugénie." A short whistle of appreciation burst from his roundly puckered lips. "Wait'll you get a load of her. Or her sister, Julie. Julie's single and sharp, but razor-sharp. Old Man Delacroix, he's top banana on the Council of State and a buddy of Old Man Courdet. Fontaine hates his guts."

"Courdet's?"

"Both of 'em."

So it went on mile after mile as they ran past Terre Delacroix and into Anse à Goulet where they got out of the car to stand and stare up at the massive granite walls of Fort Maraboux, ancient, and abandoned as unsafe now, rising up from between two camel-like humps that marked Mont Souffrance.

"Means suffering," Walker offered gratuitously, "and they weren't just kidding. Thousands of poor slobs died building that fort—that's how it got the nickname Fort Massacre, but"—admiringly now—"it did the job for the old General back in the early 1800's when the French fleet came into Anse à Goulet here. Old Maraboux blew 'em all to hell and gone, right out of the water, with his cannon, then ran burning oil down the mountainside to kill off the ones the cannon didn't get. Some bugger, Maraboux."

Back in Port Amitié, Gerard asked Walker to drop him near the waterfront area and take the car back to the embassy. As he moved through the slum district afoot, the acrid stench of human misery rose up to engulf him. It was like being back in the Far East, appallingly crowded with humanity and animal life, but filthier; its unpaved alleyways—hardly streets—were deeply rutted, strewn with fragments of palm fronds, coconut husks, fruit peelings, garbage, human and animal ordure. The rows and rows of incredibly rickety, unpainted board shacks were densely populated, their inhabitants staring with hollow curiosity at the strange *blanc* who walked among them, their eyes uncaring, a study in human futility and despair. Children ran, crawled, ate, played, and relieved themselves in the open, slept in unbelievable squalor, vulnerable to insects, rodents, and disease.

He turned eastward, crossed several streets until he came to Rue Félicité, lined with cheap bars, eating places, and pleasure palaces. He heard a hissing and shrill giggling, and looked up. In each of the four windows across the upper floor of Chez Irénée, garishly painted faces and pairs of voluptuous bosoms, covered with transparent material, leaned out over the sills to attract his attention. They beckoned, called out endearments and promises, using their hands in vulgar gestures to indicate their willingness to share themselves with him. One very dark, unusually buxom girl framed herself in one of the windows and pulled aside the gauzy stuff that covered her to expose a pair of immense breasts, her bare hips undulating erotically to advertise her special dexterity. In other windows on both sides of the street, other girls and women peered down, called out and waited hopefully, then turned back to aimless waiting and staring as Gerard passed by without showing interest. He walked to the corner where he found a cab and asked to be driven to the embassy.

11.

At four o'clock, he put aside the bound volumes of *Le Temps* and *Voix* he had asked Suzanne to bring him from the embassy library for his examination, and walked down the hall to Nora's office. Her secretary told him she was telephoning and would be free in a few minutes. He sat and smoked a cigarette while he waited. When he crushed it out, the secretary picked up the instrument and spoke into it briefly, then said, "Mrs. Lund is free now, Mr. Gerard."

He went inside and found Nora in a room slightly larger than the outer office, an austere, businesslike office with no frills. Desk, chairs, filing cabinets, table, wastebasket, clothes tree, and fixtures were the same light green color as those in his own room. The only relief from the totally G.I. appearance of everything was Nora herself, in a cool gray-and-white sheath dress that added freshness and youth to the scene.

"Hello, Jim," she greeted with a smile. "Come, sit down. Coffee?"

"Good God, no. If I had to decide whether the embassy runs on paperwork or coffee, I'd have to choose coffee."

"Why not? It's the best there is; it's cheap and delicious."

"I'm more interested in picking up my raincheck from yesterday. Dinner?"

Nora surveyed the various stacks of papers on her desk ruefully. "So much to get done at the end of the month: reports, requisitions, letters—"

"Dinner, Nora. That's what I'm interested in. With you. Don't give me the busy executive bit. You've got to eat somewhere."

She laughed. "Then I'll stop trying to impress you. All right, what time?"

"Make it easy on yourself."

"How about—six-thirty?" He nodded. "I'll pick you up."

"You know where?"

"I know the house."

"See you then." He went out, feeling a fresh glow of warmth, remembering that Nora had always laughed in that same musical way when she was happy. He found the black Ford in the parking area and drove home whistling softly to himself.

The two hours since he had talked so briefly with her dragged endlessly, and then he saw the white Thunderbird turn in from Perrigeau, cross the thick wooden planks that bridged the open drainage ditch, and move along the driveway. He came down to meet her as the car came to a stop. As he opened the door and got in, "How about the Club?" she asked.

"Why don't we have a drink there and come back into town for dinner?" he countered.

"Any place special?"

"I was told that the Excelsior—"

Nora said agreeably, "It's better than most."

During the drive to the Club, they talked lightly of the Washington they had known together, of mutual acquaintances whose whereabouts neither knew nor seemed to care about now, pages out of a dimly remembered past. Both were being careful to avoid any exchange of sentiment or intimacy that had once passed between them. Nora mentioned her marriage in 1959 as casually as if she were filling a blank space on a printed job application; and he spoke easily, perhaps too glibly, of his return from Vietnam. It was almost as though they were getting acquainted for the first time.

When Nora pulled the Thunderbird into a space in a far corner of the Club parking lot, she turned the ignition key off, but made no move to get out. He had his hand on the handle when she said, "Jim, I don't like it."

"You don't like what?"

"Your taking over Alec Fletcher's job."

"It's something that has to be done, Nora."

"I know. That's been your reasoning for everything you've ever done. Because it had to be done. But why do *you* have to be the one to do it? They've already killed one man on that same job. You could be next on the list. Doesn't that mean anything to you?"

"Nora," he said softly, "please don't be angry or offended, but I can't talk about it."

"I'm not angry or offended, Jim. But I am concerned."

"Especially for me?"

"Especially for anybody," she hedged, "assigned to a job that has already caused one death. I particularly suggested to Ben Green that he assign you to other accommodations in order to keep whoever killed Alec from suspecting you might be taking his job along with his quarters."

Gerard smiled without humor and said, "That was very thoughtful of you, Nora. Thanks."

"Then why did you insist on his house?"

"Nora, has it occurred to you that if the somebody who got to Alec suspects I'm taking his job over, he might show himself again? Alec was close to something important, and I've got to find out what it was. If I can find out the *who,* I might be able to find the *what.*"

"Jim—" she began, but he reached out and put a hand over hers. "Nora," he said with a plea in his voice, "let it ride for a while, please. Shall we go in now?"

"All right, Jim. Just be careful, will you?"

"I promise you that much. Believe me, I'll be very careful."

So, he thought as they walked toward the clubhouse, it's still there. At least a part of it is alive.

Their progress along the walk and into the building was marked by called greetings and hand waving from people

108

seated at the many umbrella-topped tables outside, others seated along the broad, open veranda over drinks, and groups clustered at the long bar inside. In less than fifteen minutes, Nora had been invited to dine with no less than four couples and several men who were alone. She introduced Gerard to American, French, British, German, and Italian businessmen, planters, newspapermen, brokers, shipping agents, embassy staff members, and politicians, most of them accompanied by wives or strikingly handsome women of upper-class Libertéan families. Privacy was impossible. They pushed their way through small knots of people and tables, among them Suzanne and a group from the embassy, to the wall end of the bar where a barman held up two fingers to indicate vacant stools. The one next to the wall was occupied by a man with a short, sandy-gray crew cut and a skin that was tanned to a near cordovan shade. As Nora brushed against him, he turned toward them, looking up from his tall, dark drink.

"Oh, Mr. Reed. I'm sorry. I hope I didn't upset your drink," she apologized.

At the mention of the name "Reed," Gerard's mind turned back to the short period he had spent looking over Alec Fletcher's papers, recalled among the folders the thick one marked TOM REED, and wondered if there were some relationship between the folder and this half-stupefied character. The man peered at Nora through vacant, watery blue eyes, blinked repeatedly as though his eyes were small electric bulbs that had been placed loosely in their sockets. His deeply veined hands clutched the glass protectively as his head shook negatively, rolling loosely from side to side.

" 'Sall right, Mrs. Lund," he muttered. " 'Sall right. No damage." With apparent effort, he looked upward and over her shoulder at Gerard.

"This is Jim Gerard, Mr. Reed. Just down from Washington to join our staff. Mr. Gerard, Tom Reed. Mr. Reed owns Belle Roseau, a sugar and coffee plantation near Anse à Goulet."

So it *was* the Tom Reed of Alec Fletcher's folder. Reed extended a leathery hand, and as Gerard took it into his own he felt the alcoholic tremor in it. "Nice t'know you, Gerard," Reed acknowledged. "Didn't know—uh—" The thought, whatever it was, slipped his mind. "You meet Jake Walker yet?" he asked.

Gerard nodded. "He met me at the plane when I came in."

Reed winked one eye owlishly, and nodded. "Fine boy, Jake. Damn' fine Marine. Twenty-six years in, Navy Cross in the P'cific, Purple Heart an' Bronze star in K'rea. Hell of a guy, Jake. Have a drink, both a you."

Gerard was about to refuse, but Nora spoke up to cut him off. "Of course, Mr. Reed, if you'll have one with us." To Gerard, she added, "Mr. Reed is a former Marine and one of our old-timers. He came to Liberté back in 1936—"

"Thirty-four!" Reed corrected sharply. "Come when the Marines pulled outa Haiti that year. Been here ever since. Ain' put a foot off the island in—in—by God, thirty years!" He looked up as though surprised himself that he had been here so long. One of the barmen passed and he called out, "Hey, Albert, set 'em up here!"

The barman took their order, but before he could bring their drinks, Reed had turned back to the one he held tightly in his hands, head lowered again so that he appeared to be contemplating the contents of his glass, or asleep. Nora signaled the boy and quietly canceled the drink for Reed, who no longer seemed to be aware of their presence. Gerard looked at her inquiringly. In a low voice she said: "Poor Old Tom, he's had it for tonight. He'll sit over that one until he wakes up and goes home."

"What's it all about? Is he really a planter?" Gerard asked.

"He was. It's a long, dreary story. I'll tell you another time."

They had their drink, joined Thorne and Dorothy Truscott and their party for another, then left. They came down the hill slowly, drinking in the sight of the city below, come alive now with lights, as Nora pointed out various landmarks. They drove into the parkwayed Champs and came into Rue Pavillon, brilliantly lighted with hotels, shops, and restaurants and found the Excelsior, its sidewalk tables crowded with predinner drinkers. They moved through the center aisle to the covered veranda where others sat at tables, into the entrance to the main dining room. At a lectern, a very heavy man, dressed in a white dinner jacket, with a bow tie that was nearly hidden by the folds of his fleshy neck, greeted them with a wave of a large, leather-covered menu.

110

"Welcome, Madame Lund, and your guest. A table for two?"

"Yes, Emil, thank you," Nora replied. "This is Mr. James Gerard, a new member of the embassy staff."

Lebrun shot a pair of small bright eyes back to Gerard. "Then you are doubly welcome, M'sieu Gerard." He pronounced it Zherrah. "This way, please." He showed them to a roomy table for four, although there were tables for two available, and called a waiter with the signal of an upraised finger. "A bottle of Maréneque, Phillipe." To Nora and Jim, "Please accept with my compliments to a precious lady and a new arrival to our little paradise."

When he bowed and left them, Gerard said: "Thank heaven. From the way things were shaping up at the Club, I thought we'd end up with no less than two dozen for dinner." He thought at once of the night in Charlottesville, and wondered if his tactlessness had evoked the same memory in her. If it had, Nora showed no signs that it had.

"They're a nice, friendly crowd; always happy to see a fresh face from the outside world," she said. "For a while, you'll be a delightful novelty. Until a newer face arrives."

"I'd have thought the atmosphere, considering the political situation, would be heavier."

"One thing you'll learn about CI, Jim, is that political matters always take a back seat. The Club is a protective haven against work, politics, and other unpleasant subjects. General business conditions, new car styles, sporting events, Paris, Rome, and New York fashions, scandal, music, art, books, and lesser matters are safer grounds. Politics are taboo. *Verboten.*"

"A happy thought and I'm all for it. Shall we order?"

Nora ordered an exotic native dish for both. "Tell me more about Tom Reed," Gerard asked.

"I'll tell you what I can, but there are so many holes that need filling in, the story won't be anything near complete." She began the recital that lived up to her earlier predictions. It was long, many of its aspects dreary, and before it came to an end, they had nearly finished their meal. "And that's enough of Tom Reed for a while," Nora said. "Tell me this: how did you win the ambassador over?"

"Win him over? I don't know that I have. Why?"

"I happen to know that our Chief of Mission isn't very fond of Intelligence operations—or operators—per se."

"My natural boyish charm, I suppose. That and—"

The voice came from behind him. "Ah, Mrs. Lund. How delightful to see you again."

Gerard stood up and turned to face a smartly uniformed figure in khaki. Tall, carrying himself with precise military erectness, the man turned toward Gerard. Nora said, "Major Lamonte, may I present Mr. James Gerard, our latest addition to the embassy staff. Mr. Gerard, Major Constantine Lamonte. The major is General Batraville's security police aide."

Lamonte's hand was already extended. Gerard accepted it, felt the hard, firm grip and said, "My pleasure, Major. Will you join us for a drink?"

"I think I have time for one, thank you." He sat down, his handsome face creased with a warm smile that showed white, even teeth. "Mr. Gerard," he said musingly. "Let me see. You arrived from Washington yesterday on the Pan Am 106 flight, were met by your Mr. Shannon and Sergeant Walker and driven to the embassy, then to the house formerly occupied by your colleague, Mr. Alec Fletcher. I presume you have been assigned to take his post as—ah—assistant commercial attaché."

Gerard felt the added emphasis on Lamonte's "assistant commercial attaché" and remembered Suzanne's (and Truscott's) words about cover jobs. The major's English was precise and clipped, evidence of his schooling abroad. His long fingers accepted the cigarette Gerard offered him, and an alert waiter had already whipped out a book of matches with a flourish and put a light to the tip of it. Lamonte ordered a Scotch-and-water-no-ice for himself. "If I can do anything to make Liberté more enjoyable for you," he continued, "please do not hesitate to call on me."

"You are extremely well informed, Major," Gerard said casually.

"Modern intelligence, Mr. Gerard. It is a new status that everyone seeks to employ. The once-despised spy or snooper takes on a new title, Intelligence Agent, and *voilà!* he achieves an air of respectability. It is a modern art, this retitling, is it not?"

"Did you know Alec Fletcher?" Gerard asked.

"We have met on several occasions. He is a very friendly man, and it is difficult not to know one so willing in friendliness."

Gerard noted with interest that Lamonte was speaking of Alec in the present tense and was about to press the

112

question further, but the waiter returned with Lamonte's drink at that moment and Lamonte picked it up, saying: "One of the few things I learned to enjoy in England. The weather was beastly, the food atrocious, their social system snobbish and lacking in cordiality. But the schooling and Scotch were excellent."

"And their tailoring," Gerard added.

Lamonte preened slightly. "And their tailoring," he agreed. "Clothes seem to be another of my weaknesses."

"I shouldn't imagine you would have been unhappy anywhere in Europe, Major," Nora said. "Or anywhere else."

"Not at all. To me, England represented hard work and study. In France, later, there were Libertéans studying at the Sorbonne and other schools who helped make life extremely enjoyable. Also in Switzerland and Germany. We managed many week ends at water and ski resorts. Marcel Courdet, Julie Delacroix, Jules Fontaine—"

"The president's relative?" Nora asked.

"His son. Poor Jules was killed in a bobsled accident in Austria."

"Did you know Madame Batraville in Paris?" Nora asked.

Something of a sly grin crossed Lamonte's face. "Ah, *la belle Lénore*. But yes. Although she traveled on a higher and richer social level than we others. Her beauty, ah, she was the toast of Paris. Men went wild over her, and almost any woman would gladly have poisoned her out of sheer jealousy. In Switzerland, two men fought a duel over her. And in Italy—but that is another story. *A vôtre!*" Gallantly, he brushed his lips over Nora's hand and shook hands with Gerard.

When he left, Gerard said, "I could cheerfully kill a man with all that excess charm."

Nora laughed lightly. "It's only a beautiful act, Jim, practiced like a role in a play. But don't let that dandified exterior fool you. Major Lamonte is a serious soldier, the son and grandson of Libertéan generals."

"Then what is he doing in the security police?"

"General Batraville. He hoped to use Constantine's social prestige to make himself more acceptable in the upper social strata. Batraville is the son of a minor civil servant. And a complete snob."

"How did he rise to a general's rank so fast? He can't be more than a few years older than Lamonte."

"Let's save it for another time. I've already given you too much of a history lesson for one evening."

They left the restaurant at a few minutes before ten. In the car, Gerard said, "Are we going somewhere?"

"I'm going to drop you at 11 Rue Perrigeau and then home to bed. I hope you don't mind, Jim. I'm rather tired and I have a full day ahead of me tomorrow."

"Not at all, Nora. It's been a long day for me, and I can use some sleep, too. And thank you for a wonderful evening. I hope we can do it again some time soon."

"I can't think of a single reason why we can't."

As Nora pulled the car away from the curb, Gerard noticed a uniformed figure get up from a sidewalk table and hurry toward a car that had been parked behind them. Jacketed and booted as Lamonte had been, but not Lamonte, Gerard thought. A moment later he turned back and saw a pair of headlights cut out from the curb, overtake two cars, then cut back in the line of traffic behind them, with only one car separating them. He heard Nora saying: "Jim, let me give you a small, friendly warning. Whatever it is you're going to do, please play it straight with the ambassador. You may have heard that in his last post, in the Middle East, he was the innocent victim of some CIA shenanigans and was declared *persona non grata* and forced to leave the country. No ambassador likes to have an embarrassment like that on his record, even when it happens through no fault of his own. What happened to Alec Fletcher has upset him dreadfully, so if you stumble into a snafu, he won't reach out a hand to help you up. Neither will Thorne Truscott."

"Thanks for the tip." Gerard reached for his cigarettes and said: "Nora, all I want to be allowed to do is the job I've been sent here to do. I don't even know what I'm after at the moment, so I can't even begin to guess who is out to trip me. If I stumble, I won't look for the ambassador or the counselor to help me up to my feet again. I'll have to fall flat on my own face."

Nora flushed. "I should have remembered that you don't need help from anyone, do you, Jim? Not now or before."

"Please, Nora, don't make me out so indifferent or unfeeling. I know you're more understanding than that."

"Perhaps I should be, but there can be a limit to understanding. I can remember waiting for so many months for some word of you, or from you, that you were alive somewhere, anywhere, in the world. How much understanding should one give without consideration?"

Some of the Irish fire was back in her eyes that flashed a quick glance at him, and he could feel the smoldering tension under this sudden impulse to let him know her underlying feelings that had been stored in her thoughts for so long. "Not as much as I'd expected, I suppose," he said. "I'll only add this: if I had found you in Washington when I returned from that assignment, all of hell couldn't have stopped me from quitting and finding another job, and doing anything else to make it up to you. I hope you believe that, Nora."

Her sudden petulance evaporated, and she addressed herself to guiding the car through the heavier traffic in the Champs de Révolution. Gerard turned toward her and glanced through the rear window. The car was still following them. When it darted out of line and drew up to a single car length behind them, he saw it was a black Plymouth. They came into the circle at the end of the Champs and followed it around to Rue Perrigeau, and Nora swung into the right lane and made the turn that led them up the hill. A half block behind them, the pair of headlights followed. When they stopped at No. 11, the Plymouth stopped and cut its lights. Nora braked the car and stared ahead through the windshield. Gerard reached for the door handle and said, "Good night, Nora—"

"Jim—Jim, I'm sorry," she said quietly. "I didn't mean to open up that—"

"It's all right, Nora. You're entitled to a few free swings. I'm only unhappy that it had to come out this way."

"You're not angry, are you?"

"Only with myself. Good night, Nora." He had turned back to her and now saw the high lights of what could have been tears welling up into her eyes. He moved closer, damning the bucket seats and the high island that separated them, making it awkward to reach her. But Nora made it easier for him by leaning toward him, her lips parted slightly. He kissed her gently, felt the response, and when he began to press harder, her withdrawal. Again he said, "Good night, darling," got out of the car and walked across the wooden bridge that spanned the drainage ditch, and opened the gate.

Nora hesitated for a moment before she put the car into gear and began to make the U-turn. Gerard did not waste a moment. Once inside the gates, he ran swiftly to

115

where the black Ford was parked, leaped into it, the ignition key ready in his hand. When he drove out and turned left on Perrigeau, he saw the white Thunderbird near the base of the hill, about to turn into the traffic circle. The black Plymouth was still parked at the side of the road, facing in Gerard's direction, and it gave him a sense of relief to know that it was not Nora, but himself, who was being followed.

Gerard drifted downhill at a normal pace. As he neared the circle, he saw the black Plymouth move out, make the U-turn and come slowly behind him. Gerard cut into the circle, then made a right turn into the Champs. The Plymouth dropped behind several car lengths, permitted another car to wedge in between them. Gerard continued on to Rue Pavillon, pulled past the Excelsior, and made a U-turn at the corner and came back, found a parking space several doors away from the café, and parked. He locked the car and, without a glance backward, went into the Excelsior.

All right, Mr. Falot, he said to himself, let's see if you're going to play for dollars or doughnuts.

12.

The Excelsior was still well patronized when he reached it, the dining room about half filled with late diners, smartly gowned women and well-dressed men in an atmosphere of rich comfort. Emil Lebrun greeted him with a curious look when he came in alone "M'sieu Gerard," he said with some light surprise in his voice "A table?"

"No, Emil, thanks. The bar."

Emil escorted him through the dining room to the bar. an elegantly paneled room with a dozen tables that were occupied by groups of men who talked in low excited voices. Political voices. Sharply urgent, frequently harsh, punctuated by eager gesticulations when making a point. At the bar, four men were seated on stools at the near end. A few empty stools, then a lone drinker, two more empty stools, and two more men. Gerard went to the far end of the bar and took the last stool. Emil signaled the barman, who came at once.

"Etienne, this is M'sieu Gerard. His first—no, second —visit to the Excelsior in the same evening."

Etienne smiled shyly and said, "M'sieu?" Lebrun bowed, turned, and went back to his dining-room post

116

"A daiquiri, please. A little on the tart side."

A puzzled half-frown, half-smile. "M'sieu?"

"Not too sweet."

"Ah, *mais oui. Aigre*."

When he had mixed the drink and poured it, he placed the brimming champagne-type glass on a thin sisal mat and waited for Gerard to taste it. The first sip evoked a brief nod and smile of approval. Etienne returned the smile and turned away. A few moments later he returned with a second daiquiri. To Gerard's questioning glance: "The first, M'sieu, is from the Excelsior, a welcome for a new guest. The second is the one you asked for. Your good health, M'sieu."

He turned back to the register and rang up two francs, then placed the oblong receipt on the bar. The four men at the lower end were demanding his attention, and Etienne went to them. By the time Gerard finished the second daiquiri, Etienne was back, wiping the bar in front of him. "Is okay, M'sieu?" he asked in English.

"Very okay, thank you, Etienne." Gerard pulled a billfold out, extracted a dollar bill. "You have a pencil, Etienne?"

"*Oui, M'sieu*." Etienne reached for the pencil beside the register and handed it to Gerard, who moved the receipt in front of him. As Etienne watched, he drew a triangle on it, the longer point facing east. Beside the point, he drew the figure "3." He turned it back to Etienne and covered it with the dollar bill. "Will you please give this to M'sieu Lebrun?" he asked.

The smile faded from Etienne's face. He picked up the bill and oblong receipt, folded the latter over and put it in his jacket pocket, then opened the cash drawer, deposited the dollar, and put three francs in change down in front of Gerard, who waved them aside. Etienne made no move to pick them up. Instead, he said, "Pardon, M'sieu, can you tell me the hour?"

Gerald held his left wrist up toward the barman and, as Etienne watched, moved the upper of the two stems so that the triangle moved around to the figure "3."

"Thank you, M'sieu." Etienne nodded toward the door in the far corner of the room, leaned forward and said in a low voice: "In the hallway are the *lavabos*, the rest rooms. Beyond is a stairway. On the second floor are eight rooms, four on each side. Go to the room farthest on the right. M'sieu will come to you there."

"Thank you, Etienne." Gerard took a last sip of his drink, then went to the door and stepped into the empty hallway. At the far end, he saw the stairway, and on the second floor he found the room Etienne had indicated. The room was in darkness. As Gerard flicked the light switch, he heard the whirring of the four-bladed ceiling fan start up. He crossed over to the windows and tilted the slatted louvers to enable him to look down on the opposite side of Rue Pavillon where a few late strollers walked slowly past the closed shops.

The walls of the room were covered with heavily embossed floral paper in a deep red color. The furniture was of rough, local manufacture; two sideboards, a massive table, six chairs, a sofa and one long wooden bench, all of native mahogany. The pictures on the walls were in ornate gilt frames, portraits of uniformed men, lightly clad women, all covered with a patina of age that made their subjects barely visible against dark backgrounds.

The floor was covered with a thick mat of sisal that made his movements soundless. He walked over to the large armoire that stood against the far wall and began to examine its primitive carvings, when he heard the sound of the door handle move. He turned and stood easily, loosely, on the balls of his feet as the door opened quickly. Emil Lebrun stepped inside, shut the door, and shot the locking bar into place. When he turned back to face Gerard, his face was crinkled in a friendly smile. "M'sieu?"

Gerard examined Lebrun more closely now, a ponderously heavy man with a round, moonlike face that was swarthy and moist. His head was either completely bald or had been shaved to give that effect. His neck had become a series of fleshy rings that disappeared into a white, sweat-dampened shirt that was closed tightly at the throat by a small black bow tie. His chest sat on top of a huge mound of stomach that rounded downward and disappeared into a pair of black trousers that were not only belted but additionally secured by a pair of bright red suspenders that peeped out from under his opened white dinner jacket. The hand he extended was huge and firm; and dry, Gerard noted gratefully.

"M'sieu?"

Gerard smiled. "M'sieu Lebrun, I am Argos 3. You are aware that when I was here earlier tonight, Madame Lund informed you that I am a member of the American Embassy staff."

Lebrun's smile was automatic. "Ah, so," he replied. "And I?"

"You are Alec Fletcher's principal contact in Port Amitié."

"And M'sieu Fletcher?"

"M'sieu Fletcher is known as Paros 9. He carries a watch similar to mine with the name Paros where mine shows the name Argos." Gerard held his watch up for Lebrun to see.

"Ah." Lebrun sighed with a broadened smile. "I am indeed very happy to see you, M'sieu Gerard."

"And I to find you, M'sieu Lebrun."

"How did you learn of me?" Lebrun asked. "Is there some word of M'sieu Alec?"

"No. I found Alec Fletcher's papers in the house where he lived. I am now living in that same house at No. 11—"

Lebrun nodded. "I know it well. I have been there many times."

"I have much to ask you. Can we talk here with safety?"

"Wait, M'sieu." There was a curious smile on Lebrun's face, not crafty or sly, Gerard thought, but—secret, was the word. As though Lebrun were holding something back that would give him pleasure to reveal at the proper moment. Lebrun went to the armoire, opened the lower left side, and slid the entire section of drawers to the right. Now he bent down and crawled inside. Gerard saw the back of the armoire roll back, and as Lebrun's huge posterior disappeared, heard his voice call out, "M'sieu!"

Gerard got down on hands and knees and entered the small cave and came up inside a tangle of hanging clothes. When Lebrun parted the garments, Gerard stepped out of a full-sized wardrobe into another room, furnished as a bedroom.

"We are on the second floor of the building next to the Excelsior, M'sieu," Lebrun explained with some pride. "I own it also. On the first floor is a florist and gift shop, Chez Martal, that is rented to a relative, but the second floor is sealed off from the one below. It can be entered only by a stairway from the rear. Therefore, the café, if one exercises caution, is not under suspicion."

Gerard nodded with admiring approval. "Now, M'sieu, we can talk in safety. Also, in comfort, if I may be per-

mitted to sit down. I have been long on my feet today."
He sat down heavily.

"First," Gerard said, "about Alec Fletcher."

Lebrun's fleshy face sagged into an expression of sadness. "I can tell you very little, M'sieu. He came here the last time about nine days ago. From Leone. Someone followed him from the checkpoint into the city. He borrowed Etienne's car to go to the embassy without being observed. Later, Etienne returned Alec's Ford and recovered his Citroën. From the moment he left here that night, we have not seen or heard from him."

"Or of him?"

"Or of him."

"Do you believe he was killed?"

"I do not know what to think, M'sieu."

"A guess, perhaps."

Lebrun was deliberate when he spoke next. "I have given this much thought. M'sieu. Let me explain it this way. The security police have been as eager as Alec to learn what has been happening in the back country. In some way, Alec received word in advance of the raid in Leone. Before he could return to Port Amitié, word of the raid was telephoned to the Bureau here. Also, that Alec had left Leone immediately after the raid took place. At the checkpoint here, someone followed him, perhaps Lieutenant Falot, who is the one of General Batraville's security aides whose duty it is to keep a close watch on suspected persons.

"If it was he who took Alec, there would be no point in killing him unless he knew everything Alec had learned in Leone. Alec, knowing this, would endure much before he would tell Falot. You understand, M'sieu, that Falot could not make an official arrest because of Alec's diplomatic privilege, no?"

Gerard nodded.

"Therefore, if Falot could force Alec to disclose what he knew of the events in Leone, he could rise high in the estimation of General Batraville by providing information the general has long sought. It is possible, then, that Falot may have taken Alec to some place, to hold him there until he is ready to talk."

"And if it was not Falot who took Alec?"

Lebrun shrugged his massive body heavily. "If it was a simple matter of robbery, the robbers would have killed him and his body would then have been found. I have

120

puzzled this question for many hours and I return to one conclusion: that Falot is the responsible one. There is also another matter that leads me to believe this."

"What matter?"

"It is a—personal—Mademoiselle Suzanne, the young—"

"I know Mademoiselle Suzanne. What part does she have in this?"

"An innocent one. Lieutenant Falot has been—ah—attracted to the mademoiselle since her arrival here. He was friendly and they were seen together several times. When Alec arrived, she showed a marked preference for her own countryman, which did not endear Alec to him. Falot has since become—how shall we say it?—overzealous in his conduct toward Alec. He is, of course, quite naturally suspicious that Alec is not merely an assistant commercial attaché, but a CIA agent. A spy. He has made it a point to keep a close watch, to find proof, and thus have him officially expelled from Liberté. It is a guess, but a possibility."

Gerard frowned over this added complication of jealousy. Experience should have dictated greater tact and caution to Alec. A personal involvement on the job was hardly tolerable. And suddenly it occurred to him that if the situation were reversed and he and Nora— He shook the thought aside. "Emil, I was followed here. A man in uniform driving a black Plymouth, the same car that followed me in from the airport when I arrived—"

Lebrun smiled dryly. "Falot, without a doubt. He did not enter the café behind you."

"Then he probably parked somewhere nearby and is waiting for me to leave."

Lebrun said, "If you wish to avoid him, you can leave by the rear exit without returning to the café. I can arrange a car—"

"That is exactly what I do not want, Emil. I think I am ready to have M'sieu Falot make a move in my direction."

"Then," Lebrun said with a shrug, "you have only to go below and leave."

"I will do that now. Later, I will want to talk with you again."

"At any time, M'sieu. However, do not regard Falot lightly. He is a man of many hatreds. And ambitious."

"I will keep that in mind. Thank you, Emil. I will be in touch with you soon."

"*Bonne chance, M'sieu.* And please, be careful."

The bar patrons had thinned out. He exchanged smiles with Etienne, and left through the front entrance. As he unlocked the Ford, he glanced carelessly up and down Rue Pavillon. The black Plymouth was parked four or five doors away in front of the Esplanade. It was not until he had got into the car that he saw the uniformed figure get up from a sidewalk table at the Esplanade and walk rapidly to his car. He pulled out from the curb and noted with satisfaction that before he reached the corner, the Plymouth was moving in his direction.

Gerard took a course unknown to him, turning off the main street before he reached the Champs, into a wide road that seemed to lead somewhere out of the city. Through the rear-view mirror, he saw the headlights of his tail following at an easy pace. He speeded up and widened the gap, but only for a few moments; the Plymouth matched his speed and equaled the distance between them. They had reached open country now, and the road began to narrow. Up ahead, Gerard could see a turn in the road; as he approached it, the turn became sharper. He jammed the accelerator down to the floorboard and watched as the following headlights became mere pinpoints. Falot had been momentarily taken off guard. At the turn, Gerard braked quickly, pulled the car off the road onto a level, grassy spot behind a tree, then cut the motor and turned the lights off.

The Plymouth roared into the turn and came to a complete stop. There was nothing ahead of it on the long stretch of road. Falot got out of the Plymouth and stood in the road staring ahead, then to either side of him. And then Gerard stepped up behind him and shoved the muzzle of his .38 into Falot's back.

"Do not turn around, M'sieu Falot," he said calmly, "unless you wish to die." Falot obeyed. "Now raise your hands slowly outward and fold them over your head." Falot's reaction was immediate. His hands went out and up, curled over his uniform cap. Gerard ran one hand over the lieutenant's back and legs, then moved to the right side and took the pistol from his holster and threw it behind him into the brush. "Now turn around and face me. Make no foolish moves, Lieutenant. I am quite accustomed to my work."

Falot turned, anguish and bitter frustration reflected in his eyes. He made a move to lower his arms, but Gerard, with a single upward motion of the .38, changed his

122

mind. In that moment, Falot regained his voice. "Well, *M'sieu l'Espion,* what do you think you will gain by this foolish thing?" he asked.

"What I shall gain or not gain will depend on you, Lieutenant. Keep in mind this much. If I do not gain what I seek, I shall have no alternative but to kill you. If you co-operate, you may save your life. The decision is yours to make. Yours alone."

"How?"

"I want you to take me to M'sieu Fletcher." As Falot opened his mouth to speak, Gerard shut him off with, "Hear me out, Lieutenant, before you begin your protests and denials. I have little time to waste and I am entirely serious. I know it was you who took M'sieu Fletcher nine days ago on his return from Leone. If you have already killed him, I shall lose nothing by killing you in return. If he is alive, you are the man who knows where he is, and I want to be taken to him. If you begin with denials, let me tell you that on your first such denial, my finger will send you to your reward in Hell. You have exactly ten seconds to make the decision which it will be. Life or death. Now, talk."

Whatever it was Falot had intended saying to Gerard before was now forgotten. His mouth shut tightly, but the fear that was inside him was becoming visible on the surface: the sweat beads gathering on his face, the slight trembling of his body and in his hands that were clasped over his head.

"M'sieu—" he began, then stopped.

"One," Gerard began the count. "Two."

"M'sieu, it will do no good—"

"Three." Then, "Four."

"You will be killed for this, M'sieu Gerard."

"Five. Perhaps, but you won't be here to enjoy my execution, will you, Falot? Six."

Falot's head turned from left to right, but his position was hopeless. The road was as empty now as when they had driven into this stretch. "Seven."

"If I—"

"If you what?"

A pause. "Eight. Nine. You have only one second, Falot. Quickly!" Gerard's right thumb drew the hammer back, and the *click!* made its final impression on Falot.

"Bien, bien, M'sieu! Do—do not shoot! I will take you to him!"

With a breath of relief, Gerard lowered the hammer easily, but held the .38 aimed at Falot's midsection. "All right, Falot. Where?"

"We must return to the city and take the road toward Plage Etoile. He is there."

"Who is with him?"

"An old man and his wife."

"No more than that?"

"No more."

"He is hurt?"

A moment of hesitation. "Yes. He attempted to escape, and it was necessary to stop him. It is not bad. A head wound. He has had medical care, M'sieu, and has returned almost to normal."

"All right, Falot. We will use your car to get us through a checkpoint if necessary. Do not delude yourself into heroics. I warn you now, if you give any order or call out, the first shot from this pistol will go into your brain. You'll never live to see the outcome of your treachery."

Once past the military checkpoint at the south end of Port Amitié, they took the curving shore road toward Maréchal, a well-traveled road, with trucks coming north laden with goods for tomorrow's markets. They came into Plage Etoile and skimmed along the main highway for a short distance, then turned off toward the secondary beach road. As they cut into the street that ran parallel to the sea and only fifty yards from it, Falot pulled up to a house and stopped. "It is that one," he said, pointing to a shell-pink two-storied house that looked little different from those that surrounded it.

"All right, Falot. Slide across the seat and get out of the car on my side. You have told me that there are only an old man and his woman in the house guarding Fletcher. If anyone other than those you have described appears, you will receive a bullet at the base of your skull. Do you wish to change your story now before we go inside?"

Falot shook his head. "No. It is as I have said."

Gerard followed beside and a quarter-step behind Falot. At the door, Falot began to reach into a pocket and felt the muzzle of the .38 press against his spine. "No key, Falot. Knock on the door."

Falot rapped sharply three times, then three times again. They waited in the darkness. "Knock again," Gerard ordered. Falot repeated the knocking in the same manner.

From inside, they could hear an incoherent mumbling, the snap of a lock and bolt. The door opened about three inches, and they saw the dim yellow rays of the hall light and the eyes of an old man, obviously annoyed at being wakened at this late hour. A brass chain stretched across the opening.

"It is I, old one. Remove the chain and let us in," Falot said. Still grumbling, the old man closed the door, slipped the chain from its guard slot, and opened the door wider. Gerard nudged Falot inside. Falot motioned the old man ahead of them and up the stairs. On the upper level, a door opened as they approached, and Gerard saw the trembling, withered face of an old, dark woman. At sight of them, she closed the door quickly. At the far end of the hall, the old man halted before a door that had two strong bolts on the outside. Falot nodded, and the old man shot the bolts and threw the door open. Gerard motioned the old man in first, then nodded to Falot. He came in behind them and heard the voice from the far side of the room call out, *"Qui est là?"*

From the doorway, Gerard said, "Let's have some light."

Falot reached for the wall and threw the switch upward. The lights came on, and in a corner of the room, in a large bed, Alec Fletcher lay outstretched, wrists tied to the brass uprights at the head, ankles tied in the same manner of the foot of the bed. His eyes blinked with the suddenness of the light. A large patch of bandage was taped to the left side of his head. But for the growth of hair on his face, Gerard recognized him at once from the photographs he had studied at JIA headquarters.

"Hello, Alec," he called out. "I'm Jim Gerard."

For a moment, there was silence; then he heard Fletcher's deep baritone voice reply happily, "Hello, buddy. What took you so goddam long?"

Gerard motioned the old man and Falot into an opposite corner and kicked the door shut behind him. With his left hand, he withdrew a knife from his trouser pocket, pressed a button that released a length of gleaming steel from its sheath with a *snick!* With two quick moves, he slashed the leather thongs that bound Fletcher's wrists and handed him the knife. "Can you make it, Alec?"

"Sure." Fletcher sat up slowly, leaned forward, and attacked the thongs that held his ankles, then lay back, rubbing his wrists. It took a few minutes before he could swing himself around and stand up shakily. He wore only shorts and trousers, a powerfully built man, strongly muscled, almost half a head taller than Gerard. His bearded face was smiling now, showing either high good humor or relief that he was once again in friendly hands.

"Get the rest of your clothes on, Alec, and let's get out of here as quickly as we can. We'll have to decide something about these two."

"Don't worry about the old man or his woman," Alec said. "They didn't have any part of this and didn't want any of it. They helped me a lot. It's that foul ball—"

"Get dressed and we'll decide on what to do with him. Is this all there is to the place?"

"For the night, yes. During the day, Falot had one of his boys drop by to make sure I was tied up. Soon as night came on, it was only the old man and his woman, except when buddy-boy here came out to work me over."

"Who are the old folks?"

"Falot's father and mother, but they couldn't care less for him. It's Falot's house."

"All right, let's go." Gerard turned to the old man, who had been watching them nervously, silently appealing to Alec for mercy through faded eyes. "You can go now, old man," Gerard told him. "Go to your room and stay there with your woman until we have left. No harm will come to you if you remain there quietly."

The old man threw a quick look at Falot and went out. Alec was dressed, all but his necktie, which he folded and put into his side jacket pocket. He went to Falot, spun him around to face the wall, and went through his pockets, came up with a knife not too dissimilar from the switchblade Gerard had used. This, Alec put into his own pocket, then spun Falot around again. "Well, soldier, the shoe is now on the other foot, no?"

Falot's eyes were filled with stony contempt. "Another time perhaps, *M'sieu Traître*," he spat out venomously.

Fletcher laughed shortly. "Traitor? I? To whom, *mon fou?*"

"To the color of your skin, to every black man in the world."

Alec turned to Gerard. "How in hell do you beat down that logic, Jim?" he asked.

"The question is, what are we going to do with him now that we've got him?"

"Turn him loose. He can't do us any harm officially."

"How do you figure that?"

"This was a little personal project of his own. If he makes an official report, he's got to come up with the answer to why he was operating on his own; on whose orders, other than his own, he kidnaped and attacked an American Embassy staff member. Even down here, he can't get away with that. What I owe him personally, I can overlook for the time being."

"You understand that, Lieutenant?" Gerard asked.

Falot nodded sullenly.

"Remember, Falot, we are two against you. If you open your mouth about this, our ambassador will make the strongest representations to M'sieu St. Germaine and President Fontaine. I don't think you would want that to happen."

Falot remained motionless and silent, a figure of dejection and resignation. "All right, Alec," Gerard said, "let's take him along. We came in his car. We'll go back to where I left mine, and we'll go from there."

They were back at No. 11 Rue Perrigeau, Alec in his old room and Gerard examining the wound. "Looks clean and healthy, Alec. How does it feel?"

"Stiff. No more than that. The old man and his woman were very careful. I don't know what they used on me, weeds, herbs, crabgrass, or whatever they got from their local witch doctor, but it worked. Luckily, it was concussion and not fracture."

"Good. What's next?"

Alec shook his head from side to side. "I guess now that you're here, it's your show, Jim."

"Our show," Gerard amended with emphasis. "Let's take it from Chalumeau."

"You know about him already?"

"The report you filed the night Falot snatched you. Also, from your records."

Fletcher winced as his head snapped too quickly in the direction of the bathroom door. Gerard said, "I found your files, Alec."

"You sure know how to dust a room, don't you? It took me weeks to dig and mortise that door out from the bottom. I'd have bet anything I had the safest hiding place on earth."

Gerard smiled. "You're not going to try to teach an old Connecticut country boy how to skin a rabbit, are you?"

Alec laughed good-humoredly, shaking his head slowly

from side to side. "Then you know my contact, Lebrun. And his son, Etienne."

"I made it a point to scout them this evening when I took Nora to dinner."

"Nora? Mrs. Lund?"

"Unless there's another Nora around. We're old friends from back in Washington. I went back later tonight and identified myself to Lebrun and Etienne. He was the second person to give me a hint that you might still be alive."

"Who was the first?"

"Suzanne."

"Ah, Suzanne."

"And by the way, haven't you learned about personal involvements on the job?"

Ruefully: "I've been briefed, Jim, but this one just couldn't be avoided. She was—well, it just—happened—"

Gerard smiled. "I know," he said. "Let's get back to this Chalumeau," he reminded Alec.

"Okay. Chalumeau. Until Leone, he was just a rumor, a shadow, a damned wraith. But I've seen him now. I watched one whole operation from start to finish, heard him talk to a small band of his men. Believe me, Jim, there's nothing little in what I've heard the Old Man call 'little hit-and-run raids.' This boy moves fast and hits hard. What's more, those scattered operations of his show a definite pattern that comes up smelling like a full-scale revolution being brewed."

"Who is behind him?"

"I don't know if anybody is sparkplugging him. I honestly think he's on his own."

"What can he hope to accomplish without outside support? If he had military backing, Russian or Cuban—"

"I haven't been able to pin down any connections. The only near miss I've had is that I've heard the Russian commercial attaché has been scouring the field trying to reach him. Man named Pyantenov, a short, barrel-shaped—"

"Feodor Pyantenov? You're sure?"

"You know him?"

Gerard nodded. "I've seen him operating in Vietnam. There's a fat file on him back home. He's one of GRU's top troubleshooters. Or trouble creators. If they've sent him in, you're right; this isn't a small matter by any means. Let's get back to Chalumeau."

"All I can tell you is that he's a big man wherever he goes. He has a key contact set up in advance somehow. A meeting is arranged in a quiet out-of-the-way place; jungle, mountaintop, the edge of a swamp, a field of high-growing cane. And Jim, they listen. I've heard him and watched them. They believe."

"In what?"

"In hope, freedom. No great riches or glory, just the simple things they want. Enough food and work, a decent life for all. To educate their young and allow them to grow up with a chance. He talks tough, but he sounds reasonable and sincere and makes sense. I know that Fontaine has promised them all that, and Dubonnière before Fontaine, but this is no stuffed shirt talking from behind a desk. This is a G.I. guy like themselves. What's more important, he's out there with them, leads them himself on these raids, and takes the same chances he asks them to take, so they know he's not just another ding-a-ling politician pumping out a snow job."

"Chalumeau," Gerard mused. "It's not his true name, of course."

"There's none other like it on Liberté, so we can assume it's a code name. I've heard others, possibly his lieutenants. Like Poignard in Leone, who is Jules Fabreau, a labor boss on the Leone docks."

"*Poignard*. Dagger," Gerard interpreted.

"And sharp. If you could hear Chalumeau, Jim, you'd be impressed. He's a hell of a salesman for whatever he's selling, and it looks like trouble. He makes them understand, feel the power in himself. If he can arm enough of them, he won't need the Army, the Russians, or Cubans. I wish I could make the ambassador or Truscott understand—"

"I think they do, now, Alec. The ambassador was given a clear picture in Washington. You and I are going to be working on the same side of the street from here on in. How's the head, really?"

"It had me dizzy for a while, Jim, but I'm coming out of it fine. A day or two and I'll be okay."

"We'll have to keep you out of Falot's range for a while. If you don't mind, I'll continue to share your quarters."

"Mind? I think it's great. Beautiful."

"I'll let Truscott know you're safe in the morning. He'll pass it along to the ambassador. Anyone else?"

"Uh—Shannon, maybe."

"And—Suzanne?"

"And Suzanne." Fletcher caught himself, then laughed. "She'll keep it quiet, won't she?"

"Sure. You can count on Suzy all the way."

"Good. Now what about General Batraville?"

"Okay. For one thing, Batraville is no yo-yo. He's a cold, calculating, ambitious bastard from the other side of the tracks, and resents the upper classes enough to want to be one of them. He's married to Lénore Dessez, whose father was on the General Staff. She was mixed up in some kind of scandal—or near scandal—that sent her daddy running over to Italy to bring her back home.

"Less than six months later, she married Batraville and moved into his palace apartment. He was head of the Palace Guard then, a captain. Soon after that, he shot up to major, colonel, then general at the top of Defense and Security. Papa Dessez made it to general. He retired when he balked at some of Fontaine's shenanigans and is living somewhere out in the back country near St. Michel."

"Any chance that he might be involved with—"

"Chalumeau? No. I checked that out. There was some suspicion, some dirty rumors about Fontaine and Lénore, but I've got a good contact in St. Michel, and there's no chance of a Dessez-Chalumeau tieup. He's clean."

"I met a Major Lamonte at the Excelsior. What about him?"

"He's Batraville's executive officer. I hear that Batraville brought him along from the Palace Guards to help improve his own image with the upper-class Libertéans, but it hasn't seemed to help much. Lamonte and his family are old friends of the Delacroix and the Courdets. In fact, the kids were all in Europe together at school about the same time Lénore was making her big splash there."

"How did you get on to the thing in Leone, Alec?"

"Put it down to voodoo, I guess. Somewhere, we've got a friend. Somebody who doesn't want it made public."

Gerard's forehead wrinkled into a frown. "How about spelling that out for me?"

"Well, when I first started getting around down here, I got a mysterious telephone call one morning. Within thirty seconds, I knew my cover as assistant commercial attaché was blown. The voice told me to keep an eye out for Falot, that he had orders to stay close on my heels.

"A couple of weeks later, I found a matchbook folded

130

around one of the spokes of my steering wheel. Inside, someone had written a note that hinted I might find it interesting to look closely and deeply into one Mr. Thomas Reed of Belle Roseau. That's how my file on him got so thick.

"A few days before I went down to Leone, I found a note in my post-office box that I use sometimes for local contacts. Just the box number on the envelope. Inside was a short note telling me to get a map and mark the last six or seven towns that had been hit by the mysterious raiders. When I did that, the note went on, I would notice that if the town of Leone, which hadn't been hit yet, were linked up with the others, it would make a perfect pattern; and since the hits were being spaced about three weeks apart, Leone might be due within a few days. I took the hint and went down there and talked it over with the contact Lebrun put me in touch with, a man named Meurice.

"For four days Meurice and I sat at one of the sidewalk cafés and kept an eye on every new face that came in by boat, bus, or horse. On the day it happened, this big tough man came in by bus, and Meurice followed him. It turned out to be Chalumeau."

"And you've no idea who has been tipping you off to these things?"

"Not the slightest, Jim. It's damned unnerving. I wouldn't even know who to begin to suspect. I've talked it over with Emil, and he couldn't come up with anything, either."

"What about this character Reed? I've had a little about him from Nora and Jake Walker. Why all the emphasis on him?"

"It hasn't fit into any special slot yet, but when the information began rolling in on him from Port-au-Prince, it came like a big wave, fascinating as hell. Just where it belongs in the picture, I haven't figured out yet. Reed is an anachronism. Maybe because he's what Walker calls a 'bamboo American,' married to a Haitian woman, or because he's an American, maybe he's become our local conscience—"

Gerard laughed. "Spare me the psychological interpretations, and let's stay with the facts, shall we?"

"All right," Alec said somewhat sheepishly. "To put it mildly, he's interesting. Let me take it from the beginning—"

13.

The man they knew as Tom Reed, Alec Fletcher explained, was hardly more than a caricature of the firm-fleshed, tough, tight-lipped and proudly erect man of thirty years ago. Those who remembered him when he first came to Port Amitié might recall a large man with broad, regular features; a quiet, secretive man who appeared to be introverted and moody. He had taken over the 8,200-acre Granjon plantation that lay between the present Hampton estate and Terre Delacroix, but little was seen of him in Port Amitié except on rare occasions when business matters forced him to come into town. Always, he came alone.

Efforts to make friends with the newcomer Reeds were politely, but firmly, refused. Mrs. Reed had not been in evidence when neighbors called to extend a formal welcome. They were greeted by Tom Reed, without warmth, and without an invitation to enter the Gran Maison. It was only later that they learned from their own servants that a Mrs. Thomas Reed actually existed and there was an infant son. *Un nègre.*

No one could deny that the Granjon plantation, renamed Belle Roseau by Tom Reed, had profited well by his hands. He worked hard at supervising his labor force. He rose early, went out into the fields, took no siesta period, and returned home after dark. He was a hard taskmaster, but he treated his people and his overseer, Manuelo Olivares, fairly and decently.

After the outbreak of World War II, some time during the latter part of December, 1941, Tom Reed drove into Port Amitié and applied for re-enlistment in the Marine Corps at the American Consulate. His application was received and forwarded to Washington. After a long delay, he was notified by the consular officer that his request for return to active military service had been declined with thanks. When he pressed for a reason, he was given the vague and unsatisfactory explanation that his occupation as a sugar planter was considered more important and necessary to the war effort than the role he could play in uniform.

It was Tom Reed's most desperate humiliation. Shortly afterward, he appeared in Port Amitié, rented a small house in a quiet middle-class neighborhood, and thereafter seldom returned to his Belle Roseau. He applied for membership in the Club International and, as a planter of means, was accepted. After that, Reed appeared to be charting a slow and solitary course aimed at self-destruction. All attempts by sympathetic members of the colony to reach him, to try to understand the mystery of his self-imposed loneliness, were fruitless. In time, he became an object of pity and curiosity, a quiet man bent on keeping to himself and devoting his waking hours to the consumption of alcohol.

Now fifty-seven, all that remained of the once trim, immaculate military figure was the closely cropped hair that he would have trimmed religiously every ten days to Marine Corps regulation length. He had grown careless otherwise. In his dress. Soft, flabby flesh hung dejectedly on his big frame to make him seem ten to fifteen years older. Most of his days and nights were now spent in local bars, his tastes running indiscriminately from the more expensive bars along the Rue Pavillon to the cheapest and vilest traps on the Rue Félicité that bordered the slum area. Occasionally, perhaps to perpetuate his own belief that he was still a white planter and a member in good standing with the white planter community, he bathed and dressed carefully and put in an appearance at the Club. Quiet and withdrawn, few objected to his presence, a sad, mysterious figure who sat alone at the bar until drowsiness would overtake him and a doorman would lead him to a cab. Visits to the Club were infrequent. His catholic tastes for the earthier needs of man led him to female companionship among those to whom he would owe no explanations, obligations, or responsibilities, permit him to wallow in his bottomless well of self-pity and personal despair without interference.

"What's behind it all?" Gerard asked.

"The black child. Reed's wife was a Haitian, remember."

"What about the child?"

"I don't know, Jim. I never could find out. There's some rumor that he was trouble prone. Went to jail several times, then to prison. Most people believe he's dead."

Gerard could feel a sense of holding back in Alec. "What else?"

Alec shrugged. "Black son, white father. They tell me that's the part Tom Reed couldn't take, why he came here instead of going back to the States when the Marines pulled out of Haiti in '34. Tom Reed's birth certificate shows he was born in a small town in South Carolina."

CHAPTER 4

1.

Gerard was checking over a sheet of penciled notes the next morning when Suzanne looked in, surprised to find him already at his desk and working before eight o'clock. She called out a "Good morning," came in and checked his OUT tray and found it empty. "Coffee?" she asked.

"Thanks. And will you bring your notebook, Suzanne? I'd like to dictate a report to the ambassador, copy to Mr. Truscott."

She returned a few minutes later with a cup of steaming coffee, which he accepted gratefully. "Get a cup for yourself and bring it back here, Suzanne. I want to talk with you before I start dictating."

When she was seated, he said: "The report I'm going to dictate has an indirect bearing on you. I'd like to tell you about it first so it won't come as a shock to you."

Suzanne leaned forward with interest. "Alec?" she asked.

"Alec. You were right, Suzanne. I found him last night."

"Where is he? Is he all right?"

"He's at No. 11 at the moment." He heard the heightened excitement in the gasp of breath she expelled.

"He's not—hurt?"

"He was, but not badly. A concussion. You'll get the whole story from the report. When you've finished typing it, I want the copies to go to the ambassador and Mr. Truscott, marked 'Eyes Only.' When that's done, you can take off and go to Alec. I told him to expect you."

"Oh. Thank you, Mr. Gerard. I don't know what to say —how to thank you—"

"It's all right, Suzanne. Just make sure we keep this to ourselves for the time being, shall we?"

"Yes. Yes, of course."

"Is Shannon in?"

"Not yet. He and Sergeant Walker rotate the night duty.

134

Clark was on last night, so he probably went home after the colors were raised for breakfast, to shave and change. He won't be in until around eleven."

While he waited for the report, Gerard pored over a sheaf of back-issue editorials clipped from *Le Temps* that Suzanne had marked earlier for his attention. As he digested the stinging rebukes and biting indictments against the Fontaine administration, Gerard wondered that the Courdets, father and son both, had survived so far. Or, if François Courdet was as honest and trustworthy as his frank proposals for decent government action made him out, why, in fact, was he not a candidate for the presidency, running against Charles Du Faure?

The phone rang. He pressed the lighted button at the base of the instrument, picked up the receiver, and heard Suzanne's voice. "A call for you, Mr. Gerard, but the gentleman refuses to give his name. He says it is a matter of extreme importance."

"Put him on, please." He heard Suzanne click off the line and said, "Gerard here."

In beautifully precise French the muffled voice at the other end said, "Mr. Gerard, if you will be at the airport at eleven-thirty, you may witness an event that should be of special interest to you."

"Who is this, please?" Gerard asked.

"That, M'sieu, I cannot tell you, but please believe me and spare the time. I assure you it will be rewarding."

"And if I go to the airport, what shall I look for?"

"The arrival of a Cubana airlines plane. One of the passengers should merit your attentioon."

"I see. And how will I know which—" he began, but heard the disconnecting click as his caller hung up. He sat for a moment, staring at the dead receiver in his hand, puzzling over the voice. Alec's mysterious benefactor had now become his own. He checked the time: ten-forty. He picked his hat off the clothes tree and went through Suzanne's office. "Finished?" he asked.

"Just about. Only a line or two."

He waited, signed the report, and watched as Suzanne folded the sheets and enclosed them in separate envelopes, sealed them with heavy tape, and marked them properly. "I'll be away for an hour or more. When you've handed these to Miss Bennett and Mrs. Weatherby, Alec will be waiting to see you."

Thirty minutes later, Gerard lounged at the gift counter at the Port Amitié airport. He bought a copy of *Le Temps* and, as if to show complete neutrality, a copy of the government-controlled *Voix de Liberté,* then checked through the travel folders in a rack. At eleven twenty-five he moved to a bench where he could look through a wide window into the arrival shed and the long table set up for Customs inspection. A few moments later he heard the whine of a jet overhead, watched as it nosed down to the runway, veered to the right, and came to a stop about fifty yards from the shed. It carried the familiar Cubana markings.

The debarking ladder was run up to the plane's side and the passengers began to emerge; a couple, three men, another couple, then a woman traveling alone, two men, another couple, and a man alone. As the thirteen passengers followed the arrows across the black-topped path to Customs, Gerard scanned each of them carefully, then came back to the thirteenth man. He was tall, burned a deep brown by the sun, and wore a crisp Panama hat, white suit, and dark wrap-around sunglasses. Of the lot, there was something vaguely familiar about him, but having been advised by his anonymous caller to look for an indefinite "someone," Gerard did not want to fall into the trap of wishful thinking.

The baggage was loaded from the plane into one small truck, then brought to the Customs shed and placed in a single orderly row as the passengers stood by, waiting to claim their possessions. The man in the dark sunglasses stood apart from this activity, peering out into the airport building as though he were expecting someone to meet him. Now the passengers were lined up before the two inspectors, baggage open. They moved along, answered questions, relocked bags, closed and tied packages, then moved on into the waiting room. Three pieces of luggage remained on the rack, untouched, evidently those of the man who waited alone.

A porter approached him, tipped his hat, and pointed to the three pieces and said, "M'sieu?"

The man shook his head negatively. *"Pas encore."*

The porter retreated to one of the inspectors and repeated the man's words. Another inspector stepped in to look inquiringly at the porter, then at the man. He walked over and spoke with the passenger, who shook his head, replied, then pointed to his watch.

At that moment, Gerard heard the wail of a siren, turned and watched as a police-escorted black limousine drew up to the building entrance. The chauffeur leaped out and opened the door, and the khaki-clad figure of General Batraville got out and strode into the building. Major Lamonte, also in uniform, was directly behind him.

This, Gerard decided, was no doubt what he had been told to watch for. Batraville and the major swept through the waiting room into the Customs area. The general greeted the sunglassed passenger with a warm embrace, turned and introduced the major, who saluted politely and stepped back a pace. The passenger spoke to the general, pointing to his three pieces of baggage. The general turned to the two customs inspectors and spoke sharply to them in terms of *"une affaire diplomatique."* The porter placed the three pieces on a hand truck and followed the party out to the limousine. Gerard trailed the party casually, and watched as the luggage was stowed in the trunk. As the small cortege pulled away, sirens wailing clearance for their passage, Jim Gerard identified the sunglassed arrival.

Craig Madden, alias John Mosher.

2.

High above the city where the summer home of President Louis Fontaine occupied the man-flattened top of Mont Couronne, the black Mercedes limousine came to a halt at the barred entrance while two civilian security guards peered inside the vehicle. To General Batraville's annoyance, they ordered the chauffeur to get out and open the trunk for examination. Some thirty yards ahead, four soldiers came out of the two sentry huts and stood with rifles held menacingly at ready, prepared against a possible crash-through into the grounds. Batraville could hardly complain, since he had originally established the procedure for the protection of the president.

On the rear seat, Batraville and his aide, Major Constantine Lamonte, sat on either side of the civilian, John Mosher, waiting in the humid heat for the examination to be completed. The trunk slammed shut. The two security guards dropped flat on the ground on opposite sides of the car to check the undercarriage, then got up. One of the men raised the red-and-white barrier and waved the chauffeur on. The four soldiers ahead saluted as the Mercedes passed them, then returned to their huts.

There was one more stop to be made at a small station where two more security guards waited. One of the men ordered Mosher to open his brief case, which he checked for weapons or bombs. The other recorded their names, went inside a small building, and telephoned ahead to be reassured the visit was in proper order. He returned, made a note of the license plate, and entered the time of their arrival. When they finally reached the Gran Maison, they were met by a secretary, dressed formally in cutaway, striped trousers, and wing collar, who told them there would be a thirty-minute wait before the president would be free. Other security guards were in evidence along the veranda and around the grounds.

They waited in a side room on the ground level for a full hour before the secretary returned, apologetically, to lead them to a study on the second floor. At each end of the long hallway of the right wing, an armed guard stood facing inward. The secretary rapped lightly on the door, and waited. Mosher heard a deep, muffled *"Entrez."* The secretary opened the door, entered, and stood stiffly aside to permit the party's entrance.

Behind the curving slash of a mahogany desk, glittering with multihued inlaid woods, Fontaine sat, dressed in a black suit of rippled silk, erect and with chin held high, his face registering no particular warmth at the sight of the American. His eyes flickered from Batraville to Lamonte as he nodded in acknowledgment of the introduction, then, with a stubby finger, indicated a delicate petit-point-covered Louis XIV chair for the white visitor and said, "Leave us now, General, Major."

Batraville's reaction was one of unfeigned disappointment. He hesitated for an awkward second or two, then straightened up, saluted, and withdrew, Lamonte following suit. Fontaine leaned back in his chair and turned his full attention to Mosher. "Please remove your dark glasses, sir," he said. "When I deal with a man I have a need to see his eyes."

"Pardon, Your Excellency?" Mosher replied.

"You do not speak French, Mr. Mosher?" he asked in English.

"Not as fluently as I should like, Your Excellency."

"Spanish, perhaps?"

"Yes, sir."

138

"Then we will converse in Spanish," Fontaine said in that language. "Your native tongue is not a favorite with me," he added bluntly, then repeated his original request. Mosher did not reply, but removed the sunglasses and allowed them to dangle from his left hand.

"Perhaps you wonder why, señor," Fontaine continued in an even, brittle tone. "Then let me tell you. Of the great number of your countrymen and the English who have lived on Liberté in the past and present, and who have accumulated great wealth, few have taken the trouble to learn our language beyond the few words necessary for their comfort or convenience. For a few francs a month, they prefer to employ interpreters. It is a form of foreign arrogance I despise; therefore, I prefer not to use the English language as a means of communication."

Mosher remained stiffly silent, annoyed by the brief, uncalled-for lecture. Fontaine waved a hand as though to dismiss the subject, then said: "You are late, Mr. Mosher. I was led to believe you would arrive here at least a month ago."

"It was expected that I would be here earlier, Your Excellency, but there were other matters beyond my control that prevented my scheduled departure from Havana."

"What matters, Mr. Mosher?"

Mosher opened his brief case and withdrew a leather-bound folder, saying as he handed it across the desk, "The detailed study of your requirements and the availability of the arms and other supplies to meet them."

Fontaine's ruffled feelings were not assuaged. In stony silence he took the folder and began riffling through its pages. He turned back to the item-for-item listing that took three full pages, and studied it, then began a more thorough reading of the Terms of Agreement section, his face showing no sign of satisfaction or dissatisfaction. When he looked up again, he said, "Because of Señor Urbana's delays, my plans have been seriously affected."

Mosher's own irritation and growing hostility toward Fontaine's cavalier treatment showed in a tightening of facial muscles along his jawline.

"Let us understand one another, Mr. Mosher," Fontaine continued. "I am not interested in excuses, but only in results. My time schedule has been destroyed because of" —he dropped the folder on the desk, away from himself and toward Mosher—"mere clerical work. Less than a week remains before our election day. I cannot move the date forward, and the arms I had counted on are not here. It is not a good example of the efficient co-operation I was led to believe I could expect."

"I can assure Your Excellency that if you will sign the agreement, the arms will leave Bahía de Nipe at once and be here in three days," Mosher replied.

"In the light of previous promises, Mr. Mosher, I am not so easily reassured." Fontaine pointed to the folder again. "The terms of this agreement require a thorough study before we are ready to commit ourselves to a program of co-operation with Cuba and Russia. A judgment of its contents cannot be made in a moment." Fontaine noticed now that his visitor's nervousness had extended to a clenching and unclenching of hands. His next question was designed to relieve that tension. "You are being well treated?" he asked in a softer tone.

"Extremely well, Mr. President. My suite at the Métropole is comfortable, and the service is excellent."

Fontaine nodded, toying with a huge cuff link emblazoned with a large diamond set in the center of an elaborate coat of arms. "You come highly recommended, Mr. Mosher," he said.

Mosher accepted the flattery without a smile. "I try to do my best, sir."

"Then perhaps you will give me your opinion on another matter."

"If I am able, Your Excellency."

"I have in mind a project to raise funds with which to help pay the Cuban Government in part for its assistance, a project I have named 'The Fontaine Fund.' Its purpose will be to explore untouched lands in search of oil deposits, to create dams and electric power, to search for minerals. The money will come from voluntary contributions from foreign landholders, planters, and those licensed to do business on Liberté, men who have been taking advantage of our country's generosity for many generations. Like the program in Cuba, they will be made to understand their obligation to support the government in this move by contributing—"

"Voluntarily, Your Excellency?"

"Voluntarily. Or be faced with certain proceedings—"

"Confiscation, Mr. President?"

"Legal expropriation," Fontaine amended.

Mosher considered Fontaine's semantics. "Your opinion, Mr. Mosher," Fontaine said.

"It would seem to me you are overlooking the possibility that the United States might take some conceivable action to protect the interests of her nationals and the nationals of her Western allies, sir."

With a show of unconcern, Fontaine replied: "Where life is not involved, Mr. Mosher, history speaks out against it. There was no military action or intervention in Mexico, in Cuba, in Santo Domingo, and other countries where governments have expropriated oil, communications operations, industries, and land. If demands are made, a promise of payment in the future can be made. It is difficult, is it not, to force the return of something once it has been taken?"

"It is a gamble, Your Excellency. Pressure from England, France, Germany, Italy—"

Fontaine smiled and waved the mild protest aside. "Señor Castro had no qualms. Nor shall I."

For a moment a heavy silence hung between them, then Mosher said, "The agreement, Mr. President—"

"I must study the terms carefully, Mr. Mosher. Leave it with me. I will inform you of my decision within two days."

3.

In his basement office at the palace, General Benoit Batraville paced back and forth, agitation spread over his face like a moving mask, angered by his dismissal from the conference between the president and John Mosher as though he were a lackey, an errand boy, instead of the general in command of the nation's defense and security. And to be shamed thus in the presence of Major Lamonte. *Sale fils de putain!*

At thirty-six, Batraville was the youngest man in Liberté's modern history to have attained the rank of general. He held much power, and now stood on the threshold of added greatness. He was an impressively large man, but his weight was evenly distributed throughout his six-foot-two-inch height. He was, like others close to Fontaine, dark of color, but his features were pleasantly regular, if not handsome. His uniforms were smartly tailored, and he frequently wore wide-flaring riding breeches and elegantly fitted English boots that showed the strength in his long, straight legs. From his wide belt hung a pearl-handled 9-mm. Czech automatic in a beauti-

141

fully embossed leather holster, a personal gift from Domingo Urbana as a memento of his visit to Havana. Over his left breast pocket he wore a row of colorful ribbons and the jeweled decoration in commemoration of the Castro Revolution pinned there by Fidel himself in a gesture of friendship and co-operation.

On the wall behind his desk, a large photograph of Louis Fontaine looked down upon him, but above the presidential smile the eyes were small and icy, the forehead deeply etched with lines that no smile could obliterate. Beneath the photograph, the legend, PEACE, PROSPERITY, GROWTH was printed in bold Gothic letters.

Peace, Batraville thought, with a strong military garrison in every important district to preserve it against local uprisings; *Prosperity*, for Fontaine's closest supporters and friends in exchange for unquestioned loyalty; *Growth*, in population, disease, death rate, poverty, illiteracy, and unrest. Batraville was staring at the photograph when he heard the rap of knuckles on the outer door and called out, *"Entrez."*

The general turned when Major Lamonte entered with a sheaf of papers, their light blue color indicating reports from civilian security agents in the interior. "Well?" he demanded brusquely.

Lamonte shook his head negatively. "As usual, nothing, General. As before, there is talk in the streets and in the cafés, but only after he has left. Nothing more."

Batraville uttered a vile epithet. "He is a man, not a phantom! Why can't they find him?" He went to his desk, sat down and shuffled through the reports Lamonte had put there, then angrily scattered them across the desk with an impatient sweep of his hand. "Chalumeau. Chalumeau. His very name haunts me."

"If," Lamonte offered, "the military commanders were ordered to co-operate with the security—"

"The military!" Batraville scoffed contemptuously. "Those mutinous *pous*, they would listen to him just as the peasants listen. Perhaps even join him."

"If," Lamonte suggested calmly, "the Army is not to be trusted, General—"

"Ah, yes, Constantine, your loyalty to the Army still runs deep, does it not?"

"My loyalty to Liberté runs even deeper, General," Lamonte retorted stiffly.

Batraville returned his aide's look of rebuke with in-

142

creasing anger, then looked away, unable to answer the challenge. A problem, this one, he thought, but a lesser one. Soon he will find himself in a desolate post like Sale Trou, with time to think over the insults his eyes repeat over and over again.

Lamonte had become a source of deep irritation to Batraville. Younger by two years, educated abroad, trimfigured and with charming manners, this son and grandson of Libertéan generals could scarcely conceal the contempt he felt for his superior officer. As a sublieutenant of equal rank only six years ago, Batraville had, as his own fortunes rose, personally chosen Lamonte as his aide, and the choice was warmly approved by Fontaine. But where Batraville had miscalculated in his ambitious plans was that while Lamonte retained his high social position among the *haute classe,* Batraville, the son of a minor bureau clerk, found that his aide's personal prestige and social status, if not his rank, remained far and above that of the general's. The position he had once dreamed of attaining, the possibility of a rapid emergence from obscurity into Lamonte's inner social set, had long ago evaporated. Perhaps when the new arms arrived and the Elite Corps of Civil Militia became established with Batraville in command—

"Very well, Constantine, leave these with me. I have plans to make," he said curtly.

"Oui, mon général," Lamonte replied formally and withdrew.

Batraville stared at the scattered reports, then got up and reconsidered the photograph of Louis Fontaine. Superimposed over it, he saw his own face reflected in the glass, and the thought struck him that if he were a true believer in Damballa, as Fontaine was, he could interpret this vision as a Sign of the Gods.

The Russians. The first hint from the innocuous Pyantenov, which he had dismissed. Next, the quiet call from Ambassador Vossolofsky, who dazzled him with rhetoric and hypothetical questions. Last, the suave Zharkov, who had more closely come to the point. If he could only be sure. But how does one enter total intrigue with Russians whom one does not understand? Or trust? Or, *could* they be trusted?

And how far, he wondered, would he trust Fontaine if it weren't for Lénore? The thought of Lénore was like a sudden painful twisting of a heart muscle within him.

When Louis Fontaine was raised to the presidency by military junta, Batraville, like Lamonte, had been a sublieutenant on duty with the Palace Guard Detachment. Batraville came to Fontaine's attention one day when, shortly after his inauguration, the president took his first official inspection tour of the city. Ahead of the limousine, Sublieutenant Batraville drove the lead car, filled with security guards, all armed with submachine guns held across their laps, out of view of the citizenry. Six soldier-mounted motorcycles flanked the two cars.

Within minutes of their arrival in the waterfront slum area, a mob had formed to block their passage; men, women, and children held outstretched arms toward Fontaine, chanting for aid. From the outer rim, more vociferous members of the crowd hooted and jeered. Some stones and clods of dirt were thrown at the stalled vehicles. A rock shattered the windshield of the car Batraville was driving. In a rage, he took matters into his own hands. He jammed his siren button on, gave orders to the security guards with him to fire out of either side of the lead car into the crowds. As the stunned people began to fall back, he depressed the accelerator to the floorboard. The car leaped into the slowly retreating mob and cleared a path for the presidential vehicle, but not without heavy cost. The security guards in Batraville's car continued firing as Fontaine, in his limousine, sat looking on stonily. Twelve men, women, and children were killed by gunfire, three by the vehicles. A score more lay mangled and broken when the cavalcade had passed.

On their return to the palace, Fontaine emerged unhurt, but visibly shaken, angered, and grim, his clothes splattered with mud and street offal. On the following afternoon during the formal guard-mount ceremony, the president made a personal appearance to present Sublieutenant Batraville with the Libertéan Medal for Courage, then promoted him to the rank of captain. After the ceremony, Batraville was handed orders assigning him to head Fontaine's personal corps of bodyguards.

Batraville moved from the *caserne* into the palace in order to make himself available on a twenty-four-hour basis. Here, he found a warm, close ally in Fontaine's wife, lonely Berta, a short, heavy-set woman whose family connections had given Fontaine his first political prominence in the Petite Aiguille district, and who now remained almost forgotten in the background. A motherly woman who mourned the death of their only son, more at home in the small coastal town she had known than in sumptuous and palatial surroundings, life had become overwhelmingly complicated for Berta. She felt more at ease with the young captain in her sterile household than with the husband who had outgrown his need for her or the influence of her back-country family.

Batraville's constant attendance on the president in daily routines and movement, at state and social functions, gave birth to ambitious dreams, of which the president soon became aware. Less than three months later, as they drove together to inspect a new pumping station erected by the Department of Public Works at La Rochelle, Fontaine pressed the button that raised the glass partition between the rear and driver compartments.

"How old are you, Captain?" Fontaine asked abruptly.

"I am nearing my thirtieth birthday, Your Excellency."

"And how does it happen that a man as personable as you has not married?"

"I have not given it much thought, Your Excellency."

"Ah. A man needs a wife to help him rise in the world, Captain. Or are you perhaps waiting for a true love match?"

Batraville began to sweat. He knew Fontaine was not given to idle conversation or small talk such as this. Berta, yes. She had spoken to him frequently on the subject of marriage, but in a different, motherly way, with a show of true affection for him. Now he began to feel a sense of importance in the president's roundabout questioning. "If I were to find a woman with whom marriage would be—"

"Beneficial?" the president suggested.

The word he had had on the tip of his tongue was "compatible," but Batraville had to surrender it in place of Fontaine's amendment.

"—beneficial, sir," he accepted, "I would not hesitate."

"Ah, yes. I was not wrong in you, Captain. You are wise." Fontaine's lips parted in a slow smile as one hand patted Batraville's thigh in this first sign of intimacy he had shown his aide.

"But I do not feel I am yet in a position to marry, Your Excellency."

"With the proper marriage, Captain, your position will improve to make many things possible."

The discussion was concluded. Fontaine pressed the button to lower the glass partition. Batraville relaxed with feelings that were mixed, but with an overriding elation.

It came as no surprise to him shortly afterward to receive an invitation to dinner from Colonel Theron Dessez, a member of the Army General Staff and father of Lénore Dessez, who had achieved a certain whispered notoriety in Port Amitié.

Five years of travel in France, England, and Switzerland had done much for the girl who had left Port Amitié at the age of eighteen to complete her education in a manner befitting the daughter of a member of the General Staff, a man of above-average means. From Geneva, a year before her return, Lénore had written of a scholarship award in art, and begged permission to take advantage of her treasured prize in Rome. Pleased and flattered, Colonel Dessez agreed.

Toward the end of that year, Dessez was privately advised by Foreign Minister St. Germaine that Lénore was involved in a scandal that could become a matter for the international press unless her affair with a certain Count Romano Donetti was broken off; that there was not, in fact, nor had there been, a scholarship. The *contessa* was preparing to appeal to the Vatican to dissolve her marriage of sixteen years, and threatened to name Lénore Dessez as the cause. Dessez was granted a leave of absence to fly to Rome to settle the matter and head off the threatened international scandal. Through the Libertéan Consul and the Rome police, he learned that Lénore and Count Donetti were living together at the latter's *palazzo* in Venice. Arrived there, the angry colonel found Lénore alone, coldly unrepentant, abandoned by her lover, who had been warned off by a telephone call from Rome.

The affair was hushed up, and Lénore Dessez accompanied her father home, where she at once became a spectacular addition to the gay, young social set of Port Amitié. With her, she had brought a fabulous wardrobe designed by the most famous *hautes couturières* in France and Italy, a small fortune in jewels, most of which had formerly bedecked the Contessa Donetti. Magnificently self-assured, a delightful conversationalist on subjects of international social and political import, wise beyond her years, ambitious and beautiful, Lénore was immediately projected into a position of great prominence. Her closest companion and favorite escort at the time was the attractive Lieutenant Lamonte.

Louis Fontaine, fully aware of the circumstances of Lénore's return, was one of the legion of men who were attracted to, if not captivated by, her sparkling personality. The Dessez family became frequent guests at the palace, and Lénore the favorite of Berta Fontaine, the gossip kept a secret from her.

Physically, Lénore was the masterpiece of a benevolent Mother Nature. She carried herself regally erect, her full young breasts thrust forward to give her waist a remarkable slimness. Her legs and arms were exquisitely rounded, and by day or night she was dressed in the height of casual or formal continental fashion in a manner designed to exhibit her 'sensual body in its most attractive and delectable light. Every inch of her was elegantly feline: her walk, her subtle *café au lait* coloring that was expertly heightened by a delicate tint of eye shadow, and a light reddening of lips that accented her brilliantly white teeth when she smiled

Batraville had noticed, if Berta had not, the great change in Fontaine from Lénore's first visit to the palace at an official reception for Army Staff members and their families. An immediate, explosive hit was registered on the president. Later, when Lénore asked Berta's permission to return to examine the palace art gallery, its tapestries, sculpture, rugs, furniture, and articles of historic interest, it was Fontaine, overhearing her request just as she had planned he would, who gave his personal permission.

On the following day, she was escorted through the establishment, accompanied by Fontaine, the National Historian and Director of Archives, and, as usual, Benoit Batraville. Later, the historian and archives director was dismissed while they had tea with Berta in Fontaine's private apartment on the third floor. Berta was completely enchanted with the girl, and began showing an almost proprietary interest in her, throwing frequent and knowing glances in the direction of the mildly embarrassed Captain Batraville.

Soon, as the young captain came to learn, Fontaine's interest in Lénore Dessez ripened into an attachment that was far more than avuncular. There began a series of private meetings, picnics, swimming parties at remote beaches, yachting trips, visits to Bellefonte and to the beach house at l'Arcachon, all without the knowledge of Madame Fontaine. Or others. However, there was never a pretense before the captain, who acted as personal chauffeur and bodyguard to the illicit lovers on those occasions. It was almost as though Fontaine were being deliberate in his inclusion of Batraville as witness to the affair; or was it, Batraville wondered, because the chief of state had so high a regard for discreetness and loyalty?

Inevitably, for all the care and secrecy of movement, there were rumors. Colonel Dessez, with few illusions about his daughter, adopted an attitude of rigid coolness to show his displeasure. Others of the General Staff were obviously in sympathy with their brother officer in so extremely sensitive a personal matter, and created a general air of hostility that penetrated Fontaine's conferences among certain members of his Council of State. Lénore remained oblivious to this semiofficial reaction. If she was aware of a change in the behavior of the members of her set toward her, she did not show it.

Fontaine needed a solution to the problem, and young Captain Batraville, in their conversation on the way to La Rochelle, showed an inclination to serve his president again. And why not? Batraville reasoned. The social pattern of European royalty was historically documented for all to read. How many positions of honor, title, and wealth had been granted because a wife or daughter had become mistress to a king or duke or prince? And how many men had risen to power because he had married the discarded mistress of a reigning monarch or royal prince, given his name to her illegitimate offspring?

Batraville began warming to Fontaine's subtle soundings, but showed no eagerness to act as the president's stand-in until a definite proposal for promotion, among other hinted rewards, was made.

Shortly thereafter, the engagement of Lénore Dessez to Captain Benoit Batraville was announced. Four weeks later, the marriage was solemnized in the cathedral and was followed by a reception at the palace. Lénore moved in to share her husband's enlarged apartment on the second floor. And no one could have been happier than Berta Fontaine, who had cast herself in the role of matchmaker.

The honeymoon was brief, a week aboard Fontaine's yacht that, coincidentally, was just being readied to take the president on his annual tour of Liberté's coastal cities. And a month after their return to the capital city, two promotions were posted: Colonel Dessez to the rank of general, Captain Batraville to that of colonel, assigned as chief of palace security.

148

But how, Batraville thought later, could he have known that he would fall in love with Lénore and come to regret his position as official court cuckold?

Outside the palace, peace was restored between the president and his detractors on the General Staff and Council of State; but rumor and gossip among the palace servants increased. Eventually, it reached Berta's ears. Overnight, she seemed to age by years. Since she had not for a long time shared Louis's bed, her sleepless nights grew longer and more difficult to live through; perhaps not so much because of her Louis as in the deception by Lénore and Benoit, on whom she had come to look as her own children. To leave her husband was unthinkable. Louis could not permit that.

Berta took to wandering through the halls at night, wondering behind which door and in which wing her perfidious Louis slept in love with the wife of Benoit. In time, she grew bolder. In her nocturnal prowlings, she began to play a painful game, trying one of the many bedroom doors, a different one each night, in a form of torturous Russian roulette. And then one night, the hammer of the revolver fell on the single cartridge. She entered a room, threw on the light switch, and found Lénore and Louis *in flagrante delicto*.

Lénore, awakened by the sudden explosion of light and Berta's agonizing sob, turned face downward and buried herself in the pillow. Fontaine leaped out of bed, struck Berta across her flat peasant face, and pushed her out of the room, heaping angry curses upon her. From that time on, Berta never spoke to her husband, took her meals apart from his, and kept to her room while he was in their apartment. When they encountered by accident, she glared baleful, silent accusations at him with sad, tearful eyes. Fontaine's composure, once so rigid, began to disintegrate.

And then, suddenly, Berta Fontaine died in her sleep one night. The certificate, signed by Dr. Cadeus Fombrun, stated that her death had been caused by food poisoning. Madame Fontaine's body was sent to her family in Petite Aiguille and interred there. But popular rumor of a more mysterious type of poison than botulism persisted.

In time, even these behind-the-hand whispers subsided, and then, like Berta herself, died. With her husband always close at hand to lend a certain fragile respectability to the triangular affair, Lénore Batraville became the

149

president's official hostess; the quiet gossiping among the palace servant staff remained *en famille*. If anyone suffered humiliation, it was Colonel Benoit Batraville; but having once weighed ambition against personal pride, he accepted his ignoble role with cold placidity. And if he became less humane in dealing with those who fell into his official hands, it was perhaps because this was a means to restore his ego.

Upon the death of General Paul Martine, General Theron Dessez was moved, on order of President Fontaine, to head the Army General Staff. Colonel Batraville was simultaneously promoted to the rank of general. Resentment by those of senior rank who had been passed over mounted. The inevitable result was widespread dissatisfaction and unrest within the military establishment and a general dereliction of duty. Batraville, goaded by Fontaine, was driven to expand his Bureau of National Security. His agents in civilian dress moved into key communities to patronize bars, cafés, restaurants, cockfighting arenas, and other gathering places to observe, listen, and report.

Fieldworkers, stevedores, clerks, and merchants were arrested along with military officers on charges of subversive utterances. They were questioned in private chambers, and witnesses were seldom permitted to appear before the special examiners on behalf of the defendants. Rumors of atrocities were rampant. Prisoners were spirited away and imprisoned in distant military districts. Men and women began to look upon neighbors with suspicion, on strangers with mounting horror, wondering if they were members of Batraville's legion of *les fantômes*.

Batraville's unpopularity became widespread. Within three months, four unsuccessful attempts were made on his life. Criticism of Fontaine's administration increased, and outspoken critics were thrown into already overcrowded jails or sent to the Pénitentiaire Nationale, itself hard pressed for space.

In time, the lessons of death and imprisonment became clear warnings to the rebellious. Resistance became covert. Resignations from the military "for reasons of illness" increased. Among them was General Theron Dessez, who was promptly awarded Liberté's Medal of Merit and a liberal pension for "his many years of honorable, devoted, and loyal service to his government." Dessez moved from Port Amitié to a quiet retirement home in distant St. Michel.

To counteract the coldness accorded him, Batraville ordered Sublieutenant Constantine Lamonte transferred to the new Department of Security with the rank of captain. Lamonte obeyed the directive, but took his new job with a certain reluctance that was to become a source of annoyance to Batraville. To reduce the coolness between them, Batraville promoted Lamonte to the rank of major, and assigned him as his personal aide.

In the year that passed, Batraville's own assessment of his success was somewhat shaky. True, his personal power had increased and his hold on the defense, with full powers and control, was tight; but it was a hollow achievement, for what good is victory without somone to share it? and what flavor has beauty that cannot be mirrored in another? Berta was gone, Lénore possessed by Fontaine, Lamonte as distant from him as ever. The need not to fail became an even more determined obsession.

And now, Chalumeau. This damned *esprit*, this *ombre*, the shadow of a man who plagued his days and haunted his sleepless nights. A shadow of his own failure. *Who is he? Who is his family, who are his loved ones? What can he gain in rebellion and treason that I cannot give him in exchange for his loyalty and support to me? I need to put my hands on him, to know who he is!*

Batraville pounded his fist heavily on the scattered reports with a vicious, repeated thumping. How could he show these to Fontaine, already furious with him for his continued failure to apprehend the elusive will-of-the-wisp known as Chalumeau?

4.

Batraville locked the door to his office and walked along the corridor to the door of the private elevator. He pressed the UP button, and when the car arrived he unlocked the outer door with his own key, entered, pushed the button marked "2." At the second floor, he exited, checked the outer door to see that it was locked, then stepped across the wide, thickly piled carpeted hallway, unlocked the door to his apartment, and entered. A servant took his cap and riding crop, and disappeared.

He knew at once that Lénore was in the apartment. There was a vibrant difference, the living perfume of her

151

in the air, when she was at home, a pall of gloom when she was absent. He passed her closed bedroom door with a quickening pulse, paused, then knocked lightly upon it and heard her musical voice call out, "Lavelle?"

"It is I, not your maid," Batraville replied.

"Oh. Benoit. Come in."

She sat at her ivory-toned oval-shaped dressing table, applying eye shadow with the delicacy of an artist, observing herself with narcissistic approval in the triple mirror, three Lénores to look back upon the original. It was a time of extreme enjoyment for her, this hour devoted to improving the gifts that had been bestowed upon her. She loved her face, her body, the natural wave in her hair. Every movement of her hands and arms was minimal. Everything fell into proper place at a mere touch. Yet, she took a full hour at this pleasurable task with a small, superior arrogance, knowing fully that the end result would incite desire in every male she passed; a sentry in the hall, a footman, chauffeur; Louis, Benoit, Constantine; even the phlegmatic, smoldering aide, Falot, had eventually succumbed.

Her narrow bra was a sheer wisp of frothy lace that hardly restrained her full breasts, but added to the alluring mystery of her. So with the narrow, snug briefs that could be seen hugging her hips and uppermost thighs through the light haze of a silken half-slip, bringing Batraville to a near explosive height of excitement. She did not turn, but addressed his image in the mirror.

"You are late, Benoit. You will have to hurry if you wish to bathe and change before lunch."

Batraville advanced toward the table, eyes fixed on Lénore's perfectly shaped back, the ripple of her spine, the curve running from her small waist to exquisitely swelling buttocks that flattened on the cushioned seat. He stood behind her, reached out and touched one shoulder gently. She added a last light touch to her left upper lid, put the brush down, and stood up. Before she could turn to face him, he put his arms around her. Lénore stiffened at his touch, but did not pull away from him. "Benoit, don't. We will be late."

"Lénore." His lips pressed against the back of her neck. Slowly now, she pulled away, and reluctantly he allowed her to slip out of his grasp. "Last night—" he began.

Lénore looked away, reached for the wheat-colored

shantung silk dress that was draped over a nearby chair. "Last night was last night, Benoit. Today——"

"Today he is back from Bellefonte, and the world changes," Batraville said moodily.

"Do not be difficult, *enfant*. He does not like it when you sulk."

"He still complains when I forget to bow and smile obediently? And what would he say if he knew there have been times when his lovely Lénore has found it agreeable, even enjoyable, to lie in her husband's arms?"

She had shrugged into the form-fitting dress and was pulling it down over her body, tugging it in place over her hips. She recognized the troubled mood. Benoit had had another bad day. She smiled tantalizingly and asked, "Have you been so terribly injured, Benoit?"

"And are you so brazen that you can ask that question of your husband?"

Lénore's smile broke into a tinkling laugh. "Ah, Benoit, *pauvre*, are you growing so dissatisfied with your bargain? With hundreds of women available for the handsome protégé general from which to pick and choose? Shall I name a few here in the palace alone who have already willingly succumbed to your charms? Marguerite, Francine, Nina? Under what other circumstance could you have reached such a state of blessedness, to hold a high position, personal wealth, to be married and yet completely free to enjoy the protection and favors of the President of Liberté?"

"As you are enjoying yours?" he asked with some bitterness.

She straightened up, the smile gone from her lovely face, then turned her back to him. He reached for the zipper and tugged it up slowly. "Benoit," she said, "we agreed. Do not spoil what we have. Live up to your part of the bargain, and we shall both enjoy our own private ambitions."

"And each other only when he is away?" The closure sealed, he put his arms around her again and drew her against his body with a fierce grip. Lénore pulled away from him. "It is late," she said.

He stared hungrily at Lénore with a lover's desire, then laughed briefly with a grim snort. "It is idiotic, fantastic, completely without sense or reason. I am the world's greatest fool."

"Are you really, Benoit? Why? Because you have risen

153

so high so quickly? Remember what and who you were before you married me."

"For his benefit."

"Do you think I would have married you for your own? Think again. Where would you be now——"

"Enough, enough," Batraville snapped testily. "I don't need to be spoken to like a child."

"Ah, Benoit," she said gently, cajolingly, "who knows better than I that you are not a child. But the situation serves us well, does it not? If life is ironical——"

"That life can be ironical, I am aware, but to compete with my wife's lover for her favors is irony above all ironies. I am in love with you, Lénore. Desperately."

Lénore sighed, returned to her dressing table, and gave her hair a final touch. "Lénore, Lénore—*ma chère*—"

"Benoit, don't. If you persist in being difficult, we can both lose much. He demands little enough for what he gives in return."

"And when Du Faure is elected and sits in his place, I must of necessity remain here. Where will you go to live then, with him? Or will you be handed over to the new president as part of——"

Before he could finish, the telephone rang. Her face flushed with mounting anger, Lénore went to the night table and spoke quietly into the mouthpiece, and hung up. "He is ready," she said shortly. "You will not have time to bathe and change now."

"You have not answered my question."

"Suppose you save it and ask it again at lunch," she retorted.

On the way to the elevator, he said in a low, angry voice, "What kind of woman are you who can take love from him and me without feeling shame or dishonor? Or are you a woman at all?"

She turned on him with an air of patience one would show a bellicose child. "You don't understand women like me, Benoit, nor have you from the start. My needs go far beyond those that any one man can give, needs in me that reach above physical love, just as there are in you. Do not place your animal desires above your ambitions, I warn you. It could be costly."

"If he were deposed, without power. Or dead——"

"You speak like a fool," she hissed angrily. The elevator came to a stop at the third floor. Before he could unlock and open the outer door, she added, "If such talk were overheard, even dreamed of, it could cost you your life."

"Sometimes," Batraville said musingly as he opened the door and stood aside for her, "I wonder if that would be so great a loss."

In the smaller of the two dining rooms on the third floor, the president sat in his usual place at the head of the table. Batraville and his wife sat opposite each other, a tall centerpiece of freshly cut flowers separating them. The conversation, as usual when they were three, was scanty until the coffee and brandy were served. When the servants were dismissed at a nod from Fontaine, the door closed, Fontaine dipped one end of his cigar into the brandy glass, then rolled it between his lips before he took the light Batraville held for him. Lénore said, "The ambassador, Louis."

"That one." Fontaine's sudden dark look and voice expressed complete disdain. "He is a fool, and I weary of fools. He has had his opportunity. Now it is too late. We shall go the other way."

Lénore's face showed tight apprehension. Batraville sat quietly, but inwardly he felt a strong elation. Fontaine began to smile with self-gratification. "Soon it will be over. When the public announcement of Du Faure's election is made and the ceremony is over, we shall see who emerges strongest, the American ambassador or the Libertéan government."

Batraville said, "It is a risk, is it not, Your Excellency?"

"There will be no risk. Every road, every trail, every inch of the coast that gives entrance into Port Amitié will be under heavy guard." He laughed disagreeably. "Perhaps the election will even bring Chalumeau into the open, since you cannot seem to find him otherwise."

"What if he does not attempt a movement on the night of the election, but soon after?"

"It will be too late. I have spoken to Mosher, and the terms of agreement are under study by me now. With a few changes, I will sign tomorrow. The arms will be here within three days after the news reaches Havana."

Batraville nodded, his mind on Chalumeau, but he seemed unappeased by Fontaine's confident note. The president smiled and said, "You are not happy, General?"

Batraville remained silent. "Do not be alarmed, General, It will go well," Fontaine said reassuringly.

Lénore said, "By next week it will be Du Faure who will be dealing with the Cubans—"

"Let us not look too far into the future, *ma chère Lénore*," Fontaine said with a pleasant smile. "Before next week, there is this week in which to prepare. Ease your minds, both of you. I have a plan that will give me all the time I will need for the future."

"I do not understand, Your Excellency," Batraville said.

"You will, Benoit, and very soon. Let us retire to my study, and I will outline the procedures for election day. Much will rest upon your shoulders. If you succeed, you know I will be generous. If you fail—" Fontaine did not finish the light, ominous threat, but Batraville knew from the tone of voice that he would not outlive the consequences of a failure in whatever the president was about to propose.

"Yes, Your Excellency," he replied.

"Then let us go now. There is much that remains to be done. Lénore, *ma petite*, you will excuse us now."

CHAPTER 5

On this election eve, there was an atmosphere not unlike that of the Mardi Gras. For days, long-empty hotels
began to fill up with visitors from the interior and coastal
cities. Members of the dissolved National Assembly arrived with their families, eager to be seen and heard
championing Fontaine's choice, M'sieu Charles Du
Faure, whom few really knew.

That there were actually four other candidates was in-
consequential. It was a usual custom that the president
would cause several names to be added to the candidate list to lend an air of democratic selection by the
Council of State.

Men with ambitions who had long stood on the
periphery of government came hopefully to make political
hay. Professional and businessmen rubbed shoulders and
drank with planters and industrial leaders in a holiday
spirit while their families shopped, lunched, visited,
dined, and gossiped with old friends they had not seen in
months.

The working class came. Clerks, fieldworkers, laborers,
dock-workers, fishermen, and the vendors in the great
open market place. They stood open-eyed and in awe of
the laughter and gaiety in the streets and along the boule-
vards, colorfully profuse with flags, streamers, bunting,
and garlands of flowers. Huge photographs of Charles Du
Faure smiled down benevolently upon them from overhead, from store windows, from the sides of trucks that
glided by. The unemployed came, beggars, scroungers,
self-seekers, and thieves, to mingle hopefully with the
others.

To the voteless citizenry, the clamor of speakers in the
parks, over the radio outlets, the banners and posters
meant little, and were intended only to make Fontaine's

choice of a successor palatable to them. Although there were discussions and debates in the Council, it would end as *Le Temps* had long ago predicted—with the election of Minister of Education Charles Du Faure.

In hotels, homes, and aboard yachts docked in the marina or anchored offshore, parties were in progress by day and night. Lights blazed, restaurants, bars, and clubs were filled to capacity; shopkeepers were hard pressed to supply the unprecedented demands for merchandise. Hired bands of singers followed drummers through the streets, skillfully injecting songs of praise for Du Faure while listeners danced and shuffled to exotic rhythms.

The air of excitement reached down into the teeming waterfront area, stirred the slum dwellers with hopeful anticipation. Perhaps this time, the change in the palace would bring with it a miracle to relieve their miserable lot. Outside their tin-patched, frond-thatched hovels, men began to speak with animation as their women hunkered over iron pots that stood on trivets over flaming faggots or glowing coconut husks, stirring whatever had been gleaned during the day for this meal. Children, infected with the spirit and the constant drum-beating, danced or ran uncontrolled in the rutted streets and alleyways, screamed shrilly, their barking dogs chasing, nipping their heels. In the pleasure huts and bars along Rue Félicité, business surged, music blared, and rum flowed as it hadn't since the war days of twenty years ago. In the *quartier misérable,* hope was momentarily reborn. Where for so long they had lived only for the long day that lay ahead, there was now a tomorrow to look forward to.

And, later that night, candles were secretly lighted, fetishes and *ouangas* were hung, powders and bones and cemetery dirt and other oddments peculiar to voodoo rites were ceremoniously chanted over for hours, then strewn about the corners of individual homes.

At a few minutes past eight on that Thursday night, John Mosher strolled leisurely along Rue Pavillon, pausing occasionally to inspect the merchandise displayed in the shop windows. The street, as all other nearby streets and promenades, was crowded with young men and their young women, arm in arm, heading for the park where the Army band played its nightly concert. Shoppers, sightseers, and strollers brushed one another in passing, their voices high with freshly kindled emotion, stimulated by the sense of importance in the coming event of tomorrow. They walked and talked with a rhythm that could easily be identified with the timing of the martial airs coming from the park.

Rue Pavillon's sidewalk cafés were filled with early diners. Waiters in short white or red jackets moved between crowded tables, carrying trays that were heavy with food and drink. Armed police and soldiers walked along in pairs, slowly, observing the flow of humanity, alert to the possibility that somewhere in this crush lay danger; the sudden outbreak of hostilities; wondering if they could cope with such an uprising.

At No. 28, Mosher stopped to peer into a window that featured a display of native woodcraft, and saw a number of excellent samples of a crude, yet interesting primitive art that had flourished on Liberté since its earliest known history. Between this shop and the one next to it was a doorway, painted a glossy black, the number "28" in raised silver figures affixed to it. Below the figures, a small plaque was engraved with the legend:

ZHARKOV
Petroleum Products
of the
U.S.S.R.

Mosher tried the silver-toned doorknob, turned it. The door opened into a narrow, dimly lit hallway. He stepped inside and mounted the narrow stairs to the second floor where, on one of the four doors, a plaque similar to the one below was barely visible in the yellow glare of the small naked bulb on the landing. He rapped on the door twice, waited and listened, then rapped again. He heard some movement from beyond. A moment later the knob turned and the door opened to a space of perhaps an inch or two. A pair of eyes peered out at him from total darkness, and he heard a gruff voice say, "A moment." The door closed again, and Mosher heard the rattle of a chain being disengaged. The door opened again, this time wide enough to admit him. He stepped through and found himself inside the dark room. The door closed again. He heard the click of a wall switch, and the room, a small, meagerly furnished outer office, was bathed in soft light.

Mosher smiled and said, "Basil. It is good to see you again."

Basil Zharkov replied, "Welcome to Liberté, Comrade. It is a pleasure to see a friendly face again."

Zharkov was a man in his late forties, tall, nattily dressed in a light-blue suit of tropical weight, black-trimmed white shoes, and a dark blue tie. His jacket was correctly styled with narrow lapels, and a half-inch of white handkerchief peeked from his upper-left breast pocket. The four years he had spent as an official of Amtorg in New York, dealing with Americans influential in commercial traffic, had made his conversion from drab Russian styling a simple transition.

Released from Zharkov's warm embrace, Mosher followed the Russian to an inside room that was larger, more elaborately furnished. Basil offered his guest a chair, a drink, and a cigar, all of which Mosher accepted. "You had a good flight?"

"Yes, thank you, Basil."

"And I assume you have made contact?"

"I saw Fontaine yesterday at Bellefonte."

"How were you received?"

Mosher smiled. "It went well, even though His Excellency made no pretense of eagerness or enthusiasm. However, I do not anticipate any serious problems."

"Be careful, Comrade. Fontaine is at various times a wise and cautious man, as it suits him to be, a man with dreams of great power and glory. Such a man can be extremely dangerous when crossed."

"The Cuban was dangerous at first, was he not, Basil? How dangerous can one be when his claws have been clipped?"

"A good question, my friend, but Fontaine has not yet come that close to the shears. Or has he accepted the entire program?"

"Not entirely. He is reluctant to take the full plunge."

"And the agreement?"

"The bait is tempting. I am sure he will sign it."

Zharkov nodded. "Time grows short. The election is tomorrow. Already the city is becoming overly crowded with celebrants."

"Or mourners?"

Zharkov shrugged. "Perhaps. Who knows? We expected you sooner."

"So did Fontaine. However, when word was received

160

in Havana that Washington had refused to reinstate a foreign-aid program on Liberté, Urbana thought it best to delay and allow the importance and need of the arms to impress itself more firmly on Fontaine. Also, there has been some speculation over the man who will replace him. Du Faure."

Zharkov said with a chuckle, "There is no need for concern. Du Faure will win, but Fontaine will remain the power behind the throne and the man to deal with. What objections did he offer to the agreement?"

"None, except that he needs the time to study the terms. He will let me know within another day. Perhaps two."

"You feel he will sign?"

"I have little doubt that he will. However, since Du Faure will be president by that time, it will be necessary to make changes in the signatures."

"That can be done by tomorrow. I have copies of the agreement and I will see to it." Zharkov leaned back in his chair and expelled a long breath of relief. "You have done well, Comrade. The ambassador will be pleased."

"Pleased enough, I hope, to credit my account in Switzerland as soon as possible," Mosher said.

"You have been regularly and liberally paid for your work in the past, Comrade. There is no reason to believe you will be treated differently now."

"None, Basil, but there is more involved now. I feel the need to move on to a more neutral country for a while once the Libertéan takeover is accomplished."

"Do not grow greedy, Comrade Mosher, or in a hurry. There is a job that must be done first. We pay well, but only on positive results."

"Don't worry, Basil. I have delivered before and I will deliver now."

"Then neither of us has cause to worry."

2.

Shortly after Mosher left No. 28 Rue Pavillon, Basil Zharkov drove to his home on Rue Goncourt where he bathed, shaved, and changed into dark, formal clothes. Beneath his left breast pocket he wore his cherished Order of Lenin, Order of the Red Star, medals that designated his participation in the Defense of Moscow, service in Poland, and during the fall of Berlin. The gold Hero of the

Soviet Union Star hung from his neck on an iridescent ribbon. He checked his appearance in the full-length mirror with smiling approval, then went below where a limousine waited to drive him to Ambassador Vossolofsky's reception at the Russian Embassy.

Having presented himself to Ambassador and Madame Vossolofsky, Zharkov passed through the long reception hall into a large oval room where he greeted, and was greeted by, numerous Cuban and other Communist bloc guests from surrounding Latin countries, and among whom he seemed to feel at home. Local business acquaintances called to him, and he paused to chat amiably, then went on to the long table that was heaped with imported delicacies. He moved from there into the next room that had been given over to a well-patronized bar and joined a small group that were being served champagne from well-laden trays.

A half-hour later, Basil Zharkov slipped unobtrusively into the hallway and made his way to the rear stairway, mounted it to the second floor, and went directly to a small study. He knocked on it with a private signal. A key turned, the handle was raised from within, and Zharkov entered the room, closed, and locked the door behind him.

A man perhaps ten years older, but looking far senior in age, had turned and walked toward a red plush sofa where he sat down and resumed eating from a plate of food. Zharkov followed him, and sat in a green leather chair that faced the sofa.

"Well, Comrade Feodor," he said with a smile that was somewhat patronizing, "you still do not approve of parties, I see."

Feodor Pyantenov snorted with distaste to show his disapprobation of the festivities below. "It is nonsense, a waste of time, money, and effort," he replied as he addressed himself to the heaping plate of food. "Particularly when there is work to be done."

Pyantenov was dressed in a somber, unsuitably heavy double-breasted gray suit that hung loosely from his short, heavy body. The fringe of graying brown hair was unkempt, even though trimmed close to his bullet-like head. His grim face was flat-planed with the high cheekbones of a Mongol, the flesh coarse-grained and loose around his neck. His frowning eyes slanted upward at Zharkov as he spoke, two cold, cruel orbs that had seen much on the way up the political ladder. His mouth was thin, a tight line drawn across his face.

Zharkov seemed amused, as though he were staring at a caricature of an old Bolshevik who lacked only the fore-peaked cap to put him in true character. "There is a need for occasional gaiety, Comrade," Zharkov said. "We need to present a lighter side of life to our friends."

"Ar-r-gh." The clearing of his throat was Pyantenov's critical reaction. "You met with the American?"

"Two hours ago."

"And the agreement?"

"He has presented it to Fontaine, and assures me it will be signed within a day or two at the most."

Pyantenov glowered again to indicate his displeasure.

"You are not pleased, Comrade?" Zharkov asked.

"Should I be pleased with the word of an American traitor?"

"He has performed well before."

"I still cannot bring myself to trust any traitor, no matter his performance. Nor will I be satisfied until the working agreement has been signed and is in my hands. It is vital that we have it."

"If I remember correctly, it was your decision to instruct Urbana to delay his arrival here. Mosher confirmed that as the reason for being late." A small, malevolent grin played over Zharkov's lips now, as though he had trapped his elder in an error. "Yes, as I recall, it was you who insisted that if Mosher's arrival were delayed until the last moment, Fontaine's need for the arms would be so great there would be no question of his acceptance—"

"Fontaine is a fool," Pyantenov growled.

Zharkov did not answer. However he felt about this turmoil-ridden man, Zharkov knew that Pyantenov was expert in his field. The eight medals displayed against the black of his own jacket were indeed few compared with the many honors that had been showered on Feodor Pyantenov, one of the few men who had lived through many purges, decorated personally by Stalin, Malenkov, Bulganin, publicly lauded by Beria and others now fallen in disrepute or dead. He had stood, in fact, only five away from Comrade Khrushchev during the May Day parade of 1963. That he would one day be named chief of The Center, GRU Headquarters at 19 Znamensky Street in Moscow, had been forecast many times by authoritative voices.

163

There was no mystery to Zharkov why so important a man as Feodor Pyantenov had been sent to this black hole of a country in person. At the meeting he had attended two years ago in Moscow, Pyantenov had been a silent observer. When General Sudanov had outlined the need for Plan WH2, Zharkov had watched Pyantenov nodding his head in close agreement with each step of the plan, and knew it had originated with this short, untidy man whose role in the Cuban takeover was well known.

In the over-all World Plan, China remained the single stumbling block. Elsewhere, Laos, Indonesia, Vietnam, Cambodia, Africa, and Europe, the Master Plan was moving well. The reestablishment of trade relations with Western nations was progressing. The U.S.–Soviet wheat deal. Relations between the West and Cuba, with the exception of the United States. De Gaulle, making noises like an elongated Napoleon with a dream of restoring France's stature as a first-class nation, was being helpful.

At that meeting, Sudanov had said, "While we exert every effort in Europe, Asia, and Africa, the pressure within and surrounding the Western Hemisphere must be increased. It is necessary to extend the Cuban situation by every facility available to us into an area where the United States considers herself invulnerable, eventually all of Central and South America. Our immediate goal, therefore, is to establish a second foothold, then a third, a fourth, and a fifth until we can march through the entire hemisphere on a series of steppingstones."

Zharkov stirred himself. "Fontaine a fool? No fool would have been able to put a weakling like Du Faure in office to replace himself," he said. "Tomorrow Du Faure will become president, but Fontaine will still be the man we must deal with."

"Ah, so." Pyantenov permitted himself another drink of vodka. "Then how shall we benefit our WH2 Plan, Comrade, as long as we must deal with a simpleton who is dominated by one so deeply steeped in the primitive arts and religion of voodooism, whose fanaticisms will not permit him to grant the concessions we need here? Are you not aware that Fontaine has been encouraged by his personal *houngan*, Fombrun, to regard himself as the Savior of the Black Race?"

For a scant moment, silence hung between them heavily. Zharkov's earlier self-complacency had been shaken by Pyantenov's clearer insight into the situation, and he won-

164

dered what new design or action pattern lay in this grubby little man's crafty mind. He waited.

Pyantenov emitted a small, triumphant, "So!" Then, "Your Louis Fontaine, therefore, remains the principal problem, despite the election of Charles Du Faure. Consequently, he will be of little use to us, now or later. However"—the cruel, fleshy grin flashed upward again—"if Fontaine were out of the way—" Pyantenov checked himself to gauge Zharkov's reaction, and was rewarded with a startled look from his sauve companion. "With Fontaine out of the way," Pyantenov repeated slowly, "Du Faure is but a helpless puppet, and his own replacement will become a matter of time. His government will collapse."

"Then who—"

"—will replace Du Faure?" Pyantenov finished the question for Zharkov, then waited again, taking a deep measure of delight in the confusion that was destroying his junior's self-importance. He stood up and went to the desk, opened a drawer and took out a single cigar, lighted it, then returned to the sofa. "I have already decided on the perfect choice." Again a pause as he watched the smoke curl upward from his cigar. "He is eager and ambitious, and with motive and opportunity, but without our help, the presidency is too high even for his ambitions."

Again the tormenting wait while Pyantenov poured another glass of vodka and drank it down in one quick gulp. Zharkov followed his every movement, fascinated, still waiting silently. It would not do to make an awkward guess; even worse, to make a suggestion that might prove clumsy. Pyantenov wiped his lips with the back of his hand, and said, "You are aware, are you not, Comrade, of the sordid affair that exists between M'sieur Fontaine and—"

"Madame Batraville!" The words were a soft explosion.

Pyantenov nodded. "Exactly. The motive. Benoit Batraville's hatred for Fontaine. Also his fear of the man. And who has a greater opportunity, eh? It is the weapon we will use to accomplish the elimination of Fontaine. Once he is out of the way, the overthrow of Du Faure will follow. Batraville can then take over the government by junta rule, become president, and we will have our second and most important foothold. This will not be another Caracas or Panama, Comrade, but a second Cuba, the beginning of the chain of springboards into and throughout Central and South America. Russia will not appear the aggressor. It will become a People's Revolution, supported by Cuba."

At that moment, Zharkov, aware of Pyantenov's meticulous successes in the past, had few doubts in his mind. He accepted the older man's words as he nodded complete approval, then asked, "And the man Chalumeau, Comrade, what of him?"

Pyantenov's brief smile indicated that Chalumeau was, and had been, part and parcel of his over-all strategy. "M'sieu Chalumeau will, when I give the word, be brought out into the open," he predicted. "He will join our movement."

"His whereabouts are known?"

"Not by me at the moment, but they are known. Have no fears, Comrade. He will join us. If he refuses to cooperate, there are more forceful means to give him wisdom."

The look on Zharkov's face had turned to complete respect, yet touched with perplexity. In a tutorial tone, Pyantenov continued: "Comrade, the mistake that has been made by Fontaine, by Batraville, by Vossolofsky, and yourself, has been to seek the elusive shadow of a man. On the other hand, I have worked from an opposite direction. Remember, no man with the ambitions of a Chalumeau can remain alone. Therefore, I reasoned, there must be a second person who knows his secret, and, like any secret, when it becomes known to a second person, it is no longer a secret. Eh? So I have concentrated my efforts on that second person, and I have found him. How?

"Through the simple application of logic and reason. By searching through newspaper files and studying the backgrounds of every man who has raised his voice against the government in power. Of the most prominent insurgents in the past, few remain alive. Of those, most are either in exile or too old to be of importance or effective. Thus, by the process of elimination, I was able to reduce the lot to one. Weeks ago, I set a man to watch his every movement, and discovered that messages were being passed between himself and Chalumeau. He is that second person. Pierre Duclosse.

"We have already met, Duclosse and I, and through him, I shall bring General Batraville and Chalumeau face to face for their first meeting. And you, Comrade Zharkov, will be present to witness that historical event. I need not tell you, Basil, that much will rest on your shoulders. Very much."

Zharkov's waning self-confidence was restored. It was the first time Pyantenov had ever called him by his given name. A sign, a hopeful sign. "And the American, Mosher?" he asked.

Pyantenov dismissed the question with a gruff snort. "You talked with him tonight. He is a rabbit, ready to run for safety. Once the agreement has been signed and the arms delivered, what further use will we have for rabbits, eh? Now go downstairs and enjoy your party."

3.

By noon on Friday, the word was announced by radio and spread to the most remote corners of Liberté by voice, messenger, and drum. The decision of the Council of State would be publicly announced from the balcony of the palace, and flashed simultaneously to the rest of the country by radio.

Port Amitié took on a fresh bustle of activity. On this day, declared a national holiday, stores would not reopen after the siesta. Public offices and schools would remain closed. Restaurants and bars would entertain their guests until eight-thirty, close until nine-thirty, reopen for the celebrants following the official announcement.

Shortly after the word had been broadcast over Station HHK, the roads leading into the capital city from every nearby town became clogged with trucks, buses, cars, horses, and tough, wiry *bourriques*. Long lines queued up at military checkpoints where triple the normal number of guards searched vehicles, animals, passengers, and drivers for hidden arms. By dusk, the thousands who had milled about in the streets, parks, and the open market place began to gather in the Champs de Révolution before the palace. The soft, velvety sky was sprinkled with gemlike stars, and a large orange moon rose over the dark hills that served as a theatrical backdrop for the crowded city. Beyond Mont Couronne, on the higher Mont Vainqueur, the blackness was broken by flames of many scattered bonfires. The muffled sound of beating drums floated downward in waves like muted thunder. On the slopes that rose toward the brilliantly illuminated summer home of the president, lights twinkled riotously in the colonial-styled frame houses through open jalousies and lattices,

167

on broad balconies and verandas that jutted outward to overlook the spectacular view far below. In the harbor, every ship, yacht, and smaller craft was afire with lights strung from fore to aft.

In the hub of the city, the presidential palace, magnificently white, was aglow inside, bathed from without by several hundred spotlights, aided by a half dozen huge searchlights fixed upon it. Another half dozen of the powerful arc lights hurled broad shafts of rotating beams into the sky. Outside the iron pickets that surrounded the grounds, a tremendous mass of humanity surged, shuffled, and danced back and forth, keeping time with the incessant beating of drums, chanting ancient songs.

Within the enclosure, three yards behind the iron pickets and two yards apart from each other, stood a single row of khaki-clad Palace Guards, stolid and expressionless, feet apart at ease, clutching bayoneted rifles. On the second floor of the palace, the wide balcony was empty except for several men attending a group of microphones, waiting for the moment when the Chairman of the Council of State would approach from the inner ballroom to make the official announcement that a new president had been elected to replace Louis Fontaine. From the shouts below, it was evident that Fontaine's departure from office would create few regrets.

In the ballroom, Libertéan government officials mingled with prominent citizens and those high in the ranks of the diplomatic corps, the political, military, and commercial world. In one corner at the far end of the ballroom, less formal in dress, members of the local and international press were gathered, observing the activities under escort of the palace press relations staff, not permitted to mingle with the guests until after the ceremony of acceptance would take place.

The corps of palace waiters, clad resplendently in gold-brocaded red jackets and white silk knee breeches, passed among the guests with trays laden with champagne. From behind a bank of potted palms, a stringed orchestra attempted, with little success, to make itself heard over the din of vibrant conversation.

At one end of the ballroom the four voiceless, faceless men whose names had been mentioned as possible contenders for the presidency stood with their families and a small clutch of friends, waiting until the announcement

168

would be over and they could return to their former obscurity, spared of further humiliation. In the center of the room, a large group of well-wishers surrounded Charles Du Faure, Fontaine's personal choice to succeed himself. He was a small, elderly, gray-haired man who smiled nervously, permitted his hand to be shaken by passing admirers. Beside him stood his wife, a diminutive woman who seemed uncomfortable in the glare of prominence that bathed her and her husband.

The foreign diplomatic corps stood slightly apart from the other guests and took no part in the exchange of premature congratulations Du Faure was receiving, or in the hushed whispers that were rampant in the huge room. Newspaper, radio, and magazine reporters waited quietly, resigned to the result that would come as an anticlimax, sipping drinks, eyes on watches, growing restive.

While Ambassador Chance chatted briefly with the British, French, Italian, and German ambassadors and their wives, Thorne Truscott stood nearby with Jim Gerard, identifying various guests. The formality of dress was perhaps the most glittering and colorful Gerard had ever seen. Uniforms blazed with brilliant, sparkling decorations, and in some instances outshone the splendidly bejeweled and tiara-ed women gowned in their latest Parisian, New York, and Roman imports.

Almost every shade of skin coloring was represented; from pale and suntanned white through the spectrum of beige, olive, and brown, to deepest black. The not infrequent crossing of color lines was evident in the many and various mixtures, not only in color but in hair and features, the former ranging from straight to caracul-curly texture; the latter from flattened nostrils, bridge-less noses, and thickened lips, to completely regular features. How distant from Africa, Gerard thought, and yet, how close.

Quietly and apart from the Western diplomatic fraternity, the Russian ambassador, Sergei Vossolofsky, florid, urbane, and smiling, held court to a dozen members of the Eastern bloc, among them the Cuban ambassador and his two aides. Vossolofsky beamed charmingly over the array of glittering decorations that brightened his tailcoat as he nodded, shook hands, and spoke with members of the palace diplomatic staff.

Truscott said to Gerard, "The short, heavy-set man with the gray hair is Du Faure."

"I recognize him from his photographs, but he looks so much shorter than I would have expected."

"And not too happy being cast in the principal role here tonight. I imagine he would be more comfortable if this were taking place in some country *homfort* with his own *houngan* administering the oath."

Gerard smiled. "Don't laugh, Jim," Truscott said. "It's all around you. Fontaine reputedly has his own private *homfort* in the basement of this building and another up at Bellefonte. Say what you want, with the believers, it has a lot going for it."

"Du Faure doesn't look like much of a sacrifice to the Gods. What do you suppose would happen if there were an upheaval, if the Council were to pick one of the others—"

Now it was Truscott's turn to smile. "Put down the crystal ball, Jim. It can't happen. If Delacroix had his way, that tall, distinguished-looking chap standing over there beyond the circle around Du Faure would be president. That's François Courdet, publisher of *Le Temps*. And just in case you're interested in historical statistics, something of a record is being set here tonight."

"In what way?"

"Fontaine leaving office alive. Among its last thirty presidents, twenty-four were deposed and killed in revolutions, three were poisoned at their own tables, one escaped into exile and returned to be assassinated, and two were lucky enough to have died of natural causes while in office."

"Sounds as though a miracle were about to occur."

Two couples had paid their respects to Ambassador and Katherine Chance. The two splendidly gowned, attractive young women might easily have been mistaken for Americans except for a special continental quality in the manner of one. The two youngish men with them were in black formal clothes, and leaned forward to shake Chance's hand. Truscott whispered to Gerard: "Marcel Courdet, the son of François. The other is Mark Fuller. American. Married to the older of the two girls, Eugénie. The younger is Julie, and both are Delacroix's daughters. Eugénie went to school in the States, Julie in Europe."

"Attractive couples," Gerard observed.

"Yes. Young Courdet is the author of most of the *Le Temps* editorials that have had Fontaine lathered up on more than one occasion. Sharp as a whip. He could be helpful to you with local information. He and Mark Fuller are very close. May well be brothers-in-law one day if the feedbox dope is accurate."

Eugénie Fuller was extending a white-gloved hand to Chance. The ambassador took it into his own hand and raised it to his lips. She moved on to Truscott, who introduced Gerard. Then Julie, Marcel, and Mark joined them. Fuller was the taller of the two men, a powerfully built man who at once invited Gerard to visit Terre Delacroix during any free time he might have. The party excused themselves and moved on to greet other friends nearby.

There was a flurry of movement and hushed murmuring as a stunning woman entered the room on the arm of Major Lamonte. She wore her hair in an upsweep that ended in a crown atop her head, held in place by a triple strand of pearls interspersed with diamonds. Her cloth-of-gold gown was embroidered with smaller pearls, and clung to her exquisite form as though she had been sewn into it. Heads turned in her direction as she returned smiles and nodded her way through an aisle of acquaintances, giving her hand to several men who brushed their lips over it.

"Madame Batraville," Truscott said, catching Gerard's admiring stare.

Gerard whistled softly under his breath. "Everything I've heard of her has been pure understatement."

"Not everything, I'm sure," Truscott commented dryly.

"I was referring to the physical."

"Then you're unquestionably correct."

It was fascinating to watch the faces of the men and women who were staring at Lénore Batraville as she moved through the crowd, the sexual awareness of the men, young and old, the envy—or malice—among the women for the animal desire she could arouse with her mere presence. She moved gracefully, exerting no effort, fully aware of her immense power to attract both desire and enmity. Her body was no more exposed than dozens of others, but there was a majestic magnetism that seemed to touch everyone in passing. Her eyes shone like sparkling lights; her smile, however restrained, became an invitation to share some deep, unknown, but heavenly secret. The deep V of her gown exposed the fullness of her breasts, and as she moved along, her legs caused the golden-hued gown to shimmer, clinging to her, matching her own color so that she appeared to be half naked. Gerard heard the expelled breath of those around him, sounding like small prayers, expressing their thoughts more articulately than a thousand words, a token of appreciation for a near perfect work of Nature.

Ambassador Chance turned and took a step toward Truscott and Gerard. He pulled a slim wafer of platinum from his vest pocket and looked at it. "Exactly nine o'clock," Gerard said, checking his own watch.

Chance's reply, "Lacking by seventeen seconds," was a nostalgic reminder of Dixie Harrington and the importance he placed on punctuality. Chance's watch had no sooner been replaced than a uniformed major-domo entered the ballroom and announced the imminent arrival of the president.

Fontaine came into the room wearing a full-dress suit without decorations except for a broad band of red watered silk that ran diagonally across his gleaming white shirt front. Two officer of the General Staff followed at a distance of one pace. Fontaine neither spoke to nor acknowledged anyone as he strode briskly to the large double doors, commanding the attention of everyone in the hushed room.

The four officers guarding the doors withdrew their sabers at first sight of him, turned inward to form a guard of honor, saluted smartly on command of the senior officer, and stood stiffly at attention. Fontaine stopped before the doors as the major-domo raised a white-gloved hand and knocked three times, then stepped backward behind and to one side of the president. The door was opened by the Council's recording secretary, who stepped nervously back into the deliberation chamber.

The first of the Council members to appear was Henri Delacroix, tall, dignified, and unsmiling. The second man was one whom Gerard recognized at once as Charles St. Germaine, whose picture he had taken in Havana together with General Batraville and Craig Madden, alias John Mosher. Surprised by the sudden appearance of St. Germaine, Gerard turned and looked about him as though he expected to see Batraville or Mosher. Where, he wondered, was the general on this auspicious occasion? He turned back now to see Delacroix and St. Germaine bowing stiffly to the president. Fontaine spoke some words, but since his back was to the ballroom, Gerard could not make out clearly what had been said, and now heard only Delacroix's response, "Yes, Your Excellency."

In a louder voice, Fontaine said, "Then, M'sieu Delacroix, you will make the public announcement."

Delacroix replied formally, "Forgive me, Your Excellency. It has been decided by consent of the Council that M'sieu St. Germaine will have that honor."

There was a moment of silence, and Gerard could see Fontaine's back stiffen rigidly. The president turned to face the guests now, to lead the delegation of Council members to the balcony; and Gerard noted clearly that Fontaine's face was clouded with anger. Then he felt a slight nudge from Truscott's elbow as if to call attention to the slight given the president by Delacroix.

As the president moved toward the balcony, the entire assembly waited with anticipation. The next man he would speak with would undoubtedly be the president-elect.

When Fontaine approached Charles Du Faure, the people around him gave way. Fontaine stopped in front of the candidate, smiled, and said, "Charles, *mon cher ami,* my felicitations."

Du Faure appeared to be in a state of acute distress as he wiped at his forehead with a large silk handkerchief. *"M'sieu le Présidente—"* he began in a low voice that sounded filled with terror.

Fontaine leaned closer to Du Faure and said into his ear: "Come, come, Charles. Pay no attention to the rabble below. Six years ago when I was similarly announced by the junta, did they not scream and shout for Dumont? By tomorrow they will be gone back to their homes and their work and you will be president of our great Republic. Does the thought not excite and stimulate you? Come now. We must appear together before them. It will not take long."

The procession toward the balcony continued, Fontaine's hand gripping Du Faure's arm firmly.

As the party stepped onto the balcony, the bright shafts of light that had been twirling outside came to rest above and below that focal point to add a greater brilliance to the occasion. When President Fontaine appeared on the raised platform before the microphones with Delacroix and St. Germaine on either side of him, the crowd below began shouting shrilly. St. Germaine stepped forward to the bank of microphones and held his hands outward and upward for silence. After a full minute, the shouting began to fade. The people were quiet now, eager to hear the official announcement.

"By the power vested in me as Deputy Chairman of the

Council of State," St. Germaine proclaimed strongly, "it now becomes my great pleasure and solemn privilege to present to you the next President of the Republic of Liberté"—and now the silence below was complete. St. Germaine, timing himself with studied drama, finished with —"His Excellency, M'sieu Charles Du Faure!"

For a moment, there was a silence from the crowd; and then a low murmur mingled with shouts of approval and disapproval. One group raised a large sign with one word —a name—on it: COURDET!

To one side, Charles Du Faure stood nervously, wiping his forehead with his dampened handkerchief. His wife twisted a pair of gloves between her fingers and turned from side to side as if in distress. Fontaine glanced in Du Faure's direction and motioned to him. An aide nudged the small, sweating figure toward the microphones. Tremulously, his face a sickly gray, Du Faure approached the raised platform, found it difficult to take the one step to mount it. Fontaine moved to his side and gripped his arm tightly, speaking to him in low, rapid words.

Gerard, standing directly behind Ambassador Chance, felt the pressure of a figure against his back. He moved to one side slightly and turned to see Truscott leaning toward him. Truscott said in a low whisper, "Have you ever seen a more reluctant bride?"

"Never in a political arena," Gerard replied.

St. Germaine and Fontaine were assisting Du Faure to the microphones. The noise below had diminished, and now Du Faure looked out and down upon the crowd, and began to speak in a low, halting voice.

In his bedroom, Alec Fletcher relaxed as he tuned the bedside radio to station HHK to pick up the direct broadcast from the palace. Beside him on the bed, Suzanne lay happily in the circle of his right arm, her lips nuzzling his ear, paying little attention to the announcer who was delivering a running account of the color, music, and gaiety in the Champs. The sound of drums and singing rose from the jam-packed parkway and came in clearer as the station switched to the reporter on the lower level who was identifying the prominent arrivals.

"I feel guilty keeping you away from the big show," Alec said.

"I wouldn't have gone out in that mob anyway, Alec. I'm right where I want to be, here with you, like this."

174

"You're sweet. And wonderful. And I'm the luckiest guy alive."

"You're only one one of the two luckiest. I'm the other."

Alec turned to face her. "Careful of your head, honey," she cautioned.

"It's as good as it'll ever be. Solid concrete." He kissed her, felt the warm, eager response in her lips. "Suzy, I had a talk with Jim this morning. I told him how it is with us, that we want to get married. Jim told me he'd recommend anything I want. If everything goes quiet after Du Faure takes over, he'll ask Harrington to order me back to Washington if I want that. Or if I'd rather stay on here, he'll go along with that. We could be married here. How do you feel about it?"

She lay quietly beside him, eyes closed, feeling his strength. "How about it, Suzy?"

"About getting married? Wonderful. Delicious."

"And about going back?"

"You'd like to stay on, wouldn't you?"

"Wouldn't you?"

"I don't know, Alec. When I think how it's been here, how it was back there, I don't want to leave. I've enjoyed it here. I walk out into the air and feel free. Like I'm— somebody. Somebody with a good job, a decent home, a chance to live. I can eat in any restaurant, go to any hotel, the Club, the Bacchanale, any public place—"

"I know, I know, baby. I've felt it, too. But it's not home. I've got a job to do, too, but I can't expect to stay here forever."

"I know," she said with a note of sadness. "But here, it's the first time I've ever been one of a majority instead of a minority—"

"But only for the upper classes, Suzy. Here, the majority is worse off than the minority at home. No legal vote, no education, no one to listen to a complaint. If we'd been born here, would we be where we are now, or are we better off only because we're educated Americans?"

Suzanne stirred restlessly. "God, I don't know. If we could have it like this at home, there'd never be a question in my mind. No matter how we look at it, it's bound to be wrong. Even if we could stay forever, we'd have the guilt of running away from our obligations to help our own. If we go back, we go back to a dirty, underhanded fight for decency and equality with all the odds stacked against us. I don't even know if I could fight any more. I

175

don't want to be part of a big, angry mob or the hoodlum groups. I've become an orderly person. I want to live a clean, orderly life, the kind I live here. Back there, somebody's always pushing or pulling you toward something you don't believe in, just to get the basic decent things you're entitled to."

"What do you believe in, Suzy?"

"Now? Here? For the first time in my life I've been able to believe in myself. In you. In the people I work with who couldn't care less about our color. It's gotten so I can almost work without feeling I've got to be better than everyone else in order to keep my job. I never felt that back home."

"I know, darling, but we can't run away and keep running forever. One day, you'll be ordered to a new post. Who knows where? If it will make you happier, I know they'll let me stay on here for a while longer. No matter how it turns out, they'll still want somebody here and there's no need for a Jim Gerard. The ambassador would let me stay on, and Jim could fix it with Harrington or Richards. We could have another year and a half, maybe two. But some day we'd have to go back—"

"Sh-h-h. We don't have to decide right now, do we?"

"If we did, it could settle some other things that have been on my mind."

"Like what?"

"Like this. Being together like this. All the disadvantages of not being married. I want you so badly, Suzy."

She said nothing, but drew closer to him, her long body hard against him, feeling his hands over her shoulders, across her back.

"Suzy?"

"What?"

"Suzy, you're the greatest, most inviting aphrodisiac—Oh, Suzy."

"It's all—all—right, Alec, if—you want to," she breathed into his neck.

Alec drew his head back slightly, his eyes only inches away from hers. "You don't really want to, do you, baby?" he said.

"I—I want to, Alec, but—"

"I know, darling. If you want to wait, I can wait, too."

He felt her relax, her face against his neck again, the wetness of her eyes against his skin. "Alec, I don't know why—"

176

"It's all right, Suzy. I don't want you to have to live with guilt. As long as I know it's you and me——"

Eagerly: "It is, Alec. You and me. But I want everything to be the way I've dreamed it would be."

"It's going to be just that way, honey. Just the way you want it to be." He found her yielding lips with his own, felt her body relax, the strain gone. Soft; and so lovely to touch. They lay together in total bliss, thinking their innermost thoughts in secret; the tomorrows, the months and years ahead. And then they became aware of the strangely haunted voice of Charles Du Faure invading their privacy:

"My friends and countrymen, today I have been voted the highest and most cherished honor that can be given to a Libertéan. I have been asked to accept the presidency of our great Republic, to take up the reins of leadership into these hands and lead our country forward and upward among the nations of the world. It is indeed a difficult task to follow in the footsteps of one who has been our respected and beloved leader for these last six years, who laid the foundation for better things to come during the next six years; one whose great, shining example of——"

A wave of murmuring had begun to sweep through the crowds, growing louder. Du Faure hesitated, wavered indecisively.

Alec said with a shake of his head, "Oh, boy——"

"He sounds frightened—sick——"

"Sh-h-h, let's hear what——"

Du Faure was mouthing his words mechanically. The rising thunder of voices from below echoed with hostility, but the thin voice of Du Faure continued haltingly, as though he were reading without knowing what he was saying.

4.

Across the broad Champs de Révolution and up over the swaying trees, General Benoit Batraville stood on the rooftop of the Army Headquarters building. He leaned forward against a waist-high parapet, hands clasped around a pair of strong field glasses as he viewed the ceremony at the palace. From his upper-left jacket pocket, a cord trailed upward to his ear, terminating there in a small button that was held in place by a loop of plastic wire as he listened to the transistorized radio tuned to the microphones on the palace balcony. Sweating heavily, his mouth compressed into a tight, grim line, he tilted his head downward toward the floor of the roof.

"Steady, Claude. Steady," he said.

Lying prone at the general's feet, Claude Falot, wearing dark civilian clothes, lay stretched out full length at the base of the parapet, clutching a high-powered rifle to which had been affixed a telescopic sight and through which its cross hairs had trapped Charles Du Faure in its exact center as he stood behind the bunched microphones. Falot did not reply to Batraville's command, but lay still and waited, his right index finger curled around the trigger. Batraville continued to peer through the field glasses, as he listened to the words coming through the miniature earpiece.

"—and so by the authority placed into my hands by the Council of State, I officially accept the office of President of the Republic of Liberté and do here and now swear to defend and uphold its Constitution and its laws, and to protect it from all enemies within and from without. This I swear by my God."

The official acceptance was over. "Now," Du Faure continued reading, "I would wish to thank——"

On the rooftop, Batraville said, "Ready, Claude?"

Falot whispered, "Ready, *mon général.*"

"Steady . . . *steady* . . . *Now!*"

Falot tightened the grip of his right hand slowly, firmly. The bullet sped across the trees and over the heads of the crowd below and stopped only after it had entered and lodged in the left chest of the unfortunate Charles du Faure.

Batraville watched for several seconds, heard the sudden, excited rise in the pitch of the radio's tone, the confused babbling and clamor of many voices. He turned from the parapet and headed swiftly for the door that led inside the building. Falot leaped to his feet at once and raced quickly behind the general. Batraville stopped and held a hand out. When he saw the question in Falot's eyes, he snapped, "The shell casing, fool! Where is it? Did you leave it behind?"

Falot ran back to the spot where he had lain, tapped the floor with the palm of his hand in momentary panic, located the shell casing, and ran back toward the doorway. Batraville took it from him, nodded grimly, and put it into his trousers pocket. Then both men disappeared into the building.

On the palace balcony, the shocked gathering stood on tiptoes, peering over those who huddled over and around the crumpled form of Charles Du Faure. Dr. Cadeus Fombrun rose and faced the stunned, uncertain audience.

"Gentlemen, ladies," he announced slowly, "I regret deeply to inform you that M'sieu Du Faure is dead."

5.

Charles Du Faure's body had been carried from the balcony, through the ballroom, and into the deliberation chamber of the Council of State where earlier in this day he had been designated president-elect. Rachelle, his widow, stood at her dead husband's side, holding his hand as she cried quietly. Beside her, a son and two daughters wept as a group of relatives and friends crowded closely to comfort the grieving family. "He did not want it! He did not want it!" Rachelle Du Faure sobbed. "Why should a man be killed for something he never wanted?"

Louis Fontaine, Charles St. Germaine, and other members of the Council stood at the foot of the table upon which Du Faure's body had been placed. Fontaine whispered into St. Germaine's ear, and the foreign minister went to the doors of the chamber and into the ballroom.

"Ladies and gentlemen," he announced, "in view of the tragic circumstances, I regret that I must ask you to leave. I am instructed to say that all may rest assured that the perpetrators of this unspeakably vile crime will be found and prosecuted. Later, funeral plans and a proper period of mourning will be announced for our dear and departed friend."

As he turned back into the chamber, he heard the voice of Louis Fontaine saying, "—and I must remind the members of the Council of State that there is still the matter of a president's election before them. Deliberations will commence immediately following the funeral."

Something in his voice compelled Henri Delacroix to look up from the face of Charles Du Faure to Fontaine. It was there in his eyes, a glittering brightness, a portrait of paranoia. Contempt for the dead man and those around him. Not even a flicker of compassion for the widow and children. The secret triumph of a man with a mania for power, a compulsive urge to rule others and, perhaps like

179

Hitler, the world. Eyes burning with fever, the domineering voice of a blustering autocrat.

Delacroix backed away and walked out of the chamber, into the rapidly emptying ballroom. Mme. Courdet was leaving the room with her son, Marcel, followed by Julie Delacroix, Mark and Eugénie Fuller. François Courdet stood to one side, waiting. Henri Delacroix approached him, and the two men stood silently for a few moments. Then Courdet said, "Well, Henri, it is here, no?"

Delacroix replied soberly: "He planned it, François. I know it. It is written upon his face, in his voice, his manner. Du Faure was not assassinated by a madman or a dissident. He was executed on Fontaine's order."

Courdet nodded in agreement. "Executed. An excellent and wise choice of words. By midnight, Henri, I will have the story written, printed, and on the streets. By morning it will be on people's lips in every city and village that can be reached. The word will go out by couriers and drums. I will have readers tell the people who cannot read what has truly happened here tonight—"

Delacroix said, "Old friend, you tread on dangerous ground."

Courdet did not appear to have heard. "By tomorrow night, Henri, my voice will rise so loud that it will be heard beyond the Republic. I promise you. I must go now and find Marcel to help—"

"François, you cannot—"

Courdet pulled out of his friend's grasp. "I must, Henri. He can no longer commit murder with impunity."

At the embassy, Katherine Chance had gone up to bed, and Dorothy Truscott had driven to her home in the limousine that had brought them from the palace. Chance, Truscott, and Gerard sat in the ambassador's office in an air of gloom. Roland Baker had left moments ago to send Chance's message off to Undersecretary Emerson. Mrs. Weatherby brought in a tray of coffee and went out again, visibly shaken from her normal aplomb by the tense atmosphere. Nora Lund stood at the curtained window and looked out over the garden and front gate where the two Marines stood on guard.

Chance said: "Well, that does it. What tomorrow will bring is anybody's guess."

"I still don't see how—" Nora began.

"It's unbelievable," Truscott said, "but somehow logical

180

here in Port Amitié. At the moment of his death, Charles Du Faure was President of Liberté. He had accepted the office and taken the oath, and Fontaine became the former President of the Republic. Du Faure's assassination makes Fontaine an eligible candidate for the office, since legally, he will not be succeeding himself, but Du Faure. Incredible."

"St. Germaine made it clear enough to the press," Chance said grimly. "There's no doubt now that when the Council reconvenes, it will be for the purpose of re-electing Louis Fontaine for another term of six years."

"And François Courdet?" Gerard asked. "This should put him out in front as Fontaine's prime opponent, shouldn't it?"

"Or his life in jeopardy," Chance replied shortly. Then, as though outlining it for his own benefit: "Delacroix will do his best to create a stalemate in the Council, but Fontaine will use pressure and every threat at his command to force the two-thirds majority he needs. He's killed before; he'll do it again if it becomes necessary. As for M'sieu Courdet"—he brought both hands together, turned their palms upward and outward in a gesture of doubt—"who knows? He could—or should be—the logical opponent, but if *Le Temps* comes out with an open denunciation, Courdet could be putting his life on the line. Marcel's, too."

"We'll know more about that when Shannon and Walker get back with the special edition," Truscott said. He checked the time. "Should be any minute now. It's past midnight."

"It was no idle threat," Chance said solemnly. "Henri pleaded with him not to make a direct accusation. He told me—"

There was a light rap on the door, and Polly Weatherby entered, carrying several copies of the freshly printed *Le Temps* Extra Edition, its 60-point eight-column head and four-column picture of Charles Du Faure still moist, held up so all could see. PRESIDENT EXECUTED! Behind Mrs. Weatherby, Clark Shannon and Sergeant Walker waited. Chance muttered, "That does it. Come in, Shannon, Jake."

Chance was staring at one copy of the four-page special edition. Truscott was reading another, while Gerard and Nora shared a third copy.

Shannon was saying "—and they're milling around *Le*

Temps calling for Courdet to come out and talk to them, screaming anti-Fontaine slogans. Just as we left, a truck loaded with armed security police pulled up and began breaking the mob up, arresting some—"

"All right, Shannon. Stay close. Jake, put some extra men on the gate and a couple to rotate around inside the wall, just in case there's any sign of a demonstration."

"Yes, sir." Walker saluted, executed a smart about-face, and went out, Shannon behind him.

"Thorne, you'd best ring up Sir Hugh Stewart, M'sieu Cartier, and the others, and alert them if they aren't fully aware of what's happening. That's about all we can do for now."

"What about M'sieu Courdet and his family?" Gerard asked.

"For the moment, they'll have to fend for themselves. If the security goons don't get to them first, they'll probably have to go into hiding after this"—he pointed to the paper, shaking his head dolefully. "François and Marcel Courdet are the only remaining vocal threat to Fontaine, and Louis doesn't exactly appreciate that type of opposition."

Suzanne said, "Alec. Alec, I'm afraid."

"Don't be, baby. It won't make things any easier, but it's not the end of the world, either."

"Oh, God! How can a thing like that—"

"I don't know how, but I'd give a lot to know exactly where Batraville and his goon Falot were when that shot was fired."

"Alec, you don't think it was deliberate, do you?"

"Not any more than the Reichstag fire was. From what we've just heard, that shot could have come only from one place, the top of the Army Headquarters building across the Champs from the palace. I'd like to know why there wasn't a security force, not only on the roof, but in every window that faces out."

"Alec—"

"That unholy, evil bastard. It's so reasonable now, the only possible way he could take over for another six years." Alec was sitting on the side of the bed nearest the babbling radio, shocked alert at the first moment when the hysterical broadcaster, over the crescendo of frightened voices from the balcony, shrieked, *"He has been killed! He has been murdered!"*

"Alec, you and Jim Gerard will be pulled into this."

"In one way or another, I suppose so."

"You'll be careful, won't you? Falot—"

"That misbegotten son, I'll keep my eyes wide open for him, don't you worry. Suzy, darling, I'm going to drive you home now, then come back and wait for Jim. We'll have a lot to talk about."

Chance and Truscott were back in the ambassador's office at seven in the morning, making plans with Mrs. Weatherby for the luncheon at which the Western ambassadors would be present for an informal chat to exchange unofficial opinions and feelings. When the phone rang, Truscott spoke into it and took the message, then turned to the ambassador. "That was Gerard. It's come."

"What?"

"The second mob. Between 150 and 200 anti-Courdet demonstrators have just broken into *Le Temps* and are wrecking it."

Chance nodded. "Anything on the Courdets?"

"François Courdet wasn't there. He and Madame Courdet have gone to the Delacroix home. They'll be safe there. Not even Fontaine would dare invade the home of the Chairman of the Council. Marcel was at the plant. He and the rest of the employees got out through the back just before the mob broke in."

Chance sat thoughtfully for a moment, then said to Mrs. Weatherby, "Get Mrs. Chance on the private line, please."

In the Russian Embassy, Ambassador Vossolofsky, Basil Zharkov, and Feodor Pyantenov sat in the small second-floor study over coffee. The ambassador's florid face was an enigma of perplexity and confusion, feeling a lesser authority in the presence of Pyantenov as he toyed nervously with the fob that dangled from his watch. Unsure of himself, he said nothing, and waited.

Pyantenov's head bobbed up and down, lips tightly pursed together, his forehead ridged in a dark frown. Zharkov alone seemed calm and undisturbed. He put his cup down, lighted a cigarette, and said, "Even the most carefully laid plans go astray, eh, Comrade?"

Pyantenov's head swung around to face Zharkov. In a peevish growl, he snapped: "The behavior pattern of a statesman is seldom difficult to foresee. His mental reactions are human and are therefore relatively simple to read and defend against. But who can see into the minds of animals like Fontaine?—that he would sacrifice Du Faure to his African voodoo Gods so that they would permit him to continue in office?"

"And now?" Zharkov asked with a tight smile.

Pyantenov regarded the younger man with a cool stare, as though he knew Zharkov was enjoying his setback. "So, my young friend," Pyantenov said, "nothing has changed. Merely the order of their elimination. One is gone, and we did not have to raise a hand to accomplish this. But now it becomes necessary to force the matter to a head." He turned to Vossolofsky. "Sergei, you will prepare 100,000 francs at once, in notes of assorted denominations. I will leave at once for Riam-sur-Mer and make my final arrangements with Duclosse. On my return, I will see General Batraville. I think the time is ripe to bring him face to face with M'sieu Chalumeau. You, Basil, will keep in touch with Mosher. The moment Fontaine signs the agreement, make our radio available to him. He is to contact Urbana and start the arms moving from Bahía de Nipe."

Vossolofsky was already on his way to get the 100,000 francs from his safe.

6.

The crowd of ragged, howling Libertéans, clad in rough work clothes, heads covered with floppy-brimmed straw hats, had been gathered from the waterfront area during the night. As they milled through the streets during the early hours of daylight, the heavy odor of cheap rum traveled with them, the air turned suddenly sour with the syrupy, alcoholic smell. Their cries and incoherent shouting brought people to their windows as they ran along Rue Desplaines into Alpeste, then into Montaigne, a short side street only two blocks long. Until they came to the storefronted *Le Temps* building, there had been, curiously, no sign of a police or military uniform anywhere along the route; nor had the mob inflicted any damage except to ear and eye; and now, suddenly, the huge black man who led them began to bellow: "Here they are! Down with Courdet! Death to all traitors!"

The rum-inflamed mob took up the shout, and similar cries began to ricochet from the walls on both sides of the narrow street that housed numerous small commercial establishments and enjoyed local, rather than tourist, trade. Wary merchants began lowering overhead corrugated iron closures to their entrances, racing frantically against inevitable destruction. In front of the building, the brawny black leader came to a stop, turned and threw his massive arms up and shouted: "Here! Here is the den of traitors! Find them! Kill them! Burn! Destroy them before they destroy us!"

Inside, Marcel Courdet, at the first sound of the bellowing baritone voice, looked up startled from his desk, then ran toward the front of the building. Behind him came two employees from the press room, racing for the chains that would lower the corrugated iron door, but Marcel shouted: "Let it go! It is no use! Get out and warn the others. Not the front. Through the back way. Hurry!"

The mob had come to a momentary halt to listen to their leader. Following him, as many as could do so burst through the flimsy wooden doors into the building while others smashed and hacked at the windows with clubs and machetes. Inside, the last of *Le Temps'* employees was leaping from the alley delivery platform to the ground as the first of the rioters entered. Piles of morning papers, partially loaded into two trucks, were abandoned.

Outside, on Rue Montaigne, those who could not squeeze into the building began to turn their attention to neighboring store fronts, smashing windows, breaking doors, and pulling down wooden uprights that supported overhanging balconies. They ripped out the iron door of a liquor *boutique*, began throwing bottles to their clamoring companions in the street, and the crash of breaking glass could be heard blocks away. Two men were rolling small wooden casks through the door, and these were at once set upright, their tops bashed in, and the rum scooped up by hand to mouth.

A roaring cheer arose as the largest of the two printing presses was pulled and pushed out of the doorway into the street, where it was battered apart, its rollers, plates, gears, wheels, and other mechanical parts flung aside. Type cases came flying through the broken windows, and the air was filled with small bits of metal type. Using heavy bars and rollers, the recently new linotype machine was jockeyed outside and smashed into uselessness by the frenzied, destruction-bent rioters. The second, smaller job press came rocketing through the doorway, to be torn apart amid exuberant shouting and childish, drunken laughter.

Meanwhile, those who had reduced the liquor shop to a shambles and drunk their fill temporarily, looked about for other means to satisfy the destructive urge in them, and fell upon four automobiles that were parked a short distance away, unable to get away through the crowd. These were overturned, their doors battered off, glass shattered, the upholstery ripped out. Gasoline from their tanks began running down the street toward the newspaper building, and then someone decided to put a lighted match to the small stream. The entire street seemed to catch fire. One man tore off his shirt, wrapped it around a stout bamboo club and dipped it into the still unlit gasoline, allowing the flame to reach it, then ran shouting toward the *Le Temps* structure. The flaming torch was passed from hand to hand inside, and within minutes, the building had become a roaring furnace. Those inside leaped and fought their way out, but two luckless participants emerged with their clothing afire, tearing at the burning rags on their bodies as others looked on and laughed gleefully, insanely, at the misfortune that had befallen them.

Jim Gerard had parked his car on the wider Rue Pavillon, then ran along it to Rue Montaigne and within a block of the conflagration. Where, he wondered, were the police? The Army? Police and Army Headquarters were almost within sight of the violence, certainly within hearing, yet neither police nor soldiers were present. It was at that moment that the torch was put to the building. Flames leaped out through the doorways and caught at the old, dried-out frame exterior, licked their way to the upper story, and all but consumed it within minutes; then they began to reach for the buildings on either side. As Gerard turned back, intent on pushing through the crowds of curious and frightened onlookers, he saw the familiar Plymouth sedan across the street. Behind the wheel, hatted and sunglassed, sat Lieutenant Claude Falot.

Gerard looked up to the second-story level and saw the faces of several helmeted soldiers looking down on the frenzied scene below. In other windows, he caught a glimpse of several policemen, watching and ignoring the scene. He crossed the street with difficulty, passed the sedan, then turned back to see who sat on the back seat, calmly observing the carnage up ahead. Despite the sunglasses and civilian clothing, he recognized General Benoit Batraville.

And then he heard the wailing sirens, saw two pieces of ancient fire equipment lumbering belatedly into Montaigne from Pavillon, a row of soldiers flanking either side of the trucks, bayoneted rifles held at high port. At once, the mob leader shouted the word to disperse, and led most of the mob toward the escape end of the street that was still partially unobstructed. The trucks and soldiers reached the flaming building and began to pump chemicals into it. A few of the rioters, too drunk or dazed to escape, waited to greet them, but the soldiers and fire fighters paid no attention to these, and directed their efforts toward a cause that had been long lost.

7.

"—during which, police and members of the military establishment, including General Batraville, chief of the Security Police, watched from concealment as the *Le Temps* building and presses were destroyed, thereby removing final and important opposition to former President Fontaine's bid for re-election. It can be expected that François Courdet and his family, safe for the moment, will become targets in a campaign to force them into exile, just as it is now increasingly obvious (refer to report immediately preceding) that Fontaine will regain the presidency for another term of six years. Report ends."

Chance stopped dictating, and said to Mrs. Weatherby: "I'll have a rough draft of that, Polly, triple-spaced. After I make my corrections, I'll want to send a personal note along to Mr. Emerson, eyes only. Is Baker still standing by?"

"Yes, sir."

"Tell him he'll have these to send in about an hour. When Mr. Truscott has finished making his telephone calls, have him look in on me, please."

Mrs. Weatherby got up and left the office. Chance swiveled around to face Gerard. "That about covers it for the moment, wouldn't you say?"

"I believe so, sir."

"I wonder what the devil will come next," Chance said glumly.

Gerard shook his head from side to side. "It's almost impossible to predict. What about the Courdets, sir?"

"They're safe for the moment, still at the Delacroix home. How Marcel managed to get there without being picked up is a minor miracle."

"What about asylum?"

Chance's mouth twisted in a wry grin. "If they ask for it, of course we'll give them every protection of the embassy; but I can't, by convention, offer or force it on them. Fontaine would swear we kidnaped them against their will or some other such rot."

"But if it were to be suggested to them by—"

"Jim, you can't make the offer. Technically, you are an officer of my staff, and such a move would practically constitute an unfriendly act." Chance paused to retrieve his stubby pipe from his desk drawer. He lighted it and added, "However, to ease your mind, the suggestion has already been made." He looked up quickly. "Not by me. Mrs. Chance telephoned the Delacroix home and spoke to Julie. The Courdets will get the message."

Gerard leaned back in his chair, showing relief. "I hope they'll accept the suggestion."

"We can't be too sure they will. There's still the problem of getting here without being intercepted by the security police, and that won't be any easy matter. Also, once inside these grounds, Courdet can engage in no political activity or communicate with anyone who can. I doubt if he will consent to those conditions and restrictions. Certainly, Marcel will refuse."

"I suppose so," Gerard agreed.

"All right, Jim, suppose you get along and let me write my letter to Emerson. Now, remember this. I don't want you or Alec to get openly involved in this matter. The Department has laid down some rather fine lines about these situations. Above all, we can't afford to be caught up in an intrigue that can be linked to the embassy. At this moment, on top of everything else, my expulsion, or that of any principal officer here, could cause grave embarrassment in Washington. And considerable enjoyment in other quarters."

"I understand, sir, and I'll be careful."

"Let's be sure of that. I don't want to hamper your—ah—duties or activities, but keep in mind that I am officially responsible for your behavior."

"I'll keep that firmly in mind, sir."

On his way out, Gerard thought with a half-smile over

Chance's structuring of the sentence, *I don't want you or Alec to get openly involved—*

Had the ambassador placed a particular emphasis on the word *openly,* or was it his imagination?

CHAPTER 6

1.

Alec Fletcher was pacing his bedroom when Gerard got back to No. 11. He wore slacks and loafers, but his upper body was bare, the bandage removed from his head, showing an angry flesh bruise. Gerard looked the nearly healed welt over carefully.

"It's fine, Jim," Alec said. "No trace of pain or discomfort. I'm all set for anything."

"Good. Truscott and the ambassador are anxious to see you, but I've put them off for the time being. You haven't been lonesome for company, have you?"

Alec smiled. "No. No complaints. Except that I'm getting restless with everything exploding around us. What's the official scuttlebutt?"

"Hold your steam down. We'll be getting some action soon, I think."

"What's up now?"

Gerard handed him a copy of the final issue of *Le Temps* and described what had happened during the morning. "I had a call from Mark Fuller a little while ago. He's invited me to Terre Delacroix for lunch."

"Anything special?"

"Not in so many words. Only that since I'm the latest face from the States, he and his wife would enjoy hearing some news from back home. It was the way he asked me—as though he might be afraid his phone was being monitored."

"Could be. I wouldn't rule out that possibility."

"What do you think is behind it?"

Alec shrugged. "It could be that since he and Marcel are so close—"

"I had the same sort of thought. I think I'd like to know more about Fuller. Mrs. Fuller. Terre Delacroix. Your file on them is mostly statistical. For instance, how does Mark

190

Fuller happen to be married to the daughter of the Chairman of the Council of State?"

"I'll have to take it from memory. Mark is about twenty-eight or twenty-nine. Graduate of Columbia with an engineering degree, but never practiced his profession. He met Eugénie while she was a student at Barnard—"

"That's a bit unusual, isn't it, Alec? I thought these upperclass Libertéans sent their children to Europe for their educations."

"Not in every case. Henri Delacroix has a wide circle of friends in the States. Also, his banking connections are there. Eugénie preferred New York; Julie chose Paris and Geneva, maybe because Marcel was there. Let's get back to Mark. He was some sort of football star, nominated for All-American in his senior year, and came out on AP's second team. Eugénie and he met and fell in love. Since no self-respecting daughter of high social rank would think of marrying without parental consent, Eugénie invited Mark to visit her family in Port Amitié when they were graduated. I understand there was considerable coolness on Henri's part, but Mark's interest in the country and the people, plus his expressed opinions on how much could be done to speed up progress with modern engineering methods loosened some of the resistance. Still, Henri was reluctant to give up his daughter to a foreigner for what he felt might be forever. Mark was growing impatient to get back to the States and take up his engineering career. Eugénie was torn between love for Mark and her family. Stalemate.

"I've heard it was Angélique, Eugénie's mother, who eventually suggested a way out, and Henri made the proposal to Mark. If Mark would move to Port Amitié and take over the plantation at Anse à Goulet, organize it, apply his engineering skills to its operation, and put it on a paying basis, Henri would give his consent to an immediate marriage. If after two years, Mark and Eugénie came to him and said they didn't want to remain any longer, he wouldn't block their move back to the States. Two years of their time was all he asked, during which time they could be together on Terre Delacroix. Mark thought the proposition over for a full three seconds before he accepted.

"The rest is pretty much a Cinderella story. They were married, flew back to Washington, where Mark spent the balance of the year with officials and advisers at the Department of Agriculture there and at Beltsville. When he returned with half a shipload of equipment, experimental fertilizers, trunks filled with books on tropical-soil-testing methods, plant diseases, blight, irrigation, planting and harvesting, cost data, weather information, marketing and I-don't-know-what-else, the other planters took it pretty much with tongue in cheek and sat back to watch.

"Eugénie's education in sociology and home economics helped with the natives. Both worked hard, conducted classes, put in their time in the fields, and used the brighter workers as foremen under their headman, André. At the end of eighteen months of backbreaking labor, just when Mark was on the verge of throwing in the towel, results began to show. When the other planters began showing up and asking questions, he knew he had the thing licked. At the end of the two-year period, Terre Delacroix began breaking out of the red and into the black profit column. And it was time for Mark and Eugénie to make their decision. Stay on or leave.

"At the anniversary party given for them by Henri and Angélique, Mark and Eugénie told them they wanted to stay for at least one more year. At the end of the third year, when the profits were rolling in, Henri openly defied them to leave the land by handing over the deed in their names. 'If you leave now, children,' Henri told them, 'you do not leave *my* land behind, but your own.' That settled it. They stayed."

"Any political inference there?" Gerard asked.

"With Mark? None at all. He's strictly legitimate, and keeps his mind on his work."

"Anything else?"

"Nothing I can think of. There's just the two of them. No children."

"Any special reason?"

"Now, how would I know a thing like that?"

Gerard shrugged and smiled. "How would you know so much about everything else about them? You seemed to make a point of the fact that there were no children."

"Well—it's only a guess, but there might be a question of—it's a touchy thing, Jim."

"What is?"

"The color question. In a marriage of that kind, there's the possibility of—" Alec hesitated.

"Nonwhite children?"

192

"A possibility. Light as Eugénie and the Delacroix are, they are Libertéan, and——"

"I don't know too much about the Mendelian theory, Alec, but I get the idea. I think I've got enough background."

"Jim?"

"What?"

"How about me?"

"At the moment, wait until I get back."

"Okay, but watch it, will you? The Old Man will scream like a wounded duck——"

"I know. He's already warned me. You fit for action?"

"Fit and waiting."

"All right. I'm off for Terre Delacroix. You stand by until you hear from me. Keep the phone clear in case I need you in a hurry. I'll be in touch."

2.

Lunch on the shaded terrace at Terre Delacroix had been a pleasant hour filled with light, meaningless conversation of Washington, the miracle of the 1963 World Series in which the amazing Dodgers had taken four games in a row from the fearsome Yankees, the football playoffs that gave the underdog Chicago Bears the World Championship at the expense of the New York Giants in December.

Fuller's wife was a splendidly attractive creature, even more so in slacks and boyish-cut shirt than she had been in formal gown at the palace. Her jet-black hair was cut short, with a few wisps that were trained to fall over her forehead carelessly, and he realized then that Eugénie had worn a wig the night before. Dark, luminous eyes were the most outstanding of her facial features, her nose beautifully chiseled, lips full and generous. She was slim-waisted, long-legged, and the shirt, tucked tightly into her slacks, emphasized youthful, high breasts. There was an exceptional quality of elegance in the way she moved her hands and body.

In the midst of her discussion of François Courdet's firm opinion that the people must be given the right to vote and the understanding of such voting power, Mark interrupted and said: "I'm sorry, darling, I've got to break this up or we'll spend the rest of the afternoon talking politics. I want to drive Jim out to see our experimental

193

cotton. He asked about it on the phone this morning."

Gerard looked up quickly, caught himself, nodded to Eugénie, and wondered if she was as aware as he that he had made no such request. Eugénie excused herself, invited Gerard to stay for a swim when they returned, kissed Mark, and went into the house. A young servant boy brought their hats. They went to Mark's car in the driveway and got in. Mark said to the boy, "Not this time, Ti Jacques," and drove off. "My headman's son," Mark explained. "Loves anything that moves fast." Gerard glanced back and saw the boy standing in the driveway before the Gran Maison, watching the car as it disappeared.

On both sides of the well-packed private dirt road, the fields of Terre Delacroix spread out in every direction from the Big House, or Gran Maison, to Tom Reed's Belle Roseau south, the natural deep harbor of Anse à Goulet north, the white sand beach and blue sea west, the paved main highway and mountain to the east. In the distance ahead and to their left, pieces of bright yellow agricultural equipment roared while gangs of field-workers labored under their wide-brimmed straw hats, singing while a young boy beat out a now familiar rhythm on a small, hide-covered drum that hung from his side. Gerard remarked on it.

"You'd be amazed," Fuller observed, "how much more work gets done with that youngster setting the pace." He pointed beyond to a series of stripping sheds. "In there, we use a *conteur*, a storyteller, to keep the people's minds occupied while they work."

Surrounding each field were groups of palm trees that towered regally over chinaberry, *mapou*, oleander, and pepper trees. Startlingly beautiful and strange shrubs flowered in brilliant profusion in separate private gardens behind neat rows of thatch-roofed huts of the workers. To the east, on the far side of the main highway, the ground rose in a gradual slope until it reached the sharp rise of the *mamelon*, or hillock, almost a mile away, and was covered with coffee shrubs whose bright orange berries flamed its entire side.

The heat was near stifling and the only coolness in sight was the cerulean blue of the Caribbean to the west where, a good thousand yards away, and through shimmering heat waves, Gerard could make out a beach pavilion and dock, a forty-foot (he judged) white cabin cruiser tied up.

Anchored some distance beyond the dock was a neat, seamanlike sloop that danced at the end of a line tied to a large white-and-red can buoy. Several smaller boats lay off the beach, tugging at their anchors, and in the distance, two such boats bobbed like corks as youngsters from the plantation worked over fishing nets.

Fuller drove to the far side of his experimental cotton field and pulled the small car into a wooded area that separated Terre Delacroix from the scimitar-shaped shore and beach of Anse à Goulet. Inside the woods, he tooled the car carefully among the trees, then came to a stop when passage became choked and nearly impossible. They got out and walked along a narrow path into a dense thicket, then through head-high brush until they came into a small clearing. In its center was a small hut. As they approached it, the gray, weatherbeaten door pulled inward and a man appeared in the doorway, dressed in the garb of a field-worker, with a wide-brimmed hat pulled down over his face. He wore a blue denim jumper and trousers of the same material that were tied around his waist by a long cord. In his right hand he held a revolver. Suddenly, his mouth curved upward in a smile of recognition. The revolver disappeared into the jumper pocket.

Mark said, "I believe you've met Marcel Courdet, Jim."

Gerard wiped the sweat from his forehead with one hand as he said, "I have, but you could have fooled me."

Marcel came toward them in quick steps and shook Gerard's hand. "Mr. Gerard, welcome to my humble quarters."

"Why," Gerard said, "don't we get down to a first-name basis and save ourselves a lot of unnecessary words? Now, what have we got here? I thought you were at the Delacroix house—"

Marcel said: "Don't blame Mark, please. It was I who suggested he call you. Why?" He shrugged. "I thought I detected a man"—he grinned boyishly—"who might be sympathetic to one in my situation."

"Since *Le Temps* was destroyed," Mark added, "the word is out that General Batraville's security police are quietly searching for Marcel and his father. Marcel came late last night, and I hid him here. No one but André, my headman, knows he is here. I haven't even told Eugénie yet."

"And just where do I fit into this?" Gerard asked cautiously.

"We need someone to clear the way for us with the American Embassy, to grant the Courdets asylum."

"Only for Papa and Mama," Marcel added.

"That shouldn't be difficult," Gerard said. "All you need do is have them show up."

"There are no other formalities necessary? No waiting? Permission?"

"None, if your father and mother willingly present themselves and make the request. They can move into the embassy at once. Any necessary formalities can be taken care of afterward."

"Our house," Marcel said, "is under observation. As long as my father and mother remain with the Delacroix, they are safe. Once they leave—"

Mark said: "The Delacroix house is being watched as well. It was Fontaine's order that the homes of *all* Council members would be under police or military guard for their own protection, a scheme to give him the right to keep the Courdets under observation."

"How did you manage to leave the house, Marcel?"

"I waited until dark, then climbed over the back wall. Our house is only three away, but I could see it was being watched. I walked down the hill by a back trail to a friend's house, borrowed a car, and came here."

Gerard said, "Can you make it back safely by nightfall?"

It was Mark who answered the question. "If Marcel is dressed as he is and followed the same route, he could make it."

"All right, then. Suppose you do that, Marcel. You'll need some help and another car. Mark?"

"Count on me to do anything I can, Jim."

"We'll need one or two pieces of transportation that can't be tied up with either of you."

"I think I can arrange anything we need," Mark offered.

"Then suppose we try this—"

3.

Gerard spent an hour with Alec on his return from Terre Delacroix, then drove to the embassy. The chancellery receptionist handed him a note from Nora. Four-thirty. He walked down the hall to her office and exchanged a few words with Ray Ferriss, the press officer, who was just leaving. When they were alone, he held up the note and said, "Just got back from a long lunch with the Fullers. Anything up?"

"Nothing in particular. I thought we might have a drink and dinner at the Club later."

"M-m-m. This time I'll have to ask for the raincheck. I've got a little problem to work out."

"Anything I can help you with?"

"No. No, I think not. Keep this between us, will you, Nora? Marcel Courdet slipped his halter last night. He's in hiding on Terre Delacroix. I've just seen him. He's anxious to get his parents to the embassy and into asylum."

"There's no problem about that, Jim. If they can make it inside the embassy gates on their own power, they'll be more than welcome, and without question."

"They may need some help."

"Not from you or Alec or anyone else here, Jim. I'm warning you, keep out of it. You'll do more harm than good if you're identified with them. When do they plan to come in?"

"They haven't worked out a definite time," he said evasively.

"Jim, don't get involved. I know you want to help, but aside from getting into serious trouble with the local authorities, I know the ambassador will have you on your way home ten minutes after a complaint has been filed against you. Please be careful."

"Nora, I promise you I'll be as careful as is humanly possible."

She sighed with relief. "Not only with this, Jim, but with everything else in the future. If you're going to put on your cloak and wear your dagger, make sure your slip isn't showing. This Courdet matter isn't going to be taken lightly; and there are so many other intrigues in the hopper, you could be caught up in something purely by accident. General Batraville is a mean sod to tangle with."

"Batraville himself is intriguing enough."

"And if he isn't intriguing enough, there's always the lovely Lénore."

Gerard laughed lightly. "Gossip from you, Nora?"

She flushed. "When it concerns the men, it comes under the head of information, but when it's a woman, it's gossip. Don't forget it for a moment; she fits into the picture."

"A neat arrangement."

"Don't knock it, Jim. If you were in Fontaine's shoes—"

"Don't finish the question, because you'll get no answer to it from me, Irish."

Nora's reply was a sly grin.

In his own office a few moments later, Gerard put through a call to the Délacroix house. Julie answered the phone and he asked for Mark.

"One moment, please. He has just arrived."

A few seconds passed, then, "Jim?"

"All set, Mark?"

"Waiting for the first pitch."

"Eight?"

"Eight it is."

"You've got the program in mind?"

"Down to the last detail."

"Good luck."

Gerard had no sooner hung up than Roland Baker came in with a sealed envelope addressed to him, marked EYES ONLY. He signed the pink receipt, and Baker went out again. Gerard ripped the envelope open and spent the next twenty minutes decoding the message from the radio relay station, Chieftain. When he had digested its contents, he sat staring at his penciled notes between the triple-spaced lines on the thin piece of tissue, then folded it carefully into a narrow oblong. He loosened his trousers belt and inserted the oblong inside the waistband of his shorts.

Curious, he thought, that Chieftain would commit an error of omission.

He went out, found his car in the parking area, and drove to the Café Excelsior. It was early for dinner, just six-ten. Lebrun greeted him and showed him to the bar. "Give me a few moments," Lebrun said. Gerard attracted Etienne's attention, ordered a drink, and turned on the stool to watch Emil as he ushered a party of two to a table; now a party of six; another of four.

As he seated the latter party, Lebrun glanced toward the bar, caught Gerard's eye, then deliberately placed a hand on the shoulder of the tall, coffee-colored man who wore a dark-blue suit of good linen. His face, of which Gerard had a clear side view, was as severe as his general manner. Now he turned and said something to Emil in response to a question, and sat down. At once, the three men with him leaned forward attentively as the man in blue spoke, using a table knife to emphasize his words. The talk ended briefly as a waiter appeared with a bottle of wine and four glasses, then took their orders for food. Gerard nodded to Emil to indicate that he had taken notice of the man in blue. Gerard caught Emil's nod toward the rear door. He finished his drink and made his way to the hallway, went into the men's room when he saw a janitor sweeping the hall, emerged a few minutes later to find it clear, and went up the steps.

Ten minutes later, Lebrun entered and sat down, puffing from the exertion of climbing the steps too hurriedly. "M'sieu Alec?" he asked.

"He is well. At the moment still hidden from sight at No. 11." Gerard reminded Lebrun with, "The tall light one downstairs."

"Ah, yes. He is Pierre Duclosse. In the past, he has been a thorn in the side of the Le Mans, Dubonnière, and Fontaine governments."

"A revolutionist?"

"Not in the usual sense. Some years ago, he was a strong labor leader with a considerable following. He once formed a union of dockworkers. President Le Mans broke up the organization and jailed Duclosse. In Dubonnière's time, Duclosse tried secretly to organize the water, power, and communications workers. He was arrested again, tried for political subversion, and imprisoned. In 1956, Fontaine's security police brought him in as a suspect in a student revolutionary movement. He was sentenced to ten years, but was released three years later in a New Year's proclamation of amnesty."

"And now?"

"He is the labor superintendent on an estate in Riam-sur-Mer that is owned by René Rimbaud, Fontaine's ambassador to France. Duclosse visits Port Amitié perhaps once each month to keep in touch with his old comrades. Like the three you saw at the table with him."

"So?"

"Lately, Duclosse has been seen in Port Amitié more frequently and once more seems to be affluent. It may be nothing, but he is worth watching. If there is a revolutionary movement anywhere on Liberté, you can be sure Pierre Duclosse will in some way be a part of it. For his share, he would realize a dream, to become Minister of Labor."

"And why not president?"

"He is not strong enough. He is not a—what you would call—a *physical* fighter. But he knows that if he can build

199

a strong national labor party and control it, he could possibly control the president."

"Does he have any connections in the present government?"

"To my knowledge, no."

For a moment there was a silence, then Gerard asked, "Do you believe he is in league with this Chalumeau?"

Lebrun shrugged. "It is possible, M'sieu. Not only possible, but probable. He is not one to be far removed from such an intrigue."

"I see. We'll let it stand for now. There's another matter, Emil. Less than an hour ago I received a message. You have seen the American, Mosher?" Lebrun nodded. "There is word from Havana that Mosher is here to arrange for a large shipment of supplies to Fontaine. For some days, hundreds of cases have been assembled in several warehouses at Bahía de Nipe."

Lebrun nodded and waited. "There is much activity in the vicinity. There is also no doubt that the cases contain rifles and ammunition, and many are with red markings that indicate dangerous explosives. It is presumed that the material they assemble will be shipped out soon."

"Is anything known of its exact destination?" Lebrun asked. "There are many ports where it could be landed. Ah, if those arms reach Fontaine—"

Gerard nodded grimly. Little need to add that with sufficient arms support, Fontaine would become master of the situation and as supreme a dictator as Trujillo had been in his day. Or as Castro was at this moment, even with scattered exile groups making hit-and-run attacks on the Cuban coast. Flea bites on an elephant's hide, Castro had called them, laughing them off. Then, standing behind his new arsenal, how long before Liberté would be transformed into the second Iron Curtain that Russia sought desperately to establish in this hemisphere, even while seeming to pull out of Cuba? "There is no knowledge of its exact destination, Emil, but I have reason to believe that the presence of Mosher here is an indication that Liberté could be the logical point of delivery."

"A ship could anchor off any deserted beach and land the arms," Emil observed.

"That is a gamble. Meanwhile, let every man keep his eyes and ears open. Get in touch with every contact. Anything they hear, even suspect, can be of vital use to us."

"I will do everything in my power, M'sieu. Tell M'sieu Alec I asked for him and hope to see him soon."

"You will, Emil. Soon, I hope. Now, about the panel truck I will have need for tonight—"

Alec took the decoded message from Gerard, and studied it. Gerard said, "Notice anything strange about that message?"

Alec re-examined it carefully, and nodded. "For one thing, it came directly from Chieftain without any mention of Minos 1. Usually—"

"Not usually, Alec. Chieftain has strict orders to identify the source of all messages. They've been too cautious about correct procedures in the past to get so careless now."

"How about checking back with Minos 1?"

"I've already sent a query. We should have an answer soon."

"What about this Duclosse? He sounds interesting to me."

"He's our hottest bet so far. Are you up to getting back into harness?"

"I'm just waiting for the signal to go. I can't take much more of this lying around in hiding."

"We need to find out as much as we can about Duclosse and what goes on in Riam-sur-Mer. How about a cover?"

"No problem. I can pass for a laborer looking for work. I've got the clothes to fit the act. If I can't find work around Riam-sur-Mer, that'll give me good enough reason for hanging around with the rest of the unemployed, and time to nose around."

"Identity card?"

"I've got four or five to choose from."

"And the checkpoints?"

"No problem. There's only one out of Port Amitié north. None at l'Arcachon or Riam-sur-Mer."

"Okay, Alec. You're back in business. Tonight's little mission can be your before-game warmup. If your friend Falot shows up, keep clear of him."

"That's one friend I want to meet up with before this one is over."

Gerard said: "Don't break out on your own, Alec. For the time being, keep your personal feelings out of your work. Falot is only an obstacle, like a wall that has to be scaled."

"I know, Jim. And when I scale that wall, I'm going to be wearing spiked shoes, rules or no rules."

4.

The deep night had cloaked the excitement of the day in deceptive quiet. In the hills, the incessant beat of drums continued, but this was a customary nightly occurrence, and seemed to signify nothing unusual. Bright lights glittered along the Boulevard Mont de Couronne and in the city below the Delacroix house. Only the palace area was darkened.

The supper that had brought the Courdet and Delacroix families together had been intended to relieve the strain of the past twenty-four hours, but with the tension of François, the fears of Angélique, and the anger of Marcel added to Henri Delacroix's own apprehensions for their safety, a pall of gloom had turned the meal into something less than joyful.

On the wide veranda, Marcel and Julie sat closely together in the darkness, sipping coffee, speaking in low, intimate voices.

"Trouble," Julie said, "never lasts long. Do not worry, *cher* Marcel. You remember how it was when we were children? Always trouble and unrest, revolutions every year, sometimes twice a year. It is hardly so bad as that now—"

"Ah, *ma favori,* always the comforting angel," Marcel replied. "I am not worried so much for myself as I am for them."

"They have lived through much more than we, Marcel, and so much worse."

"True, but when we were children, they were our present age, but already married, while we wait for the right time. Now they grow older and age faster, and still there is no right time for us."

"And there never will be a right time as long as we wait. The right time to do something is when you want to do it. In a short time, this will be over and once more there will be a right time, if we are sensible enough to take advantage of it."

"Ah, Julie, I wish it were so. This time is different. That *animale* has made of Papa a special target, another Du Faure awaiting execution. I am worried, *chérie.* The paper was his *life.* Mine, too."

"Marcel—"

"The paper is destroyed, the presses broken. Even if, as you say, this will blow away, what future is there? Fontaine will become president again. Nothing can stop him. Even if Papa escapes, it will mean exile."

"You take the dark side so well, Marcel, but there is another side to look at more closely. Remember, Papa is working hard. The Council is still in deliberation, and you have already elected Fontaine. So again, as it has been since we returned from Europe, there is no right time. And when we are old, there will still not be a right time—"

"Julie, Julie—"

"Marcel, listen. When your father and mother were married, was that a right time? How often have we heard them tell stories of the days when they were first married? Why must the time be so right for us when it never was for them?"

Marcel sat up, put his coffee cup on the end table, and took Julie's hand, held it tightly. "Julie, you are right as always. There will never be a right time as long as we postpone and talk."

She said happily, "Then when shall it be?"

"As soon as we can do it safely. I am too deeply in despair to wait any longer—"

Julie put two fingers to his lips. "Do not talk of despair and love in the same breath, *favori*."

"Then only of love. And I do love you, Julie. You are my world."

"Then stop talking and show it, foolish one. Kiss me."

In the sitting room, Eugénie, her mother, and Angélique Courdet sipped coffee and tried to keep their conversation from touching on the events that were foremost in their minds, each aware of the fear in the other; but their words were overshadowed by the apprehension and worry they saw in Angélique, the tremor in her hands and voice.

Across the hall, Henri Delacroix, François Courdet, and Mark Fuller took their liqueurs from the houseboy's tray and sipped solemnly. "Marcel will not do it, Henri," Courdet said.

"Then you and Angélique must. There is no time to waste, François," Henri said. "He is a madman with the dreams of a madman. And you stand in his path. You know how he acts when there is an obstacle. There is nothing he will not resort to in order to clear his way."

Courdet sat staring vacantly across the room as he listened to his friend's words. "I cannot run like a frightened animal, Henri. I could never forgive myself. Marcel—Angélique—I could never hold my head up in honor before them again."

"I need not remind you, François, of what happened to Du Faure. You were there and saw him cut down. We can be sure it was Fontaine's doing, and if he could do such a thing to Du Faure, the same thing can happen to you. Tonight. Tomorrow. Next week. Without you, there is no true opposition. As Chairman of the Council I would be forced to admit defeat and give in to him."

Delacroix felt his words striking home. "Without you, François, we will fall under the rule of an out-and-out dictatorship, just as it happened in Cuba, but with less effort on his part. You realize what this means, François? Expropriation and confiscation. Nationalization of business and industry. Land taken from us to be divided among the people in a reform movement, but held in his hands to do with as he pleases and when he pleases. Government monopoly of the press and communications, transportation, manufacture, shipping, importing and exporting. All turned over to his favorites who will then perpetuate his rule. Everything controlled by one madman's whims, desires, and lusts. You saw it happen in Santo Domingo under the Trujillos, in Haiti under Duvalier, now in Cuba. You see what is happening elsewhere. Foreign investment we depend on so much will, like our tourist trade, disappear. It will happen here if we do not stand up and face him, fight him."

"Henri—"

"I beseech you, François. For the family and country you love."

Courdet's face tightened with anxiety, unable to ignore Delacroix's sincere warning. "I cannot run away, Henri," he insisted.

"M'sieu," Mark said.

Both men were suddenly aware of him, turned toward him. "Yes, Mark," Courdet said politely.

"M'sieu, it will be senseless and useless to waste your life by fighting in the open and present Fontaine with a perfect target. Nor does it make sense to expose Madame Courdet to the same fate. Also, there is Marcel—"

At the mention of Angélique and Marcel, Courdet rose to his feet. "Stop it, Mark—" he began.

Delacroix stood up and grasped Courdet's shoulder in a firm grip. "François, listen to the boy! He is a realist. Even he realizes that there is no profit in your desire to die for no useful purpose. You and I, old friend, have been through much together, but we age, and perhaps our senses and reasoning have grown dim. But we have no right to hide from the truth or shun our duty. You owe it to your family, your friends, to Liberté, to live and help fight against this crazed man. Dead, you can do nothing but bring sadness to those you love, who love you. François, I plead with you—"

The passionate appeal of his oldest friend began to reach Courdet, forced again to think of his wife and son and their safety. "Angélique, yes. I can see that harm could befall her unjustly. But Marcel will not go into hiding. I know it."

Mark said: "Don't worry about Marcel, M'sieu. There are many places from which he can fight back without fear. From Terre Delacroix, for one place, and there are others. We are not without friends. But for you and Madame Courdet—"

"But where?" Courdet asked. "Where can we go that his butchers cannot seek us out?"

Henri said: "There is one place that is safest of all, François. One place where Fontaine and his men cannot dare reach for you. Asylum in the American Embassy."

"M'sieu Chance will grant this, Henri?"

"François, dear friend, he will not only permit it; he will welcome it. Inside that embassy, you will be as safe as if you were in the United States itself."

Courdet said sadly, "Let me talk it over with Angélique and Marcel."

"Papa, Mama, they are right," Marcel said. "Henri and Mark have only your best interests at heart. You will be safe in the embassy with all the might of the United States to prevent harm to you. But I cannot go with you. I must remain on the outside and help our friends to fight in any way I can to depose this man who would rule us with an iron fist around our throats."

"Angélique?" Courdet held out a hand and she put her own into it.

"They are right, François. And Marcel is right. We grow old. In our time we have fought against oppressions of many kinds, but our strength for fighting of this kind has passed. I will go with you, but you cannot persuade me to go alone. Nor can I ask Marcel to do less for Liberté now than we ourselves did for it when we were his age."

François Courdet let Angélique's hand drop and turned his back to wife and son. His head lowered, he said, "Very well. Will you make the arrangements, Marcel?"

Marcel said, "Papa, they have already been made."

At exactly 8:00 P.M. the violet-colored panel truck of Chez Martal drove through the gateway into the grounds of the Delacroix home and pulled up at the rear entrance to the house. The driver, clad in a suit of coveralls that matched the delicate color of the florist's truck, got out, went to the rear of the vehicle, opened one of the two doors, and removed a large basket of flowers, which he carried up the steps and into the house

From the shielded side of the house, François and Angélique Courdet, shepherded by their son Marcel, came out of the shadows and quickly got inside the truck. When the driver returned a few moments later, he slammed the rear door shut and got in behind the wheel. As he switched the ignition on, and without turning his head, he called out softly, "Marcel?"

"Everything is well, Alec," Marcel replied from inside.

Fletcher pulled his uniform cap down another half-inch, drove around to the front driveway, paused cautiously to allow a car to pass, then pulled into the Boulevard Mont de Couronne and turned west toward the city. The entire business, as his watch told him, had taken two minutes and thirty-one seconds to transact.

Four seconds earlier, Mark Fuller had come out of the front door with Eugénie and Julie. He kissed Julie lightly on the cheek, Eugénie's lips, then called, *"Bon nuit,"* and walked down the veranda steps to his dark gray Jaguar sedan and drove out of the grounds in the direction the panel truck would take a few moments later.

A quarter of a mile down the steep road, Alec Fletcher tapped his horn lightly once, twice, then once again. The Juguar dutifully pulled to the right and allowed the panel truck to pass. At the next side road, Fletcher pulled in at the side of the road and stopped behind a red Lancia that was parked. Mark Fuller drew the Jaguar in line, got out and opened the rear door of the panel truck. Marcel Courdet leaped out quickly. Together, he and Mark helped François and Angélique transfer to the Jaguar. Fletcher remained behind the wheel of the panel truck and kept the motor running. When he heard the rear door slam shut, he tapped his horn twice, pulled out sharply, and continued down the hill.

Mark Fuller got behind the wheel of the Jaguar, Marcel beside him. He tapped his horn once. In the red Lancia ahead of him, Jim Gerard switched on his lights and motor and started downward, the Jaguar following at a distance of five car lengths. During the transfer, no traffic had passed in either direction.

On the back seat of a nondescript Citroën that had been parked for most of the day in a driveway above the Delacroix home, a sharp-faced, swarthy man took the field glasses from his eyes and pondered over what he had just witnessed, questioned whether he should take official cognizance of this very normal event. Three times during the afternoon he had reported the arrival and departure of delivery trucks from grocer, laundry, and butcher, only to be told by Lieutenant Falot, "It is nothing, Georges," in a tone that indicated to Georges that he was something less than bright for wasting time with meaningless, normal household matters.

As the moments slipped by, Georges finally decided that, right or wrong, he would make the call. If it *were* something—

He reached for the radiotelephone beneath the dashboard, gave the operator a number, and added incisively, *"Vite, no? C'est pressant!"* Within a matter of seconds, a different male voice answered. *"Major Lamonte ici."*

The watcher reported what he had seen take place, and waited. *"Bien,* Georges," Lamonte replied. "Remain where you are. It may only be a ruse to draw you off. We will be on guard if they pass our station."

Behind the wheel of the Jaguar, Mark Fuller drove at a moderate rate of speed as he watched the outline of the Lancia ahead of him, one eye on his side-view mirror, restraining his desire to suddenly jam the accelerator down to the floorboard and defy anyone to catch or intercept him; but he was well aware of the risk to his passengers. The idea, as Jim Gerard had outlined it to them, was a matter of normalcy and timing. The true test, when it came, would come when they were within a few blocks of the embassy gates.

So far, so good. He threw a quick glance at Marcel, who nodded reassuringly, indicating that all was well with his father and mother on the rear seat. Still at a normal pace, Mark now pulled in front of the Lancia, as planned. Mont de Couronne was a wide boulevard that ran from the Champs de Révolution to the 1,500-foot crest with but a few cutoff roads that led to private homes in cul-de-sacs.

As the two cars neared the bottom of the hill, a small Fiat shot suddenly out of a private driveway and cut in between the Lancia and Jaguar, giving Mark and Marcel a moment of nervous fright. Evidently Gerard had captured the scene in his rear-view mirror. His brake lights flashed on. The Lancia stopped, and in the same movement its door flew open; but the offending intruder barreled recklessly downhill without pausing. The Lancia returned to normal speed, and the Jaguar followed, closing to three car lengths between them.

Traffic from the opposite direction was increasing. Several cars had also joined the downhill procession, but Marcel's body was turned at an angle to permit him to watch through the rear window. Thus far, all was still normal.

At the bottom of the hill, both cars turned right at the traffic circle. The traffic stream was heavier in all directions now, and neither Mark nor Marcel could know that the black Mercedes Benz, four cars behind them, had picked them up as they turned off Mont de Couronne into the circle. At the wheel was Major Constantine Lamonte. Beside him was Captain Robert Jérôme, and on the rear seat, Lieutenant Claude Falot. All were in civilian dress.

The Lancia crossed La Crillon, St. Gervais, d'Chappelle, Boulogne, and l'Hippodrome, the Jaguar directly behind it. There were now six blocks to Rue des Américains. Gerard swung into St. Denis and crossed Longchamps; but before Mark could follow across Longchamps, Marcel caught a glimpse of the black Mercedes as it turned from l'Hippodrome into St. Denis, looming larger with a sudden burst of speed. Mark, catching it in his rear-view mirror at the same moment Marcel gripped his arm, jammed his accelerator to the floorboard. The Jaguar leaped out, barely missing a bus in the intersection. They heard the angry blast of its air horn as the Jaguar shot past in front of it. The Mercedes was held up temporarily as the bus driver stopped to shout curses at the Jaguar, then turned on its red flasher to harass the bus driver further. The driver, in recognition of police authority, moved quickly ahead to clear the intersection.

Mark pulled up on the Lancia, jabbed at his horn three times, paused and repeated the three jabs, the danger signal. Up ahead, Gerard noted that the street was clear. Gerard pulled to the right sharply as Mark shot past him. On the back seat, François and Angélique felt the moisture of each other's hands, the tense tightening in themselves, suddenly recognizing that the danger had begun closing in on them. With outstretched hand and a smile, Marcel's attempt to reassure them was something less than comforting.

Gerard, eyes glued to his rear-view mirror, saw the Mercedes as it plunged through the intersection at an alarming rate of speed, red light flashing, the low growl of its siren rising to an ear-shattering howl. He swung the Lancia to his left, directly in the path of the oncoming Mercedes, heard the skidding and squealing of its tires as it veered to one side to avoid him. He stepped heavily on the accelerator and swerved to block the Mercedes again. Up ahead, he saw the Jaguar take a sharp right turn on two wheels into Rue des Américains, and disappear.

The Mercedes leaped forward again, swung left sharply, and brushed the rear right fender of the Lancia, forcing it over the low curb onto the narrow pavement. The Mercedes shook itself to a halt, backed off, and howled its way up the street, screaming and squealing after the Jaguar.

Gerard wheeled the Lancia back into the street and raced for the corner. He shot through the intersection to the next corner, made a right turn on two wheels, and sped through the deserted street until he came to the rear entrance of the embassy. At his horn signal, the gate opened and he tore through it, scraping the entire length of the car in order to miss the Marine sentry who could not get out of the way quickly enough.

On Rue des Américains, the bronze double gates leading into the embassy, flush with the street, were closed, a usual practice at sundown after the colors had been lowered. Inside the gates, and on either side, stood two sentry boxes. The two Marines on guard there heard the persistent signal of the Jaguar as Mark depressed his horn in short, furious bursts. A full block away, they saw the red flasher and heard the siren that accompanied it. From behind them, Clark Shannon and First Sergeant Walker were coming fast on the run, Walker shouting, "Open up! Open up! Let the first car through!"

The Jaguar made the swing into the shallow driveway approach to the gates. One sentry leaped forward to the heavy locking bar, staring through the slim bronze pickets into the headlights that were almost upon him. As his hand raised the bar, he heard the crash when the car struck. He leaped aside to safety just as the gates parted, sending the locking bar sailing over his head. At that point, the Jaguar stalled, the nose of its motor barely inside the grounds.

Behind it, the oncoming Mercedes screamed at full speed, the air filled with its howl and the smell of scorched rubber. When it was about three hundred feet from the Jaguar, the violet-colored panel truck shot out of the narrow side street and came directly in its path. The Mercedes veered to the right on two wheels, tires screaming as though in pain, righted itself on a grassy lawn, still rocking from side to side dangerously. It found the paved street again and headed directly for the Jaguar, seemingly out of control.

Apparently unable to stop in time, the Mercedes smashed head on into the rear of the Jaguar and drove it inside the embassy grounds. Meanwhile, the violet-colored florist's truck had disappeared.

The rear doors of the Mercedes burst open on impact. Lieutenant Falot emerged shakily, staggered forward a few steps, and leaned against the side of the car, straightened up, unholstered his pistol, and ran toward the open gateway. From the seat beside Lamonte, Captain Jérôme spilled out onto the ground, picked himself up, and stumbled forward to join Falot, only to find their passage blocked at the open gate by the Marine sergeant and two sentries who held their rifles at port arms, barring the way. Major Lamonte lay over the wheel of the Mercedes, apparently unconscious.

Above their angry, shouting protests, Walker and the two sentries prodded the armed civilians back into the street. Inside the grounds, Gerard came running up to join Shannon and two other Marines who had appeared on the scene. Together, they helped Marcel Courdet disentangle the elder Courdets from the rear floor of the Jaguar, then extricated Mark Fuller from the driving pit.

Fuller looked up at Gerard and said: "Sorry, old boy. Our timing was slightly off. They forced us ahead of schedule."

"It doesn't matter about the Courdets," Gerard told him, "but you and Marcel keep your heads down low. Do you think they might have spotted you?"

"I don't know how. They were never that close to us until they rammed us."

"Lucky for you they did; otherwise you'd still be in their territory. Keep in the shadows and get into the main building. Go along with the Courdets until our friends have left. I'll try to get rid of them and come back to you."

Once the Courdets and Mark Fuller had disappeared into safety, Shannon gave the signal and the entire front of the embassy was bathed in light. Spotlights from the gateposts were trained on the Mercedes, where the two security police were exchanging threat and insult with Walker and the two sentries, who stood their ground with firm, implacable silence. Gerard skirted the group and went to the Mercedes. When he threw the beam of his flashlight into the car, Major Lamonte looked up groggily, and blinked.

"Major, are you all right?" Gerard asked.

"I think so."

"The chase is over, Major. M'sieu and Madame Courdet are safely inside the embassy. The ambassador has granted them protective asylum."

"So," Lamonte said slowly, "the hares have eluded the hounds."

"Yes. Will you call off your two men?"

Lamonte sat up and ran a hand across his forehead. "We shall give you no further trouble, Mr. Gerard. If we are able to move the car, we will be on our way. Robert! Claude!"

The two men turned away from the gate, Falot reluctantly, and came back to the car. It was not until he saw Gerard that Falot stopped muttering to Jérôme. He averted his glance and turned toward Lamonte. "Good evening, Lieutenant," Gerard said.

Falot ignored him with stony silence. Lamonte said, "The vehicle that crossed our path as we were approaching the sedan. Did either of you see any identifying marks on it?"

Jérôme shook his head negatively. Falot said: "No, Major. It came too suddenly. I had my eyes on the sedan."

"Eh. Then I am afraid the entire evening has been profitless." He turned the ignition key. The motor turned over, sputtered, and died. On the next attempt, it caught and held. Lamonte put the car in reverse. The motor shuddered and died again. Falot and Jérôme went to the front of the car and tugged the left fender outward where it was biting into the tire. Gerard picked up a part of the front bumper that had dropped off and put it in the rear compartment. Both headlights were smashed and the radiator was dented badly, but it was not leaking. Lamonte started the motor again and backed off. He turned on the roof spotlight and centered it on the road ahead, then ordered Falot and Jérôme inside. The car turned and began moving slowly up the street.

"Good night, gentlemen," Gerard said.

Lamonte nodded. Falot's mouth opened as if in response, then closed. He settled for a malevolent glare at Gerard.

By nine-ten the elder Courdets were settled in a third-floor suite in the embassy with the Chances and Truscotts doing everything to make them comfortable. Marcel had refused Truscott's offer of asylum, and left to meet Mark and Gerard at the rear of the grounds where the red Lancia was parked.

Three blocks away on the parking lot of the darkened Trans-Oceanique Shipping Company building, they found the violet-colored truck and pulled up beside it. Alec stepped out of the doorway of the building and greeted them. The overalls and uniform cap he had worn earlier were lying on the seat of the truck; Alec was in his normal dark business suit.

Mark declined Gerard's offer to drive him and Marcel back to Terre Delacroix in the embassy Ford. "There's no need, Jim," he said confidently.

"What about the checkpoint? Falot will have notified every station to be on the lookout for this Lancia."

"We won't be in the Lancia. I'll pick up another car and leave the Lancia in a safe place. The friend who delivered it to you tonight has already reported it stolen as of eight-thirty. There are only two checkpoints to pass, the one out of Port Amitié and at Maréchal. It's simple. I drop Marcel before we reach them. While I am being checked, he circles around on foot and I pick him up on the other side. It's done all the time. Thanks for everything, Jim. I'll keep in touch with you."

Mark and Marcel drove off in the Lancia. Alec and Gerard walked the three blocks back to the embassy. The panel truck would remain on the parking lot overnight until Lebrun would have Martal's driver pick it up. The Jaguar had been pushed into the grounds and stood in front of the motor pool. When they reached the Ford on the embassy parking lot, Gerard said, "Well, that was a pretty fair warm-up, wasn't it?"

Alec laughed. "How about that Lamonte ramming the Jag through the gates?"

"If he were on our team, it couldn't have come off neater. It was a mighty close shave at that." They got into the car, and Gerard said, "Your friend M'sieu Falot wasn't exactly happy about the whole thing."

"That's another one he'll add to the revenge score. I'd like to have seen his face."

"It wasn't pretty. Where to now?"

"How about dropping me at No. 11. I've got to get myself ready for my next character part."

"All right, Alec. I'm going to cruise around for a bit before I turn in. I might even drive up to the Club and decompress myself with a drink or two to celebrate. Sure you won't come along?"

"I think not. I've had enough for one evening."

5.

At the Club, Gerard found only a few cars on the parking lot, the one he sought not among them. Inside, the bar was virtually deserted, the lights in the game and reading rooms turned off for lack of patrons. He had a double Scotch at the bar. Only four tables in the main dining room were occupied; on the veranda, a man and woman sat in rocking chairs over their drinks, looking down on the quiet city, officially in mourning for Charles Du Faure. Gerard ordered another drink, then left the dreary atmosphere.

As he passed the palace, there was less than the normal heavy traffic on the Champs. A larger number of pedestrians strolled past the ghostly building, staring at it with curiosity. Others stood across the parkway, looking up at the balcony where Du Faure had been so dramatically assassinated. The sentries in front of the gates wore black armbands, and two black streamers trailed from the muzzles of their rifles. Atop the darkened building, the flag flew at half-mast, startlingly bright in the light of several rooftop spotlights.

Purely from instinct, Gerard checked his rear-view mirror as he made a turn or pulled out of one lane into another. It wasn't until he was three or four blocks beyond the palace that he caught a glimpse of a familiar shape, the sweeping tailfins of— He shot ahead suddenly, pulled sharply into the right lane, and slowed down behind a Renault, watching the rear-view mirror. There it was again. The black Plymouth pulled out to pass two cars, then cut into the lane behind a passenger bus and a Fiat directly behind the Ford.

Falot. Gerard changed his mind about going back to No. 11 Rue Perrigeau. He crossed left to the center lane, and when he was certain the Plymouth had followed, swung into the extreme left lane, showing no undue haste. At Rue Centrale, he turned off the Champs into Charlemagne, then into Place Maraboux. The Plymouth followed at a cautious distance. Gerard cut his speed to allow the tail to come closer, hoping to see if there were more than one man in the car, but the Plymouth cagily kept the same distance between them, another car between them when possible.

Gerard decided then to branch off into a street or road where the traffic was more sparse. He stepped on the accelerator and pulled into the next crossing and turned sharply to his right, a dimly lit residential street. As he passed the light pole, he caught the name on the plaque —Rue Blanche, recalling at once that this was the street where Nora shared a small house with Sarah Bennett. The street began to rise sharply, and he felt the motor drop back into a lower gear. The number of Nora's house. What was it? Then he remembered: 717. He looked out and saw a number on a closed gate: 113.

And then he saw the headlights of the Plymouth as it turned into Rue Blanche, a block behind him. He speeded up, watching the numbers on the gates; the 100 series, then the 200, 300. Keep going, or make a break for 717? If Rue Blanche, like so many of these hilly streets, led into a blind cul-de-sac, he would be trapped. If he made a fight for it, the embassy would no doubt become involved in the matter and—well, he thought now, there goes the old ball game. He made his decision.

At 701, he was ready. The car behind him was closing the distance between them. No. 709, 711, 713. Gerard braked the car to a quick stop, leaped out on the right side, felt himself falling into the drainage ditch beside the road. He didn't hear the shot, but felt the slug whistle past him, then the jarring tug of the second as it ripped into his upper left sleeve, just below the shoulder. Rifle, he thought. Rifle shots, and with someone on the business end of it who knows how to use it. At least one more besides the driver.

He landed in the bottom of the ditch and was lying face down in slimy ooze, stones, and branches, listening for the sound of the motor. He heard it somewhere above him, going away. A second or two later he heard the clash of gears and realized that it had pulled into a driveway, was backing out, and would come downhill searching for him. Then Gerard began to feel the numbness in his upper left arm, the burning sensation around the edges of the wound. Using his right arm and elbow, he began to crawl uphill toward the wooden overpass that bridged the ditch into the entrance to No. 717.

The motor growl ceased and there was an awful silence. He remembered the old feeling of being hunted. He got to his knees and felt for the service revolver in his shoulder holster, loosened it, and rose in a crouch, careful to keep his head below the rim of the ditch. Now his upper left arm was beginning to stiffen, and he could feel the blood-soaked sleeve of his jacket plastered to his arm, the warm wetness of his own blood running down his arm.

Gerard got the revolver out of its holster and pushed his gun hand into the dirt wall to help him up. Still crouching cautiously, he peered over the rim; as his eyes cleared the edge, he saw the Plymouth parked on the opposite side of the road, now facing downhill. The few lights he had seen in the surrounding houses while driving up Rue Blanche were now blacked out. Few people, he knew, would be curious enough to risk possible involvement in an affair that did not concern them.

As his eyes grew accustomed to the dim light from the pole some twenty yards below them, Gerard saw the protruding rifle muzzle moving along the ledge of the rear side window, obviously searching for him; and he knew that if he did nothing, it was likely that someone would get out of the car and come looking for him. He raised his revolver over the brim, took aim at a point some three feet behind the moving rifle muzzle, and fired twice, silently blessing the inventor of the flashless, noiseless device. He saw the rifle muzzle jerk upward, heard muffled shouts or curses, saw the muzzle come down again. The man behind the wheel twisted around and pointed in the general direction of the ditch. Gerard ducked low for safety as two more shots came winging over his head, the first too far to the right, the second too far to the left. He raised up and fired twice again, heard the metallic slap as one bullet buried itself into the body of the car, then the light tinkle of broken glass. The marksman called out loudly to the driver as he pumped four more shots that spat viciously into the earth behind Gerard. And then he heard the motor as it caught, the growl of gears as the Plymouth began to move downhill. Gerard stood up. Two more rifle shots splatted erratically nearby in angry defiance, and as a parting salute Gerard fired his last two shots into the back end of the Plymouth before it disappeared from sight.

He sank to his knees again, overly tired and slightly nauseated. The burning in his arm increased. He shook his head to clear it, then began crawling toward the wooden overpass again. When he reached it, he shoved the revolver into his waistband and put a hand up to the jagged tear of his jacket. Then the gate to No. 717 opened slightly and a small head poked out nervously, pulled back, and spoke to someone behind him. The gate was thrown open wider, and Gerard looked up and saw Nora standing over him, startled and pale. She bent over and called out: "Who is it? Who is down there?"

"It's me, Nora, Jim."

"Jim! Are you hurt?" She was on her knees now, holding his right hand. "Isidor! Isidor!" she called anxiously to the small man. "Quickly!" The man reappeared and fell to his knees beside her. "Help me, Isidor. He is a friend. He is hurt."

Isidor leaped nimbly into the ditch and put his shoulders to Gerard's buttocks and raised himself as Nora hugged his chest and pulled upward. Once on the narrow wooden overpass, Gerard stood up, somewhat shakily, using Isidor's offered body for support.

"It's all right, Nora," he said. "I can make it fine now."

"Let's get inside quickly."

"There's no danger now. They've gone."

"Your arm, Jim." His left sleeve was soaked with blood, some of it dripping from his fingers. "Hurry!"

In the kitchen, Nora helped Gerard out of his jacket, unstrapped and removed the shoulder holster, and cut away his shirt sleeve while the basin of water was heating on the stove. Isidor handed Gerard a stiff drink of rum and called for someone named Tina, who came shuffling in with several towels. She stood to one side with Isidor, watching with fascinated interest as Nora cleaned the angry-looking four-inch-long furrow, then bandaged and taped it. She made a sling for his arm, then told Isidor to pour another drink for Gerard. "It's not bad, Jim," she said. "Thank God the bullet isn't somewhere inside you. But it should be looked after."

As though he were reading her mind, he said: "No doctor, Nora. You've done fine. Remind me to order a Florence Nightingale merit badge for you."

"Let me call Dr.—"

"Please, Nora, no."

"How does it feel?"

"Stiff as a board." He handed the empty glass to Isidor and got to his feet slowly, Nora's arm supporting him. He examined his muddied, bloodied trousers and grinned ruefully. "I'm a first class 100 per cent mess. How about giving me a lift home? My car is parked outside, but I don't think I can handle it with one arm."

"I think you'd better rest for a while, Jim," Nora urged. "Tina and Isidor can clean your shoes and do something about your suit. I'm afraid there isn't much we can do for your shirt—"

"Okay, I'm sold. Where's Sarah?"

"She took Suzanne and two of the other girls to the USIA library in my car. They're showing a Parisian movie, and the girls are trying to improve their conversational French. Luckily, I wasn't in the mood. She should be back in another hour."

"What time is it now?"

"Almost ten-thirty. Let's get you out of the rest of your clothes, and I'll start Tina and Isidor working on them."

In her bedroom, Isidor helped Gerard undress. Nora sent Tina with a large beach towel, and when he had

217

wrapped himself in it Nora came back with a large basin of hot water.

"Now, you lie back and relax and let the women take over," she ordered. Tina was already peeling back the upper part of the towel and began washing away the dried blood and caked mud. When they had finished his bed bath, Tina was sent away to help Isidor. Nora sat on the edge of the bed.

"You could stay here for the night, Jim. I can double up with Sarah. It would be much better that way. You won't have to move around so much, and I'll be able to dress the wound in the morning. You can't do it by yourself."

"How about Sarah? I can't afford to let Truscott or the ambassador find out about this."

"Don't worry about Sarah. She'll be on your side."

"How about a cigarette?"

She lighted one and handed it to him. "Would you want me to call Alec and tell him about this?"

"I think not. Alec has his hands full for the moment. He'll need this night of sleep."

"Jim, can you tell me what it's about?"

"Off the record?"

"Off the record."

He told her of the Courdet escape into asylum and the irony of a security police car actually having effected their dramatic delivery at the very last moment. "If the Mercedes hadn't rammed the Jag through the gate, there could have been some nasty complications."

"After I'd warned you—Jim, you're incorrigible."

"Nora, I'm sorry, but there wasn't much of an alternative. If they'd tried to make it on their own, the Courdets would be tucked away somewhere in one of Batraville's private cells, and nobody could have done a thing for them then. But all's well that ends well, isn't it?"

"Did it really end so well? If so, who tried to kill you just now? Who knew you were coming here tonight?"

"That part was pure coincidence. I'm sure it was Falot, looking for some way to pay me back for the incident with Alec, now with the Courdets. I don't know exactly where he picked me up. I was trying to lead him off onto a quiet street and got onto Rue Blanche accidentally. Once on it, I didn't know if it ended in a cul-de-sac or not. Then I remembered you lived here, and gambled on getting into No. 717 before he could get to me. What's at the top end of Rue Blanche?"

"A cul-de-sac."

Gerard grinned. "I made the best choice."

"Jim——"

"I was careless. It happens that way sometimes. Don't let it worry you, Nora. I'll be on my toes from now on."

"You could have been killed out there. Doesn't that worry you?"

"It could, but I can't afford to let it."

"It's your *life*, Jim. Are you so ready to die that the possibility of death doesn't matter to you?" She took the inch of cigarette from him and ground it out in the tray with angry stabs.

"If I could believe it matters that much to you," Gerard began, but she had swung around to face him, her green eyes flashing. "Does caring for your own life hinge on how much it matters to me? Or to anyone else?"

"In a way, yes, Nora."

"Jim, I can't believe that. I——"

"Listen to me, Nora. Please." She began an angry retort, then compressed her lips tightly. "Thanks. Will you light another cigarette for me?"

She lighted the cigarette and put it between his outstretched fingers. "You smoke too much, you know. You weren't always a chain smoker."

Gerard drew on the cigarette and laughed softly. "What's so darned funny about that?" she asked.

"Not funny, Irish. Nice. Maybe I like the idea of you being concerned whether I get killed by a bullet or by nicotine. I haven't had anybody worrying or caring about me since——" The laugh faded, and the sentence hung unfinished in the air.

"Don't——"

"To be exact," he continued, "since the day after that night in Charlottesville. I remember that I asked you to marry me. You were reluctant. I asked you again the next night in Washington. You were worried that I wouldn't be able to find anything I'd like as much as what I was doing. You thought we should think it over before we decided. The next morning my job took the decision away from both of us. It was there waiting for me when I reported in, the assignment they'd been setting me up for. When I called you that noon, I didn't know how long I'd be away, or that I'd be buried somewhere behind lines where

I couldn't get word out to you. When I came back, you were gone. I tried to trace you, and couldn't. There was another assignment waiting and there wasn't any reason left why I shouldn't stay on."

"It wasn't all my fault, Jim. Don't blame—"

"Let's not talk about fault or blame, Nora. It was one of life's bad breaks. But there have been good ones, too. Like finding you here in Port Amitié."

"Four years and one husband later," she said, and he felt the heaviness in her words, something akin to reproachfulness.

"Nora, don't—"

"I waited, Jim," she said hollowly, the words seeming to come from some distant far-off place. "I died waiting. I felt like a scrap of paper caught in a rainstorm, flying in any direction the wind takes it, beaten, wet, unable to fight clear—"

"Nora, darling, please. You're only torturing—"

"Maybe I need to so I can forget it. You were very special to me, Jim. Someone strong whom I needed, and yet, someone who needed me. Bill Noyes warned me the night he introduced us. He said you'd been living in a woman-proof world for so long you were girl-shy. A quiet-living, female-uncomplicated man, were his exact words, but I didn't let that stop me. I set out deliberately to make you fall in love with me. And it finally happened. I knew it, but you didn't.

"So I let circumstances take over. A crowded town, a motel on a road with only one room. And a double bed. And a shabby old woman with her hair in curlers with the key to that room became my fairy godmother. I remember how guilty you looked when you told her we'd take the room, as though it were your own, private idea. But it worked, and the next day you asked me to marry you. You were ready to give up a job that meant so much, change your whole life, to sell—what was it, Jim?— vacuum cleaners, insurance? It sounded so horrible and cheap. And then I began to feel guilty for having cheated you.

"A day after you'd gone, I knew I'd have married you on any terms to have you back again. But it was too late. I didn't even know where or whom to call to find out if you were still alive—"

Gerard saw the tears begin to glisten in her eyes as she spoke, and he took one of her hands into his own.

"Nora," he said contritely, "what did I do to you? I wanted the same things—"

She went on as though he hadn't spoken, unashamed, compulsively, not looking at him. "I wasn't in love with Braden Lund, Jim. You may as well know that, too. I was lonely. Desperately lonely. When you left, the bottom dropped out of my world. Month after month without a word from you. I wanted to leave Washington, but I couldn't. I kept saying there would be a letter the next day, a message the day after, or a phone call after that. And then almost a whole year had passed. Somewhere around that time, Braden Lund came back to Washington from Buenos Aires for a leave of absence and reassignment. He was an older man, a widower. And he was kind and understanding and gentle—"

"Nora, please, you don't—"

"No, let me finish, Jim. This isn't out of. guilt. I'm sure Braden suspected that I didn't love him the way he might have expected or wanted, but he was lonely, too. He didn't ask for too much beyond companionship with another lonely person. And he was happy during the time we were together. At least, I was able to give him that much. It was—a great loss—to me when he died."

There was an awkward silence between them for a few moments; then Gerard said, "How long does your assignment here run, Nora? And where to next?"

"It was a two-year assignment. I've been here nearly eighteen months. Next? I don't know. I haven't even given it a thought. What about yours?"

"I'm due for a change from active line duty. Harrington wants me back in Washington. Richards is retiring, and I've been tabbed for his job as assistant to the deputy director. It means a permanent spot in Washington."

"Are you going to accept?"

Gerard seemed to be thinking over his reply. After a few moments, he said: "I've wanted it. I expected it after the Cuba assignment. Now I don't know."

"I don't understand, Jim."

"I don't know if I can explain and make it sound logical, because you've suddenly become involved with it. I don't mean to be talking in circles, Nora, but if there's the slightest chance that I can make up for what I've lost, I'd like to know it. If there isn't, you'll make it easier for me to decide on the future."

"I'd still have to know how you feel about your job, Jim. If you could really give up the danger part of it."

"I was ready to give it up after Cuba."

"But you took on this assignment instead."

"Only because it was an extension of the Cuban thing. And I found you—"

"You didn't take it because you knew I was here, Jim. That was an accident. You're married to danger, aren't you?"

"No, Nora, don't think that. I hate it."

"You didn't always hate it. You loved it."

"No. I've never loved it. Something—I don't know myself just what—drew me into it. You can speculate all you want on the death-wish theory, but to me it was a job that needed to be done. They had men like me on their side, and we needed their counterparts on our side. I remember Dix Harrington saying, 'Gerard, you'll learn it's not a popular profession when there isn't a hot war going on, but if the capable people like you won't come forward to do the job, why should anyone else concern themselves?'

"I'd never seen real combat, only the cold war. Or the phony peace. Subversives. Infiltrators. Saboteurs. Defectors. And the need for someone to spotlight them, uncover them, yes, and even murder them before they split us apart from our allies and overran us. Call it what you want, patriotic brainwashing, if you will, but the job is there and still needs doing. If we stop, we'll be steamrollered to death.

"But, like any job, there comes a time when a man outlives his usefulness in the field. Maybe Harrington saw something I was only beginning to feel—that I needed to be brought in from the field—when he offered me the Washington assignment."

"If I'd known all this—" Nora began.

"I couldn't tell you then, Nora. I couldn't tell you a lot of things. The service is publicity-shy. We don't expect medals or public acclaim, and we get none. I don't like to remember some of the things I've had to do to survive, but this isn't an Olympic sport we're playing. Some day, I hope I can forget that part of it, believe me, Nora."

"But if it—like tonight—before you can quit, it—"

"Catches up with me? That's the chance everyone takes, isn't it? Who ever really knows the right time to quit a job, take one, buy a certain stock or sell it, walk away from a poker game, buy a house, plant a crop, get married—or make so many other decisions that face men and women every day of their lives? Everything, life itself, is a gamble. Like a man who comes through a war without a scratch and gets killed in a traffic accident within sight of his own home."

In the brief silence that followed, both had become conscious that their hands were linked tightly together. Nora said, "Jim, are you seriously considering the Washington assignment?"

"Will you believe me if I tell you that whether I accept or not depends on you?" Something in what he said caused him to laugh briefly as he added, "As lefthanded as that may have sounded, it's the second proposal of marriage I've ever made. And to the same girl."

Nora leaned forward without hesitation and said, "If it means we can be together, Jim, yes. Yes. Gladly."

His body arched upward toward her. He felt the lightning stab of pain in his left arm, and winced. Nora pushed him back gently and leaned down over him, found his lips with her own. He cradled her in the circle of his right arm and held her tightly, feeling the warmth and perfume of her yielding body, remembering—"Nora, Nora darling, I'll make up every lost hour, every minute—"

"We'll make it up together, Jim."

"Now that it's here, I can't wait, Nora. I've been so long without you, too long—"

Nora burrowed closer to him, careful of his immobilized arm. "Jim, I'll hurt you—"

"I won't feel it—"

"It's too risky. Tina—she never knocks on a door—"

"Nora—"

"Jim—be careful. Oh, Jim, I love you so much—"

And then, above their whisperings, they heard the car motor and the horn signal for Isidor to unbar the gate. Nora pulled away reluctantly, heard Gerard's whispered "Damn!"

"That's Sarah. Leave her to me." Quickly, she arranged her hair and applied fresh lipstick.

"Nora, about us. You'll break it to Truscott and the ambassador, won't you? No stalling?"

"At the proper time. Leave that to me, too, you idiot." She turned back to him, whirled around in a complete circle joyously, and laughed with sheer happiness, then leaned over and touched her lips to his lightly, brushed a finger over his mouth. "That is, if you're lucky enough to live through this last assignment," she said in sober afterthought.

"I will, darling," Gerard promised, believing it. "You'd better keep repeating that to yourself over and over again."

6.

In the long, narrow conference room next morning, Ray Ferriss outlined the official embassy version of the Courdet escape into asylum. François Courdet sat at the table beside him and nodded as he listened to the press officer give the curt details to the seven press representatives present. During the brief question period, Ferriss, in his solemn voice, merely repeated the statements he had made earlier.

"Will Ambassador Chance resist any goverment efforts to gain the release of the Courdets?" the *Times* correspondent asked.

"As the ambassador has stated, we do not anticipate any such violation of existing conventions," Ferriss replied.

"But if—" The question came again in another form.

"In that event, as I have stated previously, we shall act to prevent such an action."

"Mr. Ferriss, may we question M'sieu Courdet directly?" the New York *News* man asked.

"You may. If M'sieu Courdet pleases not to answer a question, he must not be subjected to—harassment."

The *Picayune* man said in a whisper to the *Globe* man, "What a flake, that Ferriss."

The *Globe* man chuckled. "And he complains about Fontaine's Ministry of Misinformation."

François Courdet answered the questions put to him in short, flat statements, as though he were completely disinterested in the entire proceedings. Yes. He had requested asylum for himself and Mme. Courdet because he believed their lives were in danger.

From whom?

From powerful opposition political forces.

President Fontaine?

M'sieu Fontaine, he replied, emphasizing the *M'sieu,* was not at the moment President, but the former President, a civilian without official powers or connection with the government.

Had M'sieu Courdet been threatened by M'sieu Fontaine?

Not publicly.

If privately, under what circumstances?

Courdet refused to answer the question.

And Mme. Courdet?

A shrug.

Is your son at present in Port Amitié?

Another meaningless shrug.

Do you know where your son is?

Ferriss interrupted. "Please, gentlemen. M'sieu Courdet will not answer the question."

Would M'sieu Courdet now enter the race for the presidency?

Very definitely yes, if permitted.

At the end of the conference, the photographers had their moment while an assistant to Ray Ferriss handed out mimeographed copies of Ambassador Chance's statement to each correspondent. The brief show was over.

CHAPTER 7

1.

In Louis Fontaine's office, General Benoit Batraville and Major Constantine Lamonte stood stiffly at attention before the masssive desk while Fontaine, with little attempt to restrain his anger, held forth. *"C'est une affaire maladresse,"* he snapped caustically at his chief of security. "You permitted them to escape. They were in your hands, and all you needed was to close your fingers into a fist. You had knowledge of their whereabouts at all times. Your agents had them under surveillance. You were notified when they left the Delacroix house. And yet you allowed them to escape into safety with the Americans." Unable to control himself further, he burst out with, "Fools! Idiots! How can I have faith and trust in men of such incompetency?"

"Your Excellency," Batraville pleaded sadly, "it was unavoidable. It is true we had them under our eyes. Even when they emerged, they were under observation. It was our intention to apprehend them in the act of defection. Major Lamonte had them within range of capture as they drew closer to the embassy, but a drunken *imbécile* pulled in front and blocked his path. Lamonte rammed the car out of the way, but it was too late. They—"

"Enough! Enough! I know what they did. I am not interested in your elaborate explanations of failure, General. Why were you not personally in charge? You knew how important this was to me. Courdet represents a personal threat as long as he remains free. You had him in your hands and permitted him to escape. That is the essence of your failure. Now he is not only free, but a symbol of martyrdom to my enemies."

In the heavy silence, Lamonte said, "Your Excellency, as General Batraville has explained, it was an unavoidable situation. Captain Jérôme and Lieutenant Falot were witness to—"

226

"M'sieu le major," Fontaine growled, "do not belabor the point. I am neither interested in your explanations nor in those of your subordinates." He stood up and skewered both men with a single glance. "In the past, gentlemen, I have rewarded you for your successes. Therefore, you must be prepared to receive the penalties of your failures."

Batraville's face turned a shade grayer. Lamonte stood rigidly at attention, staring over Fontaine's head as the rebuke was delivered. "And what success, General, have you to report of Chalumeau?" Fontaine taunted. "You have had complete freedom, at great cost and much time, to organize and establish a chain of communications throughout the country. You have openly boasted that you are privy to the conversations of the commandants of every military post, that you have eyes and ears in every potential trouble zone. Then why, General, Major, can your ears and eyes not detect the presence and voice of this Chalumeau who is able to come and go at will?" He pounded the desk with his fist as he asked the question and demanded, "Why? *Why?*"

Batraville's agony was monumental, aggravated by the presence of Lamonte. Beads of perspiration gathered at his hairline and began to roll down his forehead. "Your Excellency—"

"Not a day goes by that I do not hear of new signs that he has visited and inflamed a mountain village, a valley of fieldworkers. Even in the Pénitentiaire prisoners speak hopefully of him, await his coming to set them free, as though he were the Christ himself. His agents mingle with your agents to lure them to his side. Some have defected and become *his* agents. *Do you know of this, General?*" Fontaine asked with heavy sarcasm. "*Do you?*"

"I have heard—" Batraville's futile effort was cut off with Fontaine's bitter indictment. "*You have heard!* Then why was what you have heard not included in your private daily reports to me? Why have I had to learn from others of your incredible deficiencies?"

Batraville remained mute with helplessness. Never before had Fontaine lashed him so mercilessly. The angry man sat down again, his voice probing like a knife, seeking a new and more sensitive spot. "And have you heard also the names of his agents, *mon cher espion extraordinaire?* Let me recite them for you: M'sieu Flèche. M'sieu

Couteau. M'sieu Harpon. M'sieu Poignard. M'sieu Epée. You recognize these *faux noms,* these aliases behind which they hide? Arrow. Knife. Spear. Dagger. Sword. Instruments of death! *Assassination! Revolution!* Lightning rages, and you do not see. Thunder roars, and you cannot hear."

Again the heavy silence in the room. Then: "I warn you, General, Major, the time grows short. If I cannot depend upon your resourcefulness, I will be forced to move outside for help. If it is necessary for me to do that, and I will do it reluctantly, I will be forced to depose you. You have little time left, gentlemen. I want Chalumeau and I want the Courdets. Deliver them to me or else—"

"Your Excellency—" It was the pleading of Batraville.

"I will hear no more. Get out now and busy yourself with these two simple problems. I have many more of greater importance to consider. I will speak with you again later, but remember my words well. You are dismissed."

As the men turned to leave, Fontaine was speaking into the intercom box on his desk. To his secretary in the outer office he said, "Tell the American ambassador I am engaged and cannot see him. Ask him to see M'sieu St. Germaine."

2.

In the privacy of his own office, an embittered Batraville writhed with the indignity he had suffered at the hands of Fontaine, his face pinched with rage at the thought of Lamonte a witness to his disgrace. He could also expect that Lénore would soon hear of his fall from high estate, and this further humiliation was even harder to bear; he who had boasted of his expert handling of the Cuban arms arrangement, of Fontaine's total dependency on himself. Now she would see him as a floundering bungler.

First, Chalumeau.

Now, the Courdet affair.

I will be forced to move outside for help. . . . depose you. . . .

The feeling of defeat weighed heavily on the general. If he refused Pyantenov's proposal, what then? The "outside help" Fontaine had spoken of was, of course, Russian help. If he, Batraville, turned a deaf ear to Pyantenov, the Russians would have no choice but to deal with Fontaine. As in Cuba, they would come in with their "technicians" and "instructors," infiltrate every strategic garrison, the Army General Staff, the Defense and Security establishment, the very palace itself. Key men would be shipped off to Moscow for training, to return as Marxist theorists and slaves to a new ideology. Fontaine, like Castro, would remain a captive puppet, true; but for himself, what?

The choice was still his to make. Pyantenov had given him until midnight. If he accepted or not, Liberté would still become a part of their Caribbean Curtain. The difference, if he acquiesced, would be that he, and not Louis Fontaine, would become president.

The throne of a puppet, or oblivion. Choose by midnight.

He thought again of Pyantenov and Vossolofsky. A complicated and confusing people. Which, in fact, was master here; the bland, smiling ambassador or the reptilian-eyed "commercial attaché" who commanded polite silence from the ambassador when he spoke and controlled the thread of their entire conversation?

The whole affair had an aura of evil about it, yet the proposal was exhilarating to contemplate. A power more absolute than Fontaine had ever imagined. Let the Americans rant and rave; they would no more risk total nuclear war over Liberté than Russia had over Cuba. It was tempting. Too tempting to dismiss. He remembered the grubby Pyantenov's words, "You are a mere policeman now, General," then, quoting Aristotle, " 'States decree the most illustrious rewards, not to him who catches a thief, but to him who kills a tyrant.' "

Never before had he imagined himself beyond his present rank or status, but now the presidency of the republic was being held out to him. And why not? he thought. There is no true head of state to overthrow. If it happens before Fontaine is re-elected, I will simply be stepping in to take over a leaderless government just as Fontaine did in 1958. Who could find fault with that?

And Lénore. He envisioned himself now as president with Lénore standing beside him in the receiving line, sitting at his table as hostess to the government and diplomatic colony, willing and eager to please him not only as a man but as head of state—

The telephone rang. Clinging to the invigorating theme of his dreams, Batraville ignored the instrument. It rang again and he paid no attention, irritated by its soft but persistent and disturbing intrusion. Then the rapping on the door; louder now.

"What is it?" he called out.

The door opened and admitted Sergeant Lescaux. "General—"

"Did I not tell you I was not to be disturbed?" Batraville barked waspishly. "What is it?"

"A gentleman to see you, General. He says it is a matter of utmost importance and must see you personally."

"Tell him I am engaged. Send him to Major Lamonte. Or Lieutenant Falot."

"The major is not in his office, General, nor is Lieutenant Falot in his. The gentleman insists you will be angry if I do not tell you he is here. He said to speak the word 'Flèche' to you."

Batraville bolted into an upright position, electrified by the word. "Send him in and see that we are not disturbed. Not for anyone. If there is a telephone call, I am not in my office. You understand, Sergeant?"

"Yes, General." Lescaux went to the door, nodded to the man in the outer office, and stood to one side as he entered, then backed out, closing the door. Batraville sat eyeing the man from between narrowly slitted eyes, a man at ease, smiling, dangling a soft straw hat from one hand. His visitor was burned a deep color by much exposure to the sun, his face lean and severe, with small, alert eyes that looked out from under wide hoods, his mouth thin-lipped over a jutting chin. His chest was broad and his belly flat, a formidable man in good physical trim. He wore a dark suit that hung loosely from his angular frame. It was his eyes that held the general's attention: cold, piercing, unafraid; tinged with confidence —perhaps arrogance—despite the thin smile. He stood waiting for Batraville to speak.

"You are familiar to me, M'sieu," Batraville said finally. "We have met before, have we not?"

The man took three steps forward and replied, "My name, General, is—"

Before he could utter it, Batraville's fingers snapped. He brought his hand down on the desk in a flat slap, a gesture of minor triumph to his memory. "Duclosse! Paul—no, Pierre Duclosse!"

230

The man's smile broadened into a wider grin, but the look in his eyes did not change. "Yes, General. Pierre Duclosse."

Batraville leaned over his desk and spoke into his intercom set. "Lescaux! Bring me the file on one Pierre Duclosse. The labor leader imprisoned—" He looked up questioningly.

"In 1956," Duclosse said. "There are earlier records—"

"In 1956," Batraville repeated into the intercom, and flipped the lever down again. "Be seated, M'sieu Duclosse."

Duclosse sat in the chair Batraville indicated beside his desk. "I am interested deeply in your visit, M'sieu. You are here of your own accord?"

"Not entirely, General. A certain gentleman suggested that a talk between us could be mutually beneficial."

"Which gentleman?"

"I am not at liberty to disclose his name at this moment. Perhaps later."

The Russians, Batraville thought. "For the moment, I withdraw the question. Now I am interested in the name you spoke to the sergeant. Flèche. What can you tell me about him?"

"Ah, M'sieu—*pardon, Général*—it was but a device to gain admission to see you privately. The one I wish to speak of is known as—Chalumeau."

"Chalumeau!" The word escaped Batraville's lips like a lover's caress. "What can you tell me of M'sieu Chalumeau?"

"First, a question. There is a reward for his apprehension, is there not?"

"One hundred and fifty thousand francs."

"Ah. It is a small reward for so important—"

"It may seem so to you, Duclosse," Batraville said with a sign of impatience. "But, as you also know, to withhold information from the security police is a punishable offense."

"General, I have come here to be helpful. Let us not speak of punishable offenses, eh?"

Batraville regarded Duclosse coldly, then smiled. He pushed the pack of Chevaliers toward the confident visitor with the tip of his riding crop. Duclosse took one and lighted it. Sergeant Lescaux knocked and re-entered the room apologetically, handed a thick file to Batraville, and went out again. Batraville opened the file and leafed through its multicolored pages quickly and with visible satisfaction. He closed the file and looked up. "Very well, Duclosse. Now we shall discuss M'sieu Chalumeau. Where can I find him?"

Duclosse shrugged noncommittally, and Batraville showed signs of short-fused impatience. Play your little game, Duclosse, he thought, but before you leave here I will know everything you know else you will not have an inch of skin left on your body. This time I will not be put off. "Well?" he snapped.

"I do not know at this moment, General," Duclosse said evasively, "but I believe I have the means to arrange a—uh—meeting."

"I wish to take him. Quickly. And personally."

"That will not be an easy matter, as the general knows. If I may be permitted an observation, your security police have been less than *qui-vive*—"

Still smarting under Fontaine's verbal lashing, Batraville stirred uncomfortably. "We will dispense with your observations concerning my men in the field. Get on with it, man."

"General, I believe I can arrange to put M'sieu Chalumeau in your hands within a reasonably short time."

"Then you must indeed be close to him. Are you Flèche?"

"I?" Duclosse laughed aloud. "No, General. Flèche is one of his many lieutenants. But you are correct in one sense. I have been close to Chalumeau in the past. I will hold nothing back from you. If you will examine your files again, you will see that during my last imprisonment I was assigned to road camp No. 17 at Romizeau. Later, Chalumeau was assigned to the same camp. We were old friends, and I used persuasion on the sergeant of the guard to have him chained beside me. For many months we worked, ate, and slept side by side. Also, we talked much."

"I accept your word, Duclosse. Do you speak for Chalumeau?"

"No one speaks for Chalumeau but Chalumeau, General."

"Then what is the thing you are proposing?"

"That for a consideration I can arrange to bring you face to face with him. However," Duclosse added hastily, "I must be assured that no harm will come to him."

"And would you accept my assurance if I gave it to you?"

"In this case, I think yes. The gentleman who sent me to see you suggested that the meeting would be held privately, at some place convenient for him, or one of his associates, to be present. The gentleman of whom I speak is M'sieu Pyantenov."

Batraville studied Duclosse, now understanding the reason for his feeling of confidence. "I give you my assurance. When can you arrange the matter?"

"It will not be easy, General. The details must be carefully worked out. Certainly, Chalumeau will be reluctant to come to you voluntarily. He has reasons enough to be, eh, distrustful of the police and military. Yet there is the consideration—" Duclosse hesitated with an expressive shrug.

"How much?"

"For now, half the reward? 75,000 francs?"

"Let us first examine how you will arrange to deliver him into my hands. If your plan pleases me, you will receive 25,000 francs as an advance against the day Chalumeau and I come face to face."

Duclosse gone, Batraville's earlier black mood had changed to one of exhilaration. In the outer office, Sergeant Lescaux looked up as the general went to the long row of gray files and began to search through them. Lescaux said, "Can I be of help to the general?"

"No, Sergeant," Batraville replied with a rare smile, "this is something I wish to do for myself. A labor of love, one might say," he added cryptically.

Lescaux sat silently at his desk, watching closely as Batraville's examination of the files came to an end with an exultant, "Ha!" He extracted a file and began to leaf through it quickly. "Ah," he said with a happy smile, then to Lescaux, "Major Lamonte has not yet returned?"

"No, General."

"Lieutenant Falot?"

"No, General."

"Very well. You will prepare an Order of Transfer for my signature, relieving Major Lamonte of his duties with this office—temporarily. He will assume command of—ah—the garrison at Sourcier. Yes. Excellent. Draw up the order and bring it to me. Say nothing to the major. When he returns, tell him I wish to see him at four o'clock."

"Yes, General. The effective date?"

"Let us give him—seventy-two hours to make his farewells. He has many friends."

"At once, General."

"And Sergeant," Batraville added from the doorway, "you will also prepare an Order of Promotion. Lieutenant Falot to become Captain as of the date of Major Lamonte's transfer."

"Yes, General."

"When Lieutenant Falot returns, tell him I wish to see him at once—" As the door was suddenly thrust open, "Ah, he is here now. Come in, Claude. I have news—good news—" Both men disappeared into Batraville's office.

Seated, the general began to bring Falot up to date on the visit from Duclosse, Lamonte's transfer, and his own promotion. Falot flushed with pleasure and gratitude. "Thank you, General," he said.

"It is but a small reward for your personal loyalty to me. Soon, there will be many changes here. Remain loyal to me, Claude, and your rewards will mount faster than you can imagine."

"Always, General, you can count on me." Batraville smiled with his pleasant thoughts. Falot said, "General—"

"Yes, Claude."

"I have reason to believe there is a connection between the CIA spies and the American from Terre Delacroix."

"Gerard and Mark Fuller?"

"Yes. His partner, the black one, has kept himself in hiding since the arrival of Gerard. However, on the eve of the Courdet escape, Gerard visited Terre Delacroix for several hours. I have the records of the Maréchal checkpoint through which he passed in going and returning."

"What significance—"

"Fuller is the son-in-law of Henri Delacroix. Marcel Courdet and Julie Delacroix are—*amoureux*. It would not be unreasonable to suspect that Marcel Courdet is in hiding on Terre Delacroix. It is a large plantation, General, with many places where a man could easily drop out of sight."

"You are suggesting that Gerard had a hand in the matter?"

"Yes. I believe it is more than coincidence that the Jaguar that was used is owned by Mark Fuller. The Lancia that obstructed us during the chase is owned by a neighbor-friend of the young Courdet. I do not believe the report that it was stolen, but that it was borrowed for the purpose of acting as escort to the Jaguar."

"Does Major Lamonte feel this way, too?"

"General, I have not discussed any of this with the major."

"And why not, Claude?"

"Because I do not feel the major used good judgment in the entire matter. Had I been behind the wheel of the Mercedes, I would have intercepted them earlier. I have spoken of this with Captain Jérôme. He, too, feels it could have been handled more judiciously."

Batraville looked thoughtful. Falot waited. The general said finally, "You may be right, Claude. You may be right."

To himself, he thought, It could be a useful diversion to deliver Marcel to Fontaine at the proper moment, to keep his thoughts occupied with the Courdets and away from matters of much greater importance to me. To Falot, he said: "Put a man in the area to confirm your suspicions. He is to report to you and to no one else. If your assumption is correct, do nothing without my express orders. I will wish to take him myself and personally turn him over to President Fontaine. You understand, Claude? This could be the means not only of capturing him but also of using him to force the elder Courdet from the American Embassy. Also, it is possible that the American's land may be confiscated for harboring a declared traitor to the government."

"Yes, General."

"You will keep the information to yourself and for my ears only. Once it is established that young Courdet is in hiding there, remove your man and keep him confined so he can tell no one else until after Courdet has been taken."

"Yes, General."

"Good. Now see that Lescaux prepares the orders I have given him and inform the major I will see him at four o'clock."

"At once, General."

Falot went to his own office, depressed a cam on his interoffice communication set. "Sergeant Lescaux!"

"Yes, Lieutenant."

"At once. Bring your notebook."

Batraville had left the office to go to his apartment. A few minutes later, Lieutenant Falot came into the outer office, adjusted his tie in the mirror, and said to Lescaux, "You will have the orders ready for signature in the morning?"

"Yes, Lieutenant. Please accept my congratulations on your promotion."

"Thank you, Lescaux. Who has the watch tonight?"

"I have, Lieutenant."

"Very good. I will keep you informed of my whereabouts. Good night."

"Good night, Lieutenant." Lescaux resumed his typing.

An hour later, he examined the orders carefully for errors, found none, then placed the typed matter in the tray marked LIEUT. FALOT. He went to the door, opened it, looked out into the hallway, called to the sentry on duty there, and asked him to use the guard phone to call the barracks and have them send his supper to the office. That, he knew, would take half an hour. He closed the door, locked it, and returned to his desk.

Lescaux removed the left bottom drawer of his desk, got down on his knees, and reached into the cavern. His hand came in contact with an oblong box that seemed to be part of the desk itself. Deftly, he lifted out a reel of tape, snapped a fresh roll into place that automatically engaged itself in the recorder. He replaced the drawer and pocketed the five-inch reel he had extracted and slipped it into a Manila envelope, then placed it beneath some papers in the middle drawer.

Next, he entered the general's office and saw the two files lying on top of the desk. He marked their positions clearly so that he would be able to replace them exactly as they were. He took the two files to his own office, uncovered the photocopying machine, and began to duplicate each page in both files. When he finished, he returned the files to the general's desk. He arranged the duplicate sheets in proper order, stapled them together, and tucked them inside the Manila envelope with the roll of tape and sealed it carefully.

Finally, he dialed an outside number on the telephone, and when the voice replied, said, *"M'sieu le major,* the tabulation of field reports you asked for is ready."

Major Lamonte replied, "Excellent, Sergeant. I shall be passing by within the hour."

Lescaux hung up, went to the outer door and unlocked

it, then returned to his desk to await the arrival of his supper. And Major Lamonte.

3.

When Ambassador Chance was seated, St. Germaine dispensed with the usual formal greetings and introduced his subject bluntly. "M'sieu Chance, our Minister of Justice informs us that you refuse to release the Libertéan subjects whom you are holding in your embassy illegally."

Chance, coolly prepared for the interview he had anticipated, replied, "M'sieu La Tour's requests have been received. He has been informed that the Courdets are not being held illegally. They entered the American Embassy grounds of their own free will as political refugees, and as such, are entitled to asylum and the full protection my government can give them. They may leave at any time they wish, but of their own free will."

"M'sieu Chance, I personally assure you that M'sieu and Madame Courdet have nothing to fear from their own countrymen. They are not political refugees, and my government demands that they be released at once from your custody."

"I have already forwarded M'sieu La Tour's demand to my government. I am informed that Ambassador Levesque has made a similar demand in Washington. The Courdets will remain under our protection until I have received further instructions. However, I believe you already know what that reply will be, sir."

"And I protest that your refusal to release them is an insult to Libertéan sovereignty, a totally unfriendly and illegal act," St. Germaine replied angrily. It was hardly necessary to add the Damn you! his tone implied.

"And I must repeat, sir, that M'sieu and Madame Courdet are guests and not prisoners," Chance stated in firm, even tones. "Since they have requested asylum voluntarily, I have given it to them. I cannot and will not expel them against their expressed wishes. If you desire to send a delegation to interview them in the presence of myself and other witnesses whom I shall invite to be present, I will be delighted to extend that privilege to you."

"I shall send General Batraville and a military escort," St. Germaine began sternly, but Chance, impatient and not entirely unwilling to show his irritability with his questioner, replied: "If you do, sir, I shall bar them. Any three civil officials will be acceptable, but in fairness to all, the interview will be open to others, including representatives of the international press."

St. Germaine's face clouded with anger. "We shall not permit you to force unreasonable requirements on us, M'sieu Chance. I must remind you that you are a guest of our government, and not its master."

"And I am compelled against my will to remind you that in accordance with OAS and United Nations policies, to which your government and mine are signatories, M'sieu and Madame Courdet are entitled to sanctuary from political—ah—pressures. To violate their rights is to violate that covenant and call for force, if necessary, to provide adequate protection for them."

"M'sieu Chance, are you openly threatening a unilateral action by your country?"

"I must emphasize, sir," Chance replied icily, "that if force is used against the United States Embassy, my government will take every step necessary to defend its property, personnel, and full legal rights."

"You have made an interesting point, M'sieu Chance. I shall be delighted to inform President Fontaine of your reaction."

With equanimity, Chance accepted the challenge. "And I, sir, will be delighted to be informed of M'sieu Fontaine's opinion."

"When one is reached, you will be so informed. The interview is at an end, sir. Good day."

The fact that Chance had referred to Fontaine as "M'sieu" and not "President" was not entirely lost on St. Germaine.

4.

During the day, André and his son Ti Jacques had made several trips to the abandoned hut in the woods that bordered the extreme northern boundary of Terre Delacroix. In past years, before faster means of transportation and communication had been introduced to the plantation, it had been one of a chain of lookout stations, complete with warning bell to relay an alarm to the workers' quarters and Gran Maison in case of fire.

Inside the hut, the dirt floor and thatched walls had

been swept clean, the single room made more habitable with an iron cot, bedding, two chairs, a table, books, writing materials, candles and a gasoline lamp. It was dark now. Eugénie and Mark sat on the two chairs, Julie and Marcel on the edge of the cot. The oil lamp and candles were lighted and a black cloth draped over the single window, another over the open doorway. André kept the watch outside.

"Don't look so grim, Julie," Marcel said with an affected lightness he did not feel. "By day, it is luxurious. Before you came tonight, I had a wonderful swim in the bay."

"Be careful, Marcel, please. If you are seen——"

"It was already dark, and there was no one to see me. No one comes here but the ghosts of Fort Maraboux. The *loups-garous* visit only after midnight, but they never enter a house. I shall be——"

Julie said sharply, almost angrily, "Do not joke about such things, Marcel!"

"You see, Mark," Marcel said with an amused laugh, "even the cosmopolitan intellect of Liberté still respects voodoo, the zombies, and the walking, flying dead. It is born in us and remains in our secret thoughts forever, European schooling notwithstanding."

"Marcel!"

"Yes, Eugénie."

"Please."

"I am sorry, Eugénie. Forgive me."

Mark said: "It's nearly eight o'clock. Eugénie, I think you and Julie should return to the house with André. I've got to get moving if I'm to be in town by nine."

"He will be waiting there for you, Mark," Julie said. "Remember——"

"I've got every little detail firmly fixed in my mind, Julie. Don't worry."

"And be careful," Eugénie added. "Batraville's little hatchet man may have him watched."

The road into Port Amitié was practically clear of traffic. Mark came through the checkpoints at Maréchal and the south end of the city with minutes to spare. He drove slowly through town into the Champs and headed east, timing himself carefully. At the second traffic signal beyond the palace, a gray Chevrolet pulled out of Rue Duplesse and fell in behind him. Mark moved over into the center lane and noted with satisfaction that the gray car followed. Three blocks east, he pulled into the extreme left lane. The Chevrolet was right behind him. When they reached the end of the Champs where the lanes indicated Left, Straight Ahead, and Right turns only, Mark tapped his brake pedal lightly three times. The car behind dimmed its headlights, then brought them on full again.

Mark settled back in his seat. When the green arrow flashed on the signal column, Mark made a left turn into the traffic circle, followed it around to Rue Perrigeau, and made a right turn. There was no moving traffic on the residential street. At the next cross street, he slowed down. Only the Chevrolet was behind him. He stopped, but kept his motor running. The gray car pulled up and parked in front of him. A few moments later, Major Lamonte, in dark civilian clothes, walked back to Mark's car and got in. Mark drove on until he came to No. 11. The gates were open, and he pulled across the wooden ramp that spanned the open ditch and into the driveway. As he entered the grounds, someone closed the gates. Mark pulled around to the back of the house, and Lamonte joined him up the flight of steps, where Gerard met them.

In the first-floor study, Mark began to introduce them, but Lamonte was quick to say, "Mr. Gerard and I are not strangers, Mark. We have met on two occasions. At the Café Excelsior and at the gates of the embassy the other night, have we not?"

"And unless I am mistaken, Major," Gerard added, "we have spoken on another occasion."

"Yes," Lamonte admitted with a smile. "I telephoned to inform you of the arrival of Mr. John Mosher from Havana. I saw you at the airport later that morning."

"Thank you, Major. You have been extremely helpful. To me and to Alec Fletcher."

"M'sieu Fletcher is not here?"

"Not at the moment. He is out of town on a matter of business."

"I hope he is none the worse for his encounter with Lieutenant Falot."

"You knew Falot was involved?"

"But of course, Mr. Gerard. Had you not helped Alec make his escape from the house in Plage Etoile, it would have been arranged. Falot's little maneuver was not an official one, and no official report was made. A little *coup*, shall we say, to ingratiate himself further with the general. However, since he was unsuccessful, I am sure the general was kept completely uninformed of the abduction."

They seated themselves. Mark said, "I left Marcel and Julie less than an hour ago, Constantine. They are grateful for your willingness to help. This can't be an easy thing for you."

"Between old friends such as the Lamontes, the Delacroix, and the Courdets, Mark, there are few difficulties," Lamonte said. "Obstacles, yes, but not difficulties."

"Of course you understand Marcel's position, Constantine."

"I have always been aware of it. And you must understand, Mark, that I could not come forward openly without endangering them and their families. Thank God they are safe."

"Thanks to your ramming their car into the embassy grounds," Gerard said. "That was an exceptional piece of quick thinking."

"Thank you, Mr. Gerard. Your plan to have the second car was a great help to me. If it hadn't been there to block me, or the florist's truck later, I might have been forced to catch up with the Jaguar. Having two witnesses in my car would have given me no excuse not to. Let me warn you, however, that some suspicion has fallen upon me for that act. Falot is not as slow-witted as one might assume. He has given the general that opinion privately."

Mark said then, "Can you help us, Constantine?"

Lamonte smiled wryly and replied, "As of late this afternoon, I have been placed in a position where, had Julie not telephoned me to arrange this meeting, I should have come to her offering aid."

"What happened?"

"At four o'clock this afternoon, General Batraville handed me a transfer order. I am relieved of my duties at the palace and will assume command of the garrison at Mont Sourcier." To Gerard: "Sourcier is a small, isolated outpost with a roster of twenty men, commanded at present by a sublieutenant. It is one of a chain of lookout posts that was important many years ago, but of minor significance now."

"Did he give you a reason?" Mark asked.

"A vague, meaningless excuse. That I may feel, as he put it, the pulse of the people, listen to their talk, explore their feelings and report to him by the courier he will send to me each week. It is merely a ruse to move me away from headquarters. In the past, I have apparently had too much freedom in which to move around, too much for a man of questionable loyalty to his superior. He has not been, eh, comfortable, with me of late. Lieutenant Falot will be promoted to the rank of captain and will replace me as his aide."

"Falot again," Gerard said softly, touching a hand to his upper left arm.

"Falot, yes. Another with grandiose ambitions. Joubert, I think, once said, 'Ambition is pitiless. Any merit it cannot use, it finds despicable.' "

Gerard nodded. "When does your transfer take effect, Major?"

"The general was extremely kind and generous. I have been given seventy-two hours to arrange my private affairs before I leave."

"Do you intend to leave, Constantine?" Mark asked.

"At the moment, I have not fully decided. Much as I have preferred a field station, Sourcier falls far short—"

"If you remain, Major, you could be of invaluable assistance to us," Gerard said.

"Let me clear the air between us, Mr. Gerard. I am not so interested in being of assistance to a foreign nation as I am in helping my own. I do not consider myself in the least manner a defector from the responsibilities of my commission or in my loyalty to my country. I have thought very carefully over my behavior in the past and I will think over just as carefully what I shall do in the future. If my country is heading for an alliance with Russia or Cuba, I shall do anything I can to preserve it from Communism. At the moment, I do not consider that a true government exists in the Republic of Liberté. Therefore, I will work with anyone who has at heart the interests of keeping Liberté free. I am on the side of M'sieu Delacroix and M'sieu Courdet. If your government seeks that same goal, I will help you."

"I understand," Gerard said. Then, "For a start, Major, what do you know of Mosher's activities here?"

"He came to get President Fontaine's or the late President Du Faure's signature on a document, a working agreement that involves the acceptance of arms from Cuba."

"And in return?"

"Certain long-term trade agreements and a nonaggression pact between Liberté and Cuba. Russia's name does not appear anywhere. This will permit her to declare that the arrangement is one between two friendly Latin American countries and has no significance so far as Russian aims are concerned. This would include our acceptance of Russian-trained Cuban technicians and instructors to train Libertéans in various fields. Among them, to form a Civil Militia. Liberté would then, no doubt, form a part of the Caribbean Curtain that is eventually intended to spread throughout Central and South America."

How logical, Gerard thought. "Major, what can you tell us about the man Chalumeau?"

"Ah, Chalumeau." Lamonte crushed his cigarette in the ash tray beside him, and smiled. "Until today, Chalumeau has been a mystery within a mystery. This afternoon, the veil of secrecy has been lifted and the inner mystery becomes unraveled. His identity is known. A man named Duclosse—"

"Pierre Duclosse?" Gerard asked with heightened interest.

"Pierre Duclosse. But he is not Chalumeau, Mr. Gerard. Today, Duclosse came forward and volunteered to bring Chalumeau face to face with General Batraville. Perhaps for a price, perhaps for other reasons. I do not know which, nor the circumstances. *Alors*. During an interview Duclosse sought, a certain file was called for by the general. Later, when Duclosse left, the general sought out still another file, this without the aid of the sergeant who attends the office, a suspicious act in itself. When the general left his office for the day, the sergeant entered the office and found the two files together, as though they had been under comparison. Certain names were marked and some notations made."

Gerard squirmed with an impatience he was unwilling to show, but restrained himself from urging Lamonte to get to the point quickly. He lighted a cigarette, more to keep his hands occupied than because he felt the need. Lamonte continued in his easy, fluid manner.

"The sergeant then made photocopies of both files which, together with a tape he had made of the conversation between Duclosse and Batraville, he gave to me. I might add that Sergeant Lescaux is a close friend. Until the time of my father's death, Lescaux's father served him as a favorite orderly, just as Lescaux has served as mine. It has almost become a tradition."

"And?"

"The revelation made by Duclosse is extremely interesting and becomes of even greater interest to your ambassador, M'sieu Gerard."

"In what way, Major?"

"It would appear that Pierre Duclosse, during his last term of imprisonment, was assigned to a road gang in Prison Camp No. 17 at Romizeau. He was chained between two other prisoners, one Alcide Benet, now deceased, and the man we know as Chalumeau."

"But that was before he was known as Chalumeau?"

"Yes. At that time he was known by his true name. When I learned it today, it was like coming across an old friend. Chalumeau's true name is—Paul Reed."

"Paul Reed!" The name burst from Mark's lips like a rifle shot. "Good Lord, I'd always believed him dead. Everyone has."

"Did you know him, Mark?" Gerard asked.

"No. I've heard the usual stories about him, hints about him and Tom and Monique Reed. He was something like a myth, a legend. He disappeared from sight quite a few years ago, before I came to Terre Delacroix."

"When one considers the combined details and events," Lamonte continued, "the end result seems quite reasonable. Inevitable, one might add. When Tom Reed moved from Belle Roseau into Port Amitié in 1942, it seemed possible that his drinking habits would reach proportions that would make him a troublesome police problem. Unwilling to bring my thoughts to the attention of your consular officer, I undertook a private investigation of the matter. When sober, M'sieu Reed is uncommunicative, but under the influence he will talk to lessen his tensions. Much is unintelligible as time goes on, but when the fragments are pieced together, there is a curiously frightening and interesting story."

"Alec Fletcher seems to feel the same way. He has been in touch with the Embassy in Port-au-Prince and Marine Corps Headquarters in Washington. From those sources, his file on Mr. Reed is rather complete."

"So." Lamonte smiled again. "When Alec Fletcher first arrived here, I sent him a note anonymously, suggesting he might profit by looking into the background of the Reeds. If we put our knowledge together now, the pieces may all fall into place, eh?"

What emerged from Alec's investigation of Tom Reed's background and behavior prior to his arrival on Liberté and Constantine Lamonte's close scrutiny of what happened from 1934 to the present became a concise picture. Add to this the official police and prison record of Paul Reed, and the frame needed to hold the picture together made it complete.

First, Gerard recounted the details from Alec Fletcher's file, to which Lamonte added his findings.

Tom Reed's arrival in Port Amitié in 1934 coincided with the pullout of the United State Marines from Haiti. A gunnery sergeant there, he had an ample reason for wishing to remain in the Caribbean area, one that would have made his return to the States a personal disaster.

In 1932, after seven years of service that had taken him to the Philippines, China, and a tour of duty at Quantico, Reed had been stationed in Port-au-Prince with the HQ Company, 8th Brigade. There, he met Monique, the daughter of one Raoul Maissant, a French merchant, who was employed as a clerk-translator with the American Legation. In time, Tom and Monique progressed into an affair, and before long, Monique became pregnant.

When Raoul Maissant demanded that Reed make right his wrong, Reed put up little opposition or protest. In fact, he may in time have proposed marriage had he not believed there would be strong objections from her father toward an alliance between his daughter and an American of Tom's station; but Maissant and his wife, Jeanine, were not only delighted with Tom's willingness, but gave their blessings to the couple. As a wedding gift, they provided the newlyweds with a small, comfortable house and 30,000 *gourdes,* the equivalent of $6,000, as a dowry.

On an early spring day in 1933, in a room in the Haitian General Hospital in Port-au-Prince, Gunnery Sergeant Tom Reed looked down upon the black child that lay cradled in the arms of a white-clad Sister of Mercy, furious with rage at the carelessness of the nurse. When she persisted that this was truly his son, Reed stormed into the resident doctor's office and demanded an explanation for the outrageous error. The doctor patiently explained that the infant was the only one born in the hospital that day; in fact, was the only infant in the nursery.

Eventually, Tom Reed was forced to accept the truth; and at that moment, tiny Paul Reed's life began in a caul of bitterness, anger, hatred, and guilt.

From the hospital, Reed walked to the nearest bar. Two

hours later, he took a carriage to the Maissant home, where he learned the tragic truth. Monique was truly the daughter of Raoul, but Mme. Maissant was not her mother. She was *illégitime*, the result of a casual affair between Raoul and Mélisse, a young, black Haitian servant in the Maissant household who had run off, or been driven off by Jeanine, shortly after Monique was born.

From that night of his son's birth, Tom Reed's life changed. No longer were his noncom friends welcome in his house. No more beer parties. No more evenings of dating with his friends, drinking and eating well, visiting the post with Monique to shop at the commissary and post exchange, or to attend the regimental dances and movies. Tom spent most of his nights on the town alone or with one or two of his closest Marine friends. More than frequently he slept on post.

When in 1934 the news was made public that the Marine Brigade was pulling out of Haiti for good, Raoul Maissant, aware of the possibility that Reed would desert Monique and little Paul, throwing them back on his hands to create an impossible situation in his own household, sent for Tom. Over a bottle of good whisky, Raoul asked two blunt questions:

Did Tom intend to return to the United States?
Yes.
Did he intend to take Monique and Paul with him?
No.

Raoul, as he once bargained with dowry, now bargained seriously again. He proposed that if Tom would move to the island of Liberté and take Monique and Paul with him, Raoul would present him with the deed to an 8,000-acre plantation he owned there, taken in trade a few years earlier for considerable goods shipped to its then owner, one Lorenz Granjon. Raoul would also draw up a legal document in Tom's favor that would ensure a payment of $5,000 annually for the rest of his life, the money to be deposited each January 1st with the Libertéan National Bank.

Reed began to listen, weighed his present income as a gunnery sergeant, the wife and son who would never be accepted on any military post in or out of the States, the disgrace to himself and his family if his marriage were to become known in his home town in South Carolina. Too, the civilian depression was at its nether point. While these were considerations enough to cause him to weigh the advantages of the offer, Raoul threw in the final threat: he would demand action not only from the Marine Commandant in Washington, but go to the State Department, if necessary, and make Tom's shame known in every newspaper in America.

Reed capitulated. He requested and received permission to be discharged in Port-au-Prince from a willing commanding officer, and even before the 8th Brigade shipped out, Monique, Paul, and Tom Reed were on their way to Liberté.

Thus ended the story from what had been gleaned from embassy investigators in Port-au-Prince. Lamonte nodded as he listened. "It is a reasonable setting for their arrival here," he said. "The Reeds and their son arrived here by Dutch freighter in 1934. It explains much. His hard work and dedication to his plantation.

"The Granjon estate was run down, much of it taken over by neglect and the creeping jungle that surrounded it. For eight years, Tom Reed addressed himself to organizing his labor force with military precision in work squads, with a young Portuguese, one Manuelo Olivares, for his second in command. Only infrequently was he seen in the city, and then only to conduct his business among his brokers, supply merchants, and his bank. He paid little attention to the social life of Port Amitié.

"Then in 1942, if I remember correctly, he abandoned the estate and his family and moved to the city. For what reason, I do not know."

"I can fill that part in for you," Gerard said. "It was soon after World War II began and Tom's application for re-enlistment had been turned down. The disappointment was apparently too much for him."

"Ah, so. Another avenue of escape cut off. Eh. From that point, the facts deal mostly with details my investigators learned from time to time. He rented the house he presently occupies and—"

When Tom Reed removed himself from Belle Roseau, he returned perhaps once each quarter to visit with Olivares, hear the overseer's litany of accomplishments, examine the books, tonnage, shipment and bank receipts, ride out to inspect the land. He had little to complain about. Olivares, young and ambitious, was equal to the

247

task. If, on those rare occasions, Reed saw Monique or Paul, it was purely by accident.

Paul was then eight years old, bright and alert. Monique taught him to read and write English and French. He spoke both impeccably, the native patois fluently, this to Monique's distress. Even at that early age, he was aware of the vast difference between himself and the other children, among whom he played and spent most of his free hours. He was conscious of a certain power; for if, while at play, differences arose, they were invariably settled to his satisfaction. This developed in him a certain natural forcefulness, accepted as his *droit de seigneur*, the right of the young master.

At sixteen, big and strong, he was expelled from Port Amitié's Ecole de St. Thérèse, the fine private school attended by most foreign white and upper-class Libertéan children. He refused to continue at another school, and on his return to Belle Roseau, soon became aware that Monique and Manuelo Olivares were lovers. He saw it in furtive, intimate glances, in the subtle changes that overcame them in his presence. One night, he waited in his room, watching at his door, left open an inch. He heard Manuelo's bare feet padding up the steps, enter Monique's bedroom. Twenty minutes later, he entered the room and flicked the lights on to discover them *in flagrante delicto*. Manuelo's face went as pale as the sheet Monique hurriedly pulled up to cover her nakedness and guilt. Paul turned on his heels and walked out of the room.

The next morning, after careful study, Paul used his discovery well. He sought out Monique and demanded a car of his own and a generous monthly allowance. The alternative was public exposure of her illicit affair and whatever physical action Tom Reed might take. Both of his requests were granted. He moved into Port Amitié, to the relief of both Manuelo and Monique, where his new affluence and generosity attracted a coterie of older cronies, loyal, obedient, and expensive. With them, he drank, rutted among the better-class prostitutes, trying to appease his mounting hunger for the bizarre and exciting.

"So much," Lamonte said, "for what I have been able to piece together quietly over a period of time and numerous investigations. The rest of the story is a matter of simple observation and police, court, and prison records that concern Paul Reed. He first came to official attention in a matter of common assault that involved his father. On the occasion of his eighteenth birthday, in the company of two male and three female companions, Paul encountered Tom, who was entertaining a young woman of, shall we say questionable character at a sidewalk table at the Café Esplanade. Encouraged by the presence of his older friends, emboldened by his consumption of alcohol, and perhaps in need of proving his maturity, Paul approached his father's table, picked up the glass of whisky in front of him, and with a loud curse, threw it in Tom Reed's face.

"With the startled onlookers watching, Tom Reed got up and administered a beating to Paul that no witness to the act would soon forget. Paul's friends hauled him off, beaten and bloodied, hardly able to stand on his feet, but not before he had inflicted the scar on his father's face that Tom will carry to his grave.

"A policeman arrested Paul before he could be carried away, and three days later, Tom Reed sat as a witness against his son and heard Paul sentenced to six months in jail. From that time on—"

Released six months later, Paul began to add to his official record. By the time he was nineteen, he had been arrested twice for common assault, twice for assault with a deadly weapon, once for attempted rape of a young German girl. In the first two instances, he paid fines. In the second two, he was jailed. On the rape charge, failure of the hysterical victim to identify him positively as the assailant resulted in a dismissal, but with a severe lecture and warning from the magistrate.

At twenty, he joined a leftist labor union, and when it was broken up by President Dubonnière, he joined its leader, Pierre Duclosse, in an underground revolutionary movement, recruited members from among his followers, and began a campaign on the basis of "every member bring a member." Duclosse, extremely pleased with Paul, appointed him one of his chief lieutenants.

At the end of 1953, he was placed in charge of a group of specialists, charged with equipping their forces with arms and money. Duclosse taught him the art of manufacturing the Molotov cocktail, which Paul used as a diversionary tactic on buildings near undermanned police stations. When the gasoline bomb exploded and the building was ablaze, Paul and his men then attacked the empty police station. With stolen arms, they staged other swift and successful raids and occasional robberies to swell their anti-Dubonnière revolutionary campaign funds. Early in 1956, Pierre Duclosse was trapped by the newly elected President Fontaine's security police, tried for political subversion, and sentenced to ten years at hard labor. Paul Reed, without Pierre's organizational ability, watched as the revolutionary movement fell apart.

In June of the following year, Paul picked up an attractive mulatto café singer and drove to Petite Aiguille for a week end of drinking and sexual pleasures. Lying in bed in a drunken sleep early on Sunday morning, the two were brought rudely awake when police burst into their room and arrested them.

At the police station, they learned that they were but two of some thirty who had been arrested at the same time. When charged, Paul learned that in the basement of the hotel that night, a voodoo ceremony had taken place. A girl of fourteen had been found dead, a sacrifice to the Goddess Erzulie, the Eternal Female. The *houngan* was convicted and executed minutes later by a firing squad. The *mambu*, his wife, was sentenced to imprisonment for life. Other participants drew terms from ten to twenty-five years. Because Paul and his companion were not apprehended on the scene, they were sentenced to seven and one-half years each. There was no appeal.

By fortune, good or bad, Paul was sent to Prison Camp No. 17 at Romizeau, whose membership boasted of his old friend Pierre Duclosse, and by a stroke of rare good luck, both were released on New Year's Day of 1959 by President Fontaine's proclamation of amnesty, which happened to coincide with the president's natal day. After a brief visit to Port Amitié, Paul Reed dropped out of sight.

Tom Reed had known nothing of his son's most recent misadventures. He lived his lone, separate life, and required little more than the monthly deposits made to his personal account by Manuelo Olivares. Aside from this, he had the $5,000 annual payment made by Raoul Maissant, or his estate, which, when he received it, came as a painful reminder of the indiscretion he could never forget. He had a forty-eight-year-old wife who made no claims on him, a son whom he liked to believe was dead and no longer a threat to his self-respect.

Or what, at this stage, passed for self-respect.

"Now," Lamonte concluded, "consider the name, Belle Roseau, given to the Granjon estate by Tom Reed when he first arrived here. Translate the word 'Roseau'—"

"Reed," Mark interjected.

"Exactly. And now, consider the name Chalumeau. Translated, it also means 'reed.' In those two translations, we unite Paul Reed of Belle Roseau with Chalumeau. A fascinating story, eh? The black son of a white father who has always detested him and who, in return, hates the very sight of his father. His mother, the mistress of the Portuguese overseer, Olivares, gives Paul Reed more reasons to hate."

For a moment, the three men sat in quiet reflection of the cold, accurate summation of the lives of the three Reeds. Then Lamonte added, "Now there is the possibility of a direct involvement with your government that could become an embarrassment."

Gerard nodded. "An American citizen trapped in the act of possible revolution against a friendly foreign government," he said solemnly.

"Yes," Lamonte agreed. "One cannot overlook the thought that a *mésalliance* involving Paul Reed could be used effectively by Fontaine, the Cubans, or Russians to propagandize against your government before the Organization of American States and in the United Nations. It is almost impossible to believe they would hesitate to accuse Paul Reed of being in the pay of the CIA in an act to help overthrow the Libertéan government."

"I know," Gerard admitted heavily. "Our only chance is to get to him through Duclosse."

"But Batraville seems to have got to him first," Mark observed unnecessarily.

CHAPTER 8

1.

In 1961, at the age of twenty-eight, the Paul Reed who was believed dead was very much alive. He had the build of his father when Tom had been that same age in 1933. His six-foot frame was tautly fleshed and well muscled, thanks to two years at hard labor on a prison road gang. Bending, lifting, driving picks into hard soil, aiming heavy mauls at huge boulders, shoveling dirt and crushed rock onto trucks and tamping roadbeds had calloused his hands, broadened his chest, and made him lean and tough. The scars on his back made by jailers' whips bothered him far less than those made on his ankles by the iron cuffs he wore, linked to each other by eighteen inches of chain, to Alcide Benet on his left, Pierre Duclosse on his right by forty inches of heavier links. The deeper scars he carried, however, were embedded permanently in his mind and showed through eyes that, like mirrors, reflected the purity and depth of his hatred and bitterness.

For eighteen of the twenty-four months he had served of his seven-and-one-half-year sentence, Pierre Duclosse had tried to counsel Paul to avoid the brutality of their guards, but Paul seemed to derive a certain masochistic pleasure in goading his tormentors into beating him as if in need of more reason to despise all symbols of authority.

Duclosse was a resilient man whose wisdom, even when ignored, made sense to the tortured younger man. Pierre had been imprisoned many times, and knew his way. Permitted the luxury of receiving packages from his family, he asked only for cigarettes. Others pleaded for food, but Duclosse had long ago learned that cigarettes were the best material for barter with the guards, for whom, by virtue of his bribery, he displayed a smiling, arrogant contempt. Night after night, lying side by side in en-

252

forced companionship, Pierre and Paul grew even closer than they had been before, exchanging and sharing their most intimate thoughts and ideas; and in time, Paul began to learn much from the tough *insurgé*.

"Se calmer, mon ami," Pierre would whisper. *"Calmetoi.* You hate too hard, too childishly. Hating is an art to be practiced as one practices diplomacy. Your words, your eyes, your manners betray you; so your hatred is returned by these *sales cochons* with whips and the butts of their carbines. Do not accept physical pain as the only antidote to mental suffering. Learn to be tranquil, and one day, when you are free, you will be able to hate openly with useful purpose. Here, like this, it is only a waste of time and life."

Paul laughed grimly. "And how," he asked, "does it happen that a man so wise and philosophical lies here beside me in chains?"

"But without the scars you carry. Otherwise, Paul, you are right. I am here because I needed one final lesson in caution. I have learned it now and I will never forget."

"Tell me, so I will not forget."

"It is simple, Paul. Physical pain is fleeting; personal discomforts and scars are forgotten. The need is to remember. Remember well, and trust no man who can better his own position by betraying you. In this world, the greed of man is the greatest enemy of people like ourselves, the born revolutionaries. I have lived longer than you and endured far more, but I have gained the experience. And yet, I envy one quality you were born with that I have never possessed."

"I? I, Pierre?"

"You, Paul. You are a born leader. Do not laugh. It is in your voice, your bearing, even in your size. If I had so much, I would be a ruler instead of lying here in chains. Ah, you think I mock you and you laugh, but there is a quality of greatness in you, in anyone who can inspire others to listen and follow. I have seen it before in you. If I had that much, my strength would be that of whole armies."

Paul was stirred. "Then why should we not continue to work together, Pierre? Since we think so much alike, why—"

"Do not grow overly excited, *mon ami. Doucement, doucement."*

But there was little calm or peace in Paul now that

253

Duclosse had awakened in him this belief in his leadership. How to use it? His only concession to Pierre's cautioning was to lower his tense voice to a whisper.

Two years later, when by Fontaine's amnesty proclamation, the chains were struck from their ankles and they were freed, Paul was anxious to go with Pierre, but Duclosse explained to him that this would be unwise. "If we are to work together, we must not be seen together in public, Paul. Go your own way for the present, and I will go mine. In a month, perhaps two, come to Riam-sur-Mer, where my wife lives with her father. He is Gaston Le Beau. Seek him out quietly, and through him you will find me."

"Riam-sur-Mer. I will come to you there."

"Good. We will have much to talk over when we meet again."

Paul made his way into the port city of Cap Grande. As instructed by Pierre, he sought out Jean Tiresste, identified himself as a friend of Duclosse, and for a week worked as a stevedore until Jean could find a berth for him aboard a coastal vessel leaving for Port Amitié. Arrived at the capital city, he collected his pay of some three hundred francs after the unloading was completed, then walked to Belle Roseau, reaching there shortly after noon of the second day.

Monique was not at home, but he found Manuelo Olivares and demanded the full amount of his allowance that had stopped with his disappearance from Port Amitié two years before. Manuelo protested, refused. He battered the overseer into unconsciousness, revived him, then threatened to repeat the process. Heavy with fear, Manuelo opened the safe in the downstairs study and stood by quaking as Paul scooped up the entire eighteen thousand francs, ate the meal he ordered prepared for him, then took six bottles of rum, a pistol, some clothes, and appropriated the new Simca Ariane that stood in the driveway. He left at once for Port Amitié to relieve a physical need denied him for two long years. After three weeks of rum and a succession of women, he left Port Amitié behind.

His first stop was Riam-sur-Mer in the northeast military district, where he found Pierre Duclosse at the home of his father-in-law, who was the deputy collector of the Port of Riam-sur-Mer. Pierre had been installed as labor supervisor on the large Rimbaud estate, safe under the wing of his wife's uncle, who was the estate manager. Paul's welcome was warm and his talk with Pierre heartening.

"Go among the people, Paul," Pierre urged. "Go from town to town. Sit in the cafés, and listen. You will learn what I already know, but which you must hear for yourself, to understand them. You will see their discontent, feel their fears, recognize their need to be liberated. Live among them as one of them and you will come to know the depth of their despair. Hear them when they speak out, and they will listen when you speak to them. Give them hope, Paul, hope. And when they are aroused, tell them that *L'Aube*, The Dawn, is near, that they must hold themselves in readiness for the word.

"But be careful, *mon cher ami*. Remember the scars we carry on our ankles. Before you sleep each night, rub them with your hands so you will not forget. Hide your true identity with another name so that when the police and soldiers begin to seek you out, they will not know for whom they search. Do not sleep in the same place two nights in succession and look with distrust on every man except those to whom I will send you. In the past, these men have trusted me, and I trust them. You will find them ready to help you. Use them with care. And keep in mind that a fool cannot look into a mirror and expect a wise man to return his stare.

"It will take time, much time, Paul, but when you return, you will know that an army waits behind you, to follow you. Then we will make our plans."

In the interior, Paul Reed found conditions much as Pierre Duclosse had described them. Laborers and field-workers lived in squalor and amid disease, in hatred for the landowners and overseers who exploited their labors, in constant fear of dismissal, forced to scrounge and steal to augment their meager earnings in order to feed their families. The coastal cities were more heavily populated, and conditions worsened by greater competition for fewer jobs. Wage rates decreased as farm people came to seek relief, and thus created an oversupply of willing workers. Boys labored in the fields, in warehouses, on the docks, and grew into early manhood without ever having known the joys of youth. Girls matured early and were frequently bartered away into slavery or prostitution that the rest of a family could live for a while longer. They bore children at the ages of twelve, thirteen, or fourteen, were worn and broken at eighteen or nineteen, and aged and died long before the normal span of years had been reached.

In almost every house and shack there were signs of ancient superstitious beliefs; *houngans* and *mambus* ranged the island to prey on these believers in voodoo, blessed the people and their homes, children and meager possessions, accepting contributions of food and livestock from lean larders in exchange for *ouangas,* charms, fetishes, powders, all to ward off the evil night spirits who dispensed sickness, misfortune, poverty, and death; or to lure those spirits who could bring wealth, good health, love, and happiness.

Merchants, businessmen, shippers, and brokers in every district represented the small and only middle class. They were subjected to strict and severe regulatory laws that changed from time to time by whim, need, or desire of civil administrators who were backed by the military commanders and corrupt judges, without the right of challenge or appeal. Overseers robbed their employers by padding bills of merchants, from whom they received their share; daily food rations of fieldworkers were cut down, and the difference in cost was pocketed by headmen and overseers; receipts were accepted from shipping brokers for less than the actual tonnage of sugar, coffee, alcohol, cocoa, sisal, logwood or mahogany delivered, and again cash changed hands. Crafty agents and brokers shared in the embezzlement with the constituted local government officials rather than risk discovery and prosecution. Tax monies received were appropriated by the local collectors of revenue, and divided among the administrators. School funds, ridiculously insufficient to begin with, simply disappeared.

Paul Reed took Pierre's advice and left his car hidden on the Rimbaud estate. He traveled by bus, accepted rides on trucks, or walked from town to town. He moved without a set pattern, frequently backtracked his steps in order to throw off anyone who might be on his scent. He sought out the men whose names were listed on the scrap of paper he carried in the band of his hat, allowed himself to be known only as "Chalumeau," the friend of Pierre Duclosse, and was accepted readily into the *monde de merde.* From his funds, which he husbanded carefully now, he bought cheap rum and food for his hungry listeners. He sat with them in small cafés, stood with them at the cockfighting pits, talked with them as they huddled together in out-of-the-way huts, always assured of an audience that had been carefully screened from enemy eyes.

The name of Chalumeau began to spread. Chalumeau, the *gros chef*, a man of knowledge and substance, who was concerned with the problems and needs of the *Muets,* the silent ones, the oppressed underdogs. He spoke out vociferously, contemptuously, angrily, this man who knew and understood their desperations and futilities, poured out the bitterness and hatred he had borne since childhood on receptive audiences who were themselves familiar with hatred and bitterness. His words became flames of hope in the minds and breasts of those whose ears he reached. With each indictment against established authority, the people nodded and chanted their agreement; they understood these things; that the curse of their burden was Louis Fontaine and the foreigners who sucked the blood of Liberté dry, they and the mulatto intellect who cared only for their own luxuries, their own fat bellies, their own families, and the protection of their vast wealth.

"Together," Chalumeau told them, "it is they who have robbed you of your heritage, taken the land for which hundreds of thousands of Libertéans gave their lives to wrest from the invaders for you and your children and your children's children. Why else is there so much for so few, so little for so many? Great men, Maraboux, Thébault, Gréssier, Boussac, and others," he declaimed passionately, "fought the First Revolution to free your forefathers from slavery forever, but today you are again enslaved by the economic corruption, greed and moral default and decay of false leaders who are weak and easily seduced by those who lick at the fingertips of the Fontaines, the landholders, the politicians, and the military who know no loyalty except to a system that rapes the masses for the benefit of a few.

"And who are those leaders? Were they given their powers over you by God? No! By you? No! You who have given so much have had no right in choosing your leaders, nor have you ever had that choice. They use the excuse that you are illiterate, that you cannot read or write or understand how to vote, yet who is to blame for your illiteracy but those who give you no schools, no one to teach you or your children to read or write? Those, who have made themselves your masters, you their slaves. Then why should you be bound by their laws that are designed

257

for their sole benefit and profit at the cost of your lives? Remember your forefathers who fought that First Revolution, and you shall be among those who will fight the Last Revolution! Your Revolution!"

So effective and appealing was his strong voice that even Chalumeau knew it must be heard by the authorities and would not be permitted to go unchallenged. Pierre Duclosse's warnings came back to him. He must keep out of sight of those who had already, he knew now, begun to search out the reason for the upsurge in restlessness and discontent among the peasants.

Thus warned, Chalumeau began to take extra precautions to cover his movements with the help of voluntary aides who, notified of his impending arrival, would arrange meetings away from the town, in nearby hills, on the fringe of a jungle. They helped him enter and leave each new district, village, or town by back trails without the need to expose himself to carefully watched roads; to avoid the military checkpoints. He was surprised to learn that disgruntled members of the middle classes, some even from the military, had been screened, and attended his meetings. It was then that he began seriously to believe in himself as a true leader, one who could command a general movement to overthrow Fontaine.

So the time passed; a year, another. The name Chalumeau became the patron saint of the poor and oppressed. The Disciple of Maraboux, he was called. And all the while, he felt the surging power in his voice and words, adding to his strength.

From Gironde Sud to Pointe Nègre, he zigzagged across the mountains to Dondon and Royan, up the valley to Rollière, Carcasonne, and Marcellin; and even in Liberté's second largest city of St. Michel, the people came to hear the *gros homme,* to look upon him as they would a *gangan,* a superpriest of voodoo. When they approached or addressed him, it was with solemn respect and admiration. When he spoke, they heeded with intent reverence.

"We have become a nation of slaves," he declared, now identifying himself as one of them, "of servile cowards who accept poverty and oppression and disease and death from the misguided wretches who have themselves become cowardly tools of the aliens who have stolen our lands and taken our daughters to serve their sickly white bodies. We have lost pride in our rich color because a handful of whites have created a half- and quarter-white aristocracy and divided us into weakness. The sin is ours! That we cringe submissively before them and accept their unwritten and unjust laws, yes. Yes! But we have a law of our own, the law of superior numbers and force and strength, a law of determination to drive them out as Maraboux and Gréssier and Boussac and Thébault led our oppressed forefathers to victory and greatness in the past. We can do it! Chalumeau tells you! We can do it and we shall do it if we have the courage and will to do it!"

Yet, for all the fervor and desire of his listeners, their willingness to become a part of Chalumeau's righteous crusade against injustice and corruption, he felt a desperation and futility of his own; this, when he was asked the two questions he could not answer.

How?

When?

To these questions, Chalumeau was forced into vague promises. "Soon. Soon, my friends. When L'Aube comes, I will send you word through my own trusted agents. They will come among you, and when you hear their names, Flèche, Poignard, Harpon, Couteau, Epée or Lance, you will know that the message they bring comes from Chalumeau. Flèche, Poignard, Couteau, Epée, Harpon, Lance. Remember those names as you remember your own. They will speak of L'Aube, a new day, a new life. The Dawn. When you receive that word, act at once. Fail me and you fail yourselves, your futures."

He moved on and on. Perreville, Mimes, Clermont, then Montbussone. Here, he received word from Pierre Duclosse through Hubert Douvres, the owner of Le Chat Noir. It would be wise, Pierre's message said, to return to Riam-sur-Mer at once.

On his way, anxious now to reach his friend and mentor, he tallied his travels in terms of districts. Almost all had been covered; towns, villages and cities he could not revisit unless he would be ready to move in an act of finality. The two questions that had plagued him most, still remained to be answered:

How?

When?

How was the most aggravating of the two. How? To answer the first was to find the answer to the second. Machetes against machine guns? Clubs against bullets? Knives against rifles? Rocks against artillery? Running

259

feet against vehicles? Having lived so long with frustration had heightened his own impotence; hatred deepened his anger; and anger, his impatience. He knew that the moment of truth was near at hand. He must move against the core of government and destroy it or must himself pass into oblivion. Somehow, he must discover the means to arm his followers, rouse them to simultaneous uprising across the island, and overthrow Fontaine.

Now he took heart from Duclosse's message. He was ready.

2.

Paul Reed came into Riam-sur-Mer late one night and went directly to the home of Duclosse's father-in-law, Gaston Le Beau. Gaston at once telephoned the Rimbaud estate, and within the hour, Pierre Duclosse and Paul Reed had embraced and sat down to a meal and a full account of Paul's travels in the interior. Later, as they relaxed over a bottle of rum, Paul concluded his detailed story on a note of hopelessness. To his surprise, Pierre was inexplicably enthusiastic.

"It goes well, *mon cher* Paul. Extremely well. You have accomplished much more than I dreamed was possible. I have heard excellent reports from our friends."

Paul's doubt was heavy. "They are ready, Pierre," he said. "Across the island, they wait and hope for L'Aube, but they are ill equipped. Only a handful are armed and trained. Unless we can find a way to provide them with the means to strike, they will lose heart. It is like a grain of sand trying to hold back the sea; an old, weak man spitting into a strong wind."

"Do not despair, Paul," Duclosse said reassuringly. "I have been busy, too. It was for a good reason that I sent word to you to come here."

Reed's large body came erect and his eyes, alert, focused on Duclosse's face. "Tell me, Pierre, what—"

"Rest at ease, M'sieu Chalumeau. L'Aube is closer than you think. Listen. Matters have taken a turn to our advantage. If we play our hand wisely, the Dawn we seek can come with such suddenness as to blind you."

"Tell me—"

"For many months, as you already know, there has been a reward on your head. At first, 10,000 francs, which was raised later to 25,000, then 50,000. Over a month ago, through a friend in the old labor movement, I learned that the amount had been increased by still another 100,000 francs—provided you are taken alive. Curiously enough, the increase in the reward was not made by the government."

"Then by whom?"

"By General Batraville. Since the official reward still stands at 50,000 francs, why, I asked myself, would Batraville quietly announce in certain quarters that he was willing to add another 100,000 francs—with the stipulation that you must be taken alive, eh?"

Paul Reed frowned. "You speak of 50,000 francs, 100,-000. It is nothing, Pierre. We need millions. But the greatest need of all is a supply of arms with which to equip—"

"Do not underestimate or anticipate me, Paul. Hear me out. I began to make further inquiries through other sources. Recently, after Du Faure was assassinated, a man named Pyantenov, who passes himself as a commercial attaché of the Soviet Embassy, sought me out. He is a persuasive man, and I permitted him to persuade me. We talked. I told him a little, enough to whet his appetite. We met a second time. By then I had learned that he is in fact an official of high stature. On his third visit, he paid me a token sum of 100,000 francs. We talked more, and he disclosed a plan that would do credit to Judas Iscariot.

"Paul, the Russians are behind that *sale pou* Batraville. They are willing to back him in a *coup* to overthrow Fontaine, all the while seeming to support Fontaine with a massive supply of arms from Cuba. Ha, Paul?"

But Paul Reed, perhaps overly tired, had not quite caught the full significance of Duclosse's statement. "I do not understand, Pierre. Why—"

"Let me explain it more clearly. After six years of attempting to deal with this voodoo-ridden Fontaine, the Russians realize that his cold betrayal of Charles Du Faure gives them no more faith in his reliability than they enjoyed before. Even less. Through the Soviet ambassador, they had committed themselves to an arms-support program, expecting that with the election of Du Faure, Fontaine would be out of the way. Now, if Fontaine is re-elected, and there is little doubt that he will be, they will be once again saddled with one in whom they have no confidence or trust, eh? Therefore, it is expedient to see that the arms do not reach M'sieu Fontaine's arsenal. Instead, they will be turned over to Batraville to be used to eliminate Fontaine. You understand so far?"

Paul shook his head negatively. "Pierre, what you suggest is a wild dream. Batraville is equally despised and hated by the military in the back country. They would actively resist him. Surely he knows that he would live in mortal fear—"

"Exactly, Paul," Duclosse agreed. "The Russians are as well aware as Batraville that a solution to that problem must be found. Therefore, to whom can they look for the support and strength they need in the interior in order to accomplish their *coup?*"

And then the impact of Duclosse's suggestion became apparent to Paul Reed, and showed in his lightning reaction. Duclosse followed up the point. "So at last your eyes are open, eh? Chalumeau! *Chalumeau is their only hope!* Who else can go among the back-country people and convince them that their best interests lie in supporting Batraville?"

"But the military," Paul protested.

"The military cannot stand up to the people, Paul. You have already proved that. Their garrisons have been weakened and are undermanned. In order to resist the government or revolt against it, the military must gain the support of the people. Without it, they are ineffective. But Chalumeau already has that confidence, the support of the people. When the word is given by you, and the people move in to take over local administration in every key city in the interior, the military and police can do nothing. They will be helpless. They would be overrun and slaughtered."

"How, Pierre? With machetes and stones and wooden clubs?"

"No, Paul. With a share of the arms the Russians will send in from Cuba. I have made that point clear to Pyantenov. He has seen the wisdom of that necessity, and Batraville has agreed. The final arrangements you will make with them—"

"*I* will make with them?"

"You, Paul. I have committed you only as far as to arrange a means for them to meet you face to face. From that point, they insist on direct negotiations with you."

Paul sagged back in his chair, reflecting on the swiftness with which his—and Pierre's—plans were being turned from dreams into the mainstream of reality. The rapidity of change was too sudden for Paul to contemplate. And the dangers. He waited. Pierre said, "Paul?"

"Pierre, I do not trust these schemers. Least of all, Batraville."

"Have no doubts, Paul. Until now, I was equally distrustful, but their need for your support changes the situation completely. They dare not move without you. I could see the foam bubbling from Batraville's own lips with anticipation and eagerness."

Paul was hardly moved. "To what extent have you committed yourself? And me?" he asked.

"To this extent, and only to ensure that there is serious intent and not merely words or subterfuge. Batraville has already paid me a second installment of 25,000 francs. From Pyantenov, I have received 100,000 francs of which Batraville knows nothing. I have most of the 150,000 francs here with me; little enough, but sufficient to support our modest needs for the present."

"And for 150,000 francs you have promised what?"

"As I have said, to bring you face to face with Batraville and Pyantenov, perhaps one Basil Zharkov, who is Pyantenov's representative. No more."

Duclosse felt a piercing disappointment in Paul's next words. "Pierre, you have taken their money and placed my life in jeopardy."

Duclosse's anger flared mercurially. *"Merde alors,"* he exclaimed, *"moi aussi!"* Then, as his temper subsided: "Listen to me, Paul, and trust me now as you have in the past. I have taken their money, yes, but if I cannot produce you, do you think they will permit me to live?"

"And how have you arranged the meeting? Am I to drive boldly into Port Amitié and present myself at the Soviet Embassy? Or to Batraville at the palace?"

"Paul, do not jest. To Batraville and Pyantenov, I am no more than an informer, eager to collect a reward; I am merely a means to an end. If they came to believe I am able to exert so much influence over you, your value to them would diminish while mine increased. Therefore, the question of apprehending you—"

With sudden alarm, Paul said, "What is this nonsense of apprehending me? They mean to take me by force? What—"

"Not by force. By interception. I have made it clear that I have no power to simply hand you over, or convince you that this is an ordinary business meeting. In my private talk with Pyantenov, he suggested that I arrange matters, for the sake of Batraville's sense of importance, to permit him to intercept or apprehend you quietly."

"Then why must he bargain with one whom he holds captive when he can use force, torture—"

"And how will he gain the co-operation he needs by force or torture, eh? Remember, Paul, Batraville's need for you is of far greater importance than as a prisoner in a cell, or dead. You have become the key to his success. Tell this to yourself over and over again. Convince yourself that without you, his ambitious plans are doomed. Even with you in his hands, he must bargain, grant concessions. Paul, what is the one greatest need we have for our own hopes and dreams of L'Aube?"

Now there was no hesitation; the reply came swiftly: "The arms. The arms."

"Exactly. The arms. They are within our reach if you will permit yourself to see with clear eyes. Let Batraville intercept you. No harm will come to you. The Russians will see to that because they were first to realize your value to their plan to replace Fontaine with Batraville."

Paul listened, still unsure, unwilling to commit himself willingly into the hands of an enemy he had for so long eluded. He heard Duclosse's smooth, purring voice through his own thoughts. "When you meet, aside from any promises they make of wealth, lands, high position, do not show eagerness to accept. Show restraint, reluctance. When you are finally faced with the alternatives of acceptance or refusal, you will give in, but not before you have made it clear that unless your followers can be adequately armed, you can be of no use to them. Without arms, it will be impossible to overwhelm and immobilize the police and military in the interior while Batraville is using his full strength to establish control in Port Amitié. You are his answer to fear of attack from outside. It is the only solution to his greatest problem."

"Pierre, how can you be so sure?"

"I am more sure than I have ever been in my entire life. With your co-operation, the *coup* will appear to be a *people's* revolution, and this is the main point on which the Russians insist. Otherwise they will stand condemned

264

as the perpetrators in the affair and be called to account in the United Nations. Also, without your co-operation, it is possible that Liberté could be thrown into a civil war. Be reasonable, Paul. If I am wrong, my loss will be as great as yours, and I place as high a price on my life as you do on yours. It is the only way we can get the arms we need for our own purposes. Be bold in your thinking as well as in your actions, Paul, and we will both see L'Aube together."

Paul nodded. Duclosse could scarcely contain his relief. "Later, I will telephone Batraville that you are in Riam-sur-Mer. I will also inform him that tomorrow morning, you will leave here for Port Amitié—"

3.

Late that night, Alec Fletcher went to the public telephone in the Café Carnaval in Riam-sur-Mer and gave the operator the number of the Café Excelsior in Port Amitié. When Lebrun answered, Alec said: "M'sieu, I have looked into the matter of the shipment you inquired about and learned from the freight agent that it arrived only tonight. I have seen the goods myself and can assure you that it is in excellent condition. When it leaves here, I will come with it. *Va bien. Merci, M'sieu. Bon nuit.*"

A few minutes later, Gerard looked up from the jigsaw puzzle of blue flimsies that lay in front of him to answer the telephone. "He has come," Lebrun informed him. "He arrived tonight and is with the other one. Our friend will be with him when he leaves. He will keep us informed."

"Thank you, Emil. It goes well," Gerard replied. He hung up, satisfied that Alec had seen Chalumeau and Duclosse together. From now on, he would be informed of every move Chalumeau would make.

He returned to the puzzle before him. A moment later, Roland Baker drove up and delivered the fifth in the series of radio signals that had been arriving from relay station Chieftain regarding the arms shipment at Bahía de Nipe. He decoded it and added it to the four previous messages, trying to piece the puzzle together. In proper sequence, the chain began with his inquiry to Harrington, Minos 1, in Washington, requesting the source of the original signal he had received from Chieftain. It read:

> THIS STATION SENT NO MESSAGE RE: ARMS
> SHIPMENT FROM BAHIA DE NIPE/INSTRUCTING
> CHIEFTAIN ADVISE SOURCE OF ORIGINAL
> TRANSMISSION/MINOS ONE

On its heels had come the next signal from the relay station:

> SUBJECT MESSAGE RECEIVED HAVANA DIRECT/
> MARKED URGENT AND IMMEDIATE FOR ARGOS
> THREE/CONTACTING CHIOS SIX HAVANA FOR
> CONFIRMATION/CHIEFTAIN

Chios 6 was Luis Sándoz. The third signal came from Chieftain to Gerard, with a copy for Harrington:

> CHIOS SIX DENIES TRANSMITTING ORIGINAL
> SIGNAL/HOWEVER ADDS CONTENTS SUBSTANTIALLY
> CORRECT/WAS PREPARING SIMILAR INFORMATION/
> WAREHOUSES BAHIA DE NIPE EMPTY PRESUMABLY
> LOADED FOR SHIPMENT/EXACT DESTINATION NOT
> KNOWN/SOURCE OF FIRST SIGNAL REMAINS MYSTERY/
> CHIEFTAIN

Next in order was the copy of Gerard's signal to Harrington:

> SUGGEST SEA AIR SEARCH TO LOCATE INTERCEPT
> DESTROY ARMS VESSEL AS CONTRABAND/URGENT
> AND IMMEDIATE/ARGOS THREE

The signal Baker had delivered only minutes ago read:

> YR REQUEST FOR SEA AIR SEARCH NOT FEASIBLE
> TO CARRY OUT THIS POINT/IMPERATIVE KEEP
> EVERY AVAILABLE SOURCE ON FULL ALERT/REPEAT
> IMPERATIVE/LUCK/MINOS ONE

Where, Gerard wondered again, had the first message originated?

4.

Early next morning, Pierre Duclosse returned the Simca Ariane Paul had left with him. Without stealth or effort

266

toward concealment, Paul drove into Riam-sur-Mer. He stopped at a small store on the main street that maintained a gasoline pump at the curb, ordered the tank filled, then walked across the street to a café where he ate a leisurely breakfast. Afterward, he walked back to the car, paid for the gas and oil, and started out of the city. He had noticed the too casual civilian who had sat outside the café veranda watching his every move from behind a newspaper, and was assured that this obvious member of the security police was one of General Batraville's men. In his rear-view mirror, he saw the man get up and go hurriedly into the police building next to the café, no doubt to telephone ahead.

Satisfied, Paul made a right turn into the main highway leading to l'Arcachon, fifty-one miles to the south. From there, another forty-two miles would bring him to the military checkpoint just north of Port Amitié, where he would most likely be intercepted.

Va bien. He settled down for the drive, a pleasure after so many tedious months of buses and going afoot, always in fear of capture.

He was completely unaware that even as the security policeman was making his telephone call to Port Amitié, still another watcher was making a similar call to the Café Excelsior. The call completed, Alec Fletcher got into his nondescript car and took the same road toward l'Arcachon and Port Amitié.

As he approached l'Arcachon, Paul Reed checked the time. It was nearing the noon hour. Heat waves shimmered up from the roadway, and a cloud of brown dust filtered back over his windshield, stirred up by the *camion-citerne* about seventy-five or eighty yards directly ahead of him. Suddenly the tank truck's brake lights flashed, and the huge vehicle came to a stop. Paul applied his own brakes easily to slow his approach. It wasn't until the truck had passed on that he became aware that a military checkpoint had been established here since he had last passed through. Somewhere within him, a warning signal began to flash off and on. Pierre hadn't warned him—

The truck had moved beyond the sentry box, and the long red-and-white-striped barrier came down again to block the road. Two khaki-clad sentries flagged the Simca to a stop. A third soldier, a sergeant, approached him with a salute and a smile. "Your name, M'sieu?" he asked.

"Paul Reed," Paul stated blandly.

"And where do you reside, M'sieu Reed?"

"In Port Amitié."

"Your *carte d'identité*, please, M'sieu."

Paul drew his wallet from a pocket and handed the sergeant his identification card. The sergeant scanned the card carefully, then placed it in his own shirt pocket. "Your papers are not in order, M'sieu Reed," he announced. "All *cartes d'identité* must be renewed every three years. Yours expired fully five months ago. You will—"

Exasperatedly, Paul said, "I have been traveling for a considerable time. I am on my way to my home in Port Amitié and will have it renewed as soon as I arrive. It is important that—"

"I regret that I must ask you to accompany me, M'sieu Reed," the sergeant insisted politely, but firmly. "The captain will speak to you about the matter. I am certain he will arrange a new *carte* in a matter of moments."

The sergeant signaled the sentries to lift the blockade rail, and chose one of the two men to accompany them. They got into Paul's car and drove into l'Arcachon and stopped at the small, ocher-colored military headquarters where Paul was ushered into an office at the rear of the building and into the presence of the commanding officer, Captain Lucien Mauriac. The captain and Paul eyed each other coolly while the sergeant took the offending identification card from his pocket and placed it on the desk as he explained the circumstances of M'sieu Paul Reed's detention. Mauriac listened, then dismissed the sergeant.

Without bothering to examine the card, he asked, "You are M'sieu Paul Reed of Port Amitié?"

"I am," Paul replied stiffly, trying to restrain his increasing impatience.

"Ah, so. Tell me, M'sieu Reed, what is the nature of your business that requires you to travel so extensively?"

"I am not engaged in commerce, Captain. I visit friends—"

"A simple, private citizen of means, M'sieu?" A thin smile had begun to play over the captain's lips.

Paul did not reply at once. He returned the captain's amused expression with one of the contempt he felt for the slender mulatto, a dandy who, in the stifling heat, wore tie and jacket, a highly polished belt over one shoulder, and around his waist freshly pressed riding breeches that flared sharply along his upper thighs, and a pair of expensive riding boots that shone from much rubbing. And not by his own delicate hands, Paul thought with scorn. The captain picked up the slender riding crop from the desk and tapped it lightly against one boot, then pointed its looped tip toward the identification card. "It is against the law to travel with papers that are not in order, M'sieu Reed. It is, as you no doubt know, or should, a serious offense. You could be held for trial for—"

"It was a mere oversight, Captain, a minor negligence, and no more."

The look of amusement on the captain's face heightened. "Courts," he continued, "are not in session in l'Arcachon at this time. There could be a delay of perhaps a month or two before your case might be heard."

With annoyance growing, Paul said: "Captain, you are making too much over a trifling matter. I am not a criminal. I am not wanted by the police. I am a law-abiding citizen, weary of travel and on my way home to Port Amitié. It is no more than that. Why should so much be made over a small oversight?"

"Ah. A simple, law-abiding citizen, unwanted by the police, eh, M'sieu?" The captain's smile disappeared as his eyebrows arched upward in question. He leaned forward and from a wooden tray took up a sheet of paper that had been lying face down. When he turned it up, it was covered with hastily scrawled pencil notations. Mauriac scanned the sheet intently, and Paul knew then that it was a record of his past offenses, no doubt telephoned to l'Arcachon from Port Amitié in response to the telephone call from Riam-sur-Mer. Why here? he thought now. Why not in Port Amitié, as Pierre had told him it would be? Was this a trick of some sort? And if it were, he thought with rising suspicion, was Pierre involved?

Captain Mauriac looked up at him. "This information, concerning your representations as a law-abiding citizen, M'sieu," he said with sarcasm, "was telephoned to me by the Office of Defense and Security only an hour ago. It would appear that you are a person of considerable importance to them. Do you wish to have these read to you in detail, M'sieu Reed?"

"It is not necessary, Captain. I already know what it contains."

"Ah." The captain leaned back in his chair again and took up the riding crop. "Then you are aware that at the time of your parole there remained five and one-half years of your prison term unfinished."

"What," Paul asked suddenly, "is it you wish of me, Captain? I know now that this is not merely a matter of my *carte d'identité* not being in order. Will you please explain—"

"A matter of co-operation on your part, M'sieu Reed. Nothing more. If you agree, we shall overlook the matter of your lapsed identification card, and a new one, properly dated and signed, will be issued. If you refuse, we will let the matter rest with you in a cell until a judge arrives to hear your case. Perhaps he may not even rescind your parole privilege—"

"What kind of co-operation are you asking for, Captain?"

"That, M'sieu, I cannot tell you at this time. However, if you agree to accompany me to St. Afrique, you will have a complete explanation from one who wishes to speak with you, one who is deeply interested in M'sieu Paul Reed."

So it would be at St. Afrique that the game would be played out, and not Port Amitié. Inside his head, the warning alarm was beginning to sound again as an evil thought crossed his mind. How sure could he be? Had Batraville been able to reach Duclosse with a bribe, far more substantial than the 150,000 francs Pierre had mentioned? Was it possible that a deal had been made at his own expense? Or was it simply that Batraville had not seen fit to take this popinjay of a mulatto captain into his confidence? Otherwise, why this outrageous subterfuge with his identification card, the captain's polite yet contemptuous behavior? His anger began to swell, but before it could reach its boiling point, he thought of Duclosse's words, spoken so many times in the past. *"Calme-toi, mon cher Paul. Calme-tois."* He allowed his anger to cool. There was no other way. He would learn soon enough if Duclosse had betrayed him.

"Very well, Captain," he said now, "I will co-operate."

"Ah, bien." Mauriac stood up, tugged at the bottom edge of his jacket to straighten it, and smiled with satisfaction. "We will leave at once. Your car will be safe here at the *caserne* until we return."

As they moved out to the captain's jeep, another line

270

of Duclosse's crossed Paul's mind. *There is a need to remember. Trust no man who can better his own position by betraying you.*

5.

St. Afrique was twenty-two air miles from l'Arcachon. By the narrow dirt road that was cluttered with peasants leading their small *bourriques*, heavily laden with reed baskets of farm produce, to the open market in l'Arcachon, the trip took well over two hours. They crossed the snakelike, winding Desplaines River three times, climbed and dipped from ridge to valley until they reached the top of the mountain and looked out over the lush Val de Jardin beyond a steaming jungle and treacherous swamp at its base. Here the road ended suddenly, and they veered left and began to bounce and ricochet across the rough terrain that was covered with high, spiny grass. They passed over stubbled fields and were thrown from side to side, forward and aft, as they hit one unseen chuckhole after another. They flushed wild game birds into the open and saw startled wild boar take off with angry grunts and snorts as they headed for safety in the nearby swamp where disturbed birds had begun a shrill racketing that echoed and re-echoed back to them.

They stopped at a clear stream to drink the cool water. Below them some twenty yards, six women, bared to the waist, dresses tucked up over their hips, chattered loudly as they slapped wet laundry against flat rocks to cleanse it. They got back into the jeep, and after several miles of following two deeply rutted trails they came to a cultivated plantation where broad fields stretched ahead and to either side of them. Occasionally they caught the flash of sun on metal where fieldworkers labored with machetes and other hand tools.

In the distance stood a sprawling Gran Maison of impressive size, perched on the highest hillock between themselves and a grim, rock-grained mountain, built, as many were, like a small fortress against the fear of sudden uprising, with only trusted servants permitted to remain inside the high, protective walls after dark.

The captain, who had the advantage of holding the wheel of the jeep, seemed as fresh as when they had left l'Arcachon, and was enjoying the fast drive as another

271

would have enjoyed exercising a spirited horse. When they entered St. Afrique, he did not stop at the ocher-colored military *caserne* or police headquarters, but drove through its one wide, main thoroughfare, then past the characteristic huddle of slum shacks on the edge of the commercial section. On the opposite side of the town, they reached a neatly kept residential area, and Mauriac drew up to a house that was larger and far grander than most, its heavy wrought-iron gates thrown open invitingly.

A very beautiful girl, coolly dressed in a flowered green sheath garment of fine cotton, greeted them with a silent smile. She was young, no more than seventeen or eighteen, Paul guessed, and was perhaps a shade darker than the captain, a warm, rosy-tinted brown. Her face was gently rounded like that of a very lovely child, but her softly slanted eyes and warm, full lips, like the rest of her body, were those of a fully matured woman. Her hair was a luminous black and was cut in a straight line where it touched the base of her neck. Her shoulders and long, fully rounded legs were bare, and she wore a pair of thonged slippers of a gold material that were embroidered with multicolored beads. And in her smile there was a shyness. As an old and familiar urge began to heat his blood, Paul wondered if she were Mauriac's wife or daughter; but one quick glance at the captain's possessive eyes was enough to tell him she was the former. Mauriac solved the question the moment they stepped onto the veranda.

"My wife, Nicole," he said with a tone that matched the pride in his eyes; then to the girl: "This is M'sieu Reed. He will wish to bathe. Give him a robe and have his clothes washed. We will have visitors after supper."

With downcast eyes, the girl said in a low voice, "You are welcome in our home, M'sieu."

Paul stared, but said nothing. The captain continued: "I must go to the *caserne* to use the telephone, Nicole. When I return, we will have something to eat." He held up his left wrist, taking joy from the expensive slim wafer of gold that was strapped there. "It is four o'clock. I shall return at six."

The girl nodded. To Paul, the captain said: "When you have refreshed yourself, M'sieu Reed, you may rest until I return. Nicole will show you to a guest room." Paul nodded wordlessly. The captain went down the steps and got into the jeep. Nicole and Paul watched as the jeep roared proudly into action, backed up, turned and pulled out of the grounds into the road that led back toward town.

"Please come with me, M'sieu," Nicole said. Paul turned and followed in a near trance. He found it impossible to keep his eyes and thoughts away from her. Every movement of her body, the sound of her voice, impelled his attention toward her. Mauriac's arm around her waist had infuriated him with senseless jealousy. He caught up with her in the hallway and watched the movement of her young, firm breasts, and an overwhelming desire to touch her rose in him. In his mind, he envisioned her in his arms, felt the blood pulsating through his veins at an accelerated pace.

Behind the house was a series of small buildings, each for its separate purpose: garage, laundry, kitchen, storage, servants' quarters, a separate hut for bathing. A quick word to a lounging servant brought two boys and a girl from the kitchen and laundry to draw water from two large drums in buckets. These, they carried into the bathhouse to pour into the concrete coffinlike *baignoire*. From the storage building, Nicole brought a large towel and handed it to Paul. "I will send the *blanchisseuse* to wash your clothes. They will dry quickly in the sun. She will bring you one of Lucien's robes."

Paul thanked her, and watched her swinging walk as she went into the house. The bath was ready. He went into the hut and stripped off his sweat-impregnated garments and dropped them on the dirt floor. As he stood naked, preparing to step into the concrete tub, the laundress, a buxom woman, came into the room, picked up all the washable items without seeming to notice the large man who stood watching her, evidence of his interest in her—or in Nicole—showing prominently. The woman stood up, looked at his imposing figure, giggled suddenly, and went out.

Paul got into the tub and relaxed for a few minutes, then lathered himself thoroughly with the bar of harsh yellow soap. When he was finished, he stood up to reach for the towel, but the two boys and girl returned with buckets of fresh water to throw over him, one at a time, to rinse away the soap residue. He dried himself on the large towel, just as the laundress reappeared to hand him a cotton robe and a pair of slippers. She lingered for another look, and exited once again with a high giggle.

Paul went into the main house through the back door and passed a neatly dressed house servant on his way toward the front. Nicole, cool and languid, met him there in the hallway. "I will show you to your room, M'sieu," she said and started up the stairs. Paul's eyes were glued on her slender back and swaying buttocks as she preceded him, an agonizing torment blazing throughout his body, desire screaming in his brain. At the top landing, she turned right and led him along the hall to a door. She opened it, stood to one side, and waited for him to enter. He did so slowly, hoping she would come into the room with him but she remained in the doorway.

"It is satisfactory, M'sieu?" she asked with a lazy, tantalizing smile.

"Yes. Yes. Thank you, Madame."

"Rest well, M'sieu. The captain will not return for another hour and a half," she replied, and turned to go.

"Madame," he called out, then, "Nicole."

"M'sieu?" she had turned back and looked into the room, still smiling.

"I am thirsty. Would you bring me a drink? Rum?"

"*Oui*, M'sieu. At once." She went away, and he listened to her soft steps on the stairway. The muffled sound disappeared from hearing range and he lay down on the bed and waited until he heard them again, moving softly on the stairs. Suddenly, he stood up and took off the robe, threw it on a chair, hoping fervently that she had not sent the drink to him by a servant.

And then she came into the room, holding the small serving tray with both hands, the tall glass of dark rum on it, a slice of lime affixed to its rim. Her eyes opened wider at the sight of him then averted her stare to his chest. In no other way did she show a sign that his nakedness was anything but normal. He took the glass from the tray and drank from it, his eyes fixed on her face. He paused, held the rest of the drink above the waiting tray. Her eyes were still staring straight ahead at his chest, a small line of white showing between her slightly parted lips.

Paul placed the glass on the table beside the bed, turned back to her, took the tray from her hands, and dropped it on top of the robe that lay across the chair. Nicole did not move. The tip of her tongue flicked out to wet

274

her dry lips. He put out a hand and took hers into it, and she offered no resistance. He led her to the bed, then leaned over and pulled the sheath up over her head and threw it over the chair. She stood facing him, naked now as he was himself. For another moment he stood staring at her lithe, throbbing young body, and then he picked her up easily and cradled her in his arms for a few seconds, placed her tenderly on the bed, and lay down beside her. She opened her arms to him and he drew her close against him.

When he was awakened by the sound of the jeep's tires grinding on the gravel below, he was alone in the bed. On the chair, only Lucien Mauriac's robe remained; the tray and glass were gone. It was as though a magnificent dream had come to him and, like a dream, had vanished with the opening of his eyes. The mahogany wardrobe stood open, and his white suit, washed clean and immaculately pressed, hung there. His shirt, underwear, and socks lay on a shelf next to it. His tie had been pressed and his shoes were shined. He heard the music of a piano coming from far away, and hummed the familiar tune as he dressed, pulled his necktie into place, put on his jacket, and went out into the hallway and down the stairs.

In the large front room, Lucien Mauriac sat on a small sofa with a drink in his hand, booted legs cocked up on an ottoman. Nicole, dressed in a print garment of the same style as the other, sat at the spinet piano facing him, but with her eyes on the keys as she played. Paul saw the white, lacy edge of a slip showing at her knees, and the hot, consuming desire for her began to well up in him again.

Mauriac smiled a greeting without rising. Nicole stopped playing and clapped her hands twice. A houseboy entered, and she ordered a drink for Paul, then resumed playing without speaking to him.

"You rested well, M'sieu Reed?" the captain asked pleasantly.

"Very well, thank you, Captain."

"Ah, good. We will have supper soon, and later, someone will come to visit. We shall have our talk then."

Paul looked in Nicole's direction, but her eyes were riveted on the piano keys. The music, he thought, was delightful. He must one day have such a piano. But where, he mused silently, would there be a Nicole to play for him?

6.

In the home of Basil Zharkov on Rue Goncourt, John Mosher and his host sat over their drinks, Mosher in an expansive mood. He pulled a folded document from his inner jacket pocket and laid it on the table between them. Zharkov picked it up, unfolded it, saw the scrawled signature, *Fontaine,* and the raised imprint of the presidential seal over it. "You are satisfied, Basil?" Mosher asked.

"For the moment, Comrade. You must realize that this is worthless unless Fontaine is re-elected to the presidency. Until then, it is merely a piece of paper."

"A mere formality, as you have told me yourself. There are his signature and seal. The date has been left open. On the day the Council votes him in, it will be a simple enough matter to strike in that date, and it becomes a valid instrument."

"Of course."

"Then I should like to leave this forlorn tropical paradise tomorrow."

"Not so fast, Comrade. Not until your part has been finished."

"What more is left to be done? You have the signed agreement. All you need do is radio Urbana to release the shipment. Within seventy-two hours—"

"I know. But it is required that you be present to witness my signature on the cargo manifest when the arms are delivered. Once that is concluded, you will return to Havana with the signed manifest as proof of delivery. Also, you will take with you a photo copy of this document I will have made for Señor Urbana. Then your funds will be sent to Zurich, and you may collect them there."

Mosher stood up and walked to a window that overlooked the garden. Holding his anger in check, he said, "I don't like it when the rules are changed after the game has begun, Basil."

Zharkov laughed good-naturedly. "We are not playing by local rules, my dear friend, and this is no small game. You are involved until the game is over, which in your case comes when the arms have been delivered. Do not jeopardize the good work you have done so far, Comrade. Be patient. A few more days will not harm you, and the reward will be all the sweeter. And you will excuse me now? I have an engagement I must keep in St. Afrique. A tiresome drive."

7.

At nine o'clock, they heard a car enter the grounds, and a·moment later the houseboy went to the front door. Nicole left the room with Mauriac, she toward the back of the house, the captain to the front door to greet the new arrivals. There were two men, and Paul Reed, with some shock, recognized the first of the newcomers at once: General Benoit Batraville, Fontaine's *M'sieu l'Hachette*, dressed in dark civilian clothes. He stared beyond the general's shoulders to the strange white man who accompanied him. The general went directly to Paul. "M'sieu— ah—Chalumeau?" he greeted.

"General," Paul acknowledged with a slight bow.

"You know who I am?"

"Of course, General. Any resident of Port Amitié would recognize the Chief of Defense and Security."

"Ah." The word carried a note of some small gratification with it. He motioned a hand toward his companion. "And this is M'sieu Basil Zharkov, a merchant from Port Amitié."

Paul and the white man exchanged brief, unsmiling nods. The houseboy returned with a tray of drinks, and Paul caught sight of Nicole as she glided silently past the doorway on her way to the upper floor. The houseboy left the room. When they were seated, Batraville said, "We have heard much of you from our sources of intelligence in the interior, M'sieu Chalumeau."

Paul waited, sipping at his drink. "You seem to have a rare and exceptional talent," the general continued, "the ability to instill a certain—ah—confidence and respect among the people."

"The general flatters me," Paul said.

"No, no. I have looked forward most anxiously to having this talk with you, M'sieu. When I received word that you were in Riam-sur-Mer, I telephoned Captain Mauriac and asked him to—intercept you and invite you here in order that we might have this discussion in private."

"Yes, General?"

"First, I will ask you one question before we proceed with other matters."

"Yes, General."

"How, M'sieu, would you define your loyalties to President Fontaine?"

So there it was lying before him in the open; the question loaded to the muzzle and needing only the wrong answer to have it explode in his face. A dangerous, delicate problem. Reluctant to declare himself for the man he despised and sought to overthrow; unwilling to announce himself in opposition before the general, the captain, and the white stranger without first knowing their true position. He glanced from Batraville to the Russian, who sat quietly waiting for his answer. The general broke into an enigmatic smile. "Come, M'sieu. The question is not so difficult to answer, is it?"

Paul said slowly: "I find it extremely difficult to define my loyalties to any one man, General. My first and firmest loyalty is to the people among whom I have lived during the past three years. To Liberté. Next, to those who act in interests similar to my own beliefs and principles. If the president stands for those same beliefs and principles, then we are of the same mind."

"Ah." Batraville leaned back in his chair and crossed one leg over the other. "A satisfactory answer, M'sieu, but only in part." He studied Paul for another moment, then said, "You are not Libertéan, are you?"

Paul's smile was vague. "The general should know as well as the captain, who had a copy of my dossier in his office, the circumstances of my birth. My mother is Haitian, my father an—American. Thomas Reed of Belle Roseau. I consider myself Libertéan by adoption."

"Ah, yes. You do not live at Belle Roseau, M'sieu."

"No."

"Nor with your father in Port Amitié."

"I live alone, General. I have lived alone for a long time."

"I wonder why, M'sieu."

"Although I cannot see that it matters, the explanation is a simple one. There is no place for me on Belle Roseau. It is in the hands of my mother. My father is—*white*—and he has long ago disowned me for my color." Suddenly his voice rose high and sharply with defiance. "Of which I am proud. Very proud," he added fiercely, throwing a sharp, sidelong glance at the silent Zharkov.

"Naturally," Batraville said affably. "Now, the overseer at Belle Roseau is one Manuelo—"

278

"I prefer not to speak of that one, General."

"Very well." Batraville turned as Zharkov coughed lightly, calling attention to himself. "Perhaps M'sieu Zharkov would like to make our position clearer to you."

Zharkov spoke in French that was reasonably fluent and accurate, although thickly accented. "Gentlemen," he said, "I think it is time we got down to the true business at hand." Addressing Paul directly now: "M'sieu Chalumeau, we are not children. We are mature men with a mature understanding of political matters. You, M'sieu, have a potential that can bring you high honors and wealth and power, but whatever your personal ambitions, you lack the means to bring this about. However, if we can effect a coalition of effort between us, I am sure you can visualize the advantages that would accrue to you personally.

"We have need for a man of your stature and ability, a man with the influence and persuasive powers to hold, shall we say, the restless element in check until we can put into motion a plan of prosperity for all. To do this, we are in need of time, and feel that you can be most helpful in buying that time for us. It is required to move the people in the outlying districts to support us, help us to remove those whom we consider dangerous to our plans. Or, at least, to restrain them from—eh—obstructing us. We are, I can assure you, willing to reward such a man generously for his assistance."

Paul's head was cocked to one side as he viewed the white man through half-closed eyes. He said, "You are Russian, are you not, M'sieu Zharkov?"

"I am."

"Then how does it happen that a Russian speaks in terms of 'we' and 'us'?"

Zharkov's smile was one of patient amusement. "And you, M'sieu, are an American, are you not? Therefore I might easily pose the same question to you."

"But I have renounced my American citizenship. I consider myself a Libertéan in spirit as well as in fact."

"In fact, M'sieu? Is your renunciation a matter of public declaration and record? Have you ever applied for Libertéan citizenship? No? Then, M'sieu Chalumeau, we are still on the same side of the fence, are we not?"

Paul remained silent, trapped by the Russian's pointed thrust. Zharkov said softly, "Do not make it difficult for

279

those who would be your friends, Chalumeau. There are other considerations you should take into account."

"As an instance?"

"You force me to touch on a subject that is distasteful to both of us, M'sieu." Zharkov paused to wipe his hands with a handkerchief, then continued. "You are aware, I am sure, that there are two matters of unfinished business that concern you and your future."

Paul's eyebrows arched upward in question. "There is the first matter," Zharkov went on smoothly, "of five and one-half years of a prison sentence, as yet unfinished, when you were paroled on January 1st of 1961." Paul's eyes narrowed again, his lips drawn in a tight line. "I need not tell you, naturally, that any offense against the government, however light, would automatically revoke that parole and necessitate your return to prison to serve out the remainder of the sentence at hard labor."

Another few seconds ticked by while this was allowed to sink into Paul's mind. "I have already been made aware of that situation by Captain Mauriac," Paul said.

"Then there is the second matter to explore, aside from any charge of treason for your conduct in the interior since your release from prison. Deportation. You could well be considered an undesirable alien and deported to the United States."

Paul's shock showed in his face and with the sudden jerk of his body. That ironical thought had never crossed his mind before. Deported to the United States! How true! As the son of an American citizen, he was himself a citizen of a country he had never seen, one he despised in principle as he despised Tom and Monique Reed in fact.

Batraville's coaxing, oily voice intruded into his thoughts. "However, Paul," he was saying, "I can personally assure you that these matters will be officially forgotten and all records destroyed if we can count on your full co-operation."

And with those words, Paul's reassurance returned. Duclosse was right. There was a desperate need for him. Else, why was Batraville so anxious to use sugar instead of vinegar on a fly he had already trapped? Why the simple threats of imprisonment and deportation when, as Chalumeau, and not Paul Reed, he stood condemned for treason and could be stood against a wall and shot down by a firing squad? Or, in fact, be shot down here and now, on any street, in any village, for the offered reward.

Ah, Duclosse, that clever one, to see so clearly from the start that what Batraville wanted—needed—of him was of far greater importance than his elimination. He was being given a choice. Be seduced into the general's service or be done away with. Life or death. "What are you suggesting, General?" Paul asked.

"That we join forces, Paul," Batraville replied. "Since we are working for the same cause and ideals, we can reach our goal in far less time together than by working at cross-purposes."

If, Paul thought silently, our only goal is the elimination of Fontaine. *A bas le presidente! L'enfer avec le général!* Again the Russian coughed. Paul turned back in his direction.

"Liberté," Zharkov said, "is on the verge of a great undertaking that will, in the not too distant future, benefit all her people. Her Russian and Cuban friends are well aware of her needs and have extended the hand of friendship to her. Therefore, just as she is not without enemies, she is not without friends. Russia does not wish to own land here, nor does she wish to bleed profits from your country as the American imperialists have done for so many years while Libertéans have starved and suffered humiliation. What we offer is the spirit of brotherhood, normal trade relations between our countries, a cultural exchange from which Russia, Cuba, and Liberté will benefit mutually."

"With an army of civilian technicians and military personnel such as that which now represents your country's investment in Cuba, East Berlin, and other nations it has *befriended,* M'sieu?"

The Russian replied blandly: "And do you presume that it is more desirable to supply your people with modern, scientific equipment and arms of which they have no knowledge? These men are necessary to teach, educate, and train—"

"Is this not the same excuse used by the Americans?" Paul began, but Zharkov was cutting across his words, putting the objection aside. "These are small problems that can be worked out later. At the moment—" Zharkov glanced at Batraville, who was showing an eagerness to take over the conversation again.

"At the moment, Paul," Batraville continued the thread without a break, "it is your exceptional talent and ability with people in which we are interested. I need you. Li-

281

berté needs you. What I am asking for is an expression of your loyalty to the new government I will head."

So there it was. Batraville's open declaration of his intention to take over as Chief of State. "And the coming election?" Paul asked.

"The coming election will have no bearing on our plans. Whether M'sieu Fontaine wins or M'sieu Courdet wins, it will make no difference. With your help either one will be deposed. It is inevitable."

Paul leaned forward and put his empty glass on the small table in front of him and took a cigarette and lighted it, taking his time. "The military in the interior, General—"

"I am fully aware that there are dissidents in the ranks," Batraville said easily. "Do not concern yourself with such lesser matters at the moment, Paul. Many of these men have been under suspicion, and were removed from more important and sensitive posts because they were potential troublemakers. In most cases, leniency will be shown. They must be made to understand that."

And I am to be the one to make them understand, Paul thought. "In the past, General," he said now, "the aid funds and supplies received by Liberté from the United States have been diverted for personal profit, sold abroad—"

"Imperialist propaganda!" Zharkov exclaimed. "The whole notion is ridiculous fiction, and absurd. Your people have listened to and accepted American lies as truth. It has, in fact, hardly delivered one-quarter of the goods it pretends to have sent here. Talk, promises, yes, but it has remained for Russia to show the world what a practical program of aid consists of. The people of Cuba know this. They demonstrate it every day with their respect and love for Señor Castro. You wish proof? How else do you account for the fact that he is able to appear in public as frequently as he does, among people who walk about armed, without fear of assassination? Could he allow himself this luxury or privilege if the Cubans hated him as Libertéans hate Fontaine?"

"You speak well and loudly, M'sieu," Paul said, "but the people and the military here do not accept this. It is possible that the people may be persuaded, but the military? I think not."

"Then," Batraville interjected, "they will be dealt with. The traitors must be overthrown by the people in a demonstration of loyalty to the new government." He hesitated, then added, "You can accomplish that for us, Paul. The people have listened to you and understand you. They will listen to you again."

Paul shook his head in doubt. "The military garrisons are armed. The people are not. It is an inescapable fact. One cannot expect to combat arms with bare hands."

"If you will join us, Paul," Batravillè said, "you will be more than adequately equipped for the task. New, modern automatic weapons that are far superior to anything now in the hands of the military."

Paul began to feel a sudden glow of heady warmth spreading through him. New, modern automatic weapons. The missing piece in his mosaic for power. Batraville's voice plowed on. "You can see easily that it is more important that the military in the interior be routed in a popular movement by the people than by elements of the Army. Such an action would show those in Port Amitié and the outside world that the people stand firmly behind their government."

"When, General?"

Batraville smiled as he contemplated this initial victory. "When? Let us say within a week. No longer. You will have that much time to send word to your people, to prepare them. Is this possible?"

Paul nodded, leaning back in his chair, relaxed. "It is possible."

"Then you will join hands with us, Paul?"

Without a moment of hesitation, Paul replied, "As of this moment, General, our hands are joined."

8.

At No. 11 Rue Perrigeau, Lebrun and Jim Gerard discussed the message Alec Fletcher had sent by Lebrun's man in l'Arcachon.

"Nothing more, Emil?"

"That is everything at the moment. There is but one road from l'Arcachon in the direction they took, and this leads to St. Afrique. When it was safe to follow, Alec went there by bus. He found the captain's jeep at the military garrison, and followed it back to Mauriac's house. Later, a car arrived and two men entered the house, General Batraville and the Russian, Zharkov. When they emerged finally, Paul Reed was with them. They returned

283

together to l'Arcachon. The general and Zharkov drove at once to Port Amitié. Chalumeau went to the *caserne* and is there now asleep. Alec also sleeps while my man watches the *caserne*. When Chalumeau makes his next move, Alec will follow."

"Good, Emil."

"And meanwhile?"

"Meanwhile, we shall wait."

9.

Early in the morning, Paul Reed drove into Port Amitié, following the heavy flow of trucks carrying raw sugar cane from plantations to grinding mills, sacked sugar from refineries to brokers' warehouses or to the docks for loading. To one side, back-country men and women tugged at small, tough *bourriques* that were weighted down with produce, live fowl, and the carcasses of slaughtered pigs and beef to be sold in the Port Amitié market place. In the cool, predawn hours, he did not mind the delay that gave him time to think, to plan ahead. God, there would never be all the time he would need to compress the action of months into one week.

At the Port Amitié checkpoint, he showed his new *carte d'identité*, bearing Batraville's signature, drew a smart salute from the sublieutenant in charge, and was passed through quickly. Paul drove to the Hotel Clamecy, examined with approval a room that overlooked the broad sweep of the Champs, the palace, and the imposing Army headquarters building. He unpacked his one suitcase and slept until the noon hour, then bathed, dressed, and ate a satisfying lunch. Fully refreshed, he got into the Simca and drove south from the city to Belle Roseau.

The plantation was quiet at this hour of siesta. His mother, he was told by old Mama Louise, was in her room upstairs, and he sent her, protesting and grumbling, to call Monique.

His first sight of her in five years shocked him. She had become haggard, her face gray and lined, her uncared-for teeth showing gaps as she tugged the cotton wrapper around her thickened body, unable to control her large, sagging breasts.

"You," she said balefully.

"It is I, Paul, your son. Don't you recognize me, *cher Maman?*" Paul replied with a smile of contempt on his face and in his tone. "You look beautiful. I have missed you."

"As much as I have missed you," she replied bitterly to his open sarcasm.

Paul repaid her with a light air. "It is my home, is it not, *Maman*? Why should I not come home after having been too long away from your side? And where is your charming *amant*? Upstairs hiding under your bed, or in the bed of one of his younger, more attractive charges?"

"*Cochon noir!*" she spat out. "Have you been in prison again?"

"No, *cher Maman*. I have been traveling about the country. I have seen much and done much. However, such extensive travel has depleted my purse. And where else should a son come?"

"I will give you nothing, not a centime! You hear me! Get out of my sight, you filthy pig!"

"*Maman!*" Paul's voice was filled with mock filial reproof.

"Go! Leave me in peace!"

"When it pleases me to leave, *ma chère*, I shall do so. Let me first explain to you how matters stand." His voice became cold and harsh. "I have not bothered you for five long years. I am a man now, and my needs are those of a man. You grow old and your needs are also greater, but in another way. As an instance, if your Manuelo were to— let us say, leave you, or disappear, who would you find to take his place? No decent, self-respecting man would enter into an alliance with a *sorcière*, a hag like you. Therefore, you need your Manuelo. Let us now assume that I, upon returning home from my travels, find that our overseer has taken advantage of the absence of husband and son and forced you into an *affaire de cœur* with himself. Would I not be justified in killing him? I think you will find that the courts would see the justice in such an act, committed in passionate outrage to defend the name and honor of his white father and himself, no?"

Monique stood back from him, glazed eyes wide open, her lower jaw dropped in horror, breathing hard. "You *bas pou!*" she gasped. "*Ecume!*"

"Ah, so, *Maman*. Time has not improved your temper any more than it has your charm. Then let us talk of other matters. Money. Where do you keep it hidden now?"

"I keep no money here since you last robbed me. It is in the bank in Port Amitié."

"Ah, so. Then get dressed, *cher Maman,* and you will accompany me to the bank and withdraw, let us say, 50,000 francs to show your unbounded and limitless delight with my return."

"*Fifty thousand francs! Ten thousand dollars!* You are insane. A madman and a thief!"

"As you say. All of that, even more. Now——"

From behind her came the tired voice of Manuelo who had come down the stairs quietly in his bare feet, a pair of white pants supported by a colorful ribbon for a belt around his waist, his upper body bare. "Give it to him, Monique. Give it to him and let him go. You have it in the safe. Be done with him."

"*Ah, Maman,*" Paul said with a smile. "There speaks a man who has grown wise. Give it to me and let me go. Have done with me. As you were done with me years ago. As my father was done with me from the day of my birth. Let us not argue or haggle. Your master speaks."

Standing between the two men, a sudden helplessness came over her with a shudder. She put a long, thin hand up to her face and turned from Paul to Manuelo. "Give it to him," she said in a broken voice. "Go, give it to him."

10.

On his return from Belle Roseau, Paul Reed stopped at a small waterfront café and made a call from a public telephone. To the man who answered, he said, *"L'Aube."* The man replied, *"Attendre une moment, M'sieu."* Paul waited. Another man came on and spoke slowly, giving him detailed directions, then hung up. Paul got into his car and drove through the crowded Rue Passy into the coast road until he came to a huddle of dilapidated fishing shacks. He parked near the longest of the two piers and walked to the end of it where he found an old man in a small fishing boat. He spoke the word *"L'Aube"* to the old man, who waved him into the boat.

Twenty minutes later, a small, fast cabin cruiser pulled alongside them several miles offshore, and Paul made the transfer as two men from the cruiser held the fishing boat fast against rope bumpers with long boathooks. The cruiser picked up speed and headed out toward Pointe Neuf. Inside the main cabin, Pierre Duclosse sat on a cushioned bench, waiting.

They had much to discuss, and when they parted again

at the flimsy pier, the list of names Pierre had scribbled on a sheet of paper was carefully tucked inside the sweatband of his hat. Back in town, he went to the Clamecy, found a public telephone, and began calling the names on the list. Of twenty-one, he was able to reach only eight, and in each case, the man he spoke with was expecting his call. He gave them an address on Rue Montagneux and the meeting time: six o'clock.

When the calls were completed, Paul went up to his room, packed his suitcase quickly, and checked out of the hotel. He found the house on Rue Montagneux that Pierre had rented the day before, and learned from the housekeeper, Marianne, that he was expected. Michel, her son, carried his suitcase to a bedroom on the upper floor. Marianne was already aware there would be guests later, and returned to her preparation of food for them. Paul went upstairs to lie down and think.

At six, the eight men gathered at the house. Duclosse appeared a little later with four more men. By eight-thirty, they had reached a satisfactory accord. Paul handed each man a sum of money and instructed him to go to a certain town or village and deliver a message to a man who would be waiting eagerly for some word of him. The men departed singly with the word *Accélérer!* ringing in their ears. To hasten! Time is of the essence! Be prepared when the signal is given! Do not fail Chalumeau or you fail yourselves!

At nine o'clock that night, General Benoit Batraville, deep in thought, drove to the home of Basil Zharkov on Rue Goncourt. Beside him at the wheel was Lieutenant Claude Falot. Both men were dressed in dark civilian clothes. Inside the gate, two men, obviously armed, approached the car. On the driver's side, one man opened the door a few inches to activate the dome light. The second man examined the interior of the car from the opposite side. Falot spoke in sharp anger to the man at the door, but neither guard replied. The second man motioned Falot ahead, and the lieutenant jammed his foot on the accelerator to show his annoyance.

"Damné Russe!" he exploded under his breath as he parked the black Mercedes limousine at the bottom of the steps that led to the veranda. A third guard came out from behind one of the columns, and waited. Falot said, "They guard him as though he were Damballa Himself."

287

"All men have their own fears in these times, Claude," Batraville replied.

Falot nodded. "But there is an evilness here, General. I can smell it in the very air."

"Not here alone, Claude. The odor of evil is everywhere. It becomes a part of our culture." He put a hand up to open the door. "Wait here. I shall be gone perhaps an hour. The other one should arrive soon."

Falot nodded in unwilling consent.

Inside the house, a smiling, ebullient Zharkov greeted the general in the large study. When their cigars were lighted, the brandy served, and the servant gone, the Russian asked, "You saw him?"

"Three hours ago at Bellefonte."

"He was pleased?"

"And why not? I explained that I am about to lead M'sieu Chalumeau into a trap, that he is within sight of my men. After he leads us to his key followers, I will have him. This time without fail. Without Chalumeau, Fontaine agrees that his people in the interior will be impotent to act. For the rest, he relies on me to keep the city peaceful and quiet."

"Ah, good. Very good. Then he suspects nothing."

"If he does, it is not apparent to me."

Zharkov rubbed his hands over the large bowl of the brandy glass like a man warming cold hands over a fire. "Excellent. You discussed the arrival of the arms?"

"He gave me the details as Mosher had given them to him. That they would arrive on Monday night. He then outlined his plan to have me arrange for their delivery to the arsenal in Port Amitié. On Tuesday morning the arms are to be issued to the security police and military in Port Amitié only. Fontaine intends to order the Council into continuous sessions commencing on Wednesday morning, after the members have had an opportunity to see the additional troops under full arms. He will set a deadline for their decision for Friday noon."

Zharkov nodded approvingly. "I have had confirmation from Comrade Urbana in Havana. The arms will arrive here on Sunday after dark. You will arrange to bring the barges in from Pointe Neuf to the beach at Anse à Goulet. Ten barges with four men in each. There must be ten trucks, two soldiers and four prisoners for each truck. The bargemen will bring the cargo ashore. Your prisoners will load them into the trucks. The barges will then return to

Pointe Neuf. You will deliver the shipment to the warehouse in Maréchal by eleven, if all goes well—"

Batraville nodded impatiently. What need for this continual recounting when the plan had been his own from the start? "It will go well, Zharkov," he said shortly. "The barges have been arranged for. The trucks and men are available and ready, but I will not give the order until the final moments of departure, so there will be no talking among the men."

Zharkov was obviously pleased. "Now as for M'sieu Chalumeau. When he arrives, we will take him into our confidence as we planned. He is to believe, as Fontaine believes, that the arms will arrive on Monday night. He is to bring his leaders into Maréchal at midnight of Monday night. His leaders only. They are to wait outside Maréchal until they are given the signal to come in. He will be told that he is to receive four full truckloads of the arms for distribution to his people in the interior. It is at this point that we have made a slight change in the plans concerning M'sieu Chalumeau."

Batraville looked up quickly.

"General, we have no intention of turning M'sieu Chalumeau and his maquis loose with so much firepower in their hands," Zharkov said flatly.

"Then what—"

"M'sieu Pyantenov and I have agreed that without Chalumeau, as M'sieu Fontaine has suggested to you, his people will be helpless to act. Are we agreed?"

Batraville nodded slowly. "But—"

"When he arrives at the warehouse with his leaders, they will be taken into custody and held until after you have taken over the government. By Tuesday, when you are in full command, Chalumeau and his principal leaders will be in your hands. What you do with them after that—" Zharkov's smile broadened and he raised his hands upward and outward in an expressive gesture.

There came a knock on the door. Zharkov crossed the room and unlocked the door and admitted a servant. "What is it, Yuri?"

"A man is come to see you, Comrade Zharkov. With the name Reed."

"Ah, yes. I am expecting him. Show him in."

Paul Reed nodded with apparent satisfaction over the plan as it was outlined by the Russian, for whom his distaste was increasing each moment. He listened in silence, but his mind was centered on Batraville's nervousness. Monday night, midnight. He noted Batraville's hands moving agitatedly, fingering his glass, fidgeting with his jacket, buttoning and unbuttoning it. What devil's work was here that had not been revealed to him?

Zharkov had stopped talking. "You understand, Paul?" he said at last.

"I will need time to arrange for my men to come in," Paul said.

"Bring them in no earlier than Monday. Have them at the warehouse in Maréchal by midnight. The general will have new *cartes d'identité* prepared so there will be no delays at the checkpoints. Before you leave here tonight, you will give him the names of your men and he will have their *cartes* ready by morning. How many? Let us say four men for each of four trucks. One driver, a man to ride beside him, two men on top. Sixteen in all."

Paul nodded. Sixteen false names would be easy to furnish.

"The day and time for the takeover has been set for Wednesday at one o'clock in the afternoon, when the siesta period has begun. In St. Michel, Espérance, Bonheur, Romizeau, La Rochelle, Royan, Marcellin, Sommet, and Gran Aiguille, your people must be armed and ready to put down any show of resistance from the military. This will form a protective circle around Port Amitié and leave the city free from outside disturbance or possible attack. Everywhere else, they will act in accordance with the plans you already have. The city will be the province of concern for General Batraville. Is this fully understood?"

Paul said quietly, "It is understood."

"And agreed upon?"

"And agreed upon."

"Have you the means to send word to the men you will wish to bring into Maréchal on Monday?"

"I have the means."

"We will need to be in close contact from now until the distribution of the arms is made. Tomorrow two trusted aides will be assigned to serve you. You will use them as a means of communicating between yourself and the general."

So, Paul thought, *chiens de garde*, watchdogs at my heels. Better in my sight than hidden from view, like the one who has been like a shadow to me since I left my house. He nodded. "They will be useful."

"Then we are in full agreement," Batraville said now.

Paul nodded, and replied: "Fully. Now, if I may be excused, gentlemen, I will return home to complete my plans."

"I will accompany you to the door," Batraville said, rising. "I must return to the palace now."

Both men said "Good night," to Zharkov at the doorway and walked down the steps toward Batraville's waiting car. "A favor, General," Paul said.

"What is it, Paul?"

"I have taken a fancy to your Captain Lucien Mauriac. He seems capable and intelligent."

"Ah, Mauriac. An excellent man and a good soldier."

"I should like to have him as a third aide."

"If it is your wish, Paul, you may have him."

"Thank you, General. I should like to have him report to me as soon as possible. Early tomorrow morning, if that is convenient. I wish to make use of him in a capacity no civilian could handle: to make contact with certain military men in the interior who have expressed a desire to join me. Mauriac could, with a proper message from me, reassure them with greater credibility than a civilian messenger. This will relieve me of the necessity to travel at a time when I should be close to the center of command."

"A wise move, Paul. I will telephone him as soon as I reach my office."

"I will need to keep him busy for a considerable length of time, General. I would suggest that he move into Port Amitié for the present. And," he added, "that he bring his family with him. If anything should happen, Madame Mauriac would be much safer here than alone anywhere in the interior."

Batraville threw a swift questioning glance at Paul. "Well, General?" Paul asked with a light smile.

"I will suggest it to him when I telephone," Batraville replied coolly.

Duclosse was waiting at the house on Rue Montagneux. Paul explained in minute detail the plan Zharkov and Batraville had outlined for him. "You are perturbed, Paul," Duclosse said.

"Yes. I do not trust Batraville and I trust the Russian less. Something in their manner, something—"

"What is it?"

"I cannot say exactly. It goes too easy, too convenient. I have not found, from my experience, that intrigues such as this go so smoothly."

Duclosse shrugged. "It is your imagination."

"Or let us say it is the instinct of a man who has been hunted like an animal and has learned the scent of a trap. Pierre, they will use Army trucks, soldiers, and prisoners on the beach. The Army has no barges. Where can they come from?"

"From the harbormaster in Port Amitié. It is the only source."

"Through your connections with the dockworkers, can you find out what arrangements have been made with the harbormaster?"

"Yes, of course. But why?"

"Again, instinct. Humor me, old friend. I can learn nothing of the Army's plans here, but even some slight information from your sources could be helpful, if only to remove the doubt from my mind."

Duclosse shrugged again. "When?"

"Now. At once."

Duclosse got up and went out, Paul behind him. As he got into his car, Pierre said, "I will telephone you."

Paul came back into the house. In the study, Marianne was carrying away the glasses on a wooden tray. She smiled warmly and said: "You have not eaten since supper, M'sieu. I have food for you if you wish it."

Paul stared at her for a moment and said, "I am not hungry, Marianne. Will you send a drink to my room?"

He went upstairs, stripped off his sweat-dampened clothes, threw them on a chair, then lay on the bed in the dark to relax his tense muscles and nerves, restless, aching for activity. In the quiet darkness, his eyes remained open with feverish excitement. Plans. Plans. Plans. Monday night at midnight. The arms.

And then he thought of Nicole. Nicole. He breathed her name as one would a prayer. This was woman complete, the sum and total of all women. The memory turned him into a mass of frenzy for her. He whispered her name, saw her face, her long, sensually awakened body, and his mind became a confusion of love entangled with lust, anguished and painful as he visualized her once again in his arms, feeling the hot, swift breath of her against his neck. So realistic was his dream that he could hear her call out to him, *"M'sieu! M'sieu!"* then realized that it was Marianne, standing in the faint glow of the hallway light on the threshold of his door. "M'sieu, you are awake?"

"Yes. Yes, Marianne. What is it?" he asked hoarsely.

"The drink you asked for, M'sieu."

"Yes. Bring it to me."

She came into the dark room noiselessly in her bare feet. "Here," he voice-guided her, heard the rustle of her garment beside the bed. "Put the drink down on the table."

Marianne turned and placed the glass on the night table. As she turned back, he caught at her wrist and held it tightly. "M'sieu?"

"Here, Marianne. Here. Beside me."

He heard the ringing coming from a great distance and burrowed his head into the soft, yielding bosom of Marianne. She stirred, came awake slowly and said, "It is the telephone, M'sieu."

At once, he thought of Duclosse. He leaped out of bed and ran to the hall, down the steps and to the telephone in the study. Michel was about to lift the receiver. He took it from the boy's hand and said, "Go back to your bed, petit." Into the phone, he said, "Yes?"

"Paul, it is Pierre."

"You have news?"

"Yes. Important news."

"What is it?"

"Paul, the day and the hour."

"Tell me."

"Sunday when darkness falls."

"Ah!"

"The barges and the men have been ordered for then."

"Yes, Pierre. I understand."

"Paul—" He could hear the apprehension in Duclosse's voice.

"It is all right, Pierre. As long as we know, we can plan."

"Shall I return now?"

"No. Tomorrow will be soon enough. Good night, *cher ami*, you have done well."

When he returned to his room, Marianne was asleep, her

293

mouth open slightly, snoring softly. He shook her awake. "Go back to your bed, Marianne. I have work to do."

She sat up, yawned, then got out of the bed, found her dress, and held it in front of her as she padded softly out of the room.

Paul lay down on the bed again, a cigarette between his lips, one arm folded beneath his head. Monday at midnight, Batraville had told him. And the barges were ordered to be on the beach at Anse à Goulet by dark on Sunday. Then he must bring his men here during Friday night. No later than Saturday night. Forty men. He would need to quarter them away from prying eyes, see that they were fed. To sleep out in the woods a short eighth of a mile behind the house would effect no hardship on them. Their everyday lives at home were spent in less comfortable circumstances. Needs would be minimal. He would have Duclosse send a few men separately to the open market on Friday to buy the three-day supply of rice, beans, fish, and chickens they would need, as well as utensils in which to cook them. He already had the truck that would transport them. Now the last piece was fitted into the puzzle. The beach at Anse à Goulet, where they could be hidden from view until the moment arrived.

Paul suddenly laughed loudly. How well they had planned their deceit, Batraville and the Russian! Imbeciles! Did they think he had believed them? Sixteen men!

They were alike, these city-bred minds that looked down their long noses on those who lived outside the capital city as ignorant, stupid peasants. What did they know of the back-country people? What did they know of the fire and hate that burned inside these downtrodden, sinned-against men whose blood ran as hot as it had in the veins of the slaves who had risen beside Maraboux, Boussac, Gréssier and Thébault to fight against superior odds and drive the white men from this island into the sea?

And now, his own moment would come. Chalumeau would lead his people into Port Amitié from the north, the west, the south, armed with the newest automatic weapons. And they would see, all of them, what these rough, raw men of the soil could do when properly aroused; as he had aroused them; men who cared nothing for the politics of presidents and councils and assemblies and ministers of this and of that, or the mulatto intellectuals and whites who hungered for power and wealth.

These were men who would be fighting for freedom, for the right to feed their families, clothe and house them properly and decently without fear of disease or corruption. To learn to live like free men in a free world.

They will listen to me, to Chalumeau. They will follow my words and commands now as they did when I spoke to them before. Chalumeau will deliver them as he promised. They will belong to me!

And then, the whites and their cowardly hangers-on! Ah, what a picture it would make, the sight of them leaving, running in fear of their lives, abandoning their long-held treasures and lands behind them.

Ah, what a picture! A picture that centered around himself. And Nicole. And, thinking of Nicole, he fell asleep.

CHAPTER 9

1.

Truscott's reaction was one of uneasy alarm, destroying his normal calm. He leaned forward with a quick, jerky motion that forced the coffee in his cup over the rim, running down his hand. As he dabbed at it with a piece of cleansing tissue, he said, "You're positive about this, Jim?"

Gerard's nod underscored his earlier statement. "I can only qualify it with the usual 'reliable source' answer, but it's true. My information is close enough to the picture to remove any possible doubts from my mind. We know that Chalumeau and Paul Reed are one and the same man. We know that he and Pierre Duclosse have been in contact recently and that Chalumeau met secretly with General Batraville and Basil Zharkov in St. Afrique. I think that should give us a good, clear idea—"

"Where is Chalumeau—or Paul Reed—now?"

"Established in a rented house on Rue Montagneux since yesterday. Last night he attended a meeting at Zharkov's house at which General Batraville was present. That's it for the moment."

The counselor stood up abruptly and paced the width of the room several times. "Goddam it!" he exclaimed savagely. "The situation was complicated enough without an American who has never set foot on American soil getting himself, and us, involved. Win, lose, or draw, we're the goats in this mucked-up mess."

"Whatever they're up to, it's a safe bet that Chalumeau is now involved up to his neck. We can assume by reason of a second meeting that they've reached an agreement of some kind, otherwise Batraville would have Reed in a cage somewhere. If they hadn't, well—there it is."

Truscott sat down again and considered the problem. Which way to turn? I'm boxed in. Boxed in tight. If I take it to Chance, he'll blow his stack. Whatever I suggest, he'll insist on clearing with Washington first. Before we can get a decision out of Emerson, this whole thing could explode in our faces.

He looked up at Gerard, who was waiting for a decision, realizing now the difficulties of the responsibility he was being asked to assume. He said without conviction, "If only Henri Delacroix could muster enough support and strength behind Courdet—"

But Gerard had seen through this too transparent weakness. "Let's not kid ourselves," he said bluntly. "This is no longer in the hands of Henri Delacroix or the Council. Those arms are on their way here now. If they arrive, the Council is out of business. Fontaine, the Russians, Chalumeau, no matter who gets their hands on those arms will be sitting in the saddle pulling the strings. This issue has got to be resolved within a matter of hours. All we've got are two or three days at the most."

Truscott picked up his coffee cup, sipped it briefly, and put it down again. His hand toyed with the dagger-shaped letter opener, let it fall on the leather desk pad. "Well, Jim," he said, "what's next on the agenda?"

Gerard smiled without humor. "Like 'what else is new'?"

"More like, what can we do to prevent this crazy damned involvement?"

"I wish I had an answer for you, but I don't operate with a crystal ball or a slide rule. I can't make promises, either. All I'm asking for at the moment is time."

"Time for what?"

"To play it by ear and see what develops. I made certain promises to the ambassador, but I don't know how I can be of any use if my hands are tied. If you give me a 'hands off' order, the future will take its own course. If I can go along with it for a few days—"

"How many days?"

Gerard shrugged. "I don't know. There can't be too many left, but each day, each hour, could be useful."

"And that's why you're sitting here with me instead of telling it to the ambassador, isn't it?"

"I won't give you any static, Mr. Truscott. That's exactly why. I know how the ambassador feels about people in my line of work. He knows that if I foul up, he alone will carry the responsibility, perhaps find himself on his way back to Washington to have the egg washed off his face. I know it happened to him at least once before. Meanwhile, we're sitting on a bomb waiting for it to explode. If it does, we've all played it safe, but we'll be farther and deeper behind the eight ball than we were before. I'd rather take the risk of telling you first than going directly to the ambassador."

Truscott resumed playing with the letter opener, his mind probing the decision Gerard was asking him to make. The telephone rang and he made no move to answer. It rang again. The counselor reached for the receiver and said, "Yes, Sarah." He listened, asked her to repeat something he had missed, then, "Hold it for the time being. I'll take care of it later." He swiveled around to face Gerard again. "Jim— All right, Jim. We're not going to get anywhere like this. Go ahead. I'll take the responsibility. Another day or two can't matter too much one way or the other. Just try not to get yourself fouled up with the local authorities. One slip and the ball game is over and we're all in the soup together, up to here." He drew a finger across his throat.

"I understand," Gerard said soberly, realizing how deeply Truscott was involving himself.

"If you—" Truscott began, but Gerard finished the sentence for him with a wry grin:

"—stumble, I'll have to pick the pieces up myself. I'll watch it carefully. And—thanks." He stood up and reached for his hat.

"Okay, Jim. Remember that our collective necks are on this one chopping block, will you?"

"I will, believe me. Mine is just as sensitive to the ax as yours."

"Where to now?"

"Just for openers, I might try to locate Tom Reed and see if I can learn anything from him."

"After all you've told me, I doubt if that will produce anything."

"A small effort is better than no effort at all. At least, it will give me something to do."

Truscott shrugged. "If you think so, go ahead. And keep me posted, will you?"

2.

Gerard, Fletcher, and Lebrun drank coffee laced with rum and played their game of Twenty Questions. With few answers. The only certainty in their minds was that the arms were headed for Liberté and should arrive within two days. At the latest, that should put the shipment somewhere off the island by Sunday. The biggest question: Where?

They had no idea of what kind of ship to look for: trawler, freighter, motor patrol boats. Even if they had a thousand eyes available to them, the island was large, far too large for human patrol. There were at least seven coastal ports where a vessel could dock, miles of deserted beach to permit a ship to lie offshore in the night and land its cargo by small craft. They discarded Port Amitié as being too difficult to keep out the prying eyes of possible saboteurs, to give away the game before it got started. And so they sat and pored over two maps, one of Liberté, the other of Cuba, plotting various courses from Bahía de Nipe to logical points along the north and east and southern coasts. They eliminated the west coast as too distant from the capital city, too difficult to reach over steep and dangerous roads by truck.

"There is only one thing we can do while we wait, Emil," Gerard said on a note of hopelessness. "Alert every man you can contact and tell them to keep on the move and their eyes open. Every port, every inch of the coast between ports is a possibility. What we are looking for is any vessel that comes close to the island or anchors offshore within reasonable distance of a beach. They are to report anything suspicious, no matter how minor it may seem."

Lebrun got up and reached for his hat. "I will go at once and begin to make the calls."

3.

At eight-thirty, after two hours of searching in vain, Gerard pulled into Rue Félicité, named long ago by someone in the Department of Public Works who had evidently possessed a sense of humor. Its surface was cracked, light poles were scarred and carved, bulbs broken or stolen from their fixtures and never replaced. Darkness went hand in hand with the natural commerce of the neighborhood. It was the first street that began the slum area. Here, in an atmosphere of offensive stench and human rot, were a number of dimly lit bars where prostitutes of all ages prowled, made their contacts with the willing, took them off to a nearby hovel for a few minutes

299

on a mat spread on a dirt floor, then hurried back to the bars to attract new customers.

Gerard had first checked the Club, then the bars along Rue Pavillon, searching for Tom Reed. And now, on Félicité, he found him sitting at a small table on the veranda of a cheap café, oblivious to the clamor and forced gaiety that surrounded him. Gerard parked his car at the edge of the curbless pavement and went up the two steps, eyed by the usual bevy of heavily painted whores who sat waiting. The saucy, bright-eyed girl of perhaps thirteen or fourteen who had been sitting opposite Reed hopefully got up reluctantly at a silent signal from Gerard and joined her waiting friends on the long bench. Gerard sat in the chair the girl had vacated. A waiter materialized, and Gerard ordered a refill for Reed, nothing for himself. They sat in silence, Reed eyeing Gerard with dull suspicion, until the waiter returned with the rum, which Reed tossed off in a single swallow.

"You got some business with me, Mr. Gerard?" Reed asked finally.

"I'd like to talk with you if I may, Mr. Reed," Gerard replied. The older man waved a hand, indicating that he was ready to listen. "Not here, Mr. Reed. How about taking a little ride with me?"

Reed thought this over for a few seconds. The hovering waiter moved in, tray in hand, dirty towel over one arm. Gerard ordered another drink for Reed. When it had been drunk, he paid the waiter and stood up. Reed got up unsteadily, buckled his trousers belt that hung loosely in its loops and said, "A'right. Le's go, mister."

Gerard drove through the lower end of town, came into a main thoroughfare that led out of the city to the north. They passed a sugar refinery, then the rum distillery, where Reed began sniffing the heavy, sugar-and-alcohol-laden air. When they had passed the last of a group of industrial buildings, Reed asked, "What you got on your mind, mister?"

"Mr. Reed, have you ever heard the name Chalumeau?" Gerard asked.

Reed's head bobbed up and down several times. "I've heard it. What about it?"

"Do you have any idea who he might be?"

"No. Why should I know him? What's he got to do with me?"

"He is your son, Mr. Reed. Chalumeau is Paul Reed."

300

The weariness in Tom Reed's face deepened as he slumped forward and lower in his seat, dejected with premonition at the mention of his son's name. Unconsciously, he fingered the ugly scar on his left cheek. "He up to some trouble?" he asked haltingly.

"I think so. It could be very serious trouble."

"He's no stranger to trouble, Mr. Gerard. Been in enough of it in his time. His old lady let him run wild, and wild he was. Been arrested any number of times and for as many reasons: rape, robbery, assault, just about every goddam thing on the books." Reed shook his head from side to side helplessly. "That boy was born with a hate against the world and everybody and everything in it."

Gerard noted that Reed had very conveniently exempted himself from any blame or responsibility for his son. "What the hell's he up to now?"

"Something that could be very dangerous to all of us. I hate to tell you so bluntly, but we have reason to believe he's involved in a revolutionary activity. If he is successful, it could mean an uprising against every white and near white person and their families on Liberté. A blood bath—"

"I—I seen it happen in Haiti in my time," Reed said heavily. "Been sayin' all along what we ought to do is send the M'rines in here and clean the whole damn bunch of 'em out of that palace and Army Headquarters. Hell, ain' no good ever goin'-a come of lettin' 'em niggers try to run a country. They ain't been that long outa the trees to even know the first thing about—"

"I'm afraid it isn't as simple as that, Mr. Reed." Gerard began pressing, speaking incisively, trying to penetrate into the rum-soaked mind. "World opinion has changed quite considerably since you were in Haiti. I'm sure you saw conditions then that are similar to those here. And I'm sure you remember those earlier years and what happened to white people there when the natives revolted."

"Sure. I seen some of it, too. Why, hell, Mr. Gerard, it got so bad there, the men weren't allowed in town, on duty or liberty, less they went in two's, carrying rifles with 'em. Officers and noncoms wore side arms twenty-four hours a day. I know what can happen."

"Then you know how important it is for us to try to prevent a similar occurrence if we can."

"Sure," Reed agreed. Then, morosely: "All this time, I

thought he was dead. I'n seen or heard of him since—I don't even remember when." A moment later, "Just how's Paul mixed up in this thing?"

"For several years your son has been moving around in the interior country. He's managed to build up a considerable following among the people, preaching hate and revolution to them. They've about reached the blowoff point, and if he finds the means to arm them, the life of a white or near white man, woman, or child won't be worth much on Liberté."

Reed said: "You don't know the half of it, mister. I seen some of the ways they can kill when they get rummed up and drummed up with voodoo. You'd never believe it. Nothin' can stop 'em once they make their move." Suddenly, Reed's voice rose in a high, cracked pitch. "Kill! Burn! Destroy! Drive out the white devils from Hell! Kill! Burn! Destroy!" His voice dropped to a low, harsh growl again. "Yeah. You ever hear somethin' like that in the night, you'll never forget it as long as you live. You stand there and shoot 'em down and there's another ten to take the place of every one you drop. Can't stop 'em. They come on and on from behind, steppin' over the ones that fell, screamin', swingin' machetes, puttin' the torch to everything in sight."

"It's not a pleasant thing for a white man to even think about, is it, Mr. Reed?"

"No, it ain't," Reed breathed heavily, his glazed eyes staring vacantly down at his sweating, trembling hands. "No, it sure ain't."

"And every last one of us is sitting right on top of that live bomb, waiting for it to go off any minute, any hour now."

Reed didn't appear to hear this last sentence. The message had already penetrated his brain, realizing that after thirty years among Libertéans, he had actually conditioned himself to believe he would be immune to the effects of a revolution; and if such a revolution were in the making, if the whites were to be driven into the hills or into the sea or slaughtered where found, that Tom Reed would be permitted to sit at a table in front of some bar and keep on drinking his rum. Now the memory of years long past came back and he knew that he, too, would become one of the hunted. His hands began to clench into fists and unclench again, growing wet with sweat. He clutched at the edges of his rumpled jacket, muttering under his breath, then ran one hand along his left cheek, massaging the white scar again.

"Did you say something, Mr. Reed?" Gerard asked.

"The sins of a father," Reed began. His voice drifted off once more into an indistinguishable mumble, then returned to coherence. "I had two strikes on me when I married her," he said, fumbling for words. "I knew all the time I didn't have to, but I wanted to. You'd never believe it now, but Jesus, she was somethin' to see then. Sure, I loved her. She was white. Whiter'n I was. How the hell did I know she had gook blood in her?"

The road curved away from the land, and they were running parallel to the sea, a long stretch of white beach to their left. On the right, the gradual rising slope jutted suddenly upward precipitously. Gerard slowed down and made an easy turn that headed them back toward the city.

"I'd of gone back to the States and left both of 'em there, but old Raoul outsmarted me, threatened to go to the Commandant. I had a clean record. I didn't want anything to spoil it. But I couldn't go back to the States with a tar baby. I'm from South Carolina. They'd a-strung me up to the nearest lamppost. So I let old Raoul talk me into comin' here.

"Back in '42, I tried to ship over for the war, but they turned me down. More important to raise sugar, the consul told me, but I knew what it was. They knew all about my tar baby son. I had to register him with the American consul in Port-au-Prince, so they knew all about him. After that, I couldn't stand the sight of either one of 'em. Inside, they're all alike, them and their goddam voodoo. Four years old, that boy knew as much about it as anybody on the place. It's born in 'em. I seen him playin' with their *ouangas* and *gris-gris*, their nigger magic that can kill a man. I figured one day he'd grow up and fix me one of them *ouangas* that would cripple or blind me. By the time he was eight, I had enough. I cut out and moved into town.

"Sure, he hates my guts, but no more'n I hate his. Or hers. I can't cry over that. I know I'll be on top of his list once the slaughterin' starts, mister. Number one." Tom Reed suddenly turned, lurching toward Gerard. "By God, he ain't goin'-a turn this place into no slaughterhouse, mister. No, sir. I seen enough of that kind of butcherin' to last any man a lifetime. Sometimes I wake up with the

303

shakes from dreamin' it's happening again, shakin' like I was full of malaria bugs. Christ Almighty, I couldn't stand to see another one of those. Listen. Listen."

Gerard turned toward him, waiting. "Listen, Gerard. You got to get me back to town quick. Right now. I just remembered somethin' I got to do."

They came around a sharp curve, and from this distance they could see the haze of lights that rose and hovered over the city, so incredibly soft and peaceful against the cloud-rippled darkness of the sky. After a few minutes, Tom Reed said, "You know where Paul is, Mr. Gerard?"

4.

Time sped on. At eleven-thirty Gerard bent over the newest map of Liberté's coastal waters that Fletcher had borrowed from the naval attaché. "How does one pick out a single speck of dirt from a ton of black pepper?" Fletcher asked.

Gerard shook his head and threw the pencil down on the table. "It's even tougher if you're wearing a pair of boxing gloves."

The phone rang. He reached for it, hoping it was Lebrun with some news. Any news. The voice was Clark Shannon's. "Yes, Clark, what is it?"

"Just been talking to Mr. Truscott, Jim. He told me to get in touch with you. It's Old Tom Reed."

"Reed? What about him?"

"He's at the General Hospital in pretty bad shape. Took a hell of a beating from somebody. A prowl car came across him lying at the foot of Rue Sans Souci and took him to the hospital. They called Joe Paul at the Consulate. He talked to Truscott, who called me. I hustled over to the hospital, but he's out cold. Smells like a distillery. Truscott said you'd be interested."

"I am. Where are you calling from?"

"The hospital."

"What's the latest on him?"

"He'll live, but he won't look or feel the same. Broken nose, cracked rib, cut and bruised. Body beaten pretty badly. His eyes open up now and then, but he just mumbles without making any sense."

"I'll be right over, Clark. Wait until I get there, will you?"

"Okay. Jake Walker's covering for me at the embassy, but I'll wait for you."

At the hospital, there was little more Shannon could add to what he had told Gerard over the phone. The police who found him had left after Shannon arrived to take over. The doctor said: "It was not an automobile accident, M'sieu. This was done with the hands, the hard, human *poing* by someone who indeed was in a fury."

"Was he robbed?" Gerard asked.

"No, M'sieu. He had money and a watch in his possession."

"May I see him?"

"Of course. If he is able to speak—" The sentence died with a questioning shrug of the doctor's shoulders.

Shannon left to resume his night watch at the embassy. The doctor showed Gerard to the small room where Tom Reed, his purple-bruised face painted with medication and showing bandages across his nose and chin, lay breathing hard. The doctor left him there, and Gerard sat on the chair next to the bed, touched one of the older man's hands. It moved upward and across his flat stomach.

"Tom," Gerard called softly. "Mr. Reed."

Reed's eyes opened and stared upward at the ceiling, his brows corrugated with effort to concentrate. Then his head turned slowly toward Gerard. "Mr. Gerard," he mouthed through swollen lips, but without sound.

"That's right. It's Jim Gerard, Tom. How are you?"

"Wh—where am I? I feel—like—hell."

"You've been in some sort of accident, Tom. Can you remember what happened?"

"I—think—yeah. Yeah." Reed spoke with difficulty, every word an effort.

"Can you tell me about it, Tom? What happened?"

Reed turned away. "Nothin'," he said. "Nothin' happened."

"It didn't happen by itself, Tom. And you weren't hit by a car. You went to see Paul, didn't you?"

"I tr—tried. I—" Tom Reed closed his eyes. Gerard waited, but there was no further response, nor did he need further corroboration. Rue Sans Souci, where the police had found Tom, was three or four blocks down the hill from where Paul Reed now occupied his new residence on Rue Montagneux. He looked at the older man and saw tears seeping out from between his compressed eyelids. Regret? Guilt?

He stood up, touched Reed's hand gently, and left.

5.

In his office, Lieutenant Falot was giving Sergeant Lescaux instructions for the temporary assignment as "aide" to Paul Reed. "You understand, Sergeant, the importance of keeping within sight of him every moment of the time you will be with him. If he leaves the house, you will drive him. When the Russian is watching him, use that time to slip out and telephone your report to me. I rely on you, Sergeant."

"Yes, Lieutenant," Lescaux replied.

"The assignment will last only until the middle of next week. Then you will return to your duties here. Meanwhile—"

The door opened and General Batraville entered. The two men rose and stood stiffly at attention as the general passed them on his way to his office. Over his shoulder, he said sharply, "Lieutenant, I wish to see you at once."

Falot turned back to Lescaux. "You will go at once to the *caserne quartier-maître* and have your equipment issued to you. I will check it with you when you return. Go now."

Reluctantly, Lescaux left the office. Falot knocked on the general's door and heard his, *"Entrez."*

Batraville said, "Is there anything on the morning report of interest?"

"Nothing, General. However, I have had good news from one of my men."

"What is it?"

"Marcel Courdet."

Batraville's eyes lighted up. "You have found him?"

"Yes, General, it is as I thought. He is hiding on Terre Delacroix. Last night he came to the Gran Maison from the woods after dark. He returned to the woods before dawn this morning."

As he studied this for a moment, Batraville heard Falot's eager voice saying, "With a few men, I can—"

"No. Not yet. To do so would create a disturbance and excite Henri Delacroix into some unforeseeable action. No, Claude. We will allow him to feel that he is completely safe. Withdraw your man. Courdet believes he is secure. He will not flee from a comfortable hiding place. On Sunday night, once the arms are loaded and the trucks have been dispatched to Maréchal, I will take a few men and find him, bring him into Port Amitié. On Tuesday morning, I will deliver him personally into the hands of M'sieu Fontaine. Let him then engage himself with young Courdet while his capital and the country fall around his ears, eh?"

"Very well, General. I will attend to it at once."

6.

At the house on Rue Montagneux, Paul Reed heard a report from Caesar, his link between the men who had been sent to contact his key followers in the back country. They had moved swiftly and done their work well. Paul nodded approvingly. "Then I can count positively on forty armed men to gather here before dawn on Saturday."

"It is a certainty," Caesar replied. "They will begin to arrive on Friday and make their way to the woods behind this house, singly, in order not to attract attention to themselves. Each has been well instructed and will be armed. By midnight they should all be here."

"Good. They will be taken care of. You have done well, Caesar. Now I need one more important task finished."

"Command me, M'sieu."

"Marianne will feed you. When you have finished, you will go quickly to Royan with a message for Couteau. You will tell him that on Friday, a man will arrive seeking him. He will say that I have sent him, that I wish to see Couteau here. The man will be light in color, of the same height and weight as you. He will wear civilian clothes, but will be unable to hide his stiff military bearing, *une petit-maître*.

"You will tell Couteau that the man is a captain of the security police, a spy named Mauriac, who has been sent to arrest him and bring him to Port Amitié for questioning, to squeeze from him the names of his followers. You understand me thus far?"

"I understand well, M'sieu."

"Couteau will know what to do. You will remain in Royan to help him. When the spy has been disposed of, you will return at once and report to me. Say nothing of this to anyone else. Tell Couteau that the success of our mission here rests on him. The spy must be destroyed, else we shall all fail."

Caesar nodded. "It will be done as you say, M'sieu."

Paul put a hand on Caesar's shoulder and gripped it hard. "Go now. Your food will be waiting."

7.

On Friday morning, Captain Lucien Mauriac reported to Paul Reed for special assignment as his aide-de-camp. Paul scanned the typewritten note that was initialed with the single letter "B" and tossed it to one side. To Mauriac, he said: "Your arrival is most opportune, Captain. I have a special need for you."

Mauriac said: "I am at your service, M'sieu Chalumeau. I hope you have not taken offense because of the manner in which you were treated in l'Arcachon. I was so instructed and I obeyed my orders."

"Because of your efficiency, Captain, it was I who requested you for this assignment," Paul replied with a smile.

"Thank you, M'sieu. I await my orders."

"Very well. You will proceed at once to Royan. You will wear civilian clothes and go unarmed. There is nothing to fear. On your arrival there, go at once to the Café Tambourin and ask for the owner, Louis Zabrille. When you find him, you will call him by the name Couteau, and say to him that he is to return to Port Amitié with you when night falls, that Chalumeau wishes to consult with him."

"And I am to bring him here?"

"Yes. Do not leave Royan before nightfall. I do not wish him to be seen by anyone. You understand?"

"Clearly, M'sieu."

"Where are you staying in Port Amitié?"

"At the Hotel de Paris."

"Very well. You will leave now. Take my car and leave yours here. Carry your military identity credentials so that you may pass through the checkpoints without delays."

Mauriac saluted stiffly and went out. Chalumeau followed him, gave over the keys to his car, and took Mauriac's keys to the Army car, then watched as he departed for his hotel, where he would change into civilian clothes and start for Royan. And from where, hopefully, he would never return.

He waited restlessly for a full hour before he went out to the kahki-colored vehicle and drove away slowly. At the bottom of the hill, he turned right on Sans Souci, then drove westward to Rue Blanchard. At the Hotel de Paris, the clerk, who had seen him arrive in the distinctively marked Army car, informed him that Captain and Madame Mauriac were occupying Room 12 on the second level, but that the captain had left only a few moments ago. Madame? No, Madame had not left with him.

Paul went up the steps quickly, found Room 12, and knocked on the door. He heard Nicole call out, "Who is it?"

"Open the door, Nicole. It is Paul."

"Paul!" She opened the door quickly and he entered, closed the door, and snapped the latch into place. Nicole stepped into his open arms. "Paul. Oh, *cher* Paul!"

"Ah, Nicole, Nicole," he whispered. "How I have missed you!"

"Lucien. He left only a few minutes ago."

"Did he tell you where he was going?"

"No. He said only that he would return sometime tonight."

"Do not think of him, Nicole. Think only of us."

"But he will return tonight, Paul. We must not be careless."

"Nicole, he will not return. Believe me. You will pack your things now and come with me. Let us hurry."

"Paul—"

"Trust me, Nicole. There is nothing to fear. From today, this minute, you are to forget Lucien. Do not even think of him. He no longer exists. Think only of us, Nicole."

"I am so—*confondu*—Paul."

"Do not be. Do as I say and begin to pack your things."

"What shall I take?"

"Everything that is yours. I will pack his things separately and get rid of it later."

"Paul?"

"What is it, Nicole? You want to come with me, do you not?"

"Yes! Of course. But it comes suddenly. We arrived here late last night. Less than twenty minutes ago he was here in this room. Now you tell me he is no more. I—"

"You will understand later. Now we must pack and leave. Trust me, Nicole, *ma favori*. For the rest of your life, trust me."

Shortly after the noon hour, a Citroën arrived. Two

men got out and approached him on the veranda. One of the men saluted and said, "M'sieu Reed?"

"Who are you?"

"I am Sergeant Lescaux. This gentleman is M'sieu Igor Balnoskovich. We have been sent by General Batraville to report—"

"Ah, yes. My aides. Come in, gentlemen, and make yourselves comfortable." He led the way into the house. Lescaux was a slight man in a white suit, the familiar bulge of authority showing under his left armpit through the thin jacket. He was delicate-boned and wiry, with piercing, black eyes. Igor Balnoskovich was broad and bulky, and his strength showed from his beetled brows and powerful shoulders down to his square-toed boots. There was no sign of warmth in his wide, dour face; the menace in his eyes was noticeable.

In the dining room where places were already set, Paul invited the men to be seated. He went to the doorway and called out, "Marianne, my guests have arrived. Serve them." He stopped at a cabinet and brought out a bottle of rum and one of vodka and placed them on the table.

Within moments, Marianne and the houseboy, Michel, arrived bearing platters of food. Chalumeau motioned that his guests were to be served first. The men began to fork the food into their plates and when they had taken their fill, Balnoskovich looked up, a forkful of food on its way to his mouth. "You do not eat with us, Comrade?" he asked.

"I have already eaten," Paul replied. "If you will excuse me, I will go to my room for the siesta. There is a room on this floor that you can share. Michel will bring your bags and put them there."

"You have orders for us, M'sieu?" Lescaux asked.

"For the moment, no. There will be little to do here until Monday evening. Meanwhile, enjoy your stay as my guests." He got up, bowed with a smile, and left them to finish their meal.

Duclosse came before dawn on Saturday morning, entering the house through the back, bringing six bottles of rum and two of vodka. Michel showed him into the study next to the room occupied by Lescaux and Balnoskovich. The Russian had risen earlier after a sleepless night in the small, hot bedroom and now lay sprawled out in a lounge chair on the veranda. Lescaux lay on his cot, eyes open. He heard the quiet padding of feet in the hallway, then

310

silence. After ten minutes, he heard the heavier tread of Chalumeau along the hall, the slight noise of the door in the next room open, then close.

He got off the cot, picked up his cartridge belt, and unsnapped one of the pockets. From it, he took out a bite-sized rubber pad and connected it to the amplifier he carried in his hip pocket. He placed the small plastic plug in his ear and pressed the rubber pad against the wall, sat quietly, and listened to the conversation in the study.

Duclosse said in a whisper: "I have come from the bivouac area. They are all there. Matois, Brissac, and Caesar have seen that they have been fed and have issued provisions for three days. They are armed and have ammunition. Now I will return to Pointe Neuf and keep an eye on the barges as they gather. If it is other than I have told you, I will telephone."

"Excellent, Pierre," Chalumeau replied. "Do not worry about anything except that. I will handle everything else from this end."

"And what of the two watchdogs?"

"Leave them to me, Pierre. As long as they guard me, Batraville and the Russian have no reason to be suspicious. When I have no further use for them, I will rid myself of them."

"Be careful, Paul. We are close to our dream."

"No dream this time, Pierre, but reality."

"And what of Sunday night?"

"When the barges leave Pointe Neuf for Anse à Goulet, you will join Matois and Brissac where they will be hidden at Anse à Goulet. I will attend to the two spies sometime before dawn tomorrow, then wait until I hear from you that the arms have been taken. Go now, Pierre, quietly, the same way you came."

"Very well. I will telephone you when I have news."

"I will be here waiting. There must be no talk between us. Let the phone ring three times only, then hang up. It will be the signal."

The rest of his words were lost to Lescaux as the men reached the door and went out into the hall. Lescaux at once detached the wire from the amplifier and replaced the earplug and ultra-sensitive pickup device in the pocket of the cartridge belt. He lay back on the cot now and closed his eyes, but did not sleep.

Later, as he finished his breakfast opposite the Russian,

Paul came into the dining room. "I hope you slept well, gentlemen," he greeted.

The Russian grunted. Lescaux said, "If I may be spared, M'sieu, I will take the Citroën and return to my barracks for a change of underwear and a shirt."

The Russian looked up quickly with suspicion. Paul said: "Of course, Sergeant. And when you report to the general, you can tell him that I have had word that all is well. When you return, I am sure your colleague will wish to refresh himself likewise."

Lescaux drove to his quarters in the palace barracks. He showered, changed to another suit of civilian clothes, and went to the office. Falot had not yet arrived. He left a note saying that all was well and went out. In the lower end of town, he found a café with a public telephone and put in a call to Major Lamonte at his home and quickly repeated the conversation he had heard between Duclosse and Paul Reed.

"Good, Lescaux, good. I am forever in your debt. Return to the house now, and if you learn anything else, telephone me at the house on Rue Perrigeau."

"Yes, Major."

"And be careful, Lescaux. Take no unnecessary risks."

Lescaux hung up. He had not mentioned Reed's plan to dispose of the Russian and himself. That would have to take care of itself when the time came.

In the large bedroom that fronted the house, Paul Reed held Nicole Mauriac in his arms, caressing her tenderly, speaking softly to reassure her as they lay closely together. "I am afraid, Paul," she said, and he could feel the earnest fear in her voice, in her trembling body. "Those two men below, the way they follow us with their eyes. Like jailers instead of aides. Only in here they do not follow us. I do not like it. They frighten me."

He drew her closer to him and held her tightly, confidence in his grip and words. "Nicole, Nicole, have no fears. Those two, they are nothing. Small jackals. And while they waste their hours watching me, my men have gathered in the woods behind us, under their very noses."

"There will be fighting, won't there, Paul?"

"Only for a while, Nicole. It will be swift, and fewer will die because it will be so swift."

"You will be in danger."

"I have lived all my life on the edge of danger, *ma*

favori. That is why life is sweeter to me than to most. I know its value and the need to be free. This is not work for weak, placid, passionless men, but for those who have little to lose and everything to gain. They who wait for me, listen to me, follow me, do so because I think and look ahead for them. They know that if they do as Chalumeau says, their dreams, like mine, will come true."

"Lucien believes—"

The name inspired a snort of disdain. "Lucien. That weakling. A follower, like Batraville and the rest. They clutch at the shirttails of false leaders and hope for crumbs. Nicole, listen to me and believe me as the men below in the woods believe me. It will not take long. A day, two days. And those wild men will have put us at the head of our country. They and thousands like them who have been ground under the heels of others for years. Soon they will feel the glory of their freedom as I feel the power in me now. Do not be afraid of them, Nicole. Trust me."

"I trust you, Paul, when I am in your arms."

"Then prove it. Say you are not afraid, *ma chère*."

"I am not afraid," Nicole parroted; but perhaps not as confidently as she might. Lucien was still in her mind, and although Paul held him in complete contempt, even he did not know of the violence that lay beneath Mauriac's quiescent surface. And Paul had still not explained the mystery of where Lucien had gone and why he would not be back. Friday night had passed and there was no sign of him. Now it was late Saturday night. Had he in fact returned and was now seeking her?

In the complete stillness of the house and the night, they heard the light rasp of a fingernail scratching on the bedroom door. Paul kissed Nicole quickly, drew the sheet over her, and walked barefooted across the dark room. He opened the door quietly and admitted the houseboy, Michel. "What is it?" Paul whispered.

"M'sieu Brissac sends word. He is ready, M'sieu."

"I will come at once. And the two below?"

"They sleep, M'sieu. The white man in a chair on the *portique*. The other one is in the small room downstairs."

"I come at once. Return and wait in the hall below. Here, take my shoes with you. I will put them on later." He let Michel out, closed the door again, then pulled on shirt and trousers, buckled on the wide, cartridge-studded belt with its holstered pistol, and picked up the automatic

313

machine pistol. Nicole got off the bed and went to him.

"Wait here for me, Nicole. I will be no longer than a half, three-quarters of an hour. And," he added reassuringly, "if you hear a disturbance downstairs, do not be alarmed. Remain in this room." He held her tightly in the curve of his arm for a moment and kissed her. "Lock the door behind me," he whispered.

He went downstairs noiselessly. Outside the small room in which the one aide slept, he felt Michel's hand reach out and touch him. Paul handed the machine pistol to the boy, who took it and held it close to his chest lovingly, as though he were a man fondling a woman. Paul pushed the door inward with a light touch. Its oiled hinges were quiet. He moved into the room and followed the sound of Lescaux's breathing. He waited, allowing his eyes to become accustomed to the darkness and soon, in the pale light that filtered through the single window, he began to make out the figure of the slight man on the narrow cot, face turned upward, left arm curled behind his head on the pillow. Slowly, cautiously, Paul took a step toward the cot; another. His foot touched the cool iron leg of the bed softly.

Paul stood still for a moment, each move already planned. Above all else, he must not waken the Russian who slept on the veranda no more than thirty feet away, with only a room between them. He turned slightly, reached a hand out and picked up the pillow from the other bed with his left hand. As he drew the knife from his waistband with his right hand, he felt, as much as he heard, a rustling movement in the cot.

"M'sieu," Lescaux said in a soft whisper, "it will be of no use to kill me. We have orders to kill you if either of us is harmed. If I shout—"

Paul stood frozen in his tracks.

"Put the knife away and the pillow on the floor, M'sieu Chalumeau. I have a gun in my right hand that is trained upon your chest. Before you can make a move, I will shoot. Even if I do not kill you, the Russian will."

Paul lowered the pillow and sheathed the knife. "Very well, Sergeant, the next move is up to you. What shall it be?"

"I know you have men about, M'sieu, somewhere in the woods behind this house. Therefore, even if I kill you, it is likely that I shall not escape. Let me say, M'sieu, that I am sympathetic with your movement. I could become one of you if you will permit and trust me."

"How can I be sure?"

"I will tell you. We have been sent here to watch you closely. I by General Batraville, the Russian by M'sieu Zharkov. You cannot hope to win him over with bribes or promises. He is not one of us. Let me kill him for you."

Paul thought for a moment, then said, "Do it. Now."

Lescaux rose from the cot and swung his legs around to the floor. When he stood up, he was naked to the waist, but wore his trousers. He thrust the pistol into his waistband and held out a hand. "Your knife, M'sieu. I will not make a sound."

Paul handed over the knife. Lescaux went out into the hallway, Paul behind him. They passed Michel in the dark, and Paul took the machine pistol from him.

Lescaux had reached the door that led to the veranda. He pushed it outward and it opened silently. He put his head out and saw the figure of the Russian, sprawled out in the chair to his left, his leonine head rolled down toward his right shoulder, snoring lightly. Lescaux waited. A half-minute passed before he put one bare foot out and heard the boards creak lightly beneath his weight. He paused again. The Russian slept on. He took two more experimental steps; another two. The Russian did not move. He took the last three steps that placed him directly in front of the sleeping form, standing poised on the balls of his feet, ready to lunge with the knife.

And then the Russian's eyes opened. Wide, startled, frightened eyes. His mouth opened and clamped shut again. His arm came up, reaching for the pistol in his open holster under his left arm while pushing backward in the chair. Lescaux lunged forward, driving the knife homeward toward the man's heart, but the Russian twisted to one side and the knife glanced off the leather holster, giving off the sound of tearing cloth.

Heels dug into the floor, the Russian pushed backward again, taking Lescaux's weight with him. The chair toppled over. Lescaux clutched for the Russian's throat, but Balnoskovich, alert fully now, rolled quickly to one side. He turned over twice again to be clear of his attacker and found himself momentarily in the clear. He struggled to his knee, his right hand again reaching for the automatic. He got a grip on the butt of it and started to withdraw the weapon, but Lescaux was behind him

315

and threw one arm around his throat, pulling backward, throwing Balnoskovich off balance and cutting his air supply off. Holding his one-armed grip firmly, Lescaux brought the knife up swiftly and drove it into the big man's back. For a moment the two figures formed a motionless tableau in the shadows, then the Russian gasped, grunted, and fell forward. He made an effort to push himself up, but succeeded only in turning over. Balnoskovich was dead. Lescaux stood up, exhausted, empty-handed, and saw Chalumeau standing no more than ten feet from him, the muzzle of the machine pistol aimed in his direction.

Lescaux spread his arms out and said, "You wish to shoot me now, M'sieu Chalumeau?"

The moment of tension was broken when Paul lowered the machine pistol and said, "No, Sergeant. I can make good use of a man of your courage and resourcefulness. Come, let us carry him outside." To Michel he added, "Go upstairs and tell Madame that all is well, that I will return to her in half an hour."

They carried the Russian's body through the house and down the steps to the yard below. "You will remain here and bury the Russian," Chalumeau ordered. "At this late hour, I cannot explain your presence to the others. I will return when I have taken care of another matter."

Lescaux nodded and sat on the lower step to catch his breath. Chalumeau strode to the far end of the yard, climbed over the low wall, and walked quickly toward the woods where Toussaint Brissac and Albert Matois met him.

As the three men plunged into the thick woods beyond, Chalumeau thought with deep satisfaction of these two men who had been able to hold the others in check since they had begun to arrive the morning before. Colonel Brissac, former head of l'Ecole Militaire, had been relieved from his post eight months earlier and sent to Perreville out of harm's way when he had fallen under suspicion for disagreeing with several of Batraville's stated policies. He was perfect for taking charge of the operation about to be put into effect. Major Matois, who had been moved out of the palace to make room for Batraville six years ago, also hungered for revenge. Both, on word of Chalumeau, had deserted their commands months before, taking with them several men on whose loyalty they could depend. Both would become generals in the new Army of Liberation.

"The men are all present?" Chalumeau asked.

Matois said, "All are present, General."

The gratuitous title pleased Chalumeau. General. "And the truck?"

"Ready and waiting only for the men to mount," Brissac replied.

"Good, Generals. I will speak to the men for a few minutes, and then you will leave for Anse à Goulet."

They came to the clearing some three hundred yards behind the house, and were challenged by a sentry. Brissac gave the countersign, and the three stepped into the circle of men who sat upon the ground speaking in low tones, passing bottles and flasks back and forth between themselves. They were an odd assortment of various heights and build and dress. Mostly, they wore soft straw hats, gray or blue shirts and trousers, their feet bare or in thonged, roughly made leather sandals. Duclosse had thoughtfully provided blankets that were rolled, tied, and slung over their shoulders. Each man was armed with a rifle or carbine and wore a partly filled bandolier of ammunition under his blanket, with a sharply honed knife slung from his belt. Some had pistols shoved into their waistbands, and almost all carried machetes at their sides, some nakedly open, others in crude leather scabbards. Beside each man was a cotton sack that bulged with cooked or dried meat and chunks of bread.

Someone announced, "Silence! Chalumeau comes!" The low murmur of voices rose for a moment, then fell off.

Chalumeau entered the circle, turned completely around so that each man could see him. As he spoke, he kept turning so that it seemed that he was addressing each man personally at one time or another.

"It is past midnight and our Sunday has already begun, *mes frères*," he said. "Tonight, the arms arrive. We will be ready. You have your instructions. You are armed and have food and drink to last three full days and nights. Be sparing of it. If all goes well and as planned, it should be over in two days.

"You will take your positions and be prepared to move on command of Generals Brissac and Matois. The difficult part will be the waiting, but it is one full day only, and you must not allow yourselves to be seen or heard until the word is given to attack. It will be a long and tedious day, but by nightfall, it will have been worth the waiting. Then, *mes frères*, you will act swiftly. Our one great hope is surprise. They will not expect you, so the element of surprise will rest with you. When you strike, strike quickly, strike hard. Make certain that no one escapes to spread the word. Be sure your man is dead before you go on to the next.

"Remember that if you fail, you will be dead and we shall all have failed. Kill now so that you may live. Live, so that together, we and our brothers who wait for us will be able to overthrow the despots, drive out the white ones and the yellow ones. Chalumeau has given you his word that Liberté shall be yours. Life will be good if we succeed, but the dead cannot enjoy such rewards.

"You have been well instructed. Wait for the signal to move, then move like the lightning in the skies before they can gain their wits. You will be forty armed to their twenty armed. Do not hurt the unarmed prisoners. Later, they will join us, work for us. When it is over, the trucks will be standing there, already loaded, waiting for you to take them and hold them until the rest of our people arrive from their homes in the interior and the arms distributed among them.

"Do you understand what I have told you?"

There came a rising growl of approval and assent.

"Will you carry out the orders of Generals Brissac and Matois?"

Again the fierce, eager snarls of acceptance.

"Do you believe and support Chalumeau?"

As one, the men rose to their feet, brandishing their weapons over their heads, calling out, "Yes! Yes! Yes!" He waited for a few moments, then waved his arms for silence.

"Then you will now go with your leaders. Follow them, do as they order and you will be victorious. Tonight, you will take and hold the arms we need. By dawn on Monday, I will join you. All of Monday, our people will arrive to be armed and instructed. Early on Tuesday morning, we strike. By nightfall, Liberté shall be ours—yours. Go now, and remember that L'Aube that I have promised you is within your sight."

Over the large map that lay spread open before them, Constantine Lamonte's fingertip pointed to the name POINTE NEUF. It lay nine miles south of Port Amitié, a high barren cliff that fell away sharply at its westernmost point to a small, unsheltered stretch of rocky shore where a group of abandoned fishing shacks huddled as though seeking protection from the sea.

From this extended finger of land, the shoreline curved inward, south and east, to form the deep, natural harbor of Anse à Goulet. To the north and south of that fine, sandy beach that marked the end of Terre Delacroix, lay heavy woods. To the east, Fort Maraboux towered over the placid scene.

Together, Gerard, Fletcher, and Lamonte studied the western coastline on either side of Pointe Neuf. Here, the barges would be gathered and, at nightfall, brought to Anse à Goulet.

"Anse à Goulet," Lamonte said after a while. "Perfect."

"If we can rely on Sergeant Lescaux's information," Alec added. Lamonte's cool reaction to Alec's subtle doubt was immediate. "I have every confidence in Lescaux. He has served me well before. He is more than a soldier. He is a good friend in whom I repose utmost faith."

"I'm sorry," Alec apologized quickly. "I intended no slight, I assure you."

"Of course."

Gerard said, "Let's have a final recap of the situation. As we know it now, Chalumeau has willingly accepted Lescaux and the Russian as aides. Therefore, we can assume that there is a firm level of understanding and co-operation between the Russians and Batraville. If that is so, why the men in the woods behind Chalumeau's house? Surely, Batraville has all the manpower and transportation he needs to handle the shipment. Just what devil's brew—"

"Unless," Lamonte suggested, "Chalumeau's men are to back up Batraville's soldiers—"

"Forty men?"

There was a deep silence in the room. They heard a dog bark, the voice of Jacques admonishing the dog to keep quiet, then the chirp of a restless bird in a nearby tree.

"Jim?" Alec said.

"Something doesn't add up. On paper, yes, but I can't quite reconcile myself to the fact that a man of Chalumeau's dedicated hatred for Fontaine, Batraville, and the whole system of authority could be bought off for any price."

Lamonte shrugged. "Perhaps they have found the one price to which even a Chalumeau would succumb."

"Since there's little or no alternative, Jim—" Alec began.

"You're right, both of you," Gerard said suddenly. "Either way, we've still got the same problem facing us. We'll go with what we've got and trust to luck."

Et le bon Dieu," Lamonte said in a low voice.

"And to God," Gerard echoed. "Alec, are you up to a trip to Terre Delacroix?"

"Ready, willing, and able."

"From here on in, it's going to be sticky. You can't afford to be picked up on so little as a parking or speeding violation. Falot is out there somewhere waiting to get another crack at you."

"Don't worry, Jim. If I can't outsmart him from now on, I'll go back to a filing clerk's job."

"If you can get away from him next time. All right. You go down to Terre Delacroix and talk to Mark and Marcel. Mark is to go about his business as usual. You and Marcel are to keep out of sight at all times in case someone comes nosing around to check the ball grounds before the game begins. When and if something happens, get to Mark's phone and call me from there. The major or I will answer and we'll take it from there. Use the Ford and take a couple of weapons with you. Extra ammo, just in case.

"What we've got to find out is where the stuff goes. It could be the arsenal here in Port Amitié; it could be stored at some other location. Just where, is what we'll have to find out."

"Right. On my way."

"Not yet. Wait until it's a little darker out. And keep the Ford under cover once you get there."

"No sweat, Jim."

"Major, will you stay here with me?" Gerard asked.

"But of course," Lamonte replied. "I have no decisions to make until Monday morning."

9.

On Sunday morning Marcel Courdet stood idly at the eastern edge of the woods looking up at Fort Maraboux.

Hidden in the tangled brush on the northern edge where the sand beach of Anse à Goulet began, Alec Fletcher lay quietly, his eyes scanning the empty sea.

Marcel had held the same watch from six o'clock until noon. The day was exceptionally quiet, even with Fletcher so close by for company. They had exchanged small, light conversation when André had come with a hamper of food at breakfast time, which they had eaten in relays. André would not return until dusk.

The frustration of loneliness, his longing for Julie, and the deep concern for his mother and father weighed heavily on him. Even the bird and animal sounds seemed muted, as though every living thing had gone out of the world. The roaring of Mark's agricultural equipment that had labored nearby all week and annoyed him with its noises was singularly quiet on this day of rest. Now he longed for the mechanical symphony, the chorus of workers' voices that accompanied it. Today he must be doubly careful not to attract attention of the nonworking natives who might be wandering about idly. Nor could Mark, Eugénie, or Julie visit without adding to the risk of exposing him.

To remain confined in the hut was unbearable. Marcel slipped through the woods and lay down beside Alec for a moment.

"Anything, Alec?"

"Nothing. Not even a fishing boat has passed by in the last hour."

"I think we waste our time."

"It's too early for that, Marcel. If it's going to happen, it will happen today. We'll know for sure by dark."

"This—this waiting. It is abominable," Marcel exclaimed. "It is the most difficult of all punishment to accept."

"And the most difficult quality to learn is patience," Alec said quietly. "Almost anything, no matter how difficult or intricate, is acceptable as long as the mind and body are occupied. To do absolutely nothing but wait is an art in itself. Why don't you take off for a hike somewhere where you can't be seen? It helps sometimes."

It was then that Marcel decided to make the trip to the fort. He checked the highway carefully before he scurried across it, then plunged eagerly into the growth beside the stony roadway that led up to Mont Souffrance.

It had been ages since he had come here for the sole

purpose of touring the fort. Years ago, schoolchildren were taken on regular historical pilgrimages, but later, it had been declared unsafe, and visits by students and tourist sightseers were discontinued. Once since his return from Europe, had he come to take photographs for a story he had been asked to write for a Chicago news syndicate.

He had expected, during those years, that his imagination would have projected the ancient edifice into greater proportions, but now, on closer examination, he found that his memory of it had not been exaggerated. It was an immense structure, amazing as it was gigantic; even more amazing when one considered the conditions under which it had been built: by a man with no education or training in construction, without any knowledge of engineering, with forced labor, handmade tools and materials that were purely native; fear and dread of invasion had compelled Maraboux, giving him the tremendous drive, at an overwhelming cost of life, to complete and arm the fort in an impossibly short time—hence, the more popular name by which it was known, Fort Massacre.

The heavy wooden, weather-scarred doors had long ago collapsed by their sheer weight and lay rotting on either side of the twenty-foot-wide entrance. Marcel came into it on the upper level where there were nine almost evenly spaced stone buildings, now in various stages of disrepair, that had once housed the troops that manned and served the long bronze cannon. These had been captured from French land garrisons at Cap Grande, Carcassone, Pointe Nègre and Riam-sur-Mer, and installed here after the French general had incautiously blustered in a message to Maraboux that he had sent a request to Paris for substantial Army and Navy forces to support him in teaching the impudent colonial slaves a permanent lesson.

The tallest structure, rising out of the center upper level, was a wide stone housing that covered the entrance to a paved ramp that led to the level below. Up and down that ramp men had marched to and from their watch duties. Powder and ball had been trundled up from the huge magazine to feed cannon and muskets. Huge iron caldrons on wheels, now lying about and rusted into uselessness, had once been filled with flammable oil that, in emergencies, was set afire and poured through openings to spill down the mountainside when and if foot soldiers were sent against them.

The second level was high, wide, and broad. It was completely open except for well-spaced columns of thick timber that ran from floor to ceiling overhead to support the top level. Here, several thousand off-duty men and women had lived in a vast open dormitory, and here they had slept, eaten, made and repaired clothing and equipment, and waited to relieve the watchers on duty at the gates, beside the cannon along the walls. On opposite sides of this level were two tremendous catch basins that trapped rainwater by means of a series of troughs constructed on the upper level. During the months of siege, these had been their only source of water for drinking and cooking purposes.

The entire third level, reached by a series of narrower ramps, was given over to rooms and communicating passageways. At the forward end were the officers' quarters and hospital area. A wide aisle partitioned this section from the rooms given over to food, clothing, and tool storage, an armorer's shop, smithy, and other repair shops. Another passageway, then came rows of dark, windowless prison cells, some with manacles still dangling from rusted chains embedded in the stone walls, and where the dust of men was inextricably mingled with that of time.

At the rear was a large room that had served as the kitchen, where meals for officers, the sick, and prisoners were prepared. All others would draw rations and water and cook their own over charcoal braziers on the upper levels.

Marcel moved through the rancid air and stink of ancient, musty history, a handkerchief over his mouth and nose to keep out the fetid odors, dust, and gaseous air disturbed by his passage. His flashlight picked out bats and rodents, their squeals of protest echoing in his ears. He hurried back toward the ramp, feeling the heaviness in the air like a heavy blanket, and ran up to the floor above, scarcely pausing until he reached the fresh air and reassuring quiet of the top level.

How peaceful and serene everything looked below: the white beach, the sea, the land itself lying placidly in the late afternoon sun. He contemplated the hurricanes he had seen over the years, the tragic hardships inflicted by Nature in her wildest, most capricious moods; but these had passed and were eventually overcome by man's eternal optimism and hard work.

But man's own intense greed, his blind bestiality toward his fellow man, were the most difficult of uncivilized brutalities impossible for him to comprehend; how it was able to perpetuate itself from the beginning of man's existence, generation after generation, and flourish. Even the most ancient religions of mankind asked so little that could do so much for all—that he do unto another as he would have done unto himself—but in the centuries of its practice (or lack of practice), the need to better one's lot at the expense of his brother was as strong, if not stronger, than the will to survive.

Marcel's attention was diverted by the movement of a small vehicle on the road far below. For a second, the windshield reflected the rays of the weakening sun. His eyes followed the car until it disappeared in the direction of Maréchal to the north. And then he became aware of the time that had passed. The hour was nearing five-thirty. André would be coming to the hut soon with a fresh hamper of food. He wondered hopefully if Julie would come with him.

Mam'selle Julie, André told him as he ate his supper by candlelight, had telephoned earlier that Mama Delacroix was ill, and with her father not yet returned from the palace, she must remain at home. She sent word that she had spoken with Angélique and François Courdet by telephone and that they were being well entertained at the embassy. They sent their love and asked him to be careful. M'sieu Mark and Madame Eugénie were at Gran Maison, and perhaps later, when all was quiet for the night, M'sieu might ride out to visit with him and M'sieu Alec.

As he ate his portion of the meal listlessly and without appetite, listening to André's voice, they heard the rumbling of a heavy truck pass on the main highway, its gears grinding in a protesting whine along the upgrade. Marcel stopped eating and listened. They heard another truck, then a third. André snuffed out the candles. As the next two trucks passed, André said, "They go toward Anse à Goulet," then went quickly outside to the east fringe of the woods for a look, Marcel on his heels.

There were no lights visible, only the ghostlike outlines of the trucks against the solid black background of the hillside, the whine of their engines as they passed. Soon the last in line had disappeared. André said, "I have counted ten."

"Ten," Marcel agreed. "Come with me."

They ran back to the hut where Marcel found his field glasses, then hurried through the thick woods and found Alec, already alert, lying at the extreme edge where the woods left off and sand began, peering through his own night glasses over the broad sweep of scimitar-shaped beach. André and Marcel lay down on either side of him and stared out over the pale sand and the blackness to their left that was the sea. Alec said in a whisper, "Ten trucks. Six-wheeled, two-and-a-half-tonners."

"We heard them," Marcel replied, his voice kindled with excitement. "Is there anything from the sea?"

"Nothing yet. Whatever it is, it won't show running lights. If it comes in close enough, we should be able to make it out by moonlight." Before he could turn toward his left to sweep the sea with his glasses, he felt André's hand grip his arm tightly, the hoarse whisper choking in his throat. "M'sieu! M'sieu! Look! To the far side, coming out of the shadows." André had caught sight of the barges with his naked eyes. "*Bateaux*. They are *chalands*, flat-bottomed loading barges."

"Yes, yes," Marcel said. "Alec—"

"I see them. Looks like the schedule is operating on time at this end. All we need now is the Havana Express to complete the program." In the pale moonlight, the beach had turned to silver. The trucks stood like silent prehistoric animals, waiting at the east end, still in the shadows. The barges were coming in toward the beach, swinging southward. Out of the darkness, a sleek cabin cruiser arrived, also from the direction of Pointe Neuf, showing no lights. It waited offshore as the barges drew up in a line and touched the sand beach.

André said tensely, "M'sieu Mark. Shall I—"

"Not yet, André," Alec whispered. "Let us watch. We must know more first, who will come from the sea to meet them."

They heard the smooth purring of a motor along the main highway, saw a car turn into the beach and draw up beside the line of trucks. A moment later a second car pulled in off the road and parked beside the first car. Four men got out of each of the sedans and stood in the shadows, talking together. Two men walked downshore to the water's edge where a rowboat waited. They climbed in over its stern. The two men already in the boat began pulling on their oars, headed toward the cruiser. The two passengers climbed aboard the larger craft, and within seconds two pinpoints of light, one red and one white, flickered on and off from the long slender mast, the red above the white. Three full minutes passed, then the flickering signal was repeated. Again, three minutes lapsed before the signal lights flashed on and off.

André's grip on Alec's arm tightened. When he looked up, André's body was partly raised, his head turned toward the sea. Marcel rose in a crouch and gasped, *"Le bon Dieu!"* Alec's mouth fell open, but no words came from it. They had seen it almost simultaneously. In the path of moonlight, a large black shadowy form began to rise out of the sea, far offshore, conical in shape. From high above, on its upper rim, two lights began a rapid sequence of pinpoint flashes, the top light red, the bottom one white.

Beside Alec, André's voice was trembling. *"C'est un démon de la mer!"*

Marcel, his own voice subdued to hide the strain in it, replied, "No, André, it is not a devil of the sea. *C'est une sous-marin.*"

Alec broke in swiftly. "Listen carefully, André. I want M'sieu Marcel to remain here with me. You will return to Gran Maison as quickly as you can. Tell M'sieu Mark what we have seen. The trucks. The barges. The submarine. Tell him the word in English. *Ecoutez! Une sous-marin.* Submarine."

"Oui, oui. Sob—mah—rin."

"Allez vite! Warn him. Tell him to telephone to M'sieu Gerard. Tell him it has begun, that we will telephone with more news as it happens. Hurry."

Their own excitement had deepened the infection in André. Even before the sound of Alec's voice had died away, he was racing back through the woods to the car. Marcel and Alec continued to watch the huge shadow in the sea as it began to creep closer into the harbor. The twin lights on the cabin cruiser were responding in stuttering flashes, then remained on for several minutes, acting as a beacon on which the submarine could aim its long, oval nose. It had been inching along at deck-depth, but now the black hull began to break through the surface as all activity on shore ceased and everyone on the beach came to the water's edge to watch the amazing spectacle.

Moments later, it came to a full stop. Now there began another series of lights. The cabin cruiser's mast lights responded. Back came a staccato of short flashes from the sub and then darkness. They heard the cruiser's motor start, saw it put out from its anchorage, and watched as it sped down the moonlit shaft toward the mammoth cigar-like shape. Within ten minutes it lay close beside the submarine. A line shot out from the deck of the undersea craft and was caught by one of the men on the cruiser. Hands aboard the sub hauled it in and held the smaller craft steady while its two passengers climbed over the side, and boarded. They walked aft to a ladder fixed into the side of the conning tower, climbed upward, then stepped over its rim and disappeared inside the gaping mouth.

On the far side of the beach, forty-two pairs of hidden eyes saw what Marcel Courdet and Alec Fletcher had seen from the near side. Brissac and Matois watched through their field glasses with smiling satisfaction.

Brissac said: "Pass the word for complete silence. When the activity begins, we will crawl closer to the edge, flat on our bellies. They are to lie quietly until I give the word, when the last of the cargo has been landed and loaded aboard the trucks."

Matois tapped Brissac's shoulder to indicate that he had heard, then began to crawl backward to where his impatient maquis waited.

10.

Inside the submarine, Captain Pyotr Guchakov, young, confident, and smiling with pride, led John Mosher and Basil Zharkov below to his cabin, proffered a box of cigars, then poured vodka for the three. Seated in the small, sterile room, Mosher looked about him with curiosity.

"Your first visit to a submarine, Comrade?" Guchakov asked.

"No," Mosher replied, "but this is quite different from the two I have visited before."

"There is a difference, Comrade," the captain said. "It is a new type of supply submarine. All necessary equipment, armaments, torpedoes and other excess have been removed to make room for cargo. Under present conditions, with so many eager eyes watching, it is more advisable to ship supplies under, rather than above, the sea in these areas."

"But so vulnerable," Mosher commented.

"Not so, not so. Our sister lies out there to support

me if I am detected. In such a case, she engages the attacker while I escape or lie safely on the bottom. It is a team operation that we are experimenting with. She is our eyes and ears. We carry the cargo."

Mosher nodded. "Clever," he said.

"And so far, practical."

Zharkov had finished his drink, put the glass down, and said, "And the shipment?"

"In its entirety."

"Your manifest, Comrade Captain."

"Here." Guchakov handed over a sheaf of papers he took from the compact desk. Zharkov began checking the list, handed the top sheets to Mosher as he finished with each. Mosher scanned the first sheet quickly, handed it back to Zharkov. "I can't understand this. It is in Russian."

"Of course," Zharkov replied. "The submarine base at Bahía de Nipe is under Russian control, is it not? Once we have landed the cargo and return to Port Amitié, I will have this transcribed into French and Spanish for you." He turned to the captain. "How long before you will be ready to unload? We have ten barges lying on shore ready to come alongside."

"I will give the order to prepare the unloading hatches at once. We will be ready in perhaps the time it takes your barges to reach us."

"Good," Zharkov said with a nod of approval. "Comrade Mosher and I will return to shore and start them out." He folded the manifest sheets and put them in his inside jacket pocket as the captain rose to show them back to their boat.

Ashore, they conferred briefly with General Batraville and Leiutenant Falot. Batraville gave the order to move the barges out. To the man in charge of the trucks he issued orders to prepare to receive the cargo that would be coming ashore.

11.

Mark Fuller found Alec and Marcel lying in the tangled undergrowth, and for a few minutes they watched the incredible activity in silence while Alec brought him up to the minute on what had been happening. André knelt as though in prayer, making vague signs with his hands as if to ward off a threatening evil.

328

"Did you reach Gerard?" Alec whispered finally.

"I got him," Mark replied. "I could have knocked him over by breathing a little harder into the phone. By submarine. The smart bastards."

To their left, the first of the barges had reached the beach where prisoners in red-and-white-striped penitentiary garb waded out into the water to receive the heavy wooden cases from the bargemen. One of the trucks had backed down to the water's edge so that the cases could be transferred directly to its tailgate, where other prisoners stacked them inside under the watchful eyes of armed guards. When the truck was fully loaded, it was pulled upbeach and another truck backed down to take its place. The emptied barge then moved to the far side of the cove to make room for another that had arrived. The action was swift and efficient, with occasional curses and blows from rifle butts to urge the stumbling prisoners on.

When the last of the barges had been unloaded, the darkness was again broken by a short burst of intermittent flashes from the sub. There was no reply from shore. The sub's motors began thrumming quietly, and a few moments later it had turned its stern shoreward and moved in a westerly direction toward the open sea. Within seconds it had become a part of the black night.

Marcel whispered grimly, "I would give ten years of my life for a supply of hand grenades at this moment."

"Don't be so damned generous with your years," Mark replied.

"We've got to find out where they're going to move this stuff," Alec said. "Mark, you'd better get back to the house and phone Gerard. Take André with you. Marcel, I don't think it would be wise for you to come out of hiding yet."

"What good is it for me to stay here?" Marcel asked fiercely. "At least, I can be of some use—"

"Cut it, Marcel," Alec said quickly. "We haven't time for arguing. If they get their hands on you, they can flush your father and mother right out of the embassy into Fontaine's hands. You'd never live to stand trial. When they leave, I'm going to follow behind at a safe distance. I've got the protection of the embassy behind me. Mark, tell Gerard that as soon as I know something definite, I'll find a phone and call him."

For a moment, they resumed watching. The last of the barges moved in line with the others, and the cabin cruiser led them out of the harbor along the north curve and were soon lost in the shadows as they headed toward Pointe Neuf. Alec, Marcel, and Mark now turned their full attention to the last truck where prisoners were covering the load with the canvas tarpaulin, tying it in place. The truck ground its way slowly upbeach and into line with the others. The sentries, two to each vehicle, began herding the prisoners atop the loads.

In the small knot of men that had gathered to one side, Zharkov said to Batraville: "It is all yours now, Comrade. I will return to Port Amitié and telephone Comrade Pyantenov. When you are finished with your business here, I will expect to hear from you." He nodded to the three men who had accompanied him. The foursome climbed into their sedan and drove off toward the main highway and turned in the direction of Port Amitié.

Batraville turned to Falot. "You know what to do now, Claude. Lieutenant Rolière in the lead truck, you in the rear. No lights until you are within a kilometer of Maréchal. Go directly to the warehouse and begin to unload. Keep the trucks and prisoners under guard and allow no one to leave until you receive word from me."

"Yes, General," Falot replied.

"M'sieu Mosher and I, with two others, will go to the house of M'sieu Fuller and search it for Marcel Courdet. I will take him to Bellefonte and deliver him personally to Fontaine, to keep him occupied while he waits for us to deliver the big prize to him. Chalumeau. Ah, Claude," he said, putting one arm around Falot's shoulder, "this will become a night for history to record."

"Yes, General."

"We go now." Batraville signaled to John Mosher and the two security police who stood behind the second sedan. They got in and drove onto the main road toward Terre Delacroix.

Falot turned back to the line of trucks, checking the first with Lieutenant Rolière, who got into the cab beside the driver and waited for the signal to move out. Falot continued down the line and inspected each truck, instructing its driver to keep his lights off until those of the truck in front of his were turned on, to remain closed up within fifteen feet of each other and maintain the set speed.

Alec Fletcher got to his knees and whispered to Marcel and Mark: "They're ready. I'm going back to my car and move it closer to the road as soon as they turn their engines on. When they get around the first bend, I'll follow with my lights off. When you reach Gerard, tell him that—"

They heard the sharp, insistent hiss of warning from André. "M'sieu Mark! *Messieurs! Gardez-vous!*"

At the unrestrained urgency in André's voice, Alec, Mark and Marcel threw themselves flat on their bellies, and even before they could sight along André's extended, trembling arm, the row of irregular, hunched shadows was emerging from the black nothingness on the far side of the beach, racing swiftly across the open stretch of moonlight. Noiselessly, fiercely, the low shapes came on relentlessly like a wind-driven wave, splitting into smaller, separate shadowy groups as they peeled away from the main body to attack the convoy.

At the rear of the last truck in the line of ten, one of the two soldiers turned, saw the oncoming shadowy figures with disbelieving eyes. Unable to find his voice, he pointed the muzzle of his rifle skyward and pulled the trigger. He and his companion were cut down at once. The rest of the soldiers, taken completely unaware, were stunned momentarily by the suddenness of the appearance of these night demons who had come out of nowhere. Well after the first shots had been fired and men were dropping in the sand around them, they were still struggling to unsling their rifles. They broke, ran, stumbled, and fell in the loose sand underfoot as they tried to evade the withering fire. Too late. The attackers gave them no respite to gather their wits, firing rapidly or hacking and slashing at them with a terrible ferocity. As the cries of the first wounded and dying rose, the men on the forward trucks were dismounting in fearful disorder.

Lieutenant Falot's cries to take cover and return fire went unheard or unheeded. He drew his pistol and dodged behind the fourth truck in line, where he had been caught when the first shot was fired. Lieutenant Rolière dropped from the cab of the lead truck, and before he could get his first shot off, fell dead with a bullet through his head.

The scene was one of unbelievable confusion. Soldiers were shouting and firing simultaneously, but ineffectively, helpless against superior numbers, surprise, and an inability to distinguish friend from foe, vulnerable from every direction.

Falot looked on in desperation, realizing the utter futility of trying to rally his totally disoriented men who were being all but cut to pieces, shattered by the unexpected attack. The invaders had surrounded most of the column of trucks and were conserving ammunition by methodically chopping away with sharp, wickedly long-bladed machetes at those wounded who were still alive. He heard the pitiful pleas of the wounded, the *"Cessez le feu!"* of those trying unsuccessfully to surrender, watched as they fell to their knees, arms raised above their heads, only to receive the death cut from a slashing machete with a force vicious enough to decapitate.

And then, but for the whimpering and bleating of the prisoners who had earlier been sent atop the trucks and now lay frozen and out of harm's way, there was an ominous silence. The ragged victors were moving among the dead and wounded, stripping them of arms and ammunition belts, of jackets, trousers, and shoes, calling to each other in gleeful triumph.

Falot crouched low and between the fourth and fifth trucks, sweating with fury and despair. Who? he wondered. In the name of God, who were these phantoms, these *goules diaboliques?* From what lower regions of Hell had they come? No more than twenty feet away, one who was apparently a leader was pointing to himself, calling the guerrilla mob to him, shouting orders. Falot raised his pistol and drew a careful bead on the man, then lowered it. To what results? He would only be cut down moments later. He turned and looked back to the dark brush behind him, a short ten yards away. If he could make it— He dropped from a crouch to the ground and began to burrow across the open stretch to safety. When he had reached within three feet of it, he heard swift footsteps running toward him. He turned toward the sound and looked up. A huge figure was coming at him, machete upraised. He reached for the pistol that was dragging along in the sand with him, attached to a lanyard around his neck, and as his hand closed around it the blade fell on his shoulder. He rolled away from it. The blade fell again, close to his face, catching the lower part of his ear and cheek. He struggled toward the brush, then felt himself pulled back by the collar of his jacket. A second later he was struck with what must have been

332

the butt of a rifle or a pistol as it clubbed his skull twice, then a third time. Dazed, praying for quick release from his agony, he felt a pair of hands rifling his pockets, tugging at the pistol, still attached to the lanyard. He heard a mutter of disgust or disappointment, then an oath that was followed by another crashing blow on his head. From behind closed eyes, he saw a brilliant explosion of millions of lights. Then it was over. Only darkness and peace.

Brissac and Matois surveyed their victory with complete satisfaction. The entire engagement had lasted less than ten minutes. Only two of their men were dead, three wounded. The rest were pawing over captured pistols, rifles, and personal loot. From the fringe woods where they had lain hidden came another figure now. Pierre Duclosse. He joined Brissac and Matois for a moment. Brissac turned and spoke to the men, issuing orders crisply.

The unharmed laborer-prisoners were ordered down from the truck tops; shovels were taken from the equipment box on the running board of each truck, and the men set to digging a long, shallow common grave. The slain were dragged to this point, laid into the trench, and covered over. When the gruesome chore was completed, some semblance of order was restored. The prisoners remounted the trucks, men were told off as drivers, and the vehicles began heading for the main highway.

The quartet in the woods were staggered by the swiftness, horror, and complete decimation of what had been an efficient operating force. André was on his knees, rocking back and forth, his face and shirt soaked with sweat. *"Loups-garous,"* he muttered vacantly. *"C'est les loups-garous."*

Marcel spoke into his ear in a low, sharp whisper. "Do not become foolish, old man. They are not maneating werewolves or ghosts. They are men like others, like ourselves. They did not eat them, nor did they harm the prisoners. They killed the soldiers to take their arms. Werewolves have no need for arms, but men do."

Mark said, "Who? Who in God's name are they? Where did they come from?"

"Chalumeau," Alec replied. "They are Chalumeau's men. It's a double-cross. Chalumeau was to work with Batraville, and now he's sitting in the saddle with something

333

like twenty-five tons of rifles, machine guns, ammo, and only God knows what else. They're ready to pull out. It's more important than ever to find out where they're going with this load. Get back to the house as fast as you can now, Mark, and get to Gerard. Tell him what has happened and to hang on until he hears from me. I'll try to—"

It was at that moment that they heard the clanging of the fire-warning bell from Gran Maison. From the workers' quarters, the sound was taken up as other bells began to clang out, calling everyone on Terre Delacroix to assemble at Gran Maison. Mark was already running back through the woods toward his car, looking up into the sky for a sign of flames. But there were none. Marcel and André leaped into the car behind him as it took off across the open field, heading for the dirt road. When they reached the main house, a large goup of chattering field-workers was already there; others were running toward them from their quarters to cluster at the foot of the veranda steps. They cleared a path for the car when Mark braked it to a sudden stop.

In the center of the huddle, Emilie, André's wife, sat weeping, bruised face hidden in her hands. On the veranda, held in the lap of one of the women, Ti Jacques lay unconscious. André ordered the workers to one side, ran up the steps, and gathered his son in his arms while Mark began questioning Emilie.

Between anguished cries, she sobbed out the story. Four men had come, one a white man. When Madame Eugénie met them at the door, they demanded to know where M'sieu Marcel was hidden. Madame ordered them out of the house angrily. They asked for M'sieu Mark, and were told he was not at home. Then the large dark one had pushed her aside. The white man went outside to the car. The other three then searched the house, and when they found no one, spoke together. The large dark man told Madame Eugénie that he was a general of the police and said she must accompany them back to the city. Madame refused to go with them and went to the telephone, but before she could reach it, they took her by force. Emilie had tried to assist Madame, but one of the men had beaten her off savagely. They took Madame by the arms and began to lead her away. Then Ti Jacques attacked them, and one of the men knocked him down with one blow. They put Madame in their car and drove off. Then Emilie had run outside and rung the bell.

Mark, livid with anger, rushed up the steps and into the house. In his study, he picked up the telephone receiver and called Gerard's number. He spoke heatedly for a few moments, then ran outside again. To Marcel, he said: "I'm going into town to Gerard's house. Lamonte is with him. You and André stay here and keep a watch on things."

Marcel said: "I'm going in with you, Mark. It is because of me that this has happened. They will not come back here. André can wait, but I insist on going with you."

Mark did not argue. "Let's go," he said and ran to the car.

12.

Gerard and Lamonte listened to Mark, then Marcel. At the first mention of the submarine, Gerard muttered a quiet oath as the memory of the meaning of Bahía de Nipe came back to him. Consuela Sándoz. She had told him months before in Havana that there was talk among the Russians and Urbana of a submarine pen to be constructed at Bahía de Nipe. Its significance as a means to ship arms and supplies to Communist saboteurs and subversives throughout the Caribbean became a factor of vital importance now. He must get the word back to Harrington as quickly as possible.

Gerard had already telephoned Lebrun and alerted him to keep a close watch on Zharkov's house. Lamonte was telephoning, trying to reach a palace contact, Sergeant Bonté, on whom he had often relied in the past. He spoke to Bonté, and asked to be called if Batraville returned to the palace. Gerard's attention was turned back to Mark Fuller, impressing on him the inadvisability and futility of charging about town on his own; nor would he achieve anything by calling Henri or Julie Delacroix. They must wait until they heard from Lamonte's or Lebrun's contacts. And Alec.

"God," Mark prayed silently, "let her be safe, unharmed. If they hurt her, I'll search them out and kill them if it takes the rest of my life!"

Marcel, in a highly fevered state, pleaded: "Let me go to them and give myself up. It is my fault. They were searching for me. They do not need Eugénie if they have me. I will—"

"For what purpose, Marcel?" Gerard asked. "Do you think they can afford to turn her loose now? They'll take you to force your father and mother out of the embassy and keep Eugénie to prevent Henri Delacroix from interfering. You'll only be giving them an extra trump card to play."

Lamonte said: "He is right, Marcel, Mark. We already have men out who can do far better together what you can only hope to do alone. You can at best only delay matters. It is best for us to plan what we will do when we can move."

In Gerard's and Lamonte's minds there was little doubt that the raiders had double-dealt their co-conspirators. With the Cuban arms intended for Fontaine in Chalumeau's hands, the balance of power had changed within minutes—from tyrant to vengeful despot. Lamonte turned his attention back to Mark.

"On the road to Port Amitié, Mark, you saw no trace or evidence of the truck convoy?"

"Not a sign of it, no."

"How fast were you traveling?"

"As fast as the car would go. Eighty, ninety on the straight stretches."

Lamonte shook his head. "Between the time you heard the firebell warning, reached the house, and started to drive here, no more than twenty or thirty minutes could have elapsed, could it?"

"Less than that. I don't know exactly. Marcel?"

Marcel said, "It could have been no longer than fifteen minutes, twenty at the very most."

"Then," Lamonte said, "the trucks could have no longer been on the road. Two-and-one-half-ton Army trucks are governored down to a controlled thirty-mile-an-hour maximum in order to keep the drivers from overturning on mountain roads. Fully loaded and in convoy, without lights, they could travel at no more then twenty miles an hour. If they had come directly to Port Amitié, you would have seen or passed them before they could reach Maréchal. One thing more: if you were planning such a raid, would you risk so valuable a cargo by bringing it into Port Amitié, past the military checkpoints, when you knew every source would be on the lookout for you?"

"What are you suggesting, Constantine?" Gerard asked.

"Mark and Marcel saw the convoy start off in the direction of Port Amitié on the only road that leads here. There are only two towns between Anse à Goulet and Port Amitié: De Cosset and Maréchal. A stolen convoy that large could not afford to stop at either town, nor be seen passing through. Therefore, if Mark was traveling between eighty and ninety miles an hour, even giving the convoy as much as a thirty-minute start, and they did not pass it, the convoy necessarily turned off the road somewhere between Anse à Goulet and De Cosset. It cannot be otherwise."

"But where?" Gerard asked. "Ten large trucks and between sixty and eighty men simply don't vanish into thin air or disappear in the brush beside a road."

"No. Therefore, they are somewhere off the road in the area between Anse à Goulet and De Cosset."

"Fort Maraboux!"

"That's it. Fort Maraboux," Alec repeated. "I was within a hundred yards of them when the lead truck switched its lights on and made the turn up the road to Fort Maraboux."

Gerard said with some incredulity, "That dilapidated old—"

Lamonte shrugged and nodded. "Why not? It is true that the upper level shows the wear and tear of years of exposure to the elements, but below, it is strong and sturdy and with room enough to hide ten times the number of trucks and a hundred times the number of men."

Marcel nodded in agreement. "You are right, Constantine. I was there only this afternoon. It is possible and reasonable. The second level is firm and vast in size. The ramp is strong enough to support the trucks easily, and there is more than enough room for all."

Lamonte said: "In the old days, the fort held and provided for over six thousand men under Maraboux. And who would suspect that anyone would think to use that ancient edifice for such a purpose? Chalumeau, yes. One, because it is closest to the point of his planned attack and would remove the trucks from sight quickly. Two, because having lived on Belle Roseau, he would know it well. Examine the situation if you will. First, he avoids public detection. Second, he can bring his people across the mountains and up from the south to the fort without having to pass through a single checkpoint. Third, they

337

come to the fort in the night and are armed with the new weapons. Fourth, when they are ready to move on Port Amitié, they can be transported by the same trucks, having first overwhelmed the guards at the Maréchal checkpoint, sweep through the Port Amitié checkpoint, and—"

The soft burring tone of the telephone interrupted. Gerard spoke into the instrument, then asked a few brief questions rapidly. He hung up and turned back to the others. "That was Lebrun. Eugénie was brought to the house of the Russian, Zharkov." As Mark made a sudden move to turn toward the door, Gerard said, "Wait, Mark! She is unharmed. They've evidently drugged her. She was carried into the house without offering any resistance. A moment later, a light went on in a room at the rear on the second floor. They will not harm her. They can't afford to—"

"To hell with that!" Mark spat out angrily. "I'm going over there, with or without you, and—"

"Mark!" Gerard grabbed his arms, spun him around, and held him. "Listen to me, Mark. For the time being, she is safe. For you to run around in circles will gain nothing. Believe me, we all appreciate your anxiety, but any move on your part to get her out of there now can only result in possible harm to yourself. You'll never even get past the gates, except as a prisoner. Zharkov's house is guarded almost as well as the embassy."

"Do you expect me to sit here and do nothing?" Mark asked heatedly.

"No, but unless we work according to some organized plan, we'll get nowhere. Together, we can help each other. Alone, you're only asking for more trouble."

"Damn it, Gerard, I don't want her waking up in that strange house with those hostile faces around her."

"Mark," Gerard said in more even tones, "I know it's a hard thing to ask, but try to be reasonable about this thing. They didn't take Eugénie for the purpose of harming her, but as a political weapon to use pressure against her father and the Courdets. All I'm asking is that you work with us so we can gain more with less effort. All right?"

Mark looked from Gerard to the mute, suffering Marcel, to Alec and Lamonte. Their expressions showed their belief in Gerard's logic. "All right," he agreed finally, "if we make a move. Where do we go from here?"

Gerard said: "We know that Zharkov and Batraville

338

left the area before the hijacking took place, so we can assume that they are still unaware of what happened on the beach. When their man in charge fails to telephone in after a reasonable length of time, they'll check into it and learn that their precious cargo never reached its intended delivery point. How long that will take is anybody's guess. What is certain is that when they do find out, they'll probably be damned near out of their minds trying to figure out what happened and where it is."

Alec and Lamonte nodded in agreement. Marcel and Mark merely stood and listened. Gerard said, "We might even have to find a way to let them know where it is."

"For God's sake, Gerard, are you off your rocker?" Mark shot out angrily.

"Hold it, Mark," Alec said. "Let's hear more. Go on, Jim."

"Let me take it step by step. First, I'll need an accurate map of the fort. Constantine, Marcel, can either of you draw one that will show us what there is inside, on each level? Entrances, openings, rooms, the whole works?"

"I can do that," Lamonte said. "The fort was a subject of study in our schools. There is also a scale model on exhibition in the rotunda at the palace. Fontaine is proud to show it off as a mark of General Maraboux's genius. Every level lifts up to expose the level beneath it. Marcel can help refresh my memory."

"All right, suppose you get busy. I want to work out the rest of the plan with Alec and Mark."

The phone rang again. Gerard took the call and handed the receiver to Lamonte. Lamonte spoke for a moment, listened, then hung up. To the questioning circle of faces aimed at him, he said: "That was Sergeant Bonté at the palace. General Batraville arrived there a few minutes ago. He was in a state of high exhilaration."

"All right," Gerard said. "Our most important characters are accounted for now. Zharkov and Mosher are at Zharkov's house. Batraville is at the palace. If they were aware of the hijacking they would still be together. Now, if one of them makes a move, we will know it. Let's get back to work."

Lamonte and Marcel had begun sketching on a large pad. Gerard, Alec, and Mark were quietly discussing a means of coordinating the plan Gerard was outlining to them. It was nearly eleven when Lamonte and Marcel were ready with their three sketches, one of each level.

The five men stood over the table while Lamonte moved his pencil over the sheets, describing each level, passages, ramps, rooms and cells. "And this area, the large one on the lowest level?" Gerard asked.

"The kitchens," Marcel said. "While the men were fighting or on watch at their posts, all the cooking was done on small charcoal braziers near them. In the kitchen, food was prepared for the officers, the sick, and the prisoners."

"No steps from level to level anywhere?"

"None. Only ramps. They were more simple to build and to use in moving wheeled vehicles or cannon up and down."

Gerard was studying the kitchen area closely. "What are you looking for, Jim?" Alec asked.

"For some entrance other than the only one shown on this map. There must have been some provision for drainage, for water to run off. With the cooking and other necessary sanitary needs to take care of so many men and women, General Maraboux must have had to provide a carryoff of some kind, else his people would have become sick and died off like flies, no?"

Lamonte nodded, but could give no answer. "Then," Gerard continued, "it must be somewhere in the area of the kitchen where most of the water was used. Beneath it, most likely, with the runoff leading outside. Is there a gully of some kind between the outside rear wall and the upslope to the top of the mountain behind it? On the upper hump?"

Marcel said, "Yes. From the top of the upper *bosse,* the hump of Mont Souffrance, one looks down into a steep ravine, perhaps three hundred or four hundred feet down. This forms the saddle in which the fort itself sits."

"And from the upper hump, you can also look down onto the top level of the fort?"

"Yes. Across the ravine. It is a considerable distance. The slope is a very steep one." Lamonte picked up the pencil and sketched the slope and upper hump on the drawing.

"All right. Now, is there a way of getting to that upper hump without using the main road up or being seen from the fort?"

Mark said: "There is an old back trail that leads up to the top. André took Eugénie and me up when I first came to Terre Delacroix. It was overgrown with weeds and high grass even then. No one has used it in years."

"Do you think you could find it again, Mark?"

Mark shook his head. "Not in a hundred years. And at night, not in a million. But it's very possible that André could."

"Okay. We'll have to count on that. Now, let's put the pieces together."

13.

From the closet in his bedroom, Gerard dragged out the wooden cases that had been a part of the luggage shipped down before his arrival. With pliers and a crowbar, Alec began cutting the wire strappings, forcing the lids open, removing the oblong cartons they contained. The oblongs were given to Lamonte, Mark, and Marcel to be taken downstairs. In the first-floor study, Gerard and Alec worked quickly. The first cartons contained canvas carrying bags whose contents were emptied out on the table.

To the curious Lamonte, Mark, and Marcel, Gerard explained as he and Alec worked. "This is the newest XC7 plastic explosive. Three times more powerful than TNT. Completely stable. No danger in jarring, dropping, or from friction. You can fire a bullet into it and it won't go off."

He tore a chunk of the silver-colored puttylike material from the block and said: "Each stick weighs two and one-half pounds. In these two carrying bags are twelve sticks, enough to give us thirty one-pound blocks. We're going to cut them into thirty pieces and put them back into the carrying bags." Lamonte, Marcel and Mark began measuring and cutting the two-and-one-half-pound sticks into smaller squares under Gerard's direction.

Alec unpacked a roll of five hundred feet of yellow Primacord with a red spiral stripe. He measured off about three hundred feet, looped and taped it so that it could be carried over one shoulder. Another carton contained a canvas-covered doughnut shape that held a quarter of a mile of black-coated communicating wire. From its inside rim, Alec pulled out a length and stripped three inches of its plastic covering off to expose bare wires. He used friction tape to fasten the bare ends to the outer canvas covering. The next item was a small galvanometer that would be used to check the wiring for possible breaks.

Gerard, meantime, had unpacked a ten-cap blasting machine, or hell-box, that would set off the charges. It was little larger than a pencil sharpener, flatter and more compact. He inserted the separate handle, twisted it back and forth several times, heard its growling to indicate that it was "warmed up" and ready for use. And finally, he opened the last small carton and removed a half dozen electric blasting caps, each three-inch-long cylinder in its own cardboard sleeve. He slid the caps out and removed the crimped shunts at the end of the twelve-foot lead wires and replaced the caps in their protective sleeves. These he placed in the outside pockets of the canvas carrying bags.

The thirty squares of XC7 were ready. Gerard and Alec packed them back into the carrying bags.

Gerard went upstairs, unlocked a section of his trunk, and picked out a submachine gun, a machine pistol, a .38 revolver, several extra-long clips for the larger guns, and a box of cartridges for the revolvers.

Below, he gave the .38 and cartridges to Mark, the machine pistol and two extra clips to Lamonte, and took the submachine gun for himself.

"I think we're all set," he said. "Let's run through it once more for a final check: Alec, Mark, and I will leave at once for Terre Delacroix to pick up André and get to the top of Mont Souffrance. We'll need about an hour, more or less, according to Mark, to make it to the top. Figure another hour and a half to get down into the gully inside the fort. Another hour to do what needs to be done inside, a half to three-quarters of an hour to get back to the top of the mountain. Constantine?"

Lamonte, who had been checking his watch, said, "Between 3:45 and 4:00 A.M."

"Let's throw in another half-hour for a safety factor and say four-thirty. Timing is going to be important, the key to this whole thing from your end.

"At two-thirty Constantine and Marcel will leave here for Zharkov's house. At three o'clock Marcel will make his move. No sooner than three, no later than three-fifteen. You'll let the guards find you, Marcel. They'll take you inside for questioning. Don't give in too easily or too quickly. Make them work to get it out of you. You'll have to take some rough handling, and it won't be easy or pleasant, but they need to keep you alive if they hope to force your father and mother out of the embassy."

342

Marcel nodded soberly. "Do not concern yourself with me. I will play my part."

"Keep an eye on your watch, Marcel," Gerard cautioned. "Stall them for at least a half-hour. Forty-five minutes will be better. Then give them the information they want. They'll need some time to assemble men and transportation to make the trip to the fort. By four-thirty we should be ready to welcome them."

Marcel nodded as Gerard turned to Constantine. "Major, you'll keep well in the background. When they take Marcel, you'll get around to the back of the house. If you expose yourself too soon and are caught, Marcel's part in the plan will be wasted."

Lamonte nodded. "All right, then, let's saddle up." He picked up one of the oblong carrying cases and held it as Alec slipped his arms through the loops. Next came the canvas doughnut that he slung over Mark's left shoulder, the loop of Primacord over his right shoulder. Mark now held the second canvas bag for Gerard, who winced as the weight pulled on his left arm where Falot had wounded him. The galvanometer and blasting machine went to Alec. Gerard picked up the submachine gun and moved toward the door.

"*A bonne chance, mes amis,*" Marcel said softly.

"And good luck to you, Marcel, Constantine," Gerard replied.

14.

When they arrived at Terre Delacroix just before midnight, the main house was in total darkness. André dozed in a chair on the veranda, a shotgun across his lap. Emilie and Ti Jacques were inside asleep. "They will be all right by morning," André said. "The doctor gave them medicine to make them sleep."

"Good, André," Mark said.

"And is there word of Madame?" André asked anxiously.

"Not yet. We need your help now, André. No one will come tonight, but put another man in your place here to keep watch."

"Ask anything of me, M'sieu."

"Thank you, André. We will need you to guide us up the back road to *le plus élevé* where we can look down upon the fort without being seen by anyone."

André nodded. "It will be difficult. The trail is steep and grown over, but I know the way. When, M'sieu?"

"At once, André. First, we will need some long, strong ropes from the storeroom—"

The car purred quietly along the road. There was hardly a need for headlights with the moon high in the sky and the road turned into a ribbon of silver. They used none as they came to a point in the road where Mark felt André's hand on his shoulder. "Here, M'sieu Mark."

A few yards ahead, Mark found a gap between the trees sufficiently wide enough to take the car in. He switched his lights on, pulled in, climbed over a shallow ridge of stones and low brush, and the car was soon lost from sight of the main road in a tangle of thick growth and tall grass. He felt André's hand on his shoulder again and came to a stop in a small clearing a moment later. Gerard, Alec, and Mark got out of the car behind André and found themselves in a wilderness of spiny grass and other wild growth that rose up to chest height. Mark reslung the coil of Primacord and reel of communicating wire over his shoulders while Gerard and Alec adjusted their canvas carrying bags to ride more firmly on their backs. They started out, André in the lead, parting the tall grass before them, a machete ready to cut away the more stubborn growth.

At once, they felt the rise in the ground. Overly conscious of the noise created by their passage, they soon broke through into a thick grove of trees; then they were out of it among more high grass. They picked their way through it and came on a rutty stone trail that was overgrown with vines, and as they moved on, the climb became steeper with every step. Occasionally, André stopped to check his bearings while the other three took a grateful breather.

A hundred yards later, they passed a small cave, then a larger one. Above them was a large outcropping of rock they would need to scale, since the trail had virtually disappeared under thick, tangled growth. André unwound the rope from around his waist, removed his sandals, strapped them together, then hung them from his neck. He went on for some fifteen yards and began climbing the rock. They saw him as a vague shadow as he slithered snakelike up and over the rough mound. Atop it, he looped one end of his line twice around the trunk of a

344

tree and held fast as Gerard, Alec, and then Mark used it to pull themselves over the outcropping. Once above it, André recoiled the rope around his waist, put his sandals on, and moved out to pick up the trail again.

They reached another small cave, and André called a halt. Here, the others removed their shoes, tied them together by their laces, and hung them from their necks, socks tucked into their pockets. Gerard scooped up a handful of dirt, and indicated to Alec and Mark that they were to do likewise—smear it over their hands and faces. He checked the time; but without knowing how much further they had to go, he could not establish whether they were ahead or behind their schedule. Again, André uncoiled the rope and paid it out to the others in lengths of twelve feet. They looped it around their waists and were linked to André for the final climb to the top. The mountain was almost like a wall here, and André took the lead, moving up the steep incline on hands and knees, stretching upward and using bits of rock or scrub for firm handholds. They crawled up and over a small crest, down into a short, steep valley, then upward again, digging bare feet into the earth to give them a yielding foothold. Above them, André's foot turned a loose rock into a shower of smaller stones and dirt that cascaded down over them. They held on, waiting for the minor avalanche to subside. André tugged at the line to signal them on. Another forty yards gained, they came to a small grassy meadow on the edge of a thicket of trees.

They rested for a few minutes, and André took the lead again. The going was easier now, and they moved faster. On the other side of the thicket, André stopped. When the others reached him, he pointed upward through the trees and they could see patches of sky and a part of the ragged crestline of Mont Souffrance, a thin black ridge against the lighter background of dark blue. The moon, a pale orange globe against a star-sprinkled sky, was high above the mountain, casting eerie shadows before them.

They crept cautiously up the incline, faces close to the knobby, rocky ground. Then André had reached the rim, and they pulled up quietly beside him. Below, between two hundred and three hundred feet away, lay Fort Maraboux, huge and sprawling, its thick walls running straight down into the mountain as though they were a part of the natural formation. The rear area of the fort was in darkness, in the shadow of the hump from which they spied. Between themselves and the near wall of the fort was the steep ravine Lamonte had sketched out for them, dark and frightening. The forward part of the upper level was bathed in moonlight. Gerard checked his watch again. 1:16 A.M. They had made satisfactory time. They had a little over two and one-half hours to get down and back.

They lay there at the top of the rim for a while and allowed their eyes to grow accustomed to the dim light, trying to penetrate the shadows. On the upper level, they could make out figures of men asleep on the ground, stretched out full length in individual blanket-covered shapes or with their backs against the walls of various buildings. Perhaps a dozen men, armed with rifles, moved about or stood motionless at the forward wall, leaning over ancient, now harmless cannon that were pointed toward Anse à Goulet and the sea to the east far below them. At the rear of the top level, a larger group of men lay apart from the others, asleep.

"The prisoners," Alec whispered into Gerard's ear.

"Prisoners now. By tomorrow they'll join the others to escape being thrown back into prison. Or worse." With a motion to André, he said, "It is as quiet as it will ever be."

Heads together, he spoke in whispers. The little old man listened, nodded, pointed down into the ravine, and whispered a reply. Gerard said: "We'll go down now. André will lead, I'll follow and you will come behind me, Alec. Mark, you'll wait here with the chatter gun, the blasting machine, and the glasses."

Mark nodded, disappointed at being left behind, but understanding that he would not be needed below. "Okay," Gerard said, "let's go for broke."

15.

Claude Falot's eyes opened slowly and painfully, then closed again. Where in the name of Damballa was he? he wondered. He lay motionless as consciousness began to creep back into his numbed brain and as feeling began to return to his flesh. His eyes opened again, and he found himself staring up at the moon. Several moons, in fact, dancing as they rotated clockwise. He tried to move

346

his head, but it was as though someone were holding it in a clamp.

Then he began to remember. He had been making a final check of the trucks from the head of the column toward the rear, thinking: They have gone now and Falot is in command. Tomorrow, Lamonte will be gone and I will become Captain Claude Falot. And after Tuesday, who knows how high will be my reach in President Batraville's inner corps of—

And then, with a wrenching sob, he recalled the first cries of alarm, the fusillade of rapid shots as *they* came rushing out of the black nowhere, the Furies of Hell, to begin their slaughter. He cursed himself for his failure in a basic military necessity—to have taken a squad of men and searched the area thoroughly the very moment he had arrived.

With memory, physical pain returned. He drew his legs up and tried to turn on his left side, but the excruciating stabs in his upper left arm and shoulder almost forced a scream from his throat, and he bit his lips to contain it. With his right hand he explored his left jaw, felt the dried blood caked and crusted there like a thick coating of mud, the ragged edge of his mangled ear. His head ached abominably from the blows he had taken. He withdrew his hand and retched, felt the burning in his chest, then turned on his right side, pain notwithstanding, so that he would not choke to death on the foul mass of vomit that forced itself into his mouth.

It was over, and he lay back exhausted. How long had he lain here? he wondered. When *they* attacked, the moon had already cleared Mont Souffrance and was casting long shadows from a low angle. Now it was high in the sky, smaller. Was it even the same night? And what of the others?

He made another effort, rolled over on his stomach, and fainted. When he awoke next, he felt the cold before the pain returned. His teeth were chattering, his head afire, and the pain seemed to be shooting downward from his head along his spine. He began to crawl to keep warm. Any movement was better than lying still. He pushed with his knees and feet, pulling with his right hand, clutching at the brush, the useless left arm dragging along at his side. His suffering was intense, but he knew he must keep moving if he were to survive. He heard the murmur of the sea behind him and knew the road lay ahead and to his left. He turned in that direction, gritted his teeth against the throbbing pain, and continued to crawl.

Ahead of him was the incline that led up to the highway. He lay still for a while to regenerate some strength in his weakened body, then fell into a doze. How much later it was he could not tell; it was the sound of a motor that wakened him and he began a frantic inch-by-inch effort to climb up the incline and reach the road, whimpering with frustration, trying to call out with a voice that was only a painful whisper.

He took hope when he heard the motor slow down, come to a stop. He threw himself forward on the stony incline and felt something in his shoulder tear as he gained the rim, held on, then pulled himself forward so that he could see along the road. He looked to left and right and saw nothing. It was impossible! He had heard it so clearly! And as he lay his head down on the earth, he saw the pair of headlights come on, heard the motor start again, saw the shadow of the car back up, turn right, and disappear into the woods. He could hear the sound of it thrashing in the grass and weeds. Then silence.

Who? he wondered, then, Why?

He waited, holding on tensely. Where could they have gone? Surely there was no road through the woods. Could he be dreaming? Need overcame pain. If he was to live, he must reach that car. Falot braced himself and crawled over the rim and to the other side of the road out of the light of the moon. He began the slow, painful crawl to the point where the car had turned into the woods, praying that it had not been a mirage. Fifty yards. He rested, then crawled over the brush and was inside the woods, creeping over the flattened brush, the path the car had made. Another twenty-five yards and he saw it, standing there alone, waiting. He crawled faster now, his goal in sight; and then he could touch its metal body.

He rested for a while, then began to raise himself carefully, linked his right arm around the front bumper, dragged himself up by the radiator grill. He stood up finally, dizzy and weak, then slid along the hood until he could touch the windshield, turned his body over twice until his right hand could reach the door handle. He opened the door and fell forward inside and face down on the soft leather seat.

Later, he pulled the rest of his body inside the car and forced himself to sit up. He moved upright behind the steering wheel and began to probe for the key with bloodied, trembling fingers. He found the ignition switch. The key was missing.

There was nothing he could do but wait. He tried to see the time by his wrist watch, but his eyes could not focus properly on the illuminated dial. He felt his left ear again. Blood had begun to seep from it. He tried to stem the seepage with his hand, held it there until he was too weak to keep his arm in that raised position. His hand fell away to his right side and touched his holster. It was empty, but he found the lanyard cord and tugged at it, inch by inch, until he was able to touch the butt of the pistol that dangled at its end. He pulled it into his lap and took a firm grip on it. If they came back, he would be ready for them.

16.

Bodies close to the ground, they slithered over the crest one at a time and began the slow descent, testing for handholds and footholds, grasping at rocks and any living thing to check their forward progress. At one exceptionally steep stretch, André simply turned his face to the earth and allowed his hands and feet and body to brake himself against the gravitational pull. Gerard and Alec followed suit. André signaled when he reached a depression. Alec and Gerard dropped into it easily and looked down on the upper level of the fort and waited to be certain they had not been heard. André motioned with an upraised arm and began to move downward at an irritatingly slow pace.

They were below the top level of the fort. The incline began moving steadily closer to the steep wall with each yard of descent. Time seemed endless until they reached the bottom of the ravine and crept across the open area to stand beside the thick blocks of granite that rose up from the foundation of the gigantic wall.

Gerard spoke to André and Alec in a bare whisper: "We'll try circling the wall to the north. If Lamonte's map is correct, the kitchen should be in that direction, about in line with the rear lookout tower. André, you will take the lead."

They moved off toward the right, each man with his left arm extended to touch the granite wall and feel his way with his hand. Gerard stumbled, caught himself, muttered a low curse, and recovered his balance as Alec reached him and almost tripped over him. The tedious search went on, bringing doubt to their minds. Then Gerard heard André expel a sharp hiss of breath, and drew up closer to him. André's hand, brushing the wall as he moved along, had found the rim of an old brick-lined conduit hidden behind a mass of leaves, vines, and high grass. Alec came up now. After a whispered consultation, the three men began to pull at the overgrowth, using knives to cut the stubborn tangle away from what appeared to be an opening.

"If it's like this all the way, we'll make it in time for Christmas," Alec panted.

Gerard said: "Be grateful for small favors. At least, we found it. This should be the worst of it. There'll probably be plenty of dried muck and crud inside, but it looks as though there should be plenty of room to navigate. Let's get with it."

The outer brush finally cleared to permit entrance into the mouth of the conduit, they found it blocked by a thick criss-crossing of metal bars that were spaced some six inches apart. Gerard tested the bars, felt them give with the pressure he applied. Alec came to his aid, and now both men pushed and pulled at the bars. Grains of ancient mortar spilled down as they tugged. Encouraged, they put their full strength behind the task. Soon they were rewarded as the bars began to sway noticeably. They sawed back and forth, sweating and panting with the effort. The bars began to pull loose, then came out in one piece. They laid the iron grating to one side, and Gerard wedged himself into the opening.

The inside of the conduit was clogged with webs and clods of dirt that hung from top and sides of the round passageway like screening. Gerard brought his flashlight into play and saw the accumulation of years of dust, dirt, small branches and twigs. The light of his flash and the sound of his movement stirred up some living things, and he shuddered lightly at the sight of glittering eyes as rodents scurried past and ahead of him or dug deeper into the debris for safety, setting up a communication of frightened squeals. Gerard backed out and told Alec what to expect. André, eager to precede them, was disappointed when Gerard told him he must remain at the opening until they returned, and to enter it only if it was necessary to give an alarm. Once they gained entrance to the level above, there would be room only for the two who would be concerned with the job to be done. André handed over the reel of wire to Gerard, the coil of Primacord to Alec.

They crept into the opening on hands and knees. Passage was slower ahead where the conduit was choked with chunks of rock that had fallen from above, and they were forced to move these aside. Both Alec and Gerard wondered privately if the noises they were making could possibly be heard on the next level. Gerard, remembering the thickness of the floor beams overhead from Marcel's and Lamonte's descriptions, felt somewhat safer. From the number of men they had observed on the upper level, there should be no need for guards below.

The stirred-up dust was thicker now, and they paused to tie handkerchiefs over their noses and mouths to shield themselves from the fine stuff. Up ahead, the conduit began a slow turn and upward curve into the floor above them. When they reached that point, Gerard's flashlight picked out a solid metal circle overhead, and they knew they had come to the end of the line. If the drain cover could be budged. Gerard extinguished the flashlight and put it back into his pocket. "We'll try it together, Alec," he said. "That cover hasn't been moved in ages. Let's test it lightly."

They braced themselves and extended arms upward, palms against the web and dust-covered circle, barely able to reach it. Gerard said, "Now, Alec. Push."

They could feel it give slightly, and were encouraged. They tried again. The metal disc gave a bit more, sending a shower of malodorous dirt cascading down on them. On the sixth try, they were able to raise the cover a full inch. Gerard said, "All right, Alec, let's take a break. Next time we'll lift and move it to the right at the same time."

A few moments later, Alec said, "Let's go." They braced themselves and put all their strength behind it, heaved, and moved their hands toward the right. Gerard felt along the edge and whispered with elation, "Okay. It's an opening. Now we'll keep sliding it over until there's enough room for one of us to squeeze past it."

Two minutes later, Alec braced himself, knees partly bent, and clasped both hands together to form a stirrup. Gerard put one foot into the cupped hands. Alec heaved upward, and Gerard shot up through the opening, bent

351

over as he reached the rim, then drew one leg upward and out of the hole. One more push and his entire body was on the floor of the third level. He reached down into the hole again, flying flat on his belly, and took the two reels of wire and the two canvas carriers that Alec handed up. Then he reached down again and grasped Alec's wrists and hauled him out of the yawning conduit. The two men sat on the floor for a few moments, then stood up.

Everything was dark and silent. Gerard got the flashlight out and turned it on for a split second to establish bearings. With Alec's hand gripping his trousers belt at the rear, Gerard led the way, stepping cautiously along the long communication hall, heading toward the center section of the fort. They came to a narrow ramp and stopped behind a pair of thick wooden supporting columns, two of dozens they had passed along the way. From above, they could hear nothing. No light appeared from the second level above where the trucks would be stored.

Gerard found Alec's arm and squeezed it. Alec's hand reached over and took a firmer hold on the rear of Gerard's trousers belt again. Together, they moved up the ramp, one slow step at a time until they reached the second level. Looking ahead and upward, they could make out a faint light that seeped down from the upper level, heard the muffled footsteps of a guard pacing about to keep warm in the cool night air. They waited and listened, but could not detect any sounds on the second level. Precious minutes passed.

Gerard moved forward slowly in the vast openness of this level. Alec tapped his arm and motioned toward the right. Ahead, in two lines of five each, stood the silent, giant shapes of black against the blacker background. They inched their way to the two mountainous forms until they could touch them, feel the canvas tarpaulins with their hands, the chains that held the tailgates closed. The back end of the last truck in the left line was open. No doubt a good bit of its cargo had been brought to the upper level in case it became necessary to defend themselves from attack.

Gerard knelt and motioned Alec down beside him. He took off the canvas knapsack and laid the doughnut of communicating wire beside it. Alec did likewise. Gerard said in a low whisper: "I'm going to crawl up ahead to see what the layout is. Stay here until I get back."

After five unending minutes, Gerard returned. "We're all clear. Have you ever worked with this XC7, Alec?"

"No. I hadn't gotten around to demolition training. I was strictly in investigative work when—"

"All right. We'll have to work fast. I'll give it to you as we go along."

Gerard began cutting the Primacord, twenty lengths approximately six feet in each length. He took one end of the remaining coil and ran it along the three-foot-wide aisle formed by the two rows of trucks and wrapped it twice around the upright column at the head of the aisle, then stretched it the full length back to the rear of the last truck, a distance of 125 feet. He took up one of the canvas carrying bags and motioned Alec to take the other and bring the six-foot lengths of Primacord with him. Gerard crawled under the first truck in the left line, Alec beside him. He took out one of the pound squares of XC7 and placed it in front of him, then picked up a six-foot length of the Primacord and tied a double knot in one end and kneaded the doughy compound around it firmly. He reached up and wedged the lumpy mass under the wooden bed of the truck between the right beam that ran the length of the fifteen-foot body and the seventy-five gallon gasoline tank. He moved back about eight feet to the center of the body and repeated the process, using another pound of the XC7 into which the double-knotted end of Primacord had been molded.

"Got it?" he asked.

Alec nodded. "Two pounds to each truck."

"Right. Get the XC7 set under the rest of the trucks in this line. I'll take the other row. Work as fast as you can, but make sure the Primacord is firmly in the middle of the compound and that the ball is wedged and kneaded hard against the wooden floor beam. Get going."

In the second row, Gerard continued the same process. When he got to the end of his line, Alec was only a few moments behind him. Gerard said, "You wait here while I link up."

He crawled back up the aisle to the first truck, picked up the loose end of the six-foot length and coiled it around the main line he had attached to the forward column, joining it with a girth hitch. He repeated this with each of the twenty loose lines that were joined to the

353

lumps of XC7 under each truck, dropping back. When they were all hitched to the center main line, he was back at the rear of the line with Alec. There, he removed one of the electric blasting caps from the pocket of the carrying case, coiled the end of the main line of Primacord around it and taped it securely in place with a piece of friction tape; he then drew out the twelve-foot lead wire from the blasting cap and felt for the bare wires at the end, from which he had earlier removed the crimped shunt. From the canvas doughnut of communicating wire, he untaped the shaved ends and connected them to the lead wires of the blasting cap.

"The galvanometer, Alec." Alec handed him the leather-encased instrument. Gerard ran the bare wires across the two exposed terminals. "Give me a short beam of light." Alec got his flashlight out, shielded it with his body and cupped hands, and switched it on. Gerard noted the swing of the needle to the far right with satisfaction. "Okay so far. We've got a solid contact."

"Do we go back now?" Alec asked.

"Not yet. We've used up only twenty pounds of the XC7. No use wasting the other ten pounds. If we stand up on top of the trucks, we can reach the ceiling overhead—"

"I've got you, Jim."

"Okay. The same deal. One pound over the center of each truck, wedged against the ceiling and crossbeam. Double knot in the center of each lump. Start cutting the rest of the Primacord."

The lengths cut, they mounted the trucks, placed the remaining squares of XC7 in place, and ran the Primacord down to the main line on the floor. Gerard used the girth hitch to connect it. Once again he tested the connection with the galvanometer.

"Okay, Alec, let's get the hell out of here."

Alec held out a hand and gripped Gerard's arm. Gerard listened, heard a pair of sandaled footsteps scraping and shuffling down the ramp from the upper level. Gerard motioned Alec under the truck and crawled beneath it after him, scarcely breathing. They heard the footsteps reach the floor level. A guard. He came along the outside of the truck column and stopped at the third truck, some twelve or fourteen feet from where they lay. They could feel the movement as his body leaned against the side of the truck, heard the striking of a match, the sighing sound as the man exhaled his first draw on the cigarette. The

354

guard stood there smoking for perhaps two full minutes, then they saw his feet move, turn toward the ramp. The cigarette landed on the floor, its fire disappearing under his sandal; they heard him shuffle toward the ramp, up it to the upper level. Gerard and Alec breathed simultaneously with relief.

Quickly, they crawled out from under the truck, gathered up the empty canvas carrying bags, the remaining Primacord, and the doughnut of communicating wire, paying the thin black wire out as they went. At the conduit opening, Gerard helped Alec down into the hole, handed the communicating wire to him, then moved the drain cover over as closely as he could and still leave room for his body to squeeze through. Alec helped lower him, and they reached up together to move the cover back into place, wedging a heavy piece of wood into the space between the cover and rim so that the communicating wires would not be sheared by the weight.

"Take the flashlight," Gerard said, "and the lead."

Alec lighted the way for Gerard as he began paying out the wire. "Do you think we'll have enough to get us back to the top of the hump?"

"Should be more than enough," Gerard replied. "This thing holds a quarter of a mile of wire, 1,320 feet. We'll have some to spare. What we've got to do is guard against kinks or breaks between here and the hell-box. It checks out fine so far, but the final count comes when we hook into the blasting machine. If there's no reaction on the galvanometer, there's been a break and the whole trip has been wasted. When we get out of here, André will take the lead. You'll carry the doughnut strapped on your back, and I'll be behind you to make sure it's paying out properly. Every once in a while we'll stop and I'll bury a length of it in the ground or weight it down so it won't snarl and break."

They emerged into the night where André waited for them, anxiety showing in his voice. "All is well, André?" Gerard asked.

"All is well, M'sieu," André replied with relief.

"Then you will take the lead. We will use your rope to keep together. You first, M'sieu Alec next. I will be third in line."

The climb uphill was difficult, their footing unsure over disturbed stones and loose earth, but they dug in and moved well. André would climb some fifteen or twenty yards, then halt to allow Alec and Gerard to haul themselves up to his level. With one free hand, Gerard guided the wire from the canvas doughnut on Alec's back, and at each stopping point he anchored a section of the wire around a bush or rock to secure it. Then the signal for the move ahead and upward.

The return trip was made in forty minutes. Mark was waiting at the top of the rim with a hand ready to pull each of them over the crest. When they had taken a breather, Gerard said, "Let's get a few yards below the rim." André found a reasonably level spot where they rested for a few minutes, then Gerard was busy again. He got out his knife and began to cut the two strands of communicating wire away from the rest of the coil. Suddenly he felt a twinge of pain shooting through his upper left arm, and the reaction was such that he dropped the wire.

"What is it, Jim?" Alec asked.

"Give me a bit of light here. My arm—"

Alec's flashlight came to life, and in its beam saw Gerard's left sleeve was soaked with blood, from the point where Falot had creased his arm, to its lower cuff. Droplets of blood were beginning to seep down onto his wrist and hand.

Alec handed the flashlight to Mark. "All right, Jim, let's get the jacket off."

Together, they eased the jacket off Gerard. With his knife, Alec cut the sleeve away and saw the raw lips of the angry wound, torn open by overactivity. Mark pulled the tails of his own shirt out of his trousers and ripped off several strips that Alec used to bind and tie the wound. "Lie still and quiet," Alec ordered.

"Okay," Gerard agreed. "Strip the plastic coating off the ends of the com wires. About three inches."

Alec did so, exposing the bare wire. Gerard picked up the galvanometer in his right hand. Alec held the two ends of the wire over the terminals. "The light, Mark." Mark threw the small beam on their hands. Gerard said, "Now's the time to say a little prayer. Okay, Alec, contact."

Alec touched the wires to the terminals, and they watched together as the needle swung from the zero mark at the left to the figure "25" on the extreme right of the dial, quivered back and forth, then hung steadily there.

356

Gerard breathed deeply and expelled the lungful of air slowly. "So far, so good. The hell-box, Mark."

Mark got the blasting machine and offered it to Gerard, who motioned it to Alec. He removed the handle and slid it into his trousers belt, then told Alec to loosen the screws of the terminals. When they were loosened, Alec inserted the ends of the bare com wire and tightened the screws. "What time is it, Alec?" Gerard asked.

Mark threw the yellow beam on Alec's wrist watch. "Exactly three-forty."

Gerard nodded and smiled. "All right. The rest is up to Marcel. All we can do now is relax and wait for company."

CHAPTER ☙ 10

1.

The president's summer palace, Bellefonte, looked down on Port Amitié like a queen looking over her subjects from the lofty heights of her throne. At this late night hour, the view of the city was one of total serenity. Over the rooftops of private mansions and residences that lined both sides of the Boulevard Mont de Couronne, the area dominated by the palace and government buildings in the city's center was darkened by the decree of mourning. Eastward lay the invisible black, shrouded sea. If one could ignore the heavily armed sentries who roamed the grounds and guarded its gates, Bellefonte was a haven of rest and quiet where one could forget the turmoil of the outside world.

The presidential mansion was a large, two-storied U-shaped structure that occupied the rise in the exact center of the twelve-acre estate. There were smaller houses behind it that were set aside for the use of guests, servants, and the corps of security guards and attack dogs who policed everything within the eight-foot walls around the clock.

On this night, in a windowless room in the basement of the Gran Maison, Louis Fontaine lay upon a low couch, its cover of bright red cloth embroidered heavily with designs similar to those upon the black robe he wore: a coiled snake with open mouth and striking fangs; a multicolored rooster rising up to crow in victory; a hornless goat; a winged bat in flight; a creeping iguana; a claw holding a cross with an eye in the center; zigzagging flashes of lightning; and across the chest, three vacant-eyed, grinning skulls that could only be human.

At each corner of the couch stood a four-foot ceramic urn in which a tall black candle, as thick as the arm of a man, burned. Against one wall stood three altars side by side amid a small forest of low potted plants. On each altar a bowl of incense burned, a thick red candle on its left, a black candle on its right. Over the center altar hung three human skulls. Over the one on the left, a rooster; and over the altar on the right, the stuffed head of a goat without horns.

Against the opposite wall, twelve men and women sat on the floor, naked except for loincloths, their faces and bodies painted with voodoo symbols and other significant markings. In front of them, four men, similarly dressed and marked, crouched over goatskin-wrapped drums, waiting in the near stifling, oversweetish air.

Around the couch on which Fontaine lay, Cadeus Fombrun walked slowly, murmuring low, hoarse incantations. In flowing robe of red, wearing a red skullcap, both encrusted with the symbols of his belief, he was no longer the drab, unimpressive personal physician of the president, but Father Cadeus, the powerful *houngan*, a priestlike figure. In his left hand he carried a long wand that he passed over the reclining Fontaine. In his right, he carried a large ball of wax into which feathers taken from a variety of colorful birds had been inserted and trailed down to his knees.

Father Cadeus came to a halt at Fontaine's feet. He looked down into eyes that stared unseeingly upward, then placed the ball of feathered wax on an urn, raised the wand, and began to speak in muffled tones. When his voice reached them, the drummers' fingers began to move across their drumheads in a smooth, even rhythm. The Twelve Disciples began to sway from side to side, then back and forth, crooning automatic responses, their bodies weaving and twisting with accentuated fever, eyes glazed, faces shining with sweat.

The voice of the *houngan* faded out. The drumming and writhing ceased. Fombrun clapped his hands twice. The outer door opened, and Nine Acolytes entered, five men and four women, alternating in a single line, similarly attired and painted as the others were. Glassy-eyed, zombie-like, they moved like sleepwalkers to the couch and took their stations at its head and along both sides.

From a cloth pouch that hung from his neck by a silver chain, Father Cadeus took pinches of powder and threw them toward the flaming candles, and as the powder touched flame the dim room flared into momentary brilliant illumination. He clapped his hands twice again. The door opened and three men entered.

The first of them carried a huge rooster, its tail feathers painted in startling hues of green, red, black, gold, and silver. Behind him, the next man led a white goat by a leash attached to its collar. The third man held a nude young girl, perhaps twelve or thirteen years old, by one wrist. As they passed the couch, the Nine Acolytes fell into the procession, moving somnambulistically around the room completely one time, then toward the altars where they formed a semicircle.

Father Cadeus's deep baritone voice rose now, filling the room:

"Spirit of Damballa!
Spirit of Ashtar!
Spirit of Lazarillo!
Fathers, hear me, Cadeus, Your Disciple!
    Give unto my Master the wisdom and strength to drive from this Sacred Isle his enemies, for they are Thine enemies;

"Give unto him the insight to know what lies in their hearts and innermost minds that he may know them for their treacheries, their lies, their evil plots, to know them not as they appear to be, but for what they truly are;

"Give unto him the courage to destroy the unbelievers, the unfaithful who work against Thee, against him;

"I ask this of Thee; I, Cadeus, the reincarnation of Thine Brother, Malo, for my Master who is himself the worthy reincarnation of those who liberated this Sacred Isle from its enemies;

"For these gifts I ask, Fathers and Spirits, I will sacrifice to Damballa a fowl with claws; to Ashtar, a goat with horns; to Lazarillo, one that is without claws or horns;

"This I swear to Thee who give all things to all men who are in truth Believers, as my Master who lies here in your presence is himself a True Believer."

When the voice of Father Cadeus died away, the man with the rooster placed it upon the first altar and tethered its feet to a circle of iron by a leather thong. It lay quietly, without moving. The man who held the goat lifted it and laid it down on the altar on the opposite side and strapped it down. It too, after a few weak bleats, lay peacefully. The man who had led the young girl by the

360

wrist now lifted her and placed her down on the center altar, then strapped her ankles and wrists to iron rings.

Father Cadeus stepped inside the semicircle of Acolytes. He went first to the rooster, then to the goat, then to the girl, blessing each in turn, dedicating the rooster to Damballa, the goat to Ashtar, and the girl to Lazarillo. He stepped back and began another ritual prayer. One of the women stepped forward and handed him a silver cup. Another woman approached and held a silver knife for him. When they stepped back to their places, two men moved forward, one on either side of Cadeus. To one, he handed the cup. It would catch the blood from the rooster's throat, which Cadeus would offer to Fontaine to drink. As he raised the knife over the rooster, Cadeus lifted his gleaming face upward and spoke again.

> "Father, Father, Father,
> Spirit, Spirit, Spirit,
> Damballa, Ashtar, Lazarillo,
> Hear me now.
> Give me a Sign."

He waited, arm still upraised. A few moments passed.

> "Fathers,
> Spirits,
> Damballa, Ashtar, Lazarillo,
> I await your Holy Sign."

Again he hesitated. The upraised arm began to tremble and a look of fright crossed his face, like pain. Once more he tried.

> "Fathers, it is I, Cadeus,
> Who beseeches You. Give
> Me Your Sign."

A full minute passed. He lowered his arm and turned his back on the altars, eyes burning red. He let the knife fall to the floor and walked to the couch. He clapped his hands three times over the face of Louis Fontaine. Fontaine's head turned, his eyes openly alert now. He sat up on the couch like a sleeper aroused from a dream.

"What is it, Father?" Fontaine asked.

"There is no Sign, Master. We must discontinue and wait for a more favorable time."

361

"As you wish it, Father," Fontaine said agreeably. Cadeus turned, clapped his hands three times, then twice, then three times more. The drummers rose and left the room, the Twelve Disciples on their heels. The Nine Acolytes followed. The three attendants released the rooster, the goat, and the girl and led them from the room. Fontaine stood up, divested himself of his robe and dropped it on the couch. Beneath it, he wore an open-throated shirt of white and black trousers. He took one look around him and went out. Cadeus snuffed out the burning candles and left the room, closing the door behind him.

Upstairs in the library, Fontaine, now more formally attired, found Cadeus sitting in a chair, poring over a well-worn book, muttering to himself. Fontaine seated himself in the chair that faced the *houngan*. "What is it, Father?" he asked.

Fombrun shook his head. "I do not know, Master. Something has happened. I asked for the Sign to commence the sacrifices, and received none."

"They are angry?"

"I do not know. The Sign comes only when They are in concert with the Earth Spirits."

"I asked for the ceremony to pay homage tonight, Father. Very soon, events of vast importance will begin to happen. I need to know that the Gods will show favor to me."

"It is not for man to move our Gods to action, my son. On a night when the moon is full, they do not show themselves or speak to their Disciples."

"But it is important *now*, Father. I have made plans——"

Cadeus held up a hand. "The plans of man, my son, must wait for the appropriate moment. This I have said to you many times."

"I can wait no longer, Father. I have been pushed and pulled until I am faced with the need to move at once. Father, hear me. A day, two days, and this Sacred Isle will be in the palm of my hand. I have planned it so. Soon, we shall begin to rebuild our country, and once again, as it once was in the past, it will become a symbol to the new world. Our name shall reach out across the seas, north and south of us, to Asia and Africa. We will make ourselves known to our brethren everywhere and they will rise and join our crusade to form a world federation such as has never been seen or known in man's time on earth. And we shall use our combined might and force to win back the rights that have been withheld from us for centuries.

"A Black World, Father, with a Black God at last! Think of it! All men of color will become members of the conquering race. We shall defeat the white man and enslave him as he has held us in bondage. And Liberté shall become the citadel of that freedom, the capital of the Black World."

"With the help of our Gods, my son, it will be."

"And who shall lead them, Father?"

"You shall, Master. Fontaine the First. It is your right, your destiny. It has been written in the stars. I have seen and I know. I have read them to you. It cannot be otherwise, Divine One."

"Ah, Father, you give me hope."

"I give you only what the Holy Spirits give me to tell you, Master."

Fontaine leaned back in his chair, his face turned upward. "We shall need a symbol, Father, one that will become a Holy Image to our new world. What shall it be?"

Cadeus sat thoughtfully, his eyes closed in meditation. His lips began to move slowly, a murmur that Fontaine could not hear. Then, as his thoughts crystallized, Cadeus said in a more distinct voice: "The symbol, Master, the symbol. Fort Maraboux. It was the symbol of freedom in olden days when, for a time, our people were liberated from their chains of oppression. Let it become your symbol for tomorrow's glory. They call it Fort Massacre, and this is sacrilege. Restore its proper name, Fort Maraboux, and let it become for all times that sign of freedom for the Black World."

"Yes, Father, yes. As always, you have a clear vision. Fort Maraboux, with its walls high and strong. I shall rebuild and strengthen it to serve me as it served our ancestors in their time of need and glory."

"Yes," Cadeus said with a soft sigh.

"Father, let us return to the *homfort* and try again."

"It is of little use, my son, while the moon is full. In seven days, perhaps—"

"As you wish it, Father," Fontaine said with resignation.

2.

At two forty-five Constantine Lamonte parked his car

within three blocks of the Zharkov house on Rue Goncourt and motioned wordlessly to Marcel Courdet to follow him. He picked up the machine pistol from the floor, checked it carefully, carried it close to his side. The two men walked silently along the street, hugging the shadows, until they came to the park opposite the Russian's house. Here, they crossed over and entered a grove of trees, where they crouched close to the ground. A moment later, they were joined by two men. The first was Solomon Bertol, Lebrun's man. He reported that since Eugénie had been brought to the house by General Batraville, two of his security police, and a white man, evidently John Mosher, there had been little activity until Batraville left. Two men were posted on guard on either side of the gates, concealed behind the wall. Occasionally, two others passed the gates as they patrolled the grounds from the inside.

The second man, Roget Paret, was Lamonte's man, sent to Lebrun to be used as a second pair of eyes. He had followed Batraville as far as the palace and returned to assist Bertol, since Sergeant Bonté would keep a watch on the general from inside.

Lamonte nodded and began giving instructions to the men, stationing them where, when he would need them, they could be put to most effective use. The two agents nodded and moved out to take up their positions. When another five minutes passed, Lamonte said to Marcel: "Time for you to go, Marcel. I hope they will not use you too badly. Delay them as long as you can before you give them the information. When you do, give it reluctantly."

Marcel nodded stiffly, tight-lipped and grim. Lamonte said: "Good luck and God be with you. Remember, you are not alone."

Marcel stood up and moved out of the grove. He glanced about him, stepped into the street and crossed it, then darted quickly into the shadow cast by the wall, and waited. Now he moved closer to the front gate, stood in front of it and peered inside. He saw nothing but the pale, moonstruck white house in the far background, surrounded by immaculate gardens. The gate, as he had expected, was locked. He took a grip on the bars, climbed up, and reached the overhead coping. With a sudden leap, he pulled himself upward, gained the top, then swung his legs over and dropped into the grounds. Even as he rose from his crouch, he felt the muzzle of a pistol thrust into his spine.

"Do not move or I will kill you," the guard said. "Now stand up slowly and do as I tell you. Rest your forehead against the wall with your hands spread out on both sides, your feet back from the wall a full pace."

Marcel did as the man told him, felt a hand pass over his body in search of a weapon. Satisfied that there was none, the guard called out, "Vassily!"

Another guard came on the run. The first man said, "We have caught a prize, Vassily. A fine fresh prize of good size and weight."

Vassily chuckled with mirth. "A fine prize indeed, Gregor. Comrade Zharkov will be pleased. Take him inside."

The first guard jabbed the pistol muzzle into Marcel's back with a sudden, vicious thrust. *"Marche, M'sieu,"* he ordered.

As Marcel disappeared from his view, Lamonte waited for perhaps five minutes, then sprinted out of the grove of trees across the street, followed the wall until he was directly behind the house, whose second floor he could see above the coping that was about seven feet above the ground. He found a large tree and lowered himself to the ground, sat with his back against the tree, the machine pistol cradled in his lap. He checked his watch, and found it to be sixteen minutes past three o'clock.

In his library, Basil Zharkov, still fully dressed, tried to pace off his black mood. Feodor Pyantenov sat at the desk, his expression cold and severe, fingers drumming lightly on the leather pad. He looked up and said, "Telephone him again."

Zharkov strode to the desk and picked up the receiver, barked a number into it. A moment later, when a voice replied, he asked to be connected with General Batraville. A short wait ensued before Batraville came on. "General, Zharkov here. Have you had word yet?"

"None. I cannot understand—"

Zharkov muttered a string of curses in Russian. "It is fifteen minutes past three o'clock, General. Ten trucks, twenty-five tons of supplies, sixty men and two officers cannot so easily disappear from the face of the earth. My own man has reported that no trucks passed the military checkpoint at Maréchal; therefore they must be some-where between Anse à Goulet and there. Send someone —wait, General." Zharkov had heard the insistent knock on the library door, caught Pyantenov's signal. He put down the receiver, went to the door, and shouted, "What is it?"

The doors swung open and Marcel Courdet was pushed inside, the guard behind him. "Comrade—" he began.

Pyantenov sat upright in his chair. Zharkov stared, smiled, and went back to the telephone receiver and said into it, "Yes, something. I will ring you back shortly." He hung up and turned back to the prisoner, then threw a quick look at Pyantenov. Both men listened as the guard told his story. Zharkov stepped in front of Marcel.

"It is M'sieu Marcel Courdet, is it not?" he asked.

Marcel stood sullenly silent. "Is it not?" Zharkov persisted.

Marcel nodded. "And what are you doing here, M'sieu?"

Marcel did not reply. Zharkov nodded to the guard, who jabbed the pistol muzzle into Marcel's back with a hard, quick thrust. Marcel lurched forward, regained his balance, and stood his ground. "We have ways of making a man answer a polite question, M'sieu," Zharkov said. There was no reply, only the defiant stare. Zharkov said to the guard, "Tell Mischa to come in at once."

The man went out and returned a few moments later with another man, huge and burly, his head completely shaven. He wore a Russian peasant blouse and loose, flowing trousers that were tucked into a pair of calf-high boots. Mischa was a formidable figure whose massive fore-head and black, heavy brows were out of proportion to the lower part of his face. His features were crudely hacked out of porous flesh, the nose bulbous, the lips fleshy and grinning, showing yellowed teeth. He flexed his hands into huge fists, opening and shutting them as though eager to put them to use. Zharkov spoke rapidly in his native tongue. "A job for you, Mischa. The gentleman is reluctant to talk."

Mischa grinned cruelly, flexed his spatulate fingers again, then turned suddenly and lashed out one fist, em-bedding it in Marcel's stomach. Marcel crumpled and would have fallen had not Mischa caught him and held him erect. Zharkov said: "It will be much less tiring and painful for you if you will answer a few questions. Why are you here?"

Still seated behind the desk, Pyantenov drew on his cigarette and watched with his expression unchanged. He caught a quick glance from Zharkov, and nodded approval. Zharkov turned back to Marcel. "Marcel Courdet," he said, "the son of the brave one who ran like a mouse into hiding behind the walls of the American Embassy." He rubbed his hands together. "M'sieu," he continued, "I will ask you the question only one more time. If you do not answer, you will taste far more than the small sample you have just received. The decision is yours to make. Why are you here?"

Marcel still hesitated, feeling the excruciating pain of the blow he had taken from the Russian giant. Zharkov nodded to the man, and Mischa suddenly wrapped one thick arm around Marcel's head, drew it down to the level of his knees, and began to apply pressure. Marcel could not have spoken now even if he had wished to do so. At a signal from Zharkov, Mischa released his victim. Marcel slid to the floor, dizzy and nauseated with pain. Mischa and the guard lifted him to his feet, but he was unable to stand. Zharkov motioned them toward a chair, and Marcel was thrust into it. Pyantenov now got up and came to stand in front of him, Zharkov a few paces to the left, Mischa on the right. Pyantenov said: "M'sieu Courdet, do not force us to punish you needlessly. We have more drastic means for making you speak."

Silence. Pyantenov reached forward with both hands and gripped the back of Marcel's neck firmly between his fingers. Expertly, his thumbs sought for and found the sensitive nerves that lay in the indentations behind the lobes of the near senseless Marcel's ears. He inserted a thumb in each depression and began to apply pressure. Marcel's head jerked upward and his eyes began to roll helplessly around, choking and retching with pain. Pyantenov's thumbs eased up, but still maintained a firm grip on his neck. "M'sieu, can you hear me?"

Marcel did not reply. Pyantenov increased the pressure. Marcel's head jerked forward and upward again, his mouth open as though gasping for air. Then he threw up as Pyantenov leaped to one side to avoid the liquefied mass that erupted from Marcel's mouth. Pyantenov waited until Marcel shook his head from side to side to clear it.

"There can only be much more and much worse, M'sieu, if you continue your stubbornness," Pyantenov said evenly. "Will you tell us what we want to know?"

Marcel's head moved up and down in a weak, slow motion. "Very good, then. Tell us first what are you doing here? Why did you climb over the wall? What are you seeking?"

Zharkov had moved over to a cabinet, poured a liberal drink of rum into a glass, and brought it back to the chair. He forced it between Marcel's lips. Pyantenov raised his head so he could drink. Part of the liquid ran out of one side of Marcel's mouth. Pyantenov motioned Zharkov aside with a nod of his head.

"M'sieu, I am waiting."

Marcel said slowly, "I—I was—searching—for—"

"For what?"

"For—Madame—Fuller."

"And why should you be searching for her here, M'sieu?"

"Be-because I—have reason to believe she is being held here."

"And the source of your information, M'sieu?"

Marcel's mouth closed firmly. Pyantenov signaled the eager Mischa, who stepped forward, raised Marcel's head with one hand, and slapped him hard with the other. And again.

"M'sieu, you are bringing this hardship on yourself unnecessarily," Pyantenov said with some sign of gentleness. "In one minute, we will have you removed to a room below us, where we will turn you over to our friend here. Without our presence, I can assure you that within ten minutes you will be screaming the truth. Perhaps then there will be no one to hear you. For the last time, what was the source of your information?"

Marcel reached up weakly and wiped the blood from his lips. "Some-someone—passed by here earlier and saw someone—a woman—being carried into the grounds. He did not know who she was. Later, in a café where I happened to be, I overheard him telling this to two companions." Marcel stopped and breathed deeply, then continued with effort: "When I learned later that Madame Fuller had been abducted from Terre Delacroix, I put the two incidents together and decided to investigate."

"And soon learned that you were not playing a child's game, eh, M'sieu?"

Marcel did not reply. Pyantenov said, "And where is M'sieu Fuller, the husband of the lady in question?"

"I do not know."

"Ah. You tell us you had this valuable piece of information that concerned the wife of your good friend, news of gravest importance to him, yet you did not contact him first? Come, M'sieu Courdet, for a newspaper writer you show an extraordinary lack of imagination. I warn you, sir. We are not children. Do not play your childish games with me. You have been hiding in fear of your life. No man in hiding frequents public cafés. Therefore, you are lying, and badly. Where is the husband of the lady? Outside, perhaps, waiting for you?"

Marcel shook his head negatively. Mischa stepped in front of him again and hauled him out of the chair to his feet. "Speak up!" Pyantenov snapped out angrily. "You waste my time!"

With one hand, Mischa held Marcel erect and with the other, smashed several wicked body blows into his midsection. Marcel staggered backward, but Mischa pulled him forward and pumped two more blows into him with such force that Zharkov turned away with a wince. Marcel's knees buckled. Mischa drew him up again and smashed another blow into his face that sent drops of blood and sweat flying.

Zharkov called, "Mischa! It is enough! He is hardly conscious."

Mischa released his hold on Marcel. Marcel stumbled backward, spun around in one complete directionless turn, and fell to the floor. Mischa bent over and picked him up, one fist raised, but Pyantenov said: "Wait, Mischa. I want him able to talk. Bring water."

The guard brought a carafe from the liquor cabinet and handed it to Mischa, who emptied it on Marcel's face. He shuddered awake and stared glassily around him, painful agony mirrored in his eyes. Pyantenov said, "Again, M'sieu Courdet, you have but a few seconds before you are sent below with Mischa."

Marcel watched as the bulky form of Mischa came into view, hovering over him, then felt himself being raised and placed in the chair again. He looked down at his left wrist to the face of his watch, but his eyes were blurred and he could not see it. He shook his head to clear them, raised his eyes, and barely made out the hands of the grandfather's clock behind the desk. The time was three-forty. From between puffed lips, he said, "I will—tell you—what you—wish to know."

Pyantenov waved Mischa aside. He helped Marcel to

369

his feet, guided him to a chair closer to the desk, and thrust him into it. Zharkov lighted a cigarette, carried it to Marcel, and put it between his lips. "Talk, my friend, and save yourself much pain and discomfort," he advised.

Marcel puffed at the cigarette gratefully. "M'sieu Fuller," he said simply, "is at Fort Maraboux."

"Fort Maraboux," Zharkov repeated. "And why is he there?"

"Tonight—tonight, a large shipment of arms—was delivered by a submarine to the beach at Anse à Goulet." He paused, saw the startled look that was exchanged by the two men. "Ten trucks came to take the cargo. When the trucks were loaded, the convoy was attacked by guerrilla forces who had been hiding in the woods to the north. The trucks were taken by the guerrillas to Fort Maraboux and stored there. M'sieu Fuller is somewhere in the area, waiting for friends to join him."

"And what do they plan to do there?"

Marcel shrugged. "That I do not know. Once they are gathered, they will hold a council and try to devise some means to capture the arms and put them to their own use. That is all I know. Beat me, kill me if you will, but I can tell you no more."

Zharkov started to move toward the telephone as Pyantenov snapped out: "Quickly! Get Batraville on the telephone. Tell him—tell him what we have just heard. He must gather men at once and go there."

"Comrade," Zharkov began, even as he reached for the telephone receiver, "what if he is not telling the truth—"

"It is reasonable to assume that he is. Where else could such a convoy be hidden so closely to where your colleague, M'sieu Chalumeau, would want it for his own purposes? Hurry!" As Zharkov leaped toward the desk, Pyantenov said to Mischa: "Take him below and tie him well. Do not harm him. If he escapes, I will shred your skin with a whip. And if he had lied to us, you will shred his."

At the telephone, Zharkov was shouting, "Tell the general it is M'sieu Zharkov. An emergency, you fool! Quickly!"

3.

In the house on Rue Montagneux, Nicole Mauriac lay beside Paul Reed in the dark. Even as he slept, she could feel the strength of him flow through her, the gentleness of his touch, unable to believe that so great a difference could exist between two men. Paul was the second man she had known intimately.

She had been taken from her home in St. Afrique at an age when she had hardly become aware of the fiery urgencies of sex. Captain Mauriac had had no special appeal to her as a bed partner, although she knew that other girls and women, older than herself, frequently exhibited themselves before him to attract his attention and favors. And then one day, Lucien Mauriac had come to her home and addressed himself to her father, but for what reason, she had not then known.

He returned a few days later, bringing gifts of food and cloth they could not otherwise afford. A week later he returned from a visit to Port Amitié and called with a dress for her mother, a black suit for her father, a white dress and a necklace of bright beads for herself. That night she learned, not without some inner girlish elation, that the dapper military commander of l'Arcachon and subdistrict commander of St. Afrique had asked to marry her.

On the Sunday that followed, Mauriac drove her and her parents (their first time in an automobile) into l'Arcachon where they went before the *Juge de paix*, who pronounced the solemn words over the couple in a civil ceremony. There was wine for all, and she had got dizzy and giggly and had fallen asleep during the drive back to St. Afrique. Mauriac dropped her parents off at their small house, then took Nicole with him to his much larger home. There was a fine meal with more wine, and before the supper was over, she was nodding sleepily from the effects of the wine and the excitement of the day. What a lovely outing it had been!

Mauriac picked her up gently, then, and carried her in his arms to the *salle de bains* below the house, watched intently as the housekeeper and another woman bathed her in perfumed water. She was not embarrassed. Nakedness was commonplace in the back country. He had then carried her up to the large room on the second floor and placed her on the large bed. Almost before her head could feel the softness of the pillow, she was fast asleep.

Her awakening was a rude and unpleasant memory. The room was dark, and she was sulky and petulant with sleep, unable to breathe in Mauriac's fierce grip. She tried to twist out of his arms, but he was too strong for her and countered move for move. Tired, she gave up the struggle

371

and waited, lulled by his whispering, of which she under-stood little, until she was nearly asleep again.

And then came the first searing thrust of pain and the weight of him crushing the breath from her body. She screamed. He put one hand over her mouth, and she reached up to tear it away, and in doing so, her fingers raked his face. He drew back, lashed out in anger, and struck her. She clawed out wildly and caught his face again with her nails, and this time he slapped her twice until her ears were ringing. The blows stunned her, and she cried out in painful gasps, feeling his full weight still upon her. And then his attack on her body began again, savagely, and she fainted.

Nicole was barely twelve at the time.

In the morning, she awoke gratefully to find that Mauriac had gone off to the garrison. She found her pretty new dress and ran home to her parents, hoping the fright-ening nightmare was done with and that the presents were now paid for. But she learned from her mother that this was only the beginning of her marriage and she must remain with her husband as long as he desired her.

Mauriac, in another sense, had been good to her. In the seven years of their lives together, she had never known hunger. He bought her new clothes and gifts from the shops in Port Amitié. He supplied her parents with food and occasional gifts of money. Her father had risen to the lofty position of headman on the plantation where he worked, and was now looked up to.

She was, in fact, the envy of most women in St. Afrique, even among those who had known her husband most in-timately. But she was lonesome, no longer permitted to run through the fields with the girls of her own age or even speak with the village boys. The housekeeper, who, she knew, frequently shared Mauriac with her, had begun teaching her the responsibilities of running a well-ordered household, an occupation she did not understand at that time, nor in which she showed much interest.

In bed, Nicole found no delight or pleasure that others spoke of almost unceasingly. Lucien was a passionate ani-mal with no regard for her pleasure, only his own. He was proud of her body and beauty as he was of his own strength and command over her; but she had learned to be submissive to his needs in order to keep him in good humor.

Until she saw Chalumeau in her house, she had believed

that one man would be no different from another; yet no other man had generated the awesome feeling in her that Chalumeau had with one look; a strange and indescribable something that aroused her curiosity and drew her to this stranger as a magnet attracts metal filings; something so compelling that when he had asked her to bring him a drink, she knew at once that the request had meant more; that she was to bring it to him herself and not send it with a servant; and she had needed to obey.

And then, when he had taken her hand into his own and she felt its electrifying touch, she knew she could refuse him nothing. In his arms, she had learned of gentleness and honest passion for the first time; that the physical, bodily relationship between a man and a woman was something to be enjoyed by both. And she knew, too, from that day, whatever Chalumeau would ask of her, she would give willingly and happily. It was as though she had never known Lucien Mauriac, as though he had never existed except as a memory she now longed to forget.

Somewhere in the distance of the house, the telephone rang. Paul was at once awake, listening. The bell rang three times, then stopped. He lay back on his pillow and turned to face her. She put out a hand and drew it across his chest.

"You are awake, *ma petite?*" he asked in a low whisper.

"Yes, Paul. The telephone—"

"It was the signal from Duclosse. It is almost time to go."

"No. Not yet, Paul. Please."

"Ah, Nicole *chérie*." He put his arms around her and drew her close to him, luxuriating in the feel of her flesh, the warmth and perfume of her. "If battles are to be fought and victories gained, even a sacrifice as beautiful as you must be made."

Nicole laughed with delight at his words. This was a man who knew how to make one feel completely a woman. Big, powerful, yet so gentle. Their talks together in the short time since Lucien, that pompous, preening, *petit-maître,* had left had created a closeness and intimacy she never believed could be possible. They were like one. Paul was a man with many followers, but few whom he could call friends with whom he could speak of the feelings deep within himself. They had discovered this need in each other; an understanding so penetrating that life had become rich with the knowledge that one need not keep his thoughts forever locked within himself, but could speak out and let the bitterness of life empty out and allow room for love and warmth for another; someone who cared.

"Paul, before you go—"

"Nicole, Nicole, you are a temptress, an Eve, a Delilah, to sap a man's strength and turn his mind to *gelée*. I must go to the fort—"

"Paul—" She burrowed closer to him, over him, kissing his lips.

"*Chère* Nicole," he breathed. "Tomorrow night, you will become a queen. My queen. You will live in a beautiful palace, dressed in silks and finery that only a queen should wear, grander than any other woman has ever known. We will make up to each other the years that have been stolen from us in childhood. You and I together, you and I, *favori*—"

"Tomorrow is years away, Paul. Make me your queen now."

"Now, *chère* Nicole. And tomorrow. And for all time."

4.

Below the crest of Mont Souffrance, they waited. To the east, the blue-black sky was beginning to yield to the first pale streaks of approaching dawn, and the lightening clouds signaled the end of night. Gerard, as he had done frequently since they had returned from below, checked his watch and wondered again if something had gone awry at the house on Rue Goncourt. What if Marcel had been killed by Zharkov's men in his attempt to gain entrance into the grounds and house, instead of being captured as it had been planned? Was his feeling of apprehension, however slight, being transferred to Alec and Mark, who stirred restlessly nearby, asking the same question with their eyes?

He heard Alec move up beside him. The flashlight beam flicked on, and together they examined the bandage around his upper left arm. The outer layer showed only a faint stain of blood that had now dried in the air. Alec held the jacket as Gerard allowed it to be drawn up over his left arm, then thrust his right arm through the sleeve, taking comfort in its warmth in the cool air.

At that moment they heard, then felt, the shower of stones and clods of earth rolling down from the rim, and turned to look upward. Mark crawled over to them, his hands tightening instinctively around the butt and barrel of the submachine gun. There were a few more crackling sounds, and then André slid down beside them, breathing hard with excitement, pointing the night glasses in the direction of the rim. "They come, M'sieu!" he said to Gerard.

"Where?"

"Below on the main road. The trucks with soldiers and an automobile."

"How many?"

"I could count six trucks with men standing in them. Three men descended from the automobile. Those in the fort have also seen them. They gather at the front walls."

"How many men in each truck?"

"In the dimness, it is difficult to make them out. Perhaps twenty-five or thirty men to each truck."

"The glasses, André." André took the field glasses from around his neck and handed them over. Together, the four men crept up the steep incline and edged their heads over the crest. Gerard focused the glasses on the upper level of the fort where the men were stirring. Most of them were already in position at the forward wall and on either side of the open gateway, rifles resting on the parapets as they peered down the mountain. Gerard moved the glasses and refocused them to find the action at the bottom of the mountain, and picked out the blurred movement there. Alec edged closer to him. "Anything?"

"Not yet. The trucks are still unloading below. There must be well over a hundred of them down there."

The upper level of the fort broke into action. Men were ripping boxes and cases apart, handing out heavier pieces of equipment. Two who seemed to be in charge were instructing the others in putting the equipment together. "Machine guns," Gerard relayed to Alec and Mark; ".50 caliber." Four of the assembled guns were taken to the fort opening, and two were set up at the very entrance, two more some ten yards behind them. From other cases, submachine guns and long ammunition clips were being passed around to others who stood waiting, taking them eagerly, rushing back to their positions at the wall.

Gerard said calmly: "It will begin soon. Bring the hellbox up, Mark."

Mark disappeared, following the wire trail to where Gerard had left the blasting machine. Within a minute he was back, holding the blunt piece of equipment in his hand. "The handle, Jim," he said.

"In my belt. We'll wait for a while and see how it goes."

Mark nodded. Gerard was peering through the night glasses again. There was too much darkness for full clarity at the base of the mountain, but the men on the upper level of the fort were clearly outlined in the approaching light, all but the prisoners now lining the walls expectantly. The two leaders stood a few feet behind, directing them, moving in and out to speak to the men, shifting their positions to allow more space between them.

An illuminating flare burst over the fort, a brilliant, floating white light that dangled from a tiny parachute; and then the first red flash came from below. A split second later there was an explosion almost in the center of the fort. Another landed and tore a corner of one of the buildings apart; this was followed by a sudden barrage of small bright flashes from below as shells dropped into the fort.

"Small mortars," Gerard said needlessly.

The men in the fort were holding their fire. A mortar shell fell in front of the fort, and a wide screen of dirt and stones flew into the air. A second shell dropped inside the fort, directly behind the men. One of the two leaders fell. The other leader raised the fallen man's arm and let it drop, then rushed to the parapet to look below. The wounded man tried to raise himself, then fell backward and lay still. His companion returned, bent over to touch him, then stood up again as though undecided what to do next, and finally went to the wall to direct the fire. Two men turned from the wall and pried the lid from a case and began carrying armfuls of small objects to the wall, handed them to the others, and returned for more.

Mortar shells were landing inside and in front of the fort. The men behind the walls were busy pulling pins and throwing grenades down the hill. Red flashes were bursting everywhere now. From below a sudden chattering began, and the air was filled with tracer trails from machine guns that had been emplaced midway up the mountain under cover of the mortar fire. Machine guns from the fort began to respond. A dozen more mortar shells were lobbed into the fort, almost in unison. Chunks of granite exploded in the air, and several of the guerrillas at the walls fell, victims of the flying pieces.

The men at the walls, urged by the remaining leader,

stepped up their activity, hurling grenades, firing machine guns and sub-machine guns and rifles as fast as they could. From below, the action ceased temporarily, then flared anew from positions closer to the fort. Batraville's soldiers were creeping snakelike through the brush, drawing nearer to the walls. A mortar shell from below burst among them and took an unknown toll.

Through his night glasses, Gerard saw the first of the soldiers break into the clear, only to be cut down by withering machine-gun fire from the fort entrance. Two others broke out of the brush and zigzagged up the hill, drawing full fire from the walls. Then, from out of the blackness, a truck came grinding its way up the stony road. The fire from the wall shifted to the truck. Machine guns mounted on the truck returned the fire, and several more men fell at the walls. Behind the first truck, a second followed. The men at the walls were calling to each other, confused, directing their full attention to the two vehicles that were looming larger and larger as they gained ground. The leader of the guerrillas was among his men, directing their fire at the first truck.

Machine-gun bullets poured into the lead truck. A moment later its gas tank exploded, killing the driver and another man in the cab. A third leaped to safety. Those who had been riding crouched low in its body had jumped when the first fire had struck. Now it was almost completely engulfed by flames. The second truck ground upward and to the right of the burning vehicle, using it as a shield, firing its mounted guns over and through the flames.

Meanwhile, the almost unnoticed soldiers on foot were moving up the mountain through protective brush, crouched low, running, crawling, dropping down to fire, moving again. Within minutes, they had come within seventy-five yards, then fifty, of the open entrance. A barrage of grenades was hurled into the entrance to put an end to the two machine guns and their crews that had been stationed there. From behind them, the second relay of guns took up the battle. Shadowy figures from below rushed into the opening and began firing short bursts at the guerrillas, pressed closely to the wall, firing at anything that crossed the open gateline.

And then a group of ten or twelve soldiers tore across the line of fire. Four grenades silenced the two remaining machine guns. Of the first assault wave, only four soldiers stood unharmed, turned their submachine guns on the men trapped at the walls. Through the entrance, another thirty or forty men poured onto the upper level, delivering a wall of fire that brought a cessation to the battle. Of the original defenders, fewer than fifteen men remained alive.

From the fort, a signal flare was fired high into the air. All firing from below ceased. The balance of Batraville's men moved up the hill and into the fort. It was all over.

On the crest, Gerard was poised like a scorpion about to pounce on an inferior insect as he peered down on the unbelievable sight below. He dropped the field glasses to his chest and said, "Okay, Alec, let me have it."

Alec handed the red blasting machine over, holding the trailing wires in the palm of his other hand, then paused for a moment. "Your arm, Jim," he said. "Let me."

Gerard took the handle from his waistband and held it with a tight grip. "All right, Alec," he said, "hold it for the word."

Alec took the handle, inserted it into the channel, and held it there. Mark and André looked on with expectant horror, somehow anticipating what was to come.

"Ready, Alec?"

"I'm ready."

"When I raise my right hand, get set. When I drop it, give it a full twist as far as it will go." To Mark and André, he said, "When you see my arm go up, get down to those trees below and take cover. We planted a lot of trouble down there, and all hell is going to break loose. I don't know how much of it can reach us here."

Mark and André nodded. Gerard dug himself in again, eyes glued to the glasses. There was more light in the sky now, and on the upper level of the fort, Batraville, Pyantenov, and Zharkov were pacing up and down in front of the single line of ragged guerrillas. Nearby, the prisoners in their striped garb huddled fearfully together. Batraville was speaking to them, waving his arms angrily. Four of his soldiers came up, herding eight prisoners they had flushed out of one of the buildings, and pushed them into the huddle. Pyantenov said something to Zharkov, who approached Batraville and spoke with him, then the three men turned and walked toward the ramp that led below.

As Gerard watched, he thought of the men who had been killed in the fighting and those who would die when he gave the signal to Alec Fletcher. Then he thought of the men who had died on the beach earlier and the hundreds of innocent civilians who would die if these thousands of weapons were to be put into use during the next few days. He wondered if death, to prevent death, was the compensating or justifying factor; and if it were, who should be judge and who the judged; who the executioners and who the executed. He threw a sidelong glance at Alec, who sat only six feet below him, the red hell-box in his left hand, his right gripping the handle. One twist and it would be the end of the line for every man in the fort, soldiers, guerrillas, prisoners—

He saw Batraville and the two Russians approach the ramp, and knew it would not take long before they would find the network of Primacord wires he and Alec had strung. Gerard raised his arm. Mark and André drew back and began sliding down the hill toward the grove of trees. He held it there, sweating with impatience, now wondering if, when he dropped it and Alec twisted the handle, nothing would happen; if the communicating wire had been broken somewhere along the line and all their efforts and labors would come to nought. He could hear Alec's heavy breathing.

The three men disappeared into the ramp entrance. Gerard dropped his arm. He turned away and waited only to see Alec's right hand twist the handle in the hell-box; then both men were falling and sliding downhill to where Mark and André lay face down on the ground, hands clasped protectively over the backs of their heads.

5.

Across the road from the darkened house on Rue Montagneux, Tom Reed sat with his back to a tree. The early-morning coolness chilled his tropic-thinned blood, and he reached up to draw the edges of his old khaki shooting jacket closer together over his chest and held them there, wondering dully why it would no longer button. Beneath the jacket, he wore a crumpled khaki shirt that was tucked into a pair of wrinkled once-khaki trousers, now whitened with a hundred or more washings. On his head he wore a khaki-colored hat whose stiff brim slanted forward over his eyes, its crown peaked in the campaign style worn as a Marine in the field years ago. Where the upward sloping indentations began, there was the familiar dark-bronzed Globe and Anchor of the Corps. And across his lap lay the '03 Springfield rifle he had carried through the years of active military service, old 83826, issued to him at Parris Island boot camp, purchased by him when his last enlistment had ended in 1934. Old, but its bore was as clean as a polished diamond, its stock worn and glistening from years of periodic buffing.

He raised one hand and ran it across his swollen face, felt the bruises, the tape across his broken nose. No man in his lifetime had ever given him the brutal beating Paul had when he had come here the other night to reason with him, to plead with him not to go through with his diabolical scheme. The movement of his arm sent a wave of pain through his taped body, and he winced. He got up slowly to shift his position and relieve the stiffness, then sat down again.

Through the open gateway across the road, his puffed eyes concentrated on the upper window. Three hours ago he had seen Paul at that same window as he reached out and drew the slatted shutters closed. Then, a few minutes later, the lights had gone out. At the foot of the steps in front, Paul's car stood waiting, just as Tom Reed sat waiting.

Tom's free hand picked up the bottle at his left side, and he drank deeply from it, hoping it would warm him. Ah, good rum, the necessary additive for thin blood. He put the bottle down at his side, savoring the flavor of it, and caressed the rifle stock lovingly as one would stroke the head of a favorite hunting dog. He closed his eyes for a moment and dozed, thinking over the words of Jim Gerard; that Paul was the man who stood ready to rouse the natives in the interior and bring them into Port Amitié to run wild, overthrow the government. And Tom knew what that would mean: wholesale, unrestricted slaughter of anyone who got in the way either purposely or unintentionally. Rummed-up natives racing through the streets uncontrolled, hacking, shooting, looting, and burning. One man could trigger so much violence. His own son, Paul. The son he had never acknowledged. Nor did it escape him that no white or near white would be given the slightest chance to save himself. And Tom Reed in particular. Women, children—it would make no difference to the fired-up fanatical followers of Chalumeau.

He thought of the words of a company commander

of the past under whom he had served in Haiti, struggling to remember his forgotten name. But he could recall the words, spoken moments before they were to attack a bandit camp near Las Cohobas. Or was it Mirebalais? "What this place needs is a good enema, and we're going to clean it out. When I give the word, we're going in hard and fast—"

That's what we need here, he thought. An enema. Clean the goddam bandits out of the hills, then out of the palace, and make up the bed with clean sheets and blankets tucked in at the corners for Saturday inspection. Clean up the revolutionists in the back country, in Port Amitié or anywhere else they were holed up. Go in hard and fast— This was as good a place as any to start.

He hefted the rifle, then placed its butt in the hollow of his right shoulder, hunched forward as his left arm bent to allow his hand to grip it firmly. Up came his right hand, almost automatically, to the trigger guard, index finger curling around the comma-shaped trigger, worn smooth over the long years of use. In the well-practiced sitting position, he aimed its muzzle at the second-floor window across the road as his right cheek pressed gently into the polished stock.

Through the rear peep sight, he saw no target. In the circle there was Gunny Tom Reed, marching with mechanical precision executing the sharp command, "Eyes . . . *right!*" as he passed before the reviewing officer. He had passed out of range now, and the face of Paul appeared in the peep sight, grinning to mock him, taunt him with contemptuous eyes.

He ain't goin'-a do it, Tom Reed mouthed silently. I'n goin'-a let no man do a thing like that, by God.

He lowered the rifle to his lap and felt for the bottle, found it and held it to his bruised mouth, felt the burning of the alcohol as it reached his split lip and the raw cuts inside. He put the near empty bottle down once more and began to doze.

Later, he stirred, shivered in the cold night air, and jerked himself awake. He looked about him quickly, then upward to the front window on the second floor of the house. The lights had come on in the room again. He could see the faint high lights touching the upper edges of the shutter slats. As he watched, the shutters were flung outward and he saw Paul turning back from the window, fully dressed.

Tom stood up, lifted the bottle, drained the last of the rum, threw the bottle behind him into the grass, then hefted the Springfield. He looked up at the window and saw Paul again, this time as the figure of a woman came to him, embraced and kissed him, the two silhouettes merging into one. Tom edged forward carefully, looked up and down the dirt road, then crossed it and entered the front yard. He waited, then mounted the steps to the veranda. He chose a wide, comfortable chair, turned it in the direction of the front door and sat in it and drew the rifle across his lap, his blood beginning to pound furiously.

When he heard the scraping of the front door as it opened, he threw the safety catch of the rifle to the steady position, left hand taking a firm grip on the stock, his index finger on the trigger. Paul came through the doorway, his back to Tom as he drew the door shut. Tom could see the bulge at Paul's right side, dangling from a wide cartridge-studded belt as he turned toward the steps to go to his car. At the top step he paused, looked to right and left and called in a sharp, low voice, "Lescaux! Sergeant Lescaux!" then heard the voice that came from the darkness behind him on the veranda.

"Paul!"

The big man turned quickly, startled. *"Qui est là?"* he asked as his hand reached toward the holster.

"Don't touch it, Paul," Tom's voice croaked waveringly.

It took several seconds before Paul realized who had spoken. "So. It's you again."

"Yes, it's me again, Paul."

Paul took two cautious steps toward the shadowy figure in the chair, leaned forward and stared into the dimness, then straightened up and said contemptuously, "You learned nothing from your lesson the other night?"

"Paul, listen to me. I know what devil's work you're up to. I'n goin'-a let you do it!"

Paul snickered disdainfully. "What do you know, old man?"

"I know you're goin'-a try to stir up the people to take over the government and kill off the whites. That's what I came to tell you the other night. You ain't goin'-a do it, I tell you. I'n goin'-a let you."

Paul's big head shot backward as he laughed. "You won't let me? After nearly thirty years you've come to tell me what I can do or can't do, you drunken *fou blanc?* Get out of here. Go hide yourself, old man, because by

382

this time tonight the city will be turned upside down. I'll give you that much time to hide. If I find you anywhere inside Port Amitié after that, I'll kill you with my own hands. Run, old man, run back to your Belle Roseau with your mulatto wife and her lover. Go fast, *blanc*. Later will be too late."

"Paul—" Tom Reed began to rise from his seat as Paul turned his back on him and started again toward the steps. He put one foot on the second step and turned back to Tom. "Listen, my white father. My people are this minute on their way into the city from every part of Liberté. By afternoon, they will be armed, and then nothing can stop them. I owe you nothing, but I will give you this much. By tonight, if you are not gone, there will be a machete in this hand. One chop and your head will lie on the ground at your feet. I have warned you." He spat contemptuously in Tom's direction, turned his back on him, and started down the steps. As his hand touched the side rail, he heard the piercing cry, "Paul!"

The cry had come from inside the house. It was Nicole's. He turned toward the door and started for it. As he did so, he saw the rifle in Tom's hands for the first time, raised waist-high and aimed in his direction. His head snapped around toward the door and again toward Tom, one hand outstretched in front of him. "Don't! Don't shoot! Wait!"

The rifle wavered only slightly. "You ain't goin'-a do it, Paul," Tom Reed said again. "You ain't goin'-a turn this city into a bloody pig-stickin' jamboree and I'm—"

Paul leaped forward, one hand extended toward Tom; but before he could close the distance between them by more than one step, Tom Reed had squeezed off one shot and already had pulled the bolt back, ramming another cartridge in the chamber. The bullet thudded into Paul's chest and threw him backward into the wooden post, spun him completely around, his body buckling at the knees, a look of complete surprise on his face.

Then the door opened and Nicole, screaming at the top of her voice, was standing on the threshold, her eyes wide open with fright. Before she could take a step toward Paul, he had straightened up and taken another staggered step toward Tom, reaching futilely for his own pistol, unable to co-ordinate the movement of his hand. The second bullet caught him about an inch to the left of the first hole in his chest, already wet with blood that was running down his shirt, welling up in the hollow made at his waist by his belt, then spilling over. Paul's face went blank with the stunning shock, then fell backward as Nicole caught at him. Paul made a complete turn and fell sprawling on the veranda floor, taking Nicole, crying wildly, with him.

Tom Reed lowered his rifle, then walked past the dark huddle of Paul's body, Nicole lying across his chest, weeping uncontrollably. He walked halfway down the steps and then, as if the remaining strength in him had been unaccountably drained, sat down, the rifle upright between his knees, staring vacantly up at the sky, now turned lighter. From the right side of the house, a man appeared. He looked curiously at Tom, then walked up the steps to where the weeping woman lay across the body he recognized as Chalumeau. Then he went inside the house. He picked up the telephone and gave the operator a number, but it did not answer. He gave another number, and when the Police Headquarters desk man answered, said, "This is Sergeant Lescaux of the Palace Guard. I wish to report——"

Outside, Tom Reed heard the first rumble of thunder roll across the city. He looked up again and saw the column of thick black smoke that had begun to rise to the south over Anse á Goulet.

6.

The roar that followed was the loudest noise Mark had ever heard in his lifetime, so loud that he thought for a moment that it should be visible. The whole earth seemed to rise upward and settle back in one violent tremor. Beneath him, he could feel a turbulence as though the world had split into a thousand pieces. Unable to restrain himself, he looked up toward the crest and saw rock, dirt, and blocks of stone that had been spewed into the air, high above the crest of Mont Souffrance, as though a volcano had erupted. The sky was bright with flame, brighter than the hottest sun. Then, for a moment, there was a deathlike silence.

From immediately above them, showers of small rock and stones, brush and earth descended on them. Gerard burrowed deeper into the ground, calling to Alec, Mark, and André to protect their heads and necks. And then it had passed. Gerard looked up and began to crawl out of the grove. Alec, Mark, and André followed. From here, still protected from overhead by branches and leaves, they looked out and up into the sky.

Then the second explosion came, and over the crest they saw a broad sheet of flame shoot upward, like a broad, burning curtain, carrying with it huge rocks and timbers and three large pieces that could only have been parts of trucks. The three men dropped down again, quaking either from within or from the shaking earth and trees. Gerard began to move out of the woods and up the hillside to the rim.

"Jim! No! Don't do it, Jim!"

But if Gerard heard Alec, he gave no sign of it. In a low crouch, he ran, then crawled, hand over hand, until he was at the crest, looking down into the fort—or what remained of it. Alec and Mark followed him, and then André came scrambling up behind them. Breathlessly, the four men peered downward just as the thunderclap of a third explosion rent the air, followed by a heavy rumbling and columns of black smoke from which red and orange tongues of flame licked outward. They could hear the hissing and crackling of burning matter in the immense furnace-crater that had once been Fort Maraboux. Nothing that remained now was recognizable as the symbol of Liberté's former greatness. The rear wall had been blown out from the second level up. The parapets on the upper level had disappeared completely. In the mouth of the flaming volcano there appeared to be a mangle of wood, metal, and granite blocks that had fallen into crumpled rubble. From the obscenely gaping hole, smoke and flame issued forth and climbed in a twisted spiral toward the brightening sky. Granite blocks, ancient cannon, and parts of vehicles were still rolling down the hillside in the direction of Anse à Goulet, raising tremendous clouds of dust as new trails were gouged into the face of the mountain. There came a series of smaller explosions, no doubt caused by cases of ammunition. Huge supporting timbers continued to fall, feeding the roaring furnace.

But Fort Maraboux was gone, its sides split by wide seams, ripped apart, bowels open and exposed. There was no sign of life anywhere. Alec felt Gerard's hand as it gripped his shoulder. "Let's go, Alec. There's nothing left to be done here, and we've got some unfinished business in Port Amitié."

André was already on his way down. Mark, his face

385

white and pinched, was directly behind him. At last Alec began to move away, and Gerard moved out behind him.

The trip down was quicker, each taking his own path down the mountain now that it was light enough to see by; slipping, sliding, grabbing at trees and brush for handholds, eager to be away from here. When they were within a hundred yards of the car, Gerard signaled the others around him and took the lead, cautioning them to be quiet. "Let's spread out and move quietly. They may have left a rear guard behind. No use taking chances now."

Gerard moved straight ahead, Alec to his extreme left, André between them, and Mark on the far right. The submachine was cradled in Alec's arms. Mark and Gerard held .38's in their hands. Then, over the tallest grass and weeds, Gerard saw the top of the car. No amount of caution or care could hide the noise of his movement through the grass as it rustled and swished with each step he took. He was within three feet of the door when he saw a shadowy form rise up into a seated position behind the wheel. Gerard started to raise his .38, then saw the gleam of a faint high light that ran along the barrel of the pistol in the man's hand.

"Make no foolish moves, Mr. Gerard," the low voice said coldly, "else you will be dead. Drop it."

Gerard let the weapon fall from his hand into the grass. "Come closer, closer, Mr. Gerard. Now raise your hands and bring them forward. Place them on the edge of the door and keep them in my sight."

Gerard's eyes tried to penetrate the dim interior, but could distinguish no more than the outline of the man. "Who are you?" he asked.

"If you utter one cry of warning, Mr. Gerard, it will be your last. Now call to the others and tell them to approach. If one of them makes a false move, remember, you will die first. I am wounded, but still able to use this gun."

Behind him and to the left by about twenty-five yards so that he was approaching the car from the rear, Alec stopped and called out, "Jim?"

Falot said: "Tell him to drop his weapon and join you. If he does not, I will kill you."

Gerard turned his head in Alec's direction. He saw the

386

figure of André standing frozen in his tracks, but could not see Alec. "Alec!"

"Jim, what—"

"We've got company. You are to drop your weapon and come in beside me. He's holding a gun on me."

There was no more than the merest fraction of silence, then Alec shouted, *"Duck, Jim!"* The submachine gun began chattering, and the rear of the sedan rocked and jerked as Gerard dropped to the ground and rolled under it. Bullets smashed through glass and metal, plowed through upholstery, and shattered the windshield. Burst followed burst until there were six, and then, except for their echoing and the frightened shrieks of startled birds, the woods were silent.

"Jim! Jim, are you all right?" Alec was directly behind and on the far side of the car. From under it, Gerard called out, "I'm all right, Alec. Watch out. It's Falot."

Alec called out, "Mark?"

"I'm okay here, Alec," Mark shouted from somewhere ahead and to the right of the car.

"André?"

"Bien, M'sieu."

"Hold it where you are, all of you. He may be playing possum."

Alec approached the car stealthily, the submachine gun at ready. Inside the car, nothing moved. And then he called out, "All right. It's over."

Gerard came out from under the car as Mark and André reached it. Inside the car, lying crumpled and wedged between the front seat and the floor, was Falot, the back of his head, neck, and upper shoulders riddled.

André and Gerard dragged Falot's body out and laid it on the ground. For a moment the four men stood over him and stared; then Mark walked to the car and got in. He fumbled around in his pockets, found the ignition key, and tried it. The motor turned over smoothly. André came around and got into the seat beside Mark as Gerard and Alec climbed into the rear compartment, sweeping broken glass from the seat to the floor.

Mark said, "I'll send somebody back for him later," and threw the car in gear.

7.

In Port Amitié, the four men who guarded the walled

grounds of the Zharkov house were drawn to the front gate by the sound of the first explosion that came from the direction of Anse à Goulet. Standing at the barred gate, they watched in fascinated awe as the first tall pillar of black smoke rose into the sky. From nearby houses, people rushed to their balconies, still dressed in night clothing, to stare in startled wonderment and call back and forth to their neighbors in unsteady, frightened voices.

Behind the rear wall of the house, Constantine Lamonte, at the first rumbling sound, stood up, slung his machine pistol over one shoulder and around toward his back. He ran at the wall, placed one foot against it, and leaped upward. His hands grabbed at the coping, held on firmly, then drew himself up and swung his body over the top and dropped to the ground inside. He looked around and saw no one at the rear of the house. He moved cautiously across the neatly cropped grass to the driveway, then circled toward the front of the house, stepping quickly now. As he rounded the corner, the barred gates of the front entrance were about forty yards from where he stood. The four guards, with their eyes glued to the sky, had their backs to him.

He turned quickly to examine the front of the house, and saw no one there; then he started for the steps, his head toward the front to keep watch on the guards. At that moment he heard a rustling. He turned to his right side and saw Roget Paret's head come up over the wall, halfway between himself and the guards. But the men at the gate had heard the sound as well. They turned, reaching for their automatics. Lamonte wheeled toward them, the machine pistol thrust out before him. As the first of the four guards cleared his pistol from its holster, Lamonte squeezed off a burst. Two of the guards fell. The third man staggered against the fourth, who pulled away and aimed his pistol at Lamonte and fired twice. The shots went wide and Lamonte got off a second short burst just as Solomon Bertol's head appeared over the coping on his left.

Roget was three feet away from him, Bertol running to join them. He heard the front doors open, and the bald giant, Mischa, appeared before them, holding a submachine gun in his hands. Lamonte's weapon stuttered into the shadow, and Mischa spun, fell backward, the gun in his hand firing wildly into the ceiling of the foyer.

Inside the house, Lamonte paused in the entrance hall,

gave it a sweeping glance as Bertol started toward the staircase, Paret behind him. From the floor above, a man appeared suddenly, pistol in hand, aiming it at the two men running up the stairs. Lamonte called a warning. Two shots dug into the wall as Bertol and Paret threw themselves on the steps, using the balustrade for some small cover. Lamonte pushed the muzzle of his weapon upward, but before he could fire it, he heard another shot that came from behind the man, saw the look of surprise on his face as he threw up his hands, staggered forward against the rail, spun over it, and fell to the floor below.

Paret and Bertol sprinted up the steps, Lamonte behind them. In the upper hallway, they came on John Mosher, an automatic in his hand with which he had killed the Russian. Lamonte raised the muzzle of his submachine gun, and Mosher at once allowed the automatic to fall from his hand to the carpeted floor. Paret kicked the weapon out of the way.

"I'm not resisting, Major," Mosher said. "When you are finished here, I want to see the American ambassador. Or Jim Gerard."

"Is it not a little too late for seeking protection from the Americans, Mr. Mosher?" Lamonte asked.

"I'm not asking you to understand, Major," Mosher replied. "All I want is to be able to talk to the ambassador or Gerard." As Lamonte hesitated, Mosher added: "You'll find Mrs. Fuller in the last room on this side of the hall. Marcel Courdet is in a room in the basement. He's banged up a bit, but Mrs. Fuller hasn't been harmed in the least."

Lamonte nodded to Paret, who remained with Mosher. He and Bertol went along the hallway, throwing open door after door until they came to the last one to their left. It was locked. They put their shoulders to it, but the door was too sturdily built, and resisted. Bertol fired a single shot into the lock. The door shuddered. Bertol put his shoulder to it once again and it swung open.

Inside the room, Eugénie Fuller lay on the bed fully clothed; her eyes, wide open with fright, calmed as she saw Lamonte come through the door, Mosher ahead of him. Lamonte turned to Bertol. "Search the house below and find M'sieu Courdet. Quickly." He handed over the machine pistol and took Bertol's automatic in exchange. Then he turned back to Eugénie and spoke comforting words to her.

At Bellefonte, Louis Fontaine was sleeping in his airy, sumptuous bedroom when the first thunderous roar rolled over Port Amitié and reverberated against the mountain on which the *petit-palais* sat. He wrenched awake, eyes opened wide with sudden alarm, then threw the silk top sheet to one side, leaped out of bed, rushed to the wide French windows, and out onto the broad balcony. Clutching the top rail with both hands, he looked first toward the palace and government buildings, then skyward as he saw the first massive column of black smoke to the south, rising over Anse à Goulet. The guards in the grounds below had collected in an excited, chattering knot to gaze at the alarming sight.

"What is it?" Fontaine shouted to the men below. "You, below there!"

The duty officer had come off the lower veranda to join the men just as another low, rumbling wave, like angry thunder, swept over them. He looked up at the pajama-ed figure, stood stiffly at attention as he saluted, and replied uncertainly, *"C'est un volcan, M'sieu le Président!"*

Fontaine snorted angrily. *"Quelle folie!* It comes from Anse à Goulet! There is no volcanic mountain there."

The duty officer shrugged imperceptibly and remained at silent attention. Fontaine shouted, "My limousine! Have it readied for me at once!" Back in his bedroom, he shouted for his valet, who was already waiting, his face drawn and turned chalky gray with fear. Fontaine dressed hurriedly, then ran down the stairs to the lower hallway where he came upon Father Cadeus, calm, unperturbed, wearing his regular dress.

"Father Cadeus, what is it?" Fontaine demanded.

Cadeus shook his head and mumbled, "The Spirits, Master. They are angered."

"At whom, Father? Certainly not Fontaine."

"It cannot be, Master. I must have time to communicate with them."

The third loud roar rolled across Mont de Couronne now. A sublieutenant entered the hallway, saluted, and reported the car ready. Fontaine snapped angrily, "We come at once." To Cadeus, "Come, Father, we go to the palace."

Outside, the limousine waited, chauffeur behind the

wheel, a sentry holding the door open for them. On the front seat, two bodyguards with submachine guns sat beside the chauffeur. Two motorcycles sputtered their readiness, and the cortege moved swiftly through the grounds and roared into the boulevard.

Along the way, on the roadside and on the balconies of their homes, people in various stages of dress stood and gaped at the thickening columns of smoke. And then another explosion rent the air. The traffic that was abroad that early in the morning had come to a virtual halt. Private cars were stopped; passengers stood beside their vehicles to watch the holocaust, like an evil omen, drifting skyward. Servants on their way to market clutched their panniers and watched through glazed, frightened eyes, open-mouthed in fear and wonder. Some kneeled and mumbled incoherently as others fondled personal charms, and prayed. The smoke, caught up in a breeze at a higher level, began to drift westward toward the city in the form of a huge mushroom that was startlingly realistic.

In the limousine, Fontaine's face was beaded with sweat, reflecting his puzzlement and alarm. Beside him, Cadeus's lips moved but uttered no sound. Fontaine leaned forward and cried out with sharp impatience, urging, *"Vite! Vite!"* but it was obvious even to himself that little haste could be made through the road that was partially blocked with cars and people who had stopped to witness the terrifying sight from the hillside height. The motorcycle escort dismounted and began ordering the people to move their cars to one side, but many stood fearfully gazing at the ominous clouds that billowed in the sky, drifting closer to the city. Many of the cars had been abandoned, their drivers seeking better vantage points on the steeper sides of the mountain. Finally a passage was cleared and the presidential cortege moved through it.

Further down the hill, they were forced to halt again. Another group of cars blocked the road. Fontaine's furious voice spurred his outriders to release brakes and push offending vehicles to either side without regard for bashed fenders or protests of the owners of the cars. Sirens blaring, they eventually came onto level ground of the circle, swung into the Champs, now wide enough to permit rapid passage. The small cavalcade sped toward the palace entrance.

At the gates, a group of disorganized sentries hastily

came to attention and presented arms clumsily as the limousine raced into the driveway. Already, a number of official government cars had arrived and were parked in the reserved area opposite the steps. Flustered aides stood under the portico or paced nervously. Several ran toward the presidential car as it drew up at the foot of the steps and screeched to a halt. Fontaine emerged and marched quickly into the palace, Cadeus and the two bodyguards hurrying to keep up with him.

In the rotunda, they swept past an eight-man squad under command of a lieutenant and turned toward Fontaine's office suite. In the outer office, his secretary leaped to his feet, distraught and ashen-faced. He made a move to intercept the president, but Fontaine brushed him aside. "Get General Batraville for me at once!" he ordered sharply. The secretary followed him, trying to speak again, but Fontaine cut him short with an angry "Quickly! Hurry! The general!"

The secretary put out a nervous hand, but Fontaine had reached the door before him. As he raised the handle, the doors were pulled open from within. He stepped inside and the doors closed immediately on his back.

Cadeus and the bodyguards remained in the secretary's office. The secretary began to speak to the *houngan* in a low, imperative whisper while the bodyguards hung their submachine guns on wall pegs and seated themselves side by side on a leather sofa near the outer door. As they settled down to await the president's emergence, the outer door opened. The lieutenant whom they had passed in the rotunda only moments ago entered and stood to one side to permit his squad of soldiers to pass by him. The two bodyguards stood up. The secretary broke off his whisperings with Cadeus Fombrun and said querulously, "What is it, Lieutenant? You have no business in—"

The lieutenant ignored him. To the soldiers, he said, indicating the bodyguards, "Take them. Leave their weapons on the wall." The bodyguards exchanged glances, then looked to the secretary, but saw that he and the *houngan* were flustered with uncertainty as they stared at the lieutenant's drawn pistol. Four of the soldiers led the two bodyguards away. "You will come with us, Doctor," the lieutenant said to Fombrun. "And you"—indicating the trembling secretary—"will accompany us for the moment."

The remaining soldiers formed around the two men. Led by the lieutenant, they went out.

In his office, Fontaine came to an abrupt halt. Seated in the chair behind his desk was Henri Delacroix. In a chair on his left sat the former Army Chief of Staff, General Theron Dessez, once again in uniform. In three chairs to his right sat members of the Council of State, one of whom Fontaine had in the past counted in his own personal column. Delacroix looked up, and waited.

Fontaine strode swiftly across the room and addressed himself to Delacroix, ignoring the other four men. Behind him, his back to the door, stood the armed lieutenant who had admitted him.

"M'sieu," Fontaine demanded in cold anger, "what explanation can you offer for this outrage?"

Delacroix replied calmly, "I can assure you, M'sieu Fontaine, that what we are doing here is entirely legal and within the province of our duties as members of the Council of State."

"And by what right do you occupy my office?"

"M'sieu, as Chairman of the Council of State, I am acting as head of the government in the absence of a legal head of state and until a new president can be elected."

Fontaine's labored breathing could be heard over Delacroix's soft voice. "M'sieu Delacroix," he said slowly, clipping each word short for greater emphasis, "you and your"—he indicated Dessez and the three Council members with a contemptuous wave of his hand—"brother conspirators will remove yourselves from my office immediately or be charged with treasonable conduct. At once, sir!"

With deliberate patience, Delacroix, in the same calm voice, replied: "M'sieu Fontaine, so that we may understand each other clearly, allow me a moment of explanation. Last night, in a special emergency meeting of the Council that took place in our deliberation chamber, it was agreed by a majority of eighteen members to advise you that a provisional government has been formed to act for the good and welfare of the Republic in the absence of a legal head of state. General Dessez was called back from retirement as Army Chief of Staff and will assume his duties as of this date. These gentlemen sitting with me and I have been designated as the provisional government until the new president is elected. The election will take place within three days. We have decided—"

Fontaine smashed a fist on the desk. "I do not recognize your right—" he began stormily.

Delacroix's eyes glittered. He rose to his feet and said: "M'sieu, you have no right to recognize or not recognize our actions. Your term as president came to an end when you legally surrendered your office to M'sieu Charles Du Faure. His untimely death at the hands of an assassin in no manner restored you to that office. You are a private citizen without official position, and as such are occupying this office and residence, and Bellefonte, without legal authority. You will remember your true status in further addressing this body, sir."

Fontaine, shaken by Delacroix's damning outburst, was momentarily silenced. As Delacroix resumed his chair, Fontaine turned and strode angrily toward the doors. The lieutenant remained stiffly at his post. "Stand aside, you!" Fontaine snarled. The lieutenant looked at Delacroix, who nodded consent. The lieutenant stepped to one side and opened the doors wide. Fontaine stepped into the outer office, shouting, "General Batraville! Guards! Where—"

The outer room was empty. He turned back into his office, his face murderous with rage, and pointed a trembling finger at Delacroix. "You, M'sieu!" he thundered, "you will consider yourself under arrest! And *you*"—almost speechless with fury, he took in the others with a withering stare—"ungrateful, wretched men! You and those who are acting in concert with you in this infamous act of treachery, I warn you—"

Delacroix cut off the bombastic threat with a sharp slap of his hand on the desk. "I remind you for the last time, M'sieu Fontaine, that you no longer have the power to threaten officers of the legal government of this Republic. You, M'sieu, are yourself under arrest for dealing privately with a foreign government without the knowledge or consent of this Council. Also, with your personal *houngan*, Dr. Cadeus Fombrun, you will be tried under Article 249 of the Penal Code—"

"*You* dare threaten *me*, Louis Fontaine?"

"—and lest you underestimate the seriousness of your position, M'sieu," Delacroix continued over the interruption, "let me recall it to your attention: '*Also shall be qualified as attempted murder, the employment of drugs, hypnosis or any other occult practices which produce lethargic coma or lifeless sleep. Anyone found guilty of such practice shall be tried and judged for murder, no matter what result follows; and if he should be found guilty, he shall be condemned to die by the firing squad.'*

"No one, M'sieu Fontaine, is immune from that law. Let me also inform you that we have evidence and witnesses who have been interviewed in secret and who will testify against you, witnesses who have observed your participation in such acts that have been declared by law to be acts against humanity; that you have impeached yourself by practicing this evil black art not only in the summer residence at Bellefonte, but in the basement of this very building."

Fontaine's head moved in a semicircle over the hostile faces that stared back at him. His glassy eyes seemed dead already, and he knew there was no hope left. Dessez had been long ago lost to him, but men like Chambère —the other Council members who had been loyal to him for six years, that they could now be in league with Delacroix against him! It was incredible. *Lâche canaille sans courage!* What in God's name did they want? In another term of office, they would have become independently wealthy for life. And this they preferred to give up by betraying him. For what inexplicable, stupid reason?

And studying their faces, he knew suddenly that his race for power was over, that he had lost all. His eyes came to rest on the stern, grim Dessez, and saw the pure hatred that spilled out of the general's eyes in return. He thought of the night he had first taken Lénore Dessez into his arms; then he realized that he had lost her as well. Lénore was not a woman to remain loyal to a failure, a loser. He had had Berta removed in order to possess Lénore, given her in marriage to another that he would be able to keep her—

If he could somehow manage to escape arrest, get out of the palace before they could take him into custody, request asylum from an embassy. The Russians? No, they would shun involvement with the Americans. The Americans. Anywhere. Long enough to bargain and get out of the country. Then to Switzerland where his money lay securely and secretly in unnumbered accounts.

But no. He would not get off lightly to be allowed to live in luxury elsewhere. He could see it in their faces. They would kill him; if not by execution, then prison, to live among the many he had sent there over the past six years; to wait for a knife blade one night—.

What had gone wrong? Where was Batraville? The arms. *The arms!*

His face contorted with anger and his eyes mirrored

savagery and hate as he silently damned them all, cursed them to an eternal hell; Delacroix, his archenemy; Courdet, who would eventually succeed him; the ghouls who waited in the background, estimating their victory over his ignominious downfall. And Lénore, too. Upon her he uttered a senseless, unreasonable curse. Damnation to them all. What were they waiting for? To see him fall to his knees and beg? Let them get it over with.

A low buzzing sounded. Delacroix lifted the telephone from its cradle and spoke into it. "Come in, please."

The lieutenant opened the door, and Major Constantine Lamonte entered, his civilian clothes rumpled and sweat-stained, his face etched with the weariness of the long night, a submachine gun hanging by its sling from his shoulder. He approached the desk, ignoring the central figure in the tableau, and stood at attention before Delacroix. "I apologize for being late, sir," he said. "I was unavoidably detained on a matter of government business." He leaned across the desk and spoke to Delacroix in a low tone.

Delacroix smiled and replied: "Thank you, Major. I am deeply in your debt. The security of the palace is in your charge. You will now place M'sieu Fontaine under arrest and hold him in close confinement in this building until specific charges have been drawn up against him. Remove from his person any means by which he might do harm to himself."

"At once, sir." Lamonte went to the outer chamber and returned with a squad of soldiers in charge of Sergeant Bonté. They formed a tight square around Fontaine and led him away. As they reached the doorway, Delacroix called out, "A moment, Major."

Lamonte returned to the desk. "When you have taken care of the matter at hand, you will take a limousine to the American Embassy and ask M'sieu and Madame Courdet to accompany you to my home. Say to them it is my wish that they remain with my family there until they receive word from me later this afternoon."

"With pleasure, M'sieu," Lamonte replied with a smile.

9.

In her old room at the Delacroix home, Eugénie lay on her bed while Mark sat on the edge beside her. The fright and temporary nausea were gone; her full color was restored, and she looked surprisingly well rested. From the hallway, they could hear Julie's voice raised in argument with Dr. Fornier. "I in*sist*—"

"Julie," the doctor replied firmly, "Julie, *ma petit singe*, please go and visit with your sister. She may need you."

"My sister does *not* need me, and I want to see Marcel," she said heatedly.

"When I have finished my examination, *ma chère*, you may visit with him for the rest of your life. Another half-hour, I beg you."

"But why?"

"Why! Why! Why! Because I am about to expose certain parts of his body that a young, virginal girl should not view before her marriage. That is why."

"Poof and nonsense!" Julie stormed. "He is hurt!"

"He breathes, he talks, he drinks, he smokes, he has even laughed. How hurt can one be who can do these remarkable things, eh? Also, he is idiotically happy, although considerably bruised. It is that which I cannot see of which I must be certain. If you stand here and argue like *une chat irritante*, you simply delay the examination and your great moment of reconciliation. Now, go!" Gently, but firmly, the doctor had propelled her down the hallway.

Julie stormed into Eugénie's room, eyes ablaze. "Imagine that—that—old—old— My Marcel lies critically hurt, and *M'sieu le Docteur* must complete his examination before—"

Eugénie and Mark laughed. "He is safe, Julie," Eugénie said. "Is a half-hour so long?"

"At this moment, *ma chère sœur*, it is forever!"

"Julie, Julie, go down and talk with Mama and Angélique. Show them your better nature, and remember, there is a big week ahead of us."

"Not all of us," Julie replied. "Have you seen Marcel's face? How can he appear in public so puffed and bruised?"

"You will leave it to the good doctor and Mother Nature. In one week's time those two will have worked wonders on him. Run along now."

Julie suddenly laughed happily, kissed Mark and Eugénie impulsively, then ran out of the room. As she passed the closed door behind which Dr. Fornier was busy ministering to Marcel's needs, she rapped her knuckles against it sharply and shouted, "I shall return in fifteen minutes, you hear me in there?"

Mark said, "Génie?"

"Don't look so worried, darling. I feel wonderful now. They didn't harm me."

"Génie, I'll never forgive myself for—"

"Hush, darling. It wasn't your fault, so don't blame yourself. Did Dr. Fornier get all the gummy stuff off my face where that *cochon* Batraville taped my mouth?"

Mark felt the area tenderly with his fingers. "There's only one small red spot that will disappear soon. When I think of watching those men in the fort—"

"Start forgetting, Mark. Thank *le bon Dieu* you are not in a business like Gerard and Alec Fletcher."

"And what about Mosher?"

Eugénie shook her head. "There is something about him—Mark, he acted so strangely—unwilling. When Batraville gave orders to take me into town, it was Mosher who protested. Then he wanted to take my word I would not call out, but it was Batraville who insisted on the tape. Mosher argued against the syringe they had planned to use on Marcel, but when Batraville was firm about it, Mosher gave me the injection, but apologized first. The next thing I knew, Constantine was there with that ugly gun in his hands, looking like a maquis himself, and I was awakening from a nightmare. I dreamed the whole world had blown up. I could even *smell* it—"

Mark laughed and said: "I was wide awake and had exactly the same dream. I'll tell you all about it later when I can collect my thoughts. Maybe, when we're home again, I'll tell it to you a dozen times so you can tell our children what a great hero their father was."

"Whose children?"

"Ours, Génie. Yours and mine. The children we're going to have. A dozen of them."

"Mark!"

"I mean it. We've wasted too much time already."

"Our children," Eugénie repeated happily. "It has a wonderful ring to it, hasn't it, Mark?"

"Don't talk any more now, darling. Just sleep." He bent over low to kiss her, whispered into her ear: "And we'll have to hurry. I think it's only fair that our children should be older than Julie's and Marcel's."

CHAPTER 11

1.

Gerard lay on the examination table bared to the waist as the embassy doctor re-dressed his upper left arm. He applied the final strip of bandage, taped it, and said: "You can sit up now. I'm going to fix a sling for that arm. Not that you need it, really, except as another reminder that you're not to overdo things."

Gerard sat up slowly and reached for a cigarette with his right hand. The doctor lighted it for him. "And you might try cutting down on those, too."

"Thanks, Doc," Gerard replied. "When you start taking your own advice on that score, your patients may even begin taking you seriously."

The doctor grinned. "That's the trouble with your generation. I can remember when a patient would hardly question a doctor's right to indulge in his own excesss while preaching against them. There, that about does it for now. Slip into your shirt and jacket and I'll adjust the sling for you. And I'll have another look at that tomorrow if you'll stop by. Meanwhile, get some sleep."

Gerard walked down the hallway, responding to the greetings from familiar and unfamiliar faces, disregarding the stares of curiosity. It was ten-thirty, and he hadn't been able to change or shave, and felt conscious of his crumpled, filthy suit, scarred shoes, and the bloody stain that ran along his left sleeve. He hesitated outside Nora's office, then decided not to go in, even though she had phoned the doctor and left word she would like him to look in on her when he was finished there.

His eyes were red-rimmed and leaden, his body aching with weariness, his mind a jumbled nightmare of the events of the past twelve hours. Without Alec to help fill in the gaps, it would have been impossible for him to have made an intelligent report on tape when they reached the embassy at seven o'clock after reassuring themselves that Eugénie Fuller and Marcel were safe. Mark and Marcel were with her and the Delacroix doctor on his way when they left. Alec was now asleep on the sofa in Shannon's office with a happy Suzanne sitting beside him.

Gerard found a lounge chair on the chancellery veranda and sat down to rest until the ambassador and Truscott concluded their report to Washington based on the transcript of his report. He closed his eyes and hoped for sleep. Instead, he was reliving the horror of the moment when Alec twisted the handle in the blasting machine. If, he thought, there is such a place as Hell, it could be no more horrifying and terrible than what had happened on Mont Souffrance; the flaming eruption of Fort Maraboux, the thunderous roar that had drowned out the cries of men in the agony of death. God, God Almighty—

He became aware that someone was standing beside him. He opened his eyes, and there was Nora, holding a steaming cup of coffee in her hand. "They're about ready for you again, Jim. Here, drink this."

He sipped at the strong black stuff gratefully. "I'm one hell of a mess to be calling on an ambassador, aren't I? I'd give anything for a shave and a shower and a change of clothes. I'm so tired, Nora—"

"They'll never notice, Jim," she said gently. "It won't take long. When you're finished, I'll drive you home."

"That's a deal. Where's Alec?"

"Still asleep in Shannon's office. Suzy is with him."

"Okay." He took a final sip and handed the cup back to her. "Have you told the ambassador about—us?"

"I told Thorne and Dorothy last night at dinner. Things have been so chaotic since then—"

Gerard grinned wryly. "That's as great an understatement as I've ever heard." They were at the veranda entrance to Polly Weatherby's office. Nora reached up and kissed him quickly. "Go on in and I'll wait for you in my office."

Polly Weatherby looked up at Gerard with a mixture of awe and curiosity. "You're to go right in, Mr. Gerard. They're waiting."

He crossed the room and pushed one of the two shuttered doors open, saw Ambassador Chance sitting behind his broad desk, Thorne Truscott in the chair beside him. The third man's white-jacketed back was toward him. Trus-

cott grinned and stood up with a "Hello, Jim. Come in."
The ambassador looked up and smiled, but when the third
man got to his feet and turned to face him, he saw with
some small shock that it was Craig Madden, alias John
Mosher.

Chance said, "This gentleman tells us you know him,
Jim."

Gerard, still returning Mosher's stare, replied coolly, "I
know *of* John Mosher."

Mosher smiled briefly. "Or Craig Madden?"

Unsmilingly, Gerard replied, "Or the former Captain
Madden."

"As a matter of fact," Mosher said, "it's Major Craig
Madden, Gerard, but the news of my promotion could
hardly have reached you. It's been kept secret even from
me until a little while ago when I was ordered back to
Washington."

Gerard frowned, puzzled, suddenly feeling overcome
with his weariness. "I don't know what this is all about,
but I'm ready to listen. To anybody," he added.

Chance said, "We've already had Baker authenticate Mr.
—ah—Major Madden's identity, Jim. We received the confirmation from the Defense Department about twenty minutes ago."

"Army Intelligence," Madden amplified, "on temporary
special assignment from Ordnance to G-2."

Gerard expelled a lungful of air. "You could have
made life a hell of a lot easier for a lot of people if we'd
known about this in Havana."

"I had no idea you were there then. You did too great
a job keeping under cover. Besides, I had a specific orders
not to contact anyone under any circumstances."

"Just what were you after?"

"It seems we were after the same thing. Any kind of
lead that would indicate where they were planning to
establish a second Cuba. At first it looked like Venezuela,
but when that washed out, they began beaming toward
Liberté. I managed to let that information fall into Consuela Sándoz's hands—"

"You knew about Consuela?"

Madden laughed. "Not until I accidentally discovered
that she was passing extra copies of important data on to
someone else. The trick was to keep anyone else in
Urbana's office from finding that out."

"Did you know who her contacts were?"

"No. You were too damned cute for me." Sheepishly: "This isn't my racket, really. I was pulled out of Ordnance because I was tabbed by the Russians while I was on duty in West Berlin."

"Then that business in Washington with the Russians was a setup?"

Chance interrupted at that point. "Major Madden was about to explain that when you came in. Suppose you take it from there, Major."

Madden nodded. "It began in West Berlin one night when one of their double agents made a tentative pass at me for some information. At that time I was in the technical branch of advanced armaments, observing field tests on some special small-arms weaponry that might lend themselves to nuclear devices. I reported the contact, and that's when G-2 was brought into it. G-2's CIC went to work on it, and I was asked to co-operate. We let it rest for a while to see if they would make another contact.

"It came about two weeks later and, as ordered, I made myself agreeable. From that moment, the East Berliners began keeping an eye on me to try to find out if I was reporting back. I kept apart from any contact with Intelligence.

"I don't need to tell you how they work, Gerard. They used all sorts of bait. Girls, vacation trips with all expenses paid, money that would be deposited anywhere I named, all that sort of thing. I was playing hard to get, but still agreeable. We used my wife, Peggy, as go-between with G-2. She would pass the information along through the wife of the colonel, who passed it on to him, then on to G-2.

"Meanwhile, Intelligence and Advanced Armaments worked out some clever but useless interpretations of what we called the 'weirdies,' a number of harmless but interesting-looking developments in the more or less science-fiction line: death-ray guns, laser beams, portable nuclear devices to freeze moving vehicles or equipment—and that sort of thing. When the East Berliners began to believe I would play for pay, we started exchanging scraps of information for money. We kept it up for about four months, but weren't getting anywhere. Then the Caribbean situation began getting hot, and G-2 asked for my transfer to Washington where something more important might develop and a few of the better Russian hole cards might show.

"I was assigned to the Pentagon on something more practical G-2 knew the Russians were drooling to get their hands on at that stage. Missile deployment schedules in our Polaris program. It didn't take too long before one of their embassy attachés contacted me. I played it cool then, but finally they came through with the threat to expose me for my 'co-operation' in West Berlin, complete with copies of the 'weirdies' I had given them, and sneak photographs and tapes of me in the act of actually transferring the information and receiving money in return.

"Naturally, this was what we wanted. G-2 brought Peggy into the act again. They set me up in an expensive, platonic love nest with one of their female operatives. A few months later, Peggy flew to Reno and instituted a true-enough divorce action. Since Peg's family is socially prominent, the story and a photograph of her appeared in both the Washington *Star* and *Post* and was picked up by the wire services. Now I was a set pigeon, needing money to keep up my new apartment and for the alimony Peg had asked for.

"Whenever I met my Russian contact, mostly in public buildings, the National Art Gallery or out in the open somewhere, I kept pressing for more money. Finally, they asked for the Polaris Missile Deployment data. I told them it was too risky to get. They insisted, and raised the ante. I agreed. G-2 and Naval Intelligence got together and provided me with some very authentic-looking documentation that purportedly spotted each sub and its cruising schedule for the next six months. Actually, the schedule was accurate, but it was due for complete change within four days, long enough to allow them to make a primary check for authenticity.

"It took several days before I made contact with my Russian and told him I had made some 35-mm. photostrips of the information they wanted. He gave me an address in Virginia, an estate along the Potomac. I passed it along to my contact, and they set up the disappearing act. At the moment when they broke in on us, I got out through the back way, dived into the coldest stretch of water this side of the Arctic, and was pulled out by a small Navy craft to safety. A real thriller-diller of a spy chase in the traditional Hollywood manner.

"I was taken to a house somewhere near Middleburg where I changed clothes, dyed my hair, wore glasses and grew a mustache. G-2 furnished me with an entirely new set of credentials, social security card, driver's license, money, the whole bit, then put me in a car and pointed me west. From Los Angeles, I drove to Mexico City and checked in with the Russian Embassy. That was the touchy part. I had to be checked out clean.

"They got in touch with their Washington counterparts and, after contacting Moscow, who traced me back to their East Berlin boys, they decided I wasn't a double agent. I got my free ride to Moscow where I was screened by KGB as well as GRU. Since I was an armaments expert, they assigned me to conduct special courses in modern weaponry for prospective subversives who had been shipped in through their various Commy links in Latin America.

"That's where I met Domingo Urbana, fresh in from Cuba and undergoing training for his job in Moscow.

"Urbana was a lightweight who had a tough struggle understanding his job. They assigned me to work closely with him to get the necessary information through his thick skull. I decided to concentrate on him, holding back just enough to keep him dependent on me. When Castro began putting pressure on Moscow to send him back to Havana, Urbana asked that I be sent along with him. Moscow finally agreed.

"In Havana, I was contacted by one of our own double agents and set up contact with Washington through Chieftain." He grinned at Gerard. "That's right. We were using the same transmission relay belt, but I was having some difficulty making contact. Castro's security police were all over the place. On my heels, searching my hotel room every time I left it, bugging my phone, the walls, tracking me to the cinema—"

Gerard nodded. "I know," he said. "How did you get on to Luis Sánodz's unit operating in Havana?" he asked.

"I didn't know about Luis Sándoz, but I managed to get onto Consuela Sándoz quite by accident. I opened the door to the outer office one day and saw her folding some sheets of carbon paper into a small wad. I closed the door before she was aware of me, but from that time on I was suspicious. It bothered me, so I decided to find out. One morning, I came into the office early and put a fresh new stack of carbons in her desk drawer, leaving the used sheets on top of the pile. I then called her in and dictated a good deal of ship-movement information that would make good transmitting data. I asked for an original and one carbon copy.

"When she finished the job and had left for the day, I checked the carbons again. The count of the new sheets showed four were missing.

"The day after that, I tested her with a piece of valid information when Urbana got a notion to ship some arms into Ochos Rios, Jamaica. I had Consuela type a memorandum to that effect for me and let it go through legitimately. A week or two later, we received word that the thing had been blown sky high when the fishing vessel they used had been picked up just as the arms were being put ashore. I knew then that Consuela had handed the message over to someone, that it had been relayed somehow to Washington, and from there, to the British authorities in Jamaica.

"Later, I was able to put the Venezuela information into her hands as well as other material I thought Washington would be interested in having leak through. Unfortunately, I was under strictest orders, and couldn't break secrecy to let her know we were working for the same side."

"Yes." Gerard said the word simply, accepting Madden's need to maintain cover.

"Intelligence was waiting for the big one, the sign, however small, that a second Cuba was being planned. Then, through one of your people here, JIA got onto it—"

"Alec Fletcher," Gerard said.

"Yes. I learned that this morning. That brought the State Department into it. G-2 decided to keep me where I was and let JIA develop whatever it could from this end. When your Special Ops began asking questions about John Mosher in Havana, I suppose the Defense Department held back in order to keep us working independently of each other; the assumption, I suppose, being that we might have a better chance to uncover the entire plot."

Chance muttered something unintelligible under his breath, and it was obvious to Thorne Truscott and Gerard that his private opinion did not coincide with Madden's justification for the competitive spirit encouraged between the various Intelligence agencies.

"Then you were probably responsible for the message I got through Chieftain that the arms shipment was ready to leave from Bahía de Nipe," Gerard said.

Madden nodded. "I got jammed on that one. I'd hoped to be able to keep Defense informed on the exact vessel, sailing, and arrival dates, also to pinpoint the destination. What killed that was that things had begun to slow down on the Port Amitié end, and Urbana decided to send me to speed up the signing of the agreement by Fontaine. I notified Chieftain and gave them all the information I had at the moment and asked them to get it through to you urgent and immediate. I hadn't any idea Urbana had decided to use the sub for delivery. That came from the Russians after I'd left for Port Amitié.

"Once I got here and managed to get Fontaine's signature on the agreement, I tried my best to get back to Havana so I could notify Washington and fill them in on the rest of the missing information, but Zharkov insisted I had to remain here until the stuff was unloaded. That put the ball in your hands, and I think you've got the rest of the story from that point."

"And where to now that your cover in Havana has been blown?" Gerard asked.

Happily, Madden said, "Home. Back to Washington, a long leave of absence to romance Peg and propose to her again. I'm anticipating a long honeymoon."

"I hope you make it," Gerard said. "Best wishes."

Madden had left with Jake Walker, to be driven to his hotel. The ambassador relighted his stubby pipe and said, "You knew about this all the time, Thorne?"

"Not all of it, Bill, but I'll take the responsibility for turning Jim loose so he could work freely and without official restrictions."

"Hm-m-m." Chance shot a quick glance at Truscott, then to Gerard. Somewhere in the brief exchange, the look of mild reproof and tone of gentle scolding disappeared, replaced by a faint, forgiving smile. "Well," he said finally, "thank God somebody had the good sense to do it."

There was a knock on the shuttered door, and Mrs. Weatherby came in quietly. "Yes, Polly?" Chance said.

"Excuse me, sir, but the phone simply won't stop ringing. Sir Hugh Stewart, the others—"

"I'm not in my office. Ring Sir Hugh back and ask him if it would be convenient for him to drop in around four. I'll talk to the others afterward."

"And Mr. Shannon is back."

Truscott said: "Let's have Shannon in now, sir. He's been gone a good two hours and may have picked up something useful."

Chance nodded and Polly Weatherby backed out, stood to one side as Clark Shannon, flustered with importance, brushed past her, his face the forerunner of the news he bore. He came in and sat down, shaking his head from side to side mournfully. "It was just the way Sergeant Lescaux said, sir," he began. "Paul Reed—Chalumeau— was at the morgue with two bullets in his chest you could cover with a fifty-cent piece. The woman, Madame Mauriac, was in the police chief's office in a state of shock—"

"What about Tom Reed?" Gerard interjected.

"Gone. Lescaux told me. Old Tom was sitting on one of the steps while Lescaux went up to check Paul out. A few seconds later, they heard the first big explosion, and when he looked at Tom, there he was lying on the ground at the bottom of the steps. He'd shot himself with his own rifle. He was at the morgue, too, lying there next to his—Paul—Chalumeau. Pierre Duclosse showed up at the house about the time the police and the ambulance got there. They're holding him for questioning by Major Lamonte. That's about it."

"All right, Shannon," Truscott said. "Dictate your report to Mrs. Weatherby and ask her to have it ready for the ambassador as soon as possible."

Chance was speaking into the intercommunication set. "Is Ray Ferriss back from the Ministry of Information, Polly?"

"He just came in, sir. He's waiting out here to see you."

"Have him in, please."

Ray Ferriss came in and reported quietly. "The Ministry is in a turmoil. No one seems to have the answer to anything. Same at Police Headquarters. At the palace, I picked up some talk that President Fontaine is under close surveillance in one of the cells in the basement. No sign of General Batraville or his aide, Falot. Major Lamonte is in charge. The Council of State is in emergency session, and the betting is something like ten to one that there will be an announcement before long that M'sieu François Courdet has been elected president."

"Any signs of our Russian friends?"

"None at all. Their press attaché hasn't shown up anywhere, and the embassy is handing out nothing. St. Germaine has disappeared. Someone said they've got Fontaine's personal physician, Fombrun, in jail, but there haven't been any charges released on him. One thing more."

"What?" the ambassador asked.

"Madame Batraville."

"What about her?"

"I picked it up from the Paris *Match* correspondent. She took off on the morning Pan-Am flight to Washington, booked through to New York, then to Zurich. Bag and baggage."

"Appropriate phrasing, Ferriss," Truscott said with a light chuckle.

"The rumor is that she's heading for Zurich to clean out Fontaine's safety-deposit boxes there—"

"It won't do her a bit of good," Gerard said. "Lamonte told me several hours ago that Fontaine made a deal. An agent is already on his way with Fontaine's authorization to bring back his cache of Swiss francs and United States dollars in exchange for a recommendation of mercy. He'll probably get off with imprisonment for life."

"And there's to be a formal press conference at the palace at three o'clock," Ferriss added.

"Be sure you're there. I'll want the official version as a follow-up to my own report to the Secretary. All right, Ferriss, thank you." Chance swung around and surveyed a weary, unshaven Gerard. "Are you all right, Jim?" he asked.

"It's nothing that a week of sleep won't cure."

"How is the wing?"

"Stiff but operable. It pulled open a bit last night, but it's all patched up. The sling is only for show purposes. If you don't mind, sir, I think Alec and I should take off and get a first installment on some sleep."

Chance nodded his approval. Gerard stood up and said, "No news from Ambassador Vossolofsky yet?"

Truscott said: "We hear he's been at the palace filing notes of protest as fast as they can be written, accusing the American CIA of ousting Fontaine, murdering Du Faure, and putting Courdet in as front runner to replace him. Someone asked him if he believed the rumor that Comrades Pyantenov and Zharkov had defected to the United States, and he practically went through the roof. By the time he learns what happened, he'll be ready to be taken in charge by the men in white. I've an idea our good Comrade will soon be on his way back to Moscow for a series of conferences."

"What about you, Jim?" Chance asked.

"I sent through a 'mission completed' message to JIA, and referred Harrington and Richards to Undersecretary Emerson for a copy of your report."

"I suggested to Deke Emerson that he have them in for a look at it," Chance said. "Suppose you take off now and we'll have another talk later."

2.

Once again, as it had been on another warm night a short time ago, the Presidential Palace was bathed in glittering brilliance from within and without. In the Champs, thousands of holiday-minded Libertéans gathered in a gigantic display that easily rivaled the annual Mardi Gras. The spirit was the same. Laughter, singing, clapping hands to the rhythmic beat of drums, sandaled and bare feet shuffling and dancing, the jockeying for a better vantage point from which to witness the ceremony soon to take place. Searchlights twirled and picked out the cheerful, shining faces that looked up from the street and out from the windows of the government buildings across the Champs.

Youths were high in the trees, clung to light poles, or took possession of the statue of General Maraboux, the rear of the horse holding a young girl who clutched the general's body, a boy sitting astride in front of him. Above the clamor in the street came the chant, "Courdet! Courdet! Courdet!"

Through the cleared passageway, limousines were arriving and discharging guests who were ushered up the steps and toward the ballroom. There, groups of governments officials, prominent citizens, the military and members of the international diplomatic corps stood in small groups, chatting amiably, the men in civilian or military full dress, the women handsomely gowned and bejeweled in their finest.

A tight circle had gathered around François and Angélique Courdet, offering congratulations. Close by, Marcel Courdet, his face showing signs of his encounter with Mischa that could not be hidden cosmetically, clung to Julie Delacroix's arm, linking it with his own, in animated conversation with Mark and Eugénie Fuller. The international planter-commercial-industrial set talked with Libertéan officials over glasses of champagne while the press, as usual, patronized the bar in a room from which they could observe the scene, waiting for the official announcement to be made. They had already written their stories in most complete detail. Only official confirmation remained. And yet, nothing had been filed. There was always the outside chance—

Ambassador and Ambassadress Chance entered the ballroom with Counselor and Mrs. Thorne Truscott. Behind them came the First and Second Secretaries and their wives, followed by Jim Gerard and Nora Lund, then Alec Fletcher and Suzanne Forrest. The party moved through the crowd with smiling nods and words of greeting, then paid their respects to the Courdets, who were eager to thank the ambassador publicly for the recent hospitality shown them. The party of Americans moved on to speak with their German, British, French, and Italian counterparts, accepted glasses of champagne from the liveried footmen.

Ambassador Vossolofsky arrived a few moments later and stood in a gloomy knot of Russian attachés. The Cuban ambassador's funereal manner set the pace for their mood.

Chance checked his watch. "Eight-fifty-two," he said to Truscott.

Truscott nodded. To Gerard, he said, "I hope they've taken adequate precautions—"

"You can rest assured. Every building, every window, every point from which—"

"Those windows across the Champs, the government buildings—"

"Only employees who have been checked out and searched. The big searchlights will be turned on the crowds as soon as the ceremony begins, and anyone who so much as raises a hand to scratch his head will be picked out within a second. Major Lamonte—"

Truscott interrupted. "Here it comes."

Four officers entered the ballroom and went to the double doors of the deliberation chamber. The officer in the lead knocked with a gloved fist. The doors were thrown open from inside, and as the officers stiffened to attention, Henri Delacroix emerged, a tight smile on his face. Behind him came the other Council members in twos. Delacroix went directly to François Courdet, embraced him, and said loudly enough for those clustered around him to hear, "My congratulations, *M'sieu le Président!*"

The immediate circle that surrounded them broke into a buzz of low cheers and gloved applause. In the roped-off press section, the news correspondents broke ranks to head for the section that had been set apart for them on the outside balcony. Henri Delacroix took François Courdet's arm and led the way toward the battery of microphones in view of the crowds below. As they appeared on the balcony together, the shouts, "Courdet! Courdet! Courdet!" rose in a smashing crescendo to greet them. The shouting continued until the balcony was filled with guests and members of the Courdet and Delacroix families. Henri Delacroix raised his hands and waved them for silence. When the roar decreased, he began to speak.

"My fellow countrymen, it seems that I have heard the name 'Courdet' beating in my ears for many days and nights. Therefore, I know you will receive my next announcement with as much pleasure as it gives me to make it to you. I will spare you the normal flowery prelude as, with great personal pride and happiness, I present to you the President-Elect of the Republic of Liberté, His Excellency, M'sieu François Courdet!"

Delacroix's announcement was the signal for a deafening clamor of shouting, handclapping, singing, and the beating of drums. It was as though his voice had been heard even in the upper reaches of the hills, for the fires that had been burning there seemed to leap higher into the air as the wave of drumming increased in tempo. On the Champs, gaily clad women joined in the mambic shuffle to which all seemed to have succumbed, chanting and screaming the newly elected president's name. Henri Delacroix held up Courdet's arm and waved it toward the celebrants.

A full quarter of an hour passed before the crowd could be brought to order. Courdet made several starts and was compelled by the noise from below to break it off and begin again. The crowd, urged by Delacroix's voice coming through the loudspeakers, began to settle down to listen, but the low thunder of the drums in the hills remained constant, carrying their messages across the island into areas where the telephone had not yet been seen or heard. Across jungles, over the spines of its tallest mountains, into the most remote villages and distant plantations, the news was being spread: *Fontaine il est fini. Fontaine il est fini. François Courdet il est Président de la République.*

Courdet spoke well, strongly, kindly. The people listened, soberly and thoughtfully, nodding approval as they accepted his sincere words as they were intended to be taken.

Across the parkway atop the roof of the Army Head-

411

quarters building, the lean, uniformed figure hunched forward, elbows resting on the wide ledge as he watched the proceedings through field glasses. Beside him on the ledge rested a walkie-talkie that linked him to the various security unit stations on surrounding rooftops and below. From the transistorized radio in his upper jacket pocket and through the cord that ran to his earplug-receiver, he listened to the words of President Courdet.

"—nor can there be room in our world for the supremacy of one race or one nation over another race or nation. There can be only one supremacy we must recognize, the Supremacy of World Brotherhood, toward which this free government of Liberté shall work with other free governments of the world. In this matter, as in others of grave importance, you will have a voice, a vote that will—"

The watcher-listener felt a hand on his arm, and turned aside for a moment. "Yes, Lieutenant?"

"The two-minute report, Colonel Lamonte. Each station reports all is well and under quiet control."

Lamonte smiled. "Thank you, Lescaux. All is truly well."

"—thus there will be no need for the heavy military budget that has drained off money needed for schools and hospitals and housing. I have already received assurances from our great neighbor and friend to the north. They will step in immediately to assist us in this monumental task. Within a month, a Peace Corps unit will arrive, its sole mission to teach our children to read and write and understand, to teach our adults in methods that will produce the goods we need to trade with the world, to—"

The official ceremony was over. In the streets there was bedlam as the crowds gave in to the spirit of the occasion and abandoned themselves to music and street dancing. Across the island, men and women had listened to the voice of their new president with hope in their hearts that the promise of this one would be better than the promises of the last one and the one before. Men nodded solemnly, hats held in their hands with respect for the faceless man whose metallic words spoke with reality for the tomorrows to come. At least, they said among themselves, it could not be worse than the last one.

412

In the palace, the air was festive and gay with toasts and congratulations as the assembled guests took their places in the receiving line to be greeted by President and Madame Courdet.

Having passed through the line, the party of Americans stood to one side, champagne glasses in hand as they talked and watched the enthusiastic, glittering procession. The official Western families joined them to exchange diplomatic pleasantries that smacked of a resounding victory over the Eastern bloc. Thorne Truscott leaned forward to whisper a few words in Ambassador Chance's ear. Chance turned to see Ambassador Vossolofsky bearing down on him, a thin smile on his flat face. Chance said, "Ah, Sergei. A happy occasion, is it not?"

Vossolofsky glanced at the smiling faces that seemed to be waiting for his reply. "If one sees it that way, Comrade."

"Then I take it you do not?"

Vossolofsky shrugged lightly. Still smiling, he said in a low voice for Chance to hear alone: "One wins, one loses, my dear William, but as I have learned from your own American game of baseball, the game is never over until the final inning has been played and won. Even then, my friend, the true test comes later, in the World Series, does it not? The World Series. That is the final battle." He turned to the others with a bow, and added "Zdravstvuite, my dear colleagues, ladies." He turned away, rejoined his glum-faced aides and the Cuban ambassador, who had stood coolly to one side, and made his way to the exit.

3.

"—and while I find it difficult to find words to express my thanks to you, Dix, and my admiration for, and commendations to, Jim Gerard and Alec Fletcher, the loss of one of the finest administrative officers I have ever had leaves me with a deep sense of chagrin. Although I can't charge you with that particular piece of larceny, I should somehow have expected from the first that I would come out on the short end of any cooperative effort with an Intelligence agency. To even matters, I should like to request Alec Fletcher's assignment here to be extended. Gerard will explain to you that the request is not only official, but borders on the romantic.

"You will learn from my report to Deke Emerson that the general atmosphere throughout Liberté is quiet and hopefully expectant. Augmenting my report of last night, there has been no sign of any effort on the part of Chalumeau's followers. With his death, the last indication of revolt in the interior has died. With Courdet at the helm and Delacroix on the bridge to navigate, the new Ship of State has ridden out its first storm and is for the moment safely on course. The National Assembly has been recalled, and at this moment committees are at work devising ways and means for establishing voting procedures for the public. The new aid program approved by the Secretary and forwarded to the Congress will fit admirably with President Courdet's and Council Chairman Delacroix's over-all plans and should bear sweet fruit.

"Gerard and Nora are standing by, waiting to carry this to you by hand. I hope they will find a generous leave of absence waiting for them before Jim takes up his new duties. They deserve it.

"I hope on my next visit to Washington I shall have more time to spend socially. If, meanwhile, you find an opportunity to look in on Port Amitié, my wife and I will be delighted to entertain you.

"Most cordially yours, and—to borrow a phrase from our Russian friends—Do Svidaniya."

Chance released the button on the microphone, held it for a moment, then depressed it again and said, "An original and one copy for my personal file, Polly. I'd like to sign that before I leave for the palace conference with the new foreign minister."

He rang for Mrs. Weatherby. She came in for the dictation tape and said, "Sergeant Walker is back, waiting to report."

"Let's have him in. And hurry that letter to Harrington along, will you, Polly?"

Walker came in, stood at attention, and saluted formally. "Close the door, will you, Polly, please. Come in, Jake," the ambassador said.

When the door was closed, Chance stood up and slipped out of his jacket. He relighted his pipe, gripped it firmly between his teeth as he rummaged through the top center drawer. "Ah, here they are." He threw a deck of cards to Walker and began setting pegs in the cribbage board.

"Deal 'em out, Jake," he said. "I've got half an hour to spare, and I've got a sweet hunch that the way things have been going lately, I'm going to win the pants off you today."

4.

A small private plane taxied out toward the center runway. It came to a stop, trembled violently with vibration as its motors roared a defiant challenge to the waiting sky. Pan Am's early-morning flight north wheeled into position nearby, flattening the grass in its wake as it stood poised, waiting for the small plane to take off.

From a forward window, Jim Gerard leaned across Nora's lap and looked out and down on Alec and Suzanne, Thorne and Dorothy Truscott, Clark Shannon, Roland Baker and Jake Walker. Behind them, Colonel Constantine Lamonte, who had arrived in time to hand Nora a bouquet of flowers, stood to one side. Alec's hands were cupped to his mouth, shouting words that never reached their goal. Jim and Nora smiled and waved an indefinite reply.

Then the stewardesses were checking seat belts again. The huge jet moved out to where the small plane had stood moments before. As they lifted off, the small group on the ground had its final look, then began to break up, moving out of the sun toward their cars. Alec and Suzanne remained, each with an upraised arm to shade their eyes until the plane circled toward the north, and disappeared.

Gerard unfastened his belt and lighted cigarettes for Nora and himself. "Comfortable?" He felt a shudder go through her body.

"I feel as though I'm just beginning to awaken from a horrible nightmare," she said soberly.

"At least, the end—"

"Justifies the means?"

"I was about to say, 'the end was a happy one.'"

"When you consider the cost— So much unnecessary killing."

"Who ever knows, Nora, how much is necessary and how much is unnecessary to prevent even more killing?"

"But where does it end? When?"

"A good question. As long as the East and West are divided by ideology, misunderstanding, and distrust, plus the need to spend over a hundred billions a year to prove that neither side can dominate the other, we'll go on living one day at a time until this aching world can find some means to resolve its collective problems and let its people live in peace. If we're lucky, it might happen in our time."

She shook her head to rid herself of the morbid mood into which she had fallen. "Let's talk about us for a change," Nora said.

"All right. Happy?"

She nodded, smiling. "And you, Jim?"

"I've never been so completely happy in my whole life. I can't believe it's finally happened."

"What was in the message Rolly brought to the airport for you?"

"For us." Gerard pulled the message flimsy from his pocket, unfolded it, and handed it to her. "Three months' leave of absence," he said. "Richards will stay on the job until we're back. My first leave since Vietnam."

"Three whole months," Nora breathed happily.

"Three whole months with nothing to do, nothing to think about but—"

"—but shopping for a trousseau, getting married, finding a house or an apartment, furnishing it, a honeymoon to plan—"

"Where, darling? You haven't told me yet."

"I don't know, but when we plan it, let's make one clear stipulation. No palm trees, blue lagoons, or tropic sunsets. I want to be in a crowded city, surrounded by people, traffic, neon lights, theaters, restaurants, hotels, music—"

"Where? New York, London, Paris, Rome, Copenhagen, Athens?"

She looked up quickly, breathlessly. "Why not all of them? Could we, Jim? We'll worry about the other things when we get back. I'll need something to keep me busy when you begin your new job. Besides, we'll have—"

"Why not?" Gerard said as he leaned back, relaxed and smiling, contemplating the future with Nora.

"—time to plan whether we'll live in the city or suburbs, color schemes, curtains, draperies, rugs, a 'way-out den for you—"

"The 'way-'way-outest—" Gerard agreed happily.